APR   2006

D1505357

Landscapes

Landscapes

Stories by Kevin J. Anderson

With an Introduction by Neil Peart

Five Star • Waterville, Maine

First Edition
First Printing: March 2006

Published in 2006 in conjunction with
Tekno Books and Ed Gorman

Set in 11 pt. Plantin.

Printed in the United States on permanent paper.

Library of Congress Cataloging-in-Publication Data

Anderson, Kevin J., 1962–
    Landscapes / stories by Kevin J. Anderson ; with an
    introduction by Neil Peart. — 1st ed.
        p. cm.
    ISBN 1-59414-476-1 (hc : alk. paper)
    1. Science fiction, American.   2. Fantasy fiction,
American.   I. Title.
PS3551.N37442L36 2006
    813'.54—dc22   2005030112

Landscapes

Table of Contents

THE GREAT OUTDOORS

Introduction

By Neil Peart

In the late '80s, a novel called *Resurrection Inc.* arrived in my mailbox, accompanied by a letter from the author, Kevin J. Anderson. He wrote that the book had been partly inspired by an album called *Grace Under Pressure*, which my Rush bandmates and I had released in 1984.

It took me a year or so to get around to reading *Resurrection Inc.*, but when I did, I was powerfully impressed, and wrote back to Kevin to tell him so. Any inspiration from Rush's work seemed indirect, at best, but nonetheless, Kevin and I had much in common, not least a shared love since childhood for science fiction and fantasy stories.

We began to write to each other occasionally and, during Rush's *Roll the Bones* tour in 1991, on a day off between concerts in California, I rode my bicycle from Sacramento to Kevin's home in Dublin, California. That was the beginning of a good friendship, many stimulating conversations (mostly by letter and e-mail, as we lived far apart), and regular packages in the mail, as we shared our latest work with each other—the ultimate stimulating conversation. In subsequent years I would send Kevin a few books of my own, numerous CDs and DVDs from my work with Rush, and there seemed to be a fat volume from Kevin arriving about every other month.

Back in 1991, though, Kevin was still working full-time as a technical writer at the Lawrence Livermore National

Laboratory. He spent every spare minute working on his fiction, and though he would famously collect over 750 rejection letters, there was no doubt in Kevin's mind about his destiny. Even as a child, Kevin didn't "want to be" a writer when he grew up; he was *going to be* a writer.

And so he was. To date, Kevin has published over 80 novels, story collections, graphic novels, and comic books, and he still spends every minute *being a writer*. Kevin doesn't write to live, he lives to write.

He has even found ways to weave his recreation, relaxation, and desire for adventure and physical challenge into the writing process, carrying a microcassette recorder on long hikes throughout the West, including the ascent of each of Colorado's 54 "fourteeners," (peaks over 14,000 feet).

In a recent exchange of e-mails, Kevin and I were discussing writing styles and habits, and he offered this revealing passage:

A long time ago, my friend and collaborator Doug Beason made a joking comment when I suggested that I needed a break, a sabbatical. He said, "Kevin, if you ever stop writing, your head would explode!"

And I knew he was right. My imagination is stuck in overdrive, for better or worse. Instead of a writer calling for a Muse to give him an idea, I've got a hyperactive Muse that won't leave me alone.

I feel as if my head is a pot filled with too many popcorn kernels, popping away, filling the container and pushing the lid up, and unless I keep shoveling the new stuff out, the whole thing will blow up on me. I'm writing as fast as I can to keep the growling, slavering Ideas from nipping too close at my heels.

There was a US News & World Report *article a few*

months ago about a newly "found" disease they called "hypographia," the compulsion to write. They said writers like Sylvia Plath and Tolstoy were so obsessed with writing they often wrote as much as a thousand words a day. (A thousand words? Man, I've done over 10,000 words in a day!) I guess I'm an addict.

I'm picturing you as a guy with a similar compulsion to drum, slapping your knees, the furniture, the walls, feeling a rhythm in your blood. It's what you do. For me, stories are the drumbeats inside me. I'm always fabricating stories, characters, weird locations, plot twists. I'm just not happy "relaxing." Sometimes I'm just banging around having fun, goofing with toys that I enjoy—as when I write Star Wars or comics or light books like Sky Captain; other times I'm intense and working on something I think is Really Important, like Hopscotch. The "Seven Suns" books are a little of both, the biggest and most challenging story I've ever told, but damn, I'm having the time of my life with it, too.

I've been saying for years and years, "soon I'll slow down and take more time to smell the roses." It'll never happen, I suppose, because I just love the writing so much. Three days ago I started writing Seven Suns #5, and I was in absolute euphoria plotting the 112 chapters. This happens, then this happens, then this happens—I was discovering what my beloved characters were going to do, where they would end up, who would die, who would triumph. I came up with some twists and new ideas that were revelations to me, real lightning bolts from the hyperactive Muse—and best of all, they were so logical and inevitable in the universe of the story, that it seemed as if they were sewn into the fabric of my imagination from the very beginning, but I just didn't realize it yet. Now that's cool.

So, yes, I would like to have that sense of stillness and the time to pay attention deeply to the things around me . . . but on *the other hand, I can't wait to see what happens next in the new novel that's just over the horizon.*

And Kevin Anderson's horizons are wider than most—infinite, really. His imagination roams the entire universe, creating strange new worlds and peopling them with strong, believable characters.

From the philosophical depth of *Resurrection Inc.* and *Hopscotch*, to the novelizations for *Star Wars* and *The X-Files*; from the genre of "historical fantasy" (which I think Kevin *invented*—richly-imagined tales about Jules Verne, H. G. Wells, and Charles Dickens), to the breathtaking scope of his "imagineering" in the *Seven Suns* series, there have been so many excellent works that have delighted *this* reader, and millions of others.

Among seemingly overlooked treasures, I fondly remember the fantasy trilogy, *Gamearth*, *Gameplay*, and *Game's End*, now sadly out of print, but there are also Kevin's collaborations with Doug Beason, like *Timeline* and *Ill Wind*, and the ongoing, highly-successful *Dune* series with Brian Herbert.

In writing to Kevin in response to reading one of those, *The Butlerian Jihad*, I talked about the subtle skill of his craft:

More and more I notice how truly masterful writing, yours and others', leaves the reader with an overall impression of making it all seem easy—regardless of how much work has gone into the craft, the background, the research, and the intellectual underpinnings (or maybe because of all that), it just breathes off the page in a smooth flow of seemingly-inevitable revelations.

I know I've made similar comments about drummers before: some of them try to make simple things look difficult and impres-

sive, but the true masters make the impossible seem easy.

It doesn't seem fair to the creator of that carefully-wrought illusion, undermining all the effort and experience necessary to operate at that rarefied level, but it's the ultimate nature of mastery, I guess. (It may be lonely at the top, but it must feel better than being at the bottom!)

In late 2002, toward the end of a long American tour that had me drained and feeling sorry for myself, I wrote to Kevin:

One bright spot I can report along the way is that during some idle hours in the tuning room, on the bus, and in hotel rooms, I had the great pleasure of reading Hidden Empire.

First of all, I have to tell you that if you or anyone else had any doubt, I think you have achieved a true Masterpiece with this book—meaning that term in the sense which you clarified for me years ago. It is definitely a piece of work to lay alongside those of the Masters, to be accepted by them and by the great abstraction of "the Audience" as one of the pantheon of masters yourself.

Congratulations. I really think it is a great book. I was so impressed by it at the time, and also after the fact—a true test of quality, I'm sure you'll agree.

The craftsmanship alone is sheer perfection. The architecture of the storytelling moves forward with grace and economy, combining girders and panels of deft characterizations, wondrous settings, admirable "imagineering," and all the superstructure of pure thought that has preceded all that.

(The reader will have observed by now that when Kevin asked me to write this introduction, it was easy to say yes—I

13

knew the important stuff had already been written, either by me or by him. I would only have to look it up!)

Here are some of Kevin's thoughts on "style," from a recent exchange of e-mails on the subject:

I think in a letter to you many years ago, I talked about creating believable worlds and scenes; one of the vital tricks I mentioned was to nail down a few small but very precise and mundane details (the color of a piece of lint, the brand of a gum wrapper wadded up in a gutter), and the reader will buy into the rest of what you're describing. It seems easy, seems transparent. It's simple to show off, to be flashy and flamboyant, to prance around and point at marvelous overblown metaphors. It's more difficult to be subtle.

To which I replied, in part:

Another note about writing style that occurred to me in connection with what I wrote the other day: I just finished Gabriel García Márquez's memoir, Living to Tell the Tale, *and he described his early decision as a writer to avoid all adverbs of the "ly" sort (mento in Spanish, I think), and how it became almost pathological with him, just as Hemingway tried to cut every unnecessary adjective.*

In your case, with the necessary "mission" of describing an entirely imaginary universe for the reader, it would seem especially difficult to avoid extraneous adjectives and adverbs—and yet you do, making the descriptions of planets, cities, palaces, customs, and technology fall more-or-less naturally into the ongoing narrative. And . . . you make it look so easy.

As we have discussed, that is the highest level of craft, and yet the least likely to be admired, or even appreciated. Once I offered a definition of genius, in particular reference to Buddy

Rich: "Doing the impossible, and making it look easy."

And yes, Kevin does make it look easy, though of course it's not. He works to a very high standard of quality in his writing, from the conception to the execution, and these stories are a testament to the consistency of his art.

When people have called him lucky, Kevin likes to counter, "Yes, and the harder I work, the luckier I get."

As one of his appreciative readers, I think the harder Kevin works, the luckier *we* get.

SCIENCE FICTION

Science fiction isn't just a literature of ideas. Any good writer follows the *consequences* of those ideas, asking the next question, and the next, and the next. These first five stories all center around the idea of "Alternitech"—a company that sends prospectors into alternate but similar timelines in order to exploit the differences. Imagine the small fluctuations in your day, how a few inches or a few miles-per-hour during a skid on an icy road can mean the difference between a fender-bender or a fatal accident. These tiny changes could lead to a world where the Beatles never broke up, or where Lee Harvey Oswald wasn't gunned down after the Kennedy assassination, where an accidental medical breakthrough offers an unexpected cure to certain diseases.

But a story isn't "about" that. It's about how those changes affect the people who witness them.

Music Played on the Strings of Time

He arrived, hoping to find a new Lennon, or a Jimi Hendrix. Or an alternate universe where the Beatles had never broken up.

As the air ceased shimmering around him, Jeremy staggered; with his head pounding, he sucked in a deep breath. His employers at Alternitech always made him empty his lungs before stepping through the portal. The company had strict rules limiting the amount of nonreturnable mass shuttled across timelines, even down to the air molecules. Take nothing tangible; leave behind as little as possible.

The air here smelled good, though; it tasted the same as in his own universe.

He snatched a glance around himself, making sure that no one had seen him appear. It had rained recently, and the ground was still wet. Everything about this new reality appeared the same, but each timeline had its subtle differences.

Jeremy Cardiff simply needed to find the useful ones.

The Pacific Bell logo on the phone booth had the familiar design, but with a forest-green background color instead of bright blue. He had always found a phone booth in the same spot, no matter which alternate reality he visited. Some things must be immutable in the Grand Scheme.

Jeremy reached into the pocket of his jacket and withdrew the ring of keys. One of them usually worked on the phone's coin compartment, but he also had a screwdriver and a small pry bar. His girlfriend Holly had never approved of stealing, but Jeremy had no choice—in order to spend money in this universe, he had to get it from somewhere *here,* since he could leave none of his own behind.

The third key worked, and the coin compartment popped open, spilling handfuls of quarters, nickels, and dimes—Mercury dimes, he noticed; apparently they had never gotten around to using the Roosevelt version. He scooped the coins out of the phone booth and sealed them in a pouch he took from his pack. Never get anything mixed up, the cardinal rule.

Time to go searching. Jeremy picked up the phone book dangling from a cable in the booth and flipped through the yellow pages, hunting for the nearest record store.

Before he had left his own timeline that morning, everything had happened with maddening familiarity:

"Your briefing, Mr. Cardiff," the woman in her white lab coat had said. The opalescent *Alternitech: Entertainment Division* logo shone garish on her lapel, but she seemed proud of it. Her eyebrows were shaved; her hair close-cropped and perfectly in place; her face never showed any expression. This time Jeremy saw she was attractive; he had not noticed before. Every other time he had been too preoccupied with Holly to notice.

"You tell me the same thing every trip," Jeremy said to the Alternitech woman, shuffling his feet. He felt the butterflies gnawing at his stomach. He just wanted to get on with it.

"A reminder never hurts," she said, handing him the high-speed tape dubber. It had eight different settings to accommodate the types of music cassettes most often found in near-adjacent timelines.

At least the woman had stopped giving him the "time is like a rope with many possible strands" part of the speech. Jeremy was allowed only into universes where he himself did not exist at that moment; it had something to do with exclusions and quantum principles. He chose never to stray far from his own portion of the timestream, stepping over to adjacent threads, places where reality had changed in subtle ways that might lead to big payoffs in his own reality.

Other divisions of Alternitech sent people hunting for elusive cures to cancer or AIDS, but they had been by and large unsuccessful. A cure for cancer would change history too much, spin a timeline farther and further away from their own, and thus make it harder to reach.

"Ghost music," on the other hand, was easy to find. Jeremy wanted to find new work by Hendrix or Morrison or Joplin, a timeline where these stars had somehow escaped freak accidents or avoided suicide.

"Do you have everything now?" the woman asked him.

"All set." Jeremy stuffed the tape dubber in his shoulder pack. "I've got my money bag, a snack, some blank tapes, and even a bottle to piss in if I can't hold it." Sometimes the precautions seemed ridiculous, but he wasn't here to question the rules. Alternitech would deduct from his own commission the transport cost for every gram of mass differential.

"You have five hours until you return here," she said. The portal opened, shimmering inside its chrome framework. "I trust that will be enough time for you to search."

"I've never needed more than two hours, even if I have to walk to the mall."

She ignored that. He was disrupting her memorized speech. "You are entitled to your commission on whatever new music you locate, but according to our contract we re-

21

tain all rights and royalties." She smiled. Her lips looked as if they had leaped off the screen from the *Rocky Horror Picture Show*.

"Of course," he said. He had already learned that once, with his first big payoff, finding three new albums by Buddy Holly—he had actually been looking because of Holly's name, and he had been so surprised he had almost forgotten what to do. Almost. He had coasted on the triumph for a year, but he had found nothing new in a long time. He felt the anticipation building each time, wondering what he might find.

Exhaling the air in his lungs, Jeremy went sailing into the timestream.

Shopping malls had to be the most ubiquitous structures in creation. Jeremy had never encountered a timeline where the mall did not exist.

Inside the record store, Jeremy scouted down the aisles. The new releases displayed the appropriate Big Hits; a familiar Top 40 single played on the store's stereo system. The important changes would be subtler, difficult to find.

He checked under the Beatles first. At other times he had found strange but useless anomalies—a version of *Abbey Road* that did not include "Maxwell's Silver Hammer," a copy of the White Album that actually listed the songs on the back, a release of *Yesterday and Today* that had retained the disgusting butcher shop cover censored in the U.S. But since he could not take anything physical back with him, cover variations were worthless. In this store, however, everything looked the way it should have.

Disappointed, he next tried Elvis, the Doors, Led Zeppelin, John Lennon, Kurt Cobain—those would net him the most commission if he brought an undiscovered treasure back.

He might as well have stayed home.

With a sigh, he finally searched for Harry Chapin and Jim Croce, Holly's favorites. New songs by these two wouldn't sell well back in his own timeline, but he always checked, for her. He stopped himself—it didn't matter anymore. Who gave a damn for Holly? But he looked anyway.

He thought of Chapin, killed in a car accident . . . his Volkswagen smashed under a truck, wasn't it? And Jim Croce, dead in a plane crash at age 30, two weeks after his song "Time in a Bottle" had been a theme in a TV movie: *She Lives*, one of those oh-so-typical "my lover is dying of a terminal disease" films of the early seventies. Jeremy considered the song sappy and sentimental; Holly insisted it wasn't.

"You know, if it were me saving time in a bottle," he had said to her, "I could think of a lot better things to do with it. Like find more time for my own music."

He knew just how to push Holly's buttons. After one fight, he had left a box on her doorstep for her to keep "all those wishes and dreams that would never come true." He had intended it to be ironic; she had called it cruel.

He and Holly had such different needs that they clashed often over the two years they had been together, coming close and drawing apart. He decided it was probably over now for good. Jeremy had his music, his need to write songs and work toward breaking into the business. Holly, though, just wanted to hang out with him, wasting hours in conversation that had no topic and no purpose. She said it brought them together; he resented her for draining away time that he could have used for composing.

In the house he kept his own mixer, a MIDI sequencer, synthesizers, music editing programs, a set of panel speakers mounted on marble blocks and an amp that could lift the house two inches off its foundations if he decided to crank the volume. He had all the gadgetry, he studied the hits, tried to come up with a sure-fire blockbuster. Listening to the crap on the radio, he couldn't see that his own stuff was any worse.

He just needed a lucky break. You had to know a name, get under the right label, and somebody would *make* your songs hits, crowbar you to the top of the charts. Otherwise, music people tossed unsolicited demo tapes out the window. Reject. Sorry, kid.

But Jeremy planned to get in through the side door, to make a name for himself by bringing "ghost music" back to his own timeline and taking credit for it. Then the studio execs would be ready to listen to his stuff. . . .

But it wouldn't happen here, not in this timeline, not in this record store. Jeremy sighed. No Beatles, not even any new Chapin. He flicked his gaze down to Croce.

Holly disagreed with Jeremy's approach to songwriting. She worked as a nurse and sometimes treated him like a patient with psychological problems. Therapy. Pop psychology. "You can't just find a formula and imitate it. You need the depth, the emotion. And you can only get that by drawing it from yourself, by being brave enough to look deep. But you're afraid to. You need to have something inside yourself before you can share it with anyone else."

But he knew Holly must be wrong. What did a *nurse* know about music? He played in bars on weekends, drawing a few crowds. Holly herself came to watch, sitting at a table near the stage and mouthing the words to his own lyrics that no one else recognized. Somebody would notice him. One of his songs would catch on. He needed a foot in the door and some more practice.

Startled, he found five different cassettes with Jim

Croce's name on the side. In his own timeline, Croce had made only two albums, and most of those cuts had been compiled into varied "Greatest Hits" collections. After a moment of excitement—Jeremy always felt his skin crawl at finding an obvious change—he picked up the cassettes, glancing at the titles, reading the package copy.

In this reality, Croce's plane had never crashed. In the late 70s he had changed his style dramatically, but the cassettes didn't seem to be big successes. Croce had gone for dance music, funky R&B, with more and more desperate attempts at reaching the top 40 again. Songs like "The Return of Leroy Brown" were sure danger signs of waning creativity. On his last album Croce had not even written his own material, instead doing covers of old hits. When Jeremy found "Time in a Bottle: Disco Remix" he couldn't stop from chuckling.

Personal zingers aside, the alternate Jim Croce would have little commercial value for Alternitech back in his own timeline. And Holly would hate him for bringing this stuff back, for spoiling the memories. That would be too petty. He couldn't do that to her.

Not knowing quite why he didn't want to rub her face in it, he decided against the cassettes. Alternitech wouldn't be impressed anyway, and it would be a poor shadow to those new Buddy Holly tapes he had found. Better to leave old Jim dead in his plane crash. Jeremy shook his head, feeling pleased about completing his good deed for the day.

Then he noticed another tape shelved under "Misc. C." It bore his own name: JEREMY CARDIFF—*This One's for Holly.*

He paid for the cassette by stacking up the quarters from the phone booth, one dollar at a time. The clerk looked at him strangely for paying in coins, but Jeremy was already tearing the cellophane wrapping from the tape case. The blurb sticker said "Contains the SMASH hit *For Holly!*" Promo material tended to exaggerate the magnitude of any song's success, but he felt enthralled that something of his had actually been called a hit.

By the time he emerged into the scattered crowds wandering the mall walkways, Jeremy had popped the cassette into his player. He sat down in one of the mall lounge areas, closed his eyes next to a trickling fountain, and listened.

Jeremy recognized the first two cuts as variations—sophistications, actually—on songs he had already written. The third cut was one he had just begun in his own timeline. He felt a sense of unreality drifting over him, euphoria at having achieved his dream. In at least one timeline he had succeeded. He wondered what his alternate self was doing now, how he was planning to follow up a successful first album—

Then the other part of it struck him with a force great enough that he sat bolt upright on the padded bench. He shut off the player. He could not enter another timeline where he himself still existed. Exclusion principles. The Jeremy Cardiff in this reality—the one who had been a hit musician—must be dead!

He checked the copyright date on the cassette liner. Last year. His counterpart must have died not long ago.

Jeremy had never dared to check before, had never been interested to find out what altered circumstances had erased his own existence in these other timelines. But here he had achieved his best goals, his dreams—what had happened to him? Another pointless plane crash like Jim Croce's?

Jeremy checked the timer that would send him back

through the portal to Alternitech. He had three hours to find out.

"But can you tell me how he died?" Jeremy tried to keep his voice calm on the telephone. The record company receptionist had kept him on hold long enough that he had already needed to plunk four more quarters into the pay slot.

"Self inflicted," she said. Record company receptionists must go to school to learn that perfect "go screw yourself" attitude, he thought. "You know, the old couldn't-handle-success story."

Jeremy's heart caught in his throat. *Self inflicted?* "Don't you have any other information? Please, this is important."

"Look," she answered, clearly impatient now, "he took sleeping pills, or shot himself in the head. I can't remember. Jeremy Cardiff had one hit, he made a little money, now he's dead. So what? The price of gas hasn't changed."

Jeremy swallowed as he hung up on her. "No, I don't suppose it has."

While waiting for a bus, Jeremy used the high-speed tape dubber to copy *This One's for Holly* onto a blank cassette from his own timeline, one he could take back with him. He would have to discard the original before he returned through the portal. The sky overhead was gray, as if preparing to rain again.

He listened to the rest of the tape after he had found a seat on the bus and sat back. He munched on a granola bar from his pack, careful to stow the empty wrapper back in the zipper compartment.

As the songs played, the initial astonishment wore off, and he began to hear his music with a fresh ear, like a listener would. Sadly enough, he was forced to admit that the

27

songs seemed rather empty, the "oooh, baby, baby, yeah!" kind he had always scorned. Had he been too close to them? How could he have missed it? None of them had any punch.

Until the last song, "For Holly," which stood head and shoulders above the rest of the cuts. This had been the reason for the album. This had been the demo somebody had noticed.

He couldn't put his finger on the difference here—the music, the quality of his singing voice, the words? The pain sounded real. Somehow, it combined into a punch of emotion the others had lacked. He rewound the tape and listened to the song again.

When the bus stopped, he got out. The library was three blocks away.

He flipped through eighteen back issues of *Rolling Stone* until he found his own obituary. It occupied a quarter of a page, showing the cover of his album and his photograph. Jeremy felt an eerie chill seeing his own face stare at him from a photo he did not remember ever having had taken.

The uncredited obituary stated the facts and little else. It carried the distinct flavor of an "also ran" notice. Jeremy Cardiff had had one hit, reaching #23 on the charts. He had been unhappy with his modest success, ended up washing down a bottle of sleeping pills with a pint of Jack Daniels. He would be sorely missed, but by whom it did not say.

"That's it?" He blinked up from the pages of the magazine, looking at the other people around in the library. No one noticed him, no one knew who he was. "That's all?"

He left his original cassette on the table in the library, hoping that someone would pick it up and listen to it.

★ ★ ★ ★ ★

During their last fight, Holly had said, "I hope you do become famous. I really do. Because I love you." Her voice was low with an undertone of exhausted anger, as it always was after the shouting stopped and they had both gone to their separate corners. "But you won't make room in your life for anything else. It doesn't have to be that way."

She tugged her blond hair behind her ears, keeping it out of the way. Faint mascara tracks marked her tears. Few people even recognized that Holly wore makeup, but Jeremy knew she spent half an hour each morning carefully constructing that impression.

"You'll never understand it," Jeremy said. He had tried to explain it over and over to her, but still she refused to give him the space, to let him have the time and energy he needed to devote to creating music. Instead, she was like a sponge, demanding his devotion, wrestling his attention to her own personal needs instead of to his composing.

"This isn't just a job like being an auto mechanic—" *or a nurse,* he did not add, "I really have the power to move people. I can send out a message that could make everyone think. But I have to take time to get it just right. I can't just drop what I'm working on whenever you're feeling insecure." The anger crept into his voice once more.

But Holly was having none of it. Quietly, she picked up her purse and went to the door. "Take all the time you need. Follow your yellow-brick road. I don't want to be the one responsible for you not achieving your dream."

He couldn't think of anything to say in response before she closed the door behind herself. He stood alone in his studio with the tall speakers, the amp, the MIDI equipment, and all his unfinished music. The house was very quiet.

29

* * * * *

He listened to his copy of the tape as he made his way back to where the return portal would open for him. He treasured the song "For Holly." *Would I want to go through time with you? Are you the one?*

What if he had given up everything with Holly for a chance that was ultimately a flop? What if practice and brute strength and determination were not enough? That was the way to *manufacture* songs, like the empty derivative stuff on the rest of his album. Listeners could see right through that façade. He could never send a message to the world if he had nothing to say.

As he walked along the road, Jeremy removed the last quarters from his money pouch. Since he couldn't take them with him, he tossed them in one big handful into a puddle in the gutter. Like a wishing well—but he no longer had any idea what to wish for.

He needed the substance inside himself before he could put it into the songs, but he had tried to bypass that part, to skip an important step. Sorry, no shortcuts allowed. With a sinking feeling he knew it would be a hell of a lot more difficult.

As he stood in position and waited, Jeremy listened to the last song on the tape one more time. He had managed the true inspiration once, and he could do it again. He could use "For Holly" as a model—and it would be a great gift for her. He must swallow his pride, tell her he had been stubborn.

His chronometer showed only a minute or so before he would return to Alternitech. The executives would be upset when he returned empty-handed again. But Jeremy felt anxious now, ready to start a new timeline of his own. He could get some studio to listen to "For Holly"; he could scrap the empty songs he was working on and spend the time he needed. Maybe Holly would even want to help him; he had never let her actually help him before.

Jeremy froze with his hand on the cassette player. He was not, after all, returning empty-handed. He had his own music—and the contract stated that any songs he found in alternate realities belonged to Alternitech/Entertainment. Everything. The whole copyright, hook, line, and sinker. He had signed it, knowing full well what it contained. If he tried to cross them, they would press the legal buttons and swallow him up.

He could not let that happen to a song like this. He had only one choice, but there was no use crying about it— Alternitech would deduct for the mass differential of a fallen teardrop left behind. He felt his throat trembling as he pushed the button.

The cassette made a thin whimper as it zipped through the high-speed dubber, sending his music back into nothingness, erasing it forever.

Even if he could remember the tune, the words, he could not copy the emotion that had made the song so powerful. Such things could not be imitated; they had to be felt. He didn't want to end up with a minor hit he could not repeat. He had to learn how to *do* it, not how to copy it.

The air shimmered in front of him, opening into a brief doorway back home. His chest felt like lead, but he exhaled, pushing the foreign air out of his lungs. Shifting his pack on his shoulder, he stepped into the portal.

Reality changed subtly around him. It was all right, though. He had new inspiration, new work to do. He opened his eyes in his own timeline.

It might not be the same cut he had heard on his own tape, but it would be different from his other attempts. His focus would be different. He had a song to write, for Holly.

31

Tide Pools

The return portal formed in the air like razor blades slashing through clear ice. Andrea stepped across the threshold, her mixed elation and disappointment so overwhelming that she barely noticed the skin-fizzing sensation of hopping back home from an adjacent timeline.

"I got something!" she called, unslinging the backpack from her shoulder. "How about a miracle cure for multiple sclerosis, anybody?" It wasn't what she had hoped to find, but she had to make it look good.

In the receiving room of Alternitech, portals and complex control panels surrounded her. At her announcement, technicians and other cure hunters began to pay attention. "How much follow-up do we need?" asked the chubby man in the operating booth.

"Not necessary—I got all the right data." Andrea brushed a hand through her short, sweat-rimed dark hair, feeling her cheeks grow warm.

Cure hunters like herself dreamed of such unlikely chances. Peeping into parallel timelines, digging through other-universe medical libraries, Andrea searched for effective treatments that doctors in her own timeline had somehow missed.

Who would have thought that a drug used for skin disorders would be amazingly effective against MS? When injected into the spinal columns of those suffering from the disease, the drug dissolved the small white plaques covering nerve sheaths.

No one in her own timeline *had* thought of it, but in an adjacent universe, a doctor had stumbled upon the treatment and published it to high acclaim. Alternitech would profit greatly from the discovery, and so would mankind.

The man in the operating booth spoke into his intercom, summoning verification reps to paw through her data. Other cure hunters applauded Andrea as they waited for their own gates to open. She surrendered her backpack and its contents to the security guard.

It was phenomenally expensive to haul foreign mass from other timelines. Hunters like Andrea recorded pertinent data onto the diskettes or videotapes they carried with them. Apparently, there was no cost to transfer *information* between timelines, though Andrea supposed the entropy specialists would probably come up with something sooner or later.

After the announcement of her discovery, the reporters would come, the television interviewers, the applause from the public, the heart-felt thank-you letters from MS patients given sudden new hope for their conditions. She allowed herself to revel in the times she made a find like this.

Andrea also felt a disappointment inside, despite the rewarding rush of success. After all, she had not been *looking* for a cure for MS. She had failed in her primary mission.

The problem gnawing at her was whether or not she should tell Everett. He was the one who had everything at stake.

Home at last, Andrea entered through the front door, propping it open to let in the fresh breeze. Sunlight gushed through the bay windows, warming the sunken living room.

Everett straightened from his work by the laser generator. "Andrea? Is that you?" She stood in full view, and he was staring directly at her. His eyesight grew worse every day.

"Expecting someone else to barge in and blow you a kiss?" she asked.

"I expected you home hours ago. Wait, I have to start all this up again!" He held up his hands, then felt his way around the equipment, squinting at it, careful not to stumble. "I have a surprise. Where are you? Come into the foyer—I've set that up as prime focus."

Andrea smiled to see him looking so earnest, so bustling. This was much better than the phase of moping he had gone through a month earlier. She went where he directed her and looked around the walls. Tiny faceted mirrors were mounted at strategic points around the room.

"Ta da!" Everett switched on his laser projector, and a 3-D holo-sculpture congealed around her like a spider web of light, a kaleidoscope of rainbows. Each line was split, not quite resolved, so that it was really dozens of layered images overlapping each other, partially unfocused with chromatic aberration. His grids were out of phase, and she doubted Everett even knew it.

"My masterpiece," he said. "I wanted to leave something impressive behind. I call it *Timelines*. It's for you, Andrea."

Everett was looking at her with a childish expression of delight and anticipation on his face. His gaze was slightly off.

Timelines. She looked at the fuzzed edges of the light threads, the overlapping images that were almost but not exactly like each other. Perhaps it wasn't just some jittering lack of surety caused by Everett's fading eyesight and his trembling hands; timelines nearly overlapping but subtly different. He *must* have done it on purpose; she had to believe that, or else his failure would tear her heart apart. "I think it's beautiful, Everett. I don't know how you managed it."

He lowered his head to cover his smile. She almost expected him to say "Awww, shucks." Instead, he found a soft futon and sat down. "I was going to have it done by your birthday, but now everything takes me so damned long." He sighed. "Are you going to stay home with me tonight, or are you going back to Alternitech?"

Watching him made her wince her eyes shut. What good was a multiple sclerosis cure for him? She had failed him at the time he needed her most. She had to keep searching.

Heidegger's Syndrome. The disease selectively attacked the myelin sheaths around the optic nerve, then chewed away at the medulla oblongata, deteriorating the nerves that controlled breathing and heartbeat. After a slow descent into blindness, Everett would one day just find himself without a heartbeat, then fall over and die. Andrea dreaded the morning she would wake up to find him cold in the bed beside her. She could not prevent it in any way.

Andrea stared at Everett in the living room. The solution was painful and obvious. But Alternitech had flatly denied her permission to hunt among the timelines for a cure.

She walked up behind Everett, threw her arms around his waist, then pressed her cheek against his shoulder blades. The tapestry of light glittered around them, defeating even the sunlight. *Timelines.*

"It's your best work, Everett," she said. "I love it."

Andrea fidgeted in the university office of a man she had never met. In the halls of the Neurological Wing of the Deudakis Medical Research Facility, she could hear annoying sounds of construction, hammers and saws and power drills. She had had to weave her way around scaffolding and construction barricades to reach Dr. Benjamin Stendahl's office. The hall lights flickered, but remained on.

She looked at her watch again, sat down in the only un-cluttered chair, then stood up once more. Stendahl's computer sat on a corner of his desk, glowing with a garish screen saver of multicolored lines. She ran her fingertips along the spines of the journals on his bookshelves, stacks of dusty manuscripts, technical papers held together with old rubber bands; one band near the bottom of the pile had snapped, splaying curled printouts.

A man stepped into the office breathing heavily and mumbling to himself. He came to a full stop as he saw her. His eyebrows were like fluffy gray feathers mounted on his forehead. "Oh! I forgot." He dropped a bulging briefcase atop the stacked books on his desk. "You're here to talk to me about Heidegger's Syndrome—your husband, right? Well, there's nothing I can do for him. You realize how rare the disease is? Only eight people a year are *diagnosed* with it in all of North America."

Andrea thrust her chin forward. "I've read all your papers. Looks like you were making good progress toward a cure. Why did you stop work on it?"

"Simple answer—no more money. That's the rotten part. Heidegger's isn't really an insidious bastard like cancer or AIDS. Given some research data, I could do a lot. But our rhesus monkeys were rerouted and never arrived. I could afford only one grad student, but she got married and moved to Ohio. I couldn't get her replaced before the end of the fiscal year, when my funding went away."

Stendahl sat behind his desk, jiggling the mouse so that the screen saver dissolved to display a master menu. "I think "orphan disease" is the colorful term they have for it.

With research dollars so scarce, who wants to waste time coming up with a cure for something nobody cares about?"

"*I* care about it," she said. "Eight people a year care about it, and so do their families, and everybody they know."

Stendahl looked at her with sympathy in his big, dark eyes. "Look, millions of people get cancer, leukemia, cystic fibrosis. Heidegger's just doesn't cut it. The disease was a medical curiosity when it was first reported, little more."

Andrea stared at the journals on his shelves. Pounding hammers from the hallway punctuated her sentence. "And now?"

He shrugged again. "I'm working on other things."

Andrea wanted to spend her every waking hour hunting alternate timelines for a cure, but she needed to be with Everett. Each day was like Russian roulette with him, never knowing which heartbeat might be his last.

Seagulls wheeled overhead, tiny checkmarks that screamed against the booming rush of the Pacific. The ocean and the huge sky above made the universe seem oppressive in its grandeur. Headlands sprawled out in muted browns and grayish greens to the shore, where a string of tide pools dotted the wave-chewed rock like diamonds on a necklace. Barefoot and in cut-off shorts, Andrea and Everett picked their way among the rocks.

Andrea took sandwiches out of the pack, and they split a bottle of beer. Everett squatted beside one of the pools and dangled his fingers into the water, startling two crabs that ducked for cover beneath the rocks. He squinted to make out details. Eyeglasses would not help him; Heidegger's was not a problem of focus, but of the optic nerve itself.

The tide pools were colorful, filled with life, a microcosm of unfurled pale-green anemones, tiny fish, and shells. Snails worked their tedious way across the rock surface, finding rich patches of algae. Everett tossed a rock, watching the ripples spread to the boundaries of the tide pool, but constrained by the walls so that it could not affect the other tide pools.

"Each one is like its own universe," he said. "Full of life, nearly identical to the others, but different. "I'm like an anemone in a tide pool, stuck to the bottom, waving my fronds in the hope that I'll catch something, but ultimately trapped right where I am. You, on the other hand, are more like one of those rock crabs. With Alternitech, you can scuttle over the wall and get to other tide pools, go see new places, look at what they've got, and maybe take something back with you."

Andrea didn't know what to say. She did indeed have the flashy, high-paying career. Who could imagine a world where a "research librarian" was considered a glamorous profession? Andrea was constantly being interviewed, receiving awards and applause. She had loved it—until the search had become personal, and desperate, and she had failed.

"I'm still looking for something to help you. I'll find it. Don't worry."

A wave curled against an outcropping partly out to sea, dashing spray into the air like tiny crystal droplets. Two gulls swooped down, then wheeled high overhead.

"Why help me when you can help thousands?" Everett said. His voice held a strong resignation that had emerged from his initial depression.

"As if one cure precludes another!" Andrea scowled. "Why do we pit the two types of research against each other, as if they were our only two choices? The government spends more money maintaining *flower gardens* around monuments than they do on Heidegger's research—why does one bit of science have to siphon money from other science, rather than something else? Everything isn't equal." She looked down, though she knew he couldn't see her face anyway. "Besides, if I find something, I'll just tell Alternitech that I found it by accident while doing other research. They can't prove otherwise."

Everett smiled, like a parent watching a child deliver promises with false bravado, then he reached for his sandwich. She watched him squint until he found it.

She swallowed a large bite. "We should get back. I can go out hunting at least two more times today."

Everett's face was a plain mask of disappointment, but he said nothing.

In her long search, most of the alternate universes appeared identical. Digging into the medical research libraries, sometimes she discovered even less progress on Heidegger's Syndrome, or none at all. Twice, she found minimal successes beyond her own timeline, but nothing worth bringing back. With a run of unlikely bad luck such as Stendahl's, it seemed obvious that in some other timeline he would have received his rhesus monkeys, his grad student would have stayed an extra six months.

Throughout her search, she also had to find enough other tidbits to keep Alternitech happy. They had told her not to waste time hunting a cure for an orphan disease, yet they were delighted when she found a way to artificially change eye color from blue to brown and back again. Plenty of cosmetic and commercial applications, they said. Their priorities made her sick.

She had lost count of the timelines by now. On each mission, Andrea went directly to a university's medical library and buried herself in Stendahl's publications, checking to see if he had anything new to offer. This time, according to the library, Stendahl had completed his experiments, but his crucial summary papers were "in press," which meant they were not yet published and would be available only in his office.

Andrea hurried along the dim corridor. So far, every timeline had the same chaotic construction in the west wing of the building. Perhaps chaos itself was the only constant among the timelines. Yellow barrier tape blocked off corridors, light fixtures lay on the floor, the sounds of hammers and power saws echoed in the halls. Andrea passed a pile of new-cut boards, ducked under a scaffold holding drip-splotched cans of paint. She hadn't yet been able to determine if they were building something up or tearing something down.

Stendahl's door was closed. Taped to the wall beside his office hung a handwritten note giving an address to send Get Well cards. Under that, she read a newspaper clipping that described how Benjamin Stendahl had broken his leg after stumbling in a construction area, and that he was not expected to return to teach classes for the remainder of the semester.

Stendahl's door would be locked, but all cure hunters kept lock-picking tools in their packs. If this timeline had some crucial information for Everett, she would take whatever measures were necessary. As she worked at fumbling the slim tools into the door's keyslot, construction noises drowned out the sounds of her hidden efforts. But she kept looking over her shoulder. She was not good at this.

Wrapping her sweaty palm around the knob, Andrea finally opened the door. She ducked inside and closed it behind her, flicking the light switch.

Stendahl's abandoned office smelled oppressive and long-empty, though he had been in the hospital for only a week. She switched on the computer, letting it boot up as she scanned the bookshelves. She did not have much time to find what she needed, and Stendahl's cluttered organization made the task more difficult.

She saw the title on the fresh manuscript lying on top of one pile, then found a folder filled with memos, his hand-jotted records of the experiments, raw data. She flipped through the pages. At the end of his summary Stendahl even suggested a few treatment methods. "Yes!" she said.

She glanced at her wristwatch, trying to determine how soon the Alternitech portal would come back for her. She could use her camera to photograph each page of the hardcopy summary report, but this was raw data—files and files of it—experimental records, suggested follow-up tests. It would be laborious and time-consuming to copy all of it. More time than she had. But she could store everything onto one of her diskettes—if she could find the right files on Stendahl's computer.

Andrea went to the computer, glancing at the menu and searching for Heidegger files. As she feared, Stendahl had imposed little organization in his filing system. Some of the filenames contained the word "Heidegger," but when she called them up, they were mere memos requesting supplies. Stendahl had named seven of the files REPORT1, REPORT2 . . . each taking up significant disk space. She checked the file-creation dates, then called up the most recent, but it had nothing to do with Heidegger research.

Out in the hallway, the construction workers used something that sounded like a jackhammer on the walls. Andrea tried to ignore the racket and concentrate on her work.

Finally, when she pulled up REPORT5, the words described all his tests, all his results, all his suggestions. Jackpot!

Excitement and anxiety growing within her, Andrea checked her watch again. She unzipped her pack and pulled out the various blank diskettes from her own universe. She pulled a disk out of its plastic sleeve and tried to slide it into the drive.

It was an eighth of an inch too wide. But she had other formats, other sizes to accommodate slight differences among the timelines. She tried another from her stack.

She finally found a diskette that fit. Stendahl's drive began formatting it. Alternitech experts had always been able to decode her diskettes, no matter how subtly different their computers might be. Of course, the techs might not help if she brought back something she had been instructed not to look for. She might have to call in all of the favors she had earned in her years working for Alternitech.

The disk finished formatting. It would take a few moments to copy the files. She didn't have much time; the portal would come back for her soon.

At the far end of the hall, one of the construction workers cursed as the jackhammer noise changed with an abrupt clank.

All the lights in the building went out.

Stendahl's office filled with blackness. The computer died. Andrea's hopes died with it.

By flashlight, she photographed as many pages of the draft manuscripts as she could. Working backward, Andrea snapped each image of conclusions, then the experimental method, and finally began plowing through all the raw data. She stared at her chronometer, watching the time tick down.

Alternitech's machinery cast her across the parallel universes at random like a fishhook in the water. Now that she had found a timeline that offered hope for a Heidegger's cure, chances were very slim that she would ever find herself back *here*. Frantic, she kept photographing the data, hoping that her flashlight provided enough illumination for the pictures to turn out.

Finally, when she could not wait a second longer, Andrea clicked one more photograph, then ran out of Stendahl's office, leaving the papers scattered all around. Glowing green EXIT signs shone in the darkness. She heard voices calling, complaining about the power outage. By the bobbing light in her hand, Andrea ran through the halls, dodging construction barricades. She had to get back to the portal.

A gruff voice yelled for her to bring the flashlight over so they could find the circuit panel, but she ignored it. She nearly tripped over a pile of pipes against one wall, but she caught her balance. Reaching the secluded stairwell, Andrea stumbled into the shadows just as the Alternitech portal slashed through the air.

Clutching her precious data, Andrea fell across the sea of timelines.

"Well," Stendahl said, raising his bushy eyebrows, "that's the good news." Andrea suddenly felt her stomach turn into ice.

He folded his hands on his desk and leaned toward her. Around him, she could see photocopies of the article and notes she had taken from the alternate universe. Stendahl had studied them, marked them with a red pen. She spotted several pieces of data circled, a few with exclamation points beside them. Andrea feared that she had not managed to include the *one page* that contained crucial measurements or descriptions of the one round of tests that would have allowed Stendahl to create a treatment for Heidegger's. It would all be lost.

Alternitech management had not been pleased with Andrea when she had returned with information on Heidegger's Syndrome, information she had been specifically told not to seek out. They had suspended her, until they received a phone call from an angry senator whose daughter was even now being treated for multiple sclerosis—using the prescription Andrea had brought back. The phone call seemed like a miracle cure to her situation.

Now, Everett was the only one who had something to lose.

Andrea met Dr. Stendahl's gaze. "What is it?" she said, her voice hoarse. "What's the bad news?"

"I've confirmed—er, I mean I *agree* with my own conclusions." He forced a wry smile. "This research does indeed suggest a treatment regimen that could offer hope for people diagnosed with Heidegger's Syndrome. But—"

Andrea flinched, but she didn't dare say anything else.

Stendahl looked away. "As with so many other ailments, beginning the treatment at the onset of the disease holds the key to the cure. If we could have started this right when your husband's eyesight was affected, when the disease was still confined to the optic nerve, we might have had a chance. He could have suffered a loss of eyesight, but the disease itself would be eradicated."

His feathery eyebrows rode up his forehead. "In your husband's case, the disease has already migrated to the medulla oblongata. The damage is already being done to the crucial nerves that govern involuntary functions such as heartbeat and respiration. This treatment itself purges the disease, but at the cost of destroying the nerves that are affected—somewhat like amputation."

Andrea took a long, shuddering breath. "Obviously, we can't do that in Everett's case. Not anymore." She felt a dry whispering sound in her ear, as of her own ragged hope draining away.

Stendahl was lousy at sounding optimistic. "From now on, anyone else diagnosed with Heidegger's will have a chance. You've saved those eight people a year you were so concerned about. No one else would have funded my research. You have that to show for your efforts, if nothing else."

Andrea found she couldn't listen any more.

Mist generators sent a cool fog toward the ceiling of the room, making the bright green and red laser beams stand out. Everett had been furiously working on another sculpture, fine-tuning it and trying to finish while he could still function. He had cranked up the laser intensity to the maximum safe level, just so he could discern the beams with his failing eyesight.

With the rest of the house darkened and only a few stars visible out the window, Andrea lay next to him on the floor, looking up at the laser tracery.

Everett spoke in the darkness. "There was a poet during the Boer War who said to live every day as if it were your last, for one day you're sure to be right."

"When did you start reading poetry?" Andrea said, trying to change the subject.

"I've had a lot of time to do things while you were off at Alternitech." He sighed. "But I'm glad you found the cure anyway."

"You're still going to die!" Andrea snapped. Her failure

seemed like fluttering wings around her head.

"We're all going to die," he countered. "But you've given a longer life to the other people who get the same stupid disease I did." He took a long breath. "I came to terms with this illness a long time ago. It's *you* who need to accept it."

"I had to try," she mumbled. But she began to wonder if her obsession to find a cure, her need not to fail at the task she had set for herself, was actually more for herself instead of Everett.

"I know you did," he said. "Thank you for trying, Andrea. But all those days you were gone hunting . . . I would rather have gone to the mountains with you, done a few more bed and breakfasts up the coast." Everett's words stung.

"There are plenty of other versions of *me* in other universes who *will* have a long and happy life with you. In our timeline, I had an unlucky break. I got an incurable disease that nobody's ever heard of. It just doesn't happen in this timeline, with this Everett and this Andrea."

He sat up abruptly. "We've got money saved, so why don't we spend it? Besides . . . you'll be getting a big life insurance check from me before long."

Andrea winced, but he gripped her hand. She thought of the hours she had lost in her desperate hunt. "I suppose I could take a leave of absence from Alternitech," she said haltingly, "especially now. It would give them time to cool off." She flashed him a smile that was at first forced, but gradually grew sincere as she thought of the things they could do together, now that all the restraints had been snipped away.

"All right," she said. "Let's go be alive as long as we can."

An Innocent Presumption

A freak accident. Never happen again in a million years.

Rain slicked the pavement like a black mirror, reflecting the amber lights of the tow truck and the squad car's scarlet and blue flashers. A Toyota SUV had stalled high on the span of the Oakland Bay Bridge, angled so that it disrupted two lanes of traffic. Cars slowed across the bridge, crawling forward like a slow but belligerent garden slug.

A cop stood in the cold drizzle, waving his arms and fruitlessly directing traffic while a tow truck backed up, aligning itself to remove the offending SUV. Its warning beeps sounded like high childish screams.

A placid-looking older man in a blue Mercury eased forward to change lanes and bypass the obstacle. The cop held up one hand and waved with the other. The blue Mercury lurched forward while cars in the adjacent lane struggled to stop.

A different driver jumped the gun and accelerated, then hit the brakes. He skidded forward on the slick road and crunched into the rear of the Mercury. With the impact, the older man's trunk popped open.

Disgusted, the cop walked forward, holding out both hands to stop traffic. The driver of the rear car rolled down his window to yell curses.

The older man in the Mercury opened his door, looked at the railing of the bridge high above the gunmetal-gray water. Dazed. Determined.

The frowning cop saw the young woman's bloody body

in the Mercury's trunk. Two deep and brutal slashes across her face, her cheeks sliced open to expose white teeth. Both eyes ruined by the blade. Her throat cut all the way to the windpipe and spine.

The cop yanked out his service revolver, holding it in a stance he had often practiced at the firing range but never used in the line of duty. The old man froze before he could make a run for the edge of the bridge. The drizzle continued, but everything else had fallen silent, a snapshot tableau.

After two years and seven victims, intensive manhunts and giant budgets from crack crime-solving agencies, "Slasher X" was caught because of a silly fender-bender, a mere coincidence.

Another day on the job exploring alternate timelines.

Heather Rheims shouldered her pack, looking like a nondescript student. She wore a loose flannel shirt and comfortable jeans, a look that was in style in virtually every parallel universe. Timeline prospectors had to be unobtrusive, finish their tasks without drawing attention to themselves, then slip back through the portal to the central complex of Alternitech.

With her long rusty-brown hair and large gray-blue eyes, she passed as a typical college sophomore. Only her sharp gaze and hard expression revealed that she had scars and concerns beyond looking for parties at the student union or picking up guys in her poly-sci class.

Now, inside Alternitech's main control room, portal frames gleamed in the too-white light. The air was always frigid, overly air-conditioned to pamper the dimensional equipment. One of her fellow timeline prospectors, a tall crewcut blond who looked as if he belonged in an ROTC recruiting office, came up to her. Rod's normally stony face was a mixture of sympathy and victory. "Hey, I hear they caught the bastard last night."

Heather's lips formed a grim line. She took a moment before answering to make sure her voice was steady. "Better late than never, I guess. Although if they'd caught him after victim number three instead of number seven, then I could still go biking on the headlands with my sister."

Rod squeezed her shoulder, then turned away as the tech supervisor called his name and prepared the portal for his day's assignment.

Heather said, "Still looking for novel leukemia treatments?"

"No, just novels." Rod gave a foolish smile. "Maybe Mario Puzo's sequel to *The Godfather*, or another historical epic by James Clavell. Maybe I'll find a universe where Stephen King never did retire." He went over to the dimensional doorway as the air shimmered and crackled with a smell of ozone.

Alternitech explorers like Heather sidestepped into parallel universes nearly identical with the modern world but with subtle differences: timelines where the Beatles had not broken up, where James Dean had a long and successful film career, where scientific researchers had achieved useful medical or technological breakthroughs that, for whatever reason, had been stymied in this world. A timeline prospector's job was to identify these differences and bring them back home, where Alternitech would sell them to the highest bidder.

"Oh, Ms. Rheims?" called the tech supervisor in his thick British accent. "If you would grace us with your presence, we are ready to send you."

With the news of Slasher X in all the papers, the tech supervisor didn't give Heather his usual deprecating smirk about her "embarrassing" current quest; since her patron paid a generous fee for Heather's skills, Alternitech allowed him his eccentricities.

"Money-Is-No-Object" Feldman was obsessed with the John F. Kennedy assassination. For over a month now he had sent Heather on expeditions into parallel universes in order to secure evidence that proved or disproved the conspiracy theory.

Now she shouldered her backpack, taking several deep breaths to prepare herself. She exhaled all the air, then stepped forward into the ripple—

—Without moving, she found herself in another universe that seemed identical to her own. She had three hours here, enough time to ransack the archives in the university library.

The city maps were similar in every timeline, with only the most minor deviations of street names. She knew exactly how to get to the UC San Francisco library or, failing that, the main downtown branch. For her purposes, all she needed was a microfilm archive or public access computers with newspapers dating back to 1963. Despite all the differences, the Windows Operating System seemed ubiquitous across timelines.

The routine was familiar by now. Heather even had her favorite carrel picked out. Sometimes, she had found greater evidence for a conspiracy, various shooters other than Lee Harvey Oswald; in some timelines, no assassin had ever been caught or even accused. In others, no crusader or conspiracy theorist like Jim Garrison had even raised the possibility, and Kennedy's murder went quietly into the history books as the work of a single madman.

"Money-Is-No-Object" Feldman was delighted with

each nuance, each deviation, although so far the clues added up to nothing more tantalizing than the blurry photos often used to "prove" the existence of Bigfoot or the Loch Ness monster.

In this timeline, though, Heather felt a thrill as she discovered a significant change in history: This universe's Kennedy had survived the shooting, living out his term in office paralyzed from the waist down. After the assassination attempt, however, he had no longer been a fiery leader, and his presidency was remembered as basically ineffective. No shooter had ever been caught.

She followed the history threads, surprised at how easily the timeline's broad strokes had shifted back to her version of "normal." Heather used her hand scanner to copy the documentation. Feldman would be ecstatic.

Since she had a little time remaining before she needed to find her way back to the Alternitech portal, she glanced at current events. When she stumbled on the headline of the morning edition of the *San Francisco Chronicle*, Heather sat frozen, gulping the details with her eyes.

"Slasher X Claims Eighth Victim."

Then, of course, she knew exactly what she had to do.

Parallel line after parallel line. Feldman's enthusiasm did not diminish as Heather continued to retrieve tantalizing nuggets that maintained the eccentric millionaire's funding. But she had another mission now. She no longer cared about the razzing from the tech supervisor or the other timeline prospectors who didn't consider her "tabloid work" to be worthy of Alternitech's potential.

Now, Heather was saving lives, innocent people just like her sister Janni.

In each new parallel universe, her first action was to

check the newspapers, then make an anonymous phone call to tip off the police. The story was always the same: Her own parallel universe was the only one in which a bad-luck traffic accident had exposed the serial killer's identity. *She* knew who he was.

When she delivered her bombshell of information, the detectives were sometimes skeptical, sometimes angry, other times mercifully grateful for any lead. Since the killer had been caught in her own timeline, Heather had followed the details of the case, and she could offer enough veracity to convince the investigating homicide detectives that she wasn't a crank.

She understood, for instance, that Slasher X—an older retired man with the unusual name of Eric Keric—used a fat black marker to draw an X on the faces of his victims before commencing the bloodier work. Keric slit the throats first so that the victims didn't struggle, and his thick carving knife could make precise strokes along the dark line he had marked, crossing out their faces. Many nightmares ago, Heather had been called in to identify Janni's mutilated body—her face gashed with the terrible deadly *X*, her throat cut. . . .

After a while, Heather stopped even checking the reports before she made her anonymous call. She simply tipped them off to Eric Keric and let the professionals handle it from there. It was so easy to be a good citizen, to get her revenge for Janni . . . and to make sure that Slasher X paid the price for his terrible crimes. She began to feel like a hit-and-run crusader for justice, almost like Jim Garrison tirelessly trying to track down JFK's killers.

In her work for Feldman, she also came back in triumph to Alternitech. At last, she found a parallel line where Lee Harvey Oswald had lived long enough after being shot by

Jack Ruby to blurt out a confession. With his dying breath, Oswald had fingered a man named Francis Tarryall, a shifty Dallas businessman with ties to Cuba and the Soviet Union. He'd been in trouble with the law many times but had managed to hire the best lawyers, to get evidence dismissed, and he had always walked. But after Oswald's accusation, Tarryall's trial was swift and the outcome sure. Tarryall never confessed, but the investigations by that universe's Warren Commission yielded seemingly incontrovertible evidence.

Heather copied several months of news stories so Feldman could study the aftermath.

She was rushed at the end because this time her usual call to the police had taken an excessive amount of time. The detective—not one of the familiar names usually assigned to the Slasher X case—asked too many questions, wanted to know about the killer's victims, pumped her for even the most obvious details.

Frustrated, she insisted that he check out Eric Keric, even divulging the old man's address, which she had memorized. The fact that the detective knew Keric's name and where he lived was a good sign. Perhaps the police had already been following him. . . .

Rushed and exhilarated with her new Oswald discovery, Heather hurried back to meet the Alternitech portal. She promised herself a nice restaurant meal to celebrate a productive and satisfying day.

Alternitech prospectors rarely returned to the same parallel universe, but Mr. Feldman offered a substantial bonus. He had discovered with great glee that Heather hadn't obtained the full story about Francis Tarryall.

She'd copied later articles without reading them, and

one of her last wire-service transcripts cast extreme doubts on Oswald's dying confession. Other evidence came to light that Tarryall and Oswald had been very personal enemies, their philosophies close enough that minor differences led to shouting matches and hatreds. Some of the Warren Commission's conclusions had begun to unravel . . . but Heather had not obtained the rest of the story.

She supposed that her patron wanted to seize any possibility that the conspiracy hadn't actually been solved. In his subconscious at least, Feldman perhaps needed something to hold onto. Her last mission had apparently given him the answer, but now he hoped she could cast doubt once again.

Heather stepped through the portal, backpack and equipment slung on her shoulder, and went right to work. The answer was obvious as soon as she scrolled through newspapers a few months farther ahead in time. Francis Tarryall was proven innocent, much of the evidence found to be false or misleading, Oswald's confession dismissed as a dying man's last vendetta with no relevance to the JFK assassination.

As she copied the articles, she recalled that this was the parallel reality where she had spent so much time arguing with the skeptical detective about Slasher X. Heather flipped through recent newspapers in the library, looking for headlines proclaiming that the killer had been caught, that innocent victims had been saved. She could take credit for the justice, but she alone would know it. This was her quest . . . just like Feldman's.

But she found no headline, no story whatsoever, no mention of Eric Keric or his arrest. The detective had ignored her! It was unbelievable.

With a fluttery dread, she flipped past several months and found no banner stories announcing the serial murders.

Heather brushed her rusty-brown hair behind her ear, blinking in puzzlement. It didn't seem possible that Slasher X had managed to hide all of his victims, that people like poor Janni were simply written off as missing persons, runaways, unexplained disappearances . . . maybe even alien abductions.

What if, in this alternate timeline, Eric Keric himself didn't exist?

Breathing quickly, hoping that was the answer, she pawed through the residential phone book. In her own universe, Keric did not have an unlisted number. She found him right where she expected his name to be. The address listed was the same.

The bastard hadn't been caught. She had called the police, given her information—but the idiot detective had apparently done nothing, and the killer remained on the loose.

She looked at her watch. Still more than an hour left, since she had been so quick to get the answers Feldman needed.

Indignant, Heather thought about calling the detective again, demanding to know why he hadn't acted on her information. But she would not be coming back to this parallel universe, and if she didn't make sure that Slasher X was caught, then all his later victims would be on her conscience.

She could go there herself. She had never faced her sister's killer, never even seen the madman. Eric Keric had no idea who Heather Rheims was, despite the fact that she had turned him in timeline after timeline.

She made up her mind in an instant, even though in a horror movie this was probably a very bad decision. But Alternitech would sweep her away in an hour, no matter what happened. After all, Eric Keric had no reason to suspect her, or even recognize her. Heather decided to take the risk.

The murderer's house was repulsively charming and quaint. Neat bluechip junipers lined the walkway up to his little cottage. Flower boxes held green succulents and brown perennials that had died back for winter. Heather thought of the wicked crone's gingerbread house from the story of "Hansel and Gretel."

The front door was painted a slate gray with white trim. Obviously the old sociopath took time between killings to keep his house immaculate. She drew a deep breath and glanced at her watch again before knocking on the door. Only half an hour remained before the Alternitech portal would return. In her jacket pocket, she clasped a can of pepper spray.

Eric Keric had never seen her before in his life. She convinced herself she had nothing to worry about. Heather hoped that she looked like a newspaper salesperson or some other door-to-door annoyance. Then she rang the bell.

The old round-faced man pulled back the curtains beside the door and stared at her for an instant, then ducked away. Keric opened the door, and Heather stepped forward, tense and ready to lure him into a brief but incriminating conversation.

But his hand moved like a rattlesnake, snatching her long rusty-brown hair. "I'm not taking any more of this!" He yanked her head toward him. "And I've certainly had enough of *you*."

Before she could fumble the pepper spray out of her pocket, he swung the baseball bat that he kept beside the door, striking her a harsh sharp blow on the side of the head. Heather didn't even have time to cry out. . . .

★ ★ ★ ★ ★

Pain hammered through the grogginess. She had been stunned into twilight for only a few minutes, but Eric Keric had had enough time to drag her into the kitchen and thrust her into a metal chair beside the dinette table. He had lashed her elbows and wrists with two rubbery bonds—*extension cords,* she realized as she fought her way back to full awareness. Her ears rang, and bright colors swam at the fringes of her vision.

Keric dragged a thin wooden easel across the linoleum floor, standing it in front of her. He was dressed in a checked shirt, partly unbuttoned so she could see his low-necked undershirt and wiry gray chest hair. His sleeves were rolled up on his forearms as if he was ready to get down to work.

The smells and appliances in his kitchen, speckled Formica countertops and stainless-steel sink, were the trappings she had come to associate with kindly grandfathers, but Eric Keric seemed anything but paternal as he glared at her with both fear and anger in his eyes. He pulled the easel in front of her, and Heather lifted her throbbing head to look at it.

"I don't know who you are," the old man growled, "or why you keep tormenting me. What have I done to you?"

She tried to make words, but only a groaning sound came from her slack mouth and thick tongue. The ringing in her ears grew louder. He pulled up the white cover sheet on the easel's large sketchpad, and Heather was astonished to see an accurate, painstakingly rendered pencil and charcoal sketch of her own face. Keric straightened the easel so that she was forced to look at herself. She wondered if she might be hallucinating.

"You . . . killed my sister," Heather finally blurted.

The old man scowled at her. "I didn't kill anyone—no matter what you keep saying, no matter what the police accuse me of." Heather couldn't figure out what he was talking about. "You are an evil, spiteful woman. I know you won't tell me who hired you, or who is responsible for this conspiracy, but you've succeeded in ruining my life—if that was your purpose."

He drew a deep breath, and his eyes flickered shut as if he were composing himself, then he squared his shoulders. "But I cannot change other people. I must change myself. *I must take control of my life.*"

He turned away from her as if he couldn't bear to look at Heather's face. She knew she'd been stunned for only a few minutes at best. He couldn't possibly have drawn the exquisite portrait in that amount of time.

"The police have come to my house five times, twice with search warrants. They ransacked my private possessions, everything I own, but they found nothing, won't even tell me what they think I've done or what they're looking for."

Then he pointed an accusing finger at her. Heather was so frightened she tried to squirm away. The chair screeched with her movement, but she could not break the extension cords.

"Because of your harassment, I've lost my job. It wasn't much, but I worked hard at it. They had no reason to fire me." Keric paced the kitchen floor, and his face had a pathetically desperate plea written across it. "Don't you think every day isn't enough of a struggle? I walk on the edge, but I have the strength. I know how to deal with this burden. . . ."

His voice became a low growl, and his eyes lit up. "But *you* keep piling more and more stress. You're *trying* to drive me over the edge. You want to push me into some violent action. I don't know what you have to gain by making me go . . . berserk."

He clenched his fists but then squeezed his eyes shut again, breathing deeply as if reciting a silent mantra to himself. "But I won't let you. You don't have the power. My life is under my control. You cannot force me to break the law or to hurt anyone."

He withdrew a fat black marker from his pocket and wrenched off the plastic cap with a squeak. She could smell the ink's pungent sour fumes, and her heart skipped a beat. Slasher X always scribbled his indelible mark on the faces of his victims before he cut with the heavy knife.

"You have no power over me," he said, and turned.

With a brutal swift stroke and then a backwards slash, he made a black accusing mark across the picture he had drawn, crossing out her face, obliterating the sketched eyes as if he had eliminated her.

"There," he said, satisfied. "You can no longer bother me."

Keric tore the picture off of the easel and carried it, fluttering in his hands, over to a wooden closet door beside the refrigerator. On the back of the door, skewered on a long nail, hung a stack of sketches. Now, Keric stabbed Heather's portrait on top of the others, faces of men and women, all of them X-ed out.

"Like all those others, you simply don't matter to me anymore."

Her thoughts spun with what he had said. Could it be true that in this parallel timeline Eric Keric had never become Slasher X? That he had found a way to divert his murderous rage and take it out symbolically on his sketches rather than using a knife? She felt sick.

And if this particular incarnation of Eric Keric also had deep psychological problems but retained his sanity by the thinnest of threads . . . then by making anonymous phone calls accusing him of crimes, had she driven the old man closer toward an edge he had so far managed to avoid?

He went behind her, and Heather was afraid he would strike her, cut her throat. But then she felt the extension cords tug at her elbows and wrists—and Heather found herself freed.

The old man tossed the cords onto the linoleum floor. "Go. Get out of here. You are erased from my life."

Heather stood, disoriented, still feeling the concussion. She looked at the old man, but couldn't say a word. Too many conflicting ideas clamored in her mind.

Bolting like a frightened rabbit, she ran for the front door. She had only a few moments before the Alternitech portal would appear. Keric stepped after her, not in pursuit, but eager to seal the door tight behind her. She looked over her shoulder. "I'm . . . sorry. I made an assumption, perhaps a wrong one."

She yanked open the door—and startled herself. She stood facing a carbon copy of Heather Rheims, another her. But this one held a handgun, drawn and ready to fire.

Heather's first absurd thought was that this version of herself had come more sensibly prepared than with a pocket can of pepper spray. She recovered and figured it out first. "Of course. There have to be Alternitechs in parallel timelines."

"Yes, and we both had the same idea," the other Heather said. "Did you kill him?"

Then Eric Keric stepped up, crestfallen and anguished. "Why won't you leave me alone?"

The other Heather's lip curled, and she swung up the

handgun. She said accusingly to Heather, "Why did you let him live?"

"Because he . . . isn't guilty," she said. "Did you look for the headlines in this universe? Did you see any mention of Slasher X? Did the police react strangely when you called to turn him in?"

The alternate young woman kept the pistol aimed at Keric, but her expression wavered.

"This guy might be a brutal killer in most of the parallel universes we've visited, but not here. Oh, he's got plenty of mental problems, but so far he has managed to deal with them. He hasn't hurt anybody."

"That's ridiculous," said her counterpart.

"I know . . . but it's still true."

Keric looked back and forth between the identical young women, resigned instead of surprised. Heather realized that an endless succession of parallel versions of herself had come here to accuse him.

"This one doesn't kill people," Heather insisted. "He just draws pictures."

"How can I accept that?" said her alternate. "I need to do something for Janni. This was my only chance for revenge. How can I let that go?"

"Would I lie to you?" Heather looked at her with a deeply sincere expression. And then the other part of the puzzle slammed into place with thunderous force. "And in this timeline, Janni must still be alive."

Before she could continue the argument, before she could hope to see her sister again, the Alternitech portal shimmered in the air. Heather looked at her counterpart, who wore a startled expression on her face probably identical to her own.

But she couldn't stay. The portal beckoned. She knew

she was not likely to come back to this parallel universe . . . and she had wasted her time here. Heather had no choice but to return, without seeing Janni again.

But perhaps her counterpart would use her time for something more beneficial than useless revenge.

When she returned, blinking and disoriented, Heather stepped out of the portal into the Alternitech control room. Quickly, the tech supervisor and two security men came up to surround her. Heather didn't know what had gone wrong, why they were so intent on intercepting her.

"Ms. Rheims," said the tech supervisor, "kindly hand over all of your documentation on the John F. Kennedy assassination. Your investigation is now terminated, your information forfeit."

Heather shrugged off her backpack, her mind spinning in another direction. She hadn't even thought about Feldman and his obsessive quest. "What's wrong?" She removed all her scans and copies about the frame-up of Francis Tarryall, how the JFK conspiracy remained unresolved. "I found some interesting information, but—"

"Mr. Feldman apparently deceived us and has cost Alternitech a great deal of money. He defaulted on his last several payments, and we've just discovered that he's bankrupt."

"Bankrupt? Money-Is-No-Object Feldman has no money?" She tried to wrap her mind around that shift in reality.

With his sarcastic British reserve, the tech supervisor looked at her. "Mr. Feldman insists it's a conspiracy designed to prevent him from discovering the truth about the JFK murder."

Heather felt numb. Somewhere, in another universe, an

alternate Heather Rheims was again accusing an alternate—innocent—Eric Keric of unspeakable crimes. Or maybe she was embracing a confused but warm-hearted Janni.

Swallowing hard, she stepped away from the portal. Now she could hope for a reassignment, go exploring parallel universes for a more legitimate purpose, finding medical cures, scientific discoveries, even artistic works. Heather's vigilante streak made her a poor dispenser of justice. She would no longer solve crimes, not personal ones or political ones. The truth wasn't always clear cut, even in her own timeline.

Instead, she would remember Janni, keep the fond memories, maybe do some good things in her honor. She was alive, somewhere.

That was a truth Heather could hold on to.

The Bistro of Alternate Realities

The problem with closely parallel universes is that they all look the same. Sometimes, it takes an expert to notice the subtle differences, and only a professional timeline hunter can find variations for profitable exploitation by Alternitech Corp.

Heather Rheims arrived through the portal and took a deep, sweet breath to adjust herself to seemingly familiar surroundings. Among the myriad possible realities, the technology of Alternitech could fling her into nearby universes, worlds where decisions and alternatives had just slightly frayed the course of history. Thus, the city looked the same, the people were the same, most of the daily newspapers ran similar headlines . . . but some things were different. She just had to make her assessment.

Heather was the first one to reach the coffee shop. After wavering between possibilities, she chose a large table with eight chairs, which had always been sufficient for the doppelgangers who would show up. She picked a seat, then moved her pack to a different one, where she could see the door.

Leaving her equipment and her detailed archaeological notes on the table, she went to the coffee bar where the gaunt-looking young man with a wispy goatee—it was *always* a young man with a wispy goatee, no matter what universe she was in—and stared at the variety of hot and cold drinks, caffeinated and decaffeinated, sweet and bitter. Too many choices.

Though she came to the bistro on almost every journey through Alternitech's portals, she still had trouble making up her mind. Some people ordered the same hot beverage day after day, but Heather had never settled into a comfortable routine.

Unfortunately, that led to a crisis of decision every time she was faced with ordering coffee. After vacillating, she finally asked for a cappuccino with an extra shot of espresso, since she'd been feeling rundown. She took her wide cup back to the table and opened her thinscreen laptop so she could call up the esoteric archaeological details she was supposed to know by heart.

As a timeline hunter, Heather had been sent off into parallel universes in search of everything from medical breakthroughs to new music by the Beatles to conspiracy evidence in the JFK assassination. This time, she was a proxy archaeologist. She sipped her cappuccino and wiped foam off her lips before perusing the lengthy summaries of recent findings of ancient Greece and the Peloponnesian Wars.

Archaeology was not a rigorous science of trial and error and analysis: Finding artifacts that had been buried for untold centuries in uninhabited areas was primarily a matter of serendipity and luck. Some Turkish shepherd might go looking for part of his flock and discover a pile of ancient armor, the ruins of a fallen city, or documents sealed inside airtight containers. A single accidental find, like the Dead Sea Scrolls, might change the field forever—at least that was what the passionate young researcher Bruce Wanderlos had told Heather when he'd first hired her.

"Just because someone stumbled upon the ruins of ancient Troy in our timeline, doesn't mean the same accident happened in others." His eyes were bright, his pale brown hair curly and unkempt, but with a natural looseness that made the mess appear intentional and attractive. "And thus, the *converse* must also be true."

After receiving a large university grant Bruce had taken the controversial step of contracting Alternitech rather than going himself out into the field. Heather was assigned to go through the portal and look over current archaeology journals. "It's desk research, I know, and not terribly exciting— but if you copy the records of other digs, other discoveries that haven't been made yet in our universe, then I'll know exactly where to look *here*."

"Isn't that cheating?" Heather had asked.

He seemed so taken aback by her suggestion that she found him endearing. "This is acquiring information for science and history and the enrichment of mankind. It's not a game."

Now, in the coffee shop, she scrolled through items Bruce might be particularly interested in. The sophisticated software on her thinscreen allowed her to upload online records of any number of timeline-specific archaeological journals and scan for differences. The hardest part was deciding which place to go first. On one of her initial searches for Bruce, she had stopped at Mrs. Coffee Belgian Café and Bistro, intending just to have a cappuccino or a mocha while she planned her strategy—and then she'd discovered something incredibly alarming.

The door opened, and the tinkling silver bell announced the arrival of a new customer. She looked up to see, as expected, another Heather. She wondered which one this was and how many would be arriving for today's kaffeeklatsch. The other Heather, nearly identical except for her blouse, came over to drop her backpack in the chair beside Heather.

The barista blinked in surprise, as he always did, but by now most of the employees of Mrs. Coffee were used to the unusual event, convinced by the absurd explanation that all the Heathers were part of a Lookalike Club.

The new Heather went to the counter, swept her long cinnamon-brown hair out of her eyes and tucked it behind her shoulders. She decisively ordered a cappuccino, but without a shot of espresso. Heather wondered if maybe she should have done the same; did she really need the extra caffeine? She looked up to see another identical person step through the door. They would all be arriving soon.

Since, in her own world, Alternitech sent timeline hunters to parallel universes seeking to exploit differences, it only made sense that in many of those similar realities, other Alternitechs would send other timeline hunters, many of whom would be Heather's counterparts. The first time they'd stumbled upon each other was quite a shock, then a delight. Eventually Heather and her counterparts discovered that they could pool their resources.

Two more Heathers entered the coffee shop and bistro, standing in line to order their drinks, many of which were the same, though others had subtle variations, as was to be expected. Heather sat back and watched them all.

In the mix of universes, the people weren't always the same, but by now some of her doppelgangers were familiar to her. Most obvious was the Heather with a thin childhood scar on her cheek, a mark from when an abrupt gust of wind had blown a screen door into her face. Heather remembered that incident when she was a girl, but she had ducked aside and not been cut, as had most of her counterparts.

The first alternate Heather brought her cappuccino back to the table and sat down. Her opening question immediately identified her as Gloomy Heather. They all had quick nicknames, like the Seven Dwarves. "So are you dating anyone yet? I'm not. How's life in your timeline?"

Heather took another sip from her large cup to hide her embarrassment. "Not dating anyone at the moment, but it hasn't been that long."

"That archaeology guy's awfully cute," said another Heather, the one who had earned the nickname of Intense. "If my Sasha wasn't so damned good in bed, I'd ask Bruce out in a minute."

Intense Heather had hooked up with a fiery-eyed young rock musician, and the two had gone supernova with their initial romance. Intense rarely talked about anything else, and she had shown Sasha's picture to them all, in case they had a chance to bump into him in their own parallel universes. "Don't miss your chance. I almost did. Luckiest drink I ever spilled."

Intense had accidentally stumbled in a crowded bar on her way to a table of her own, spilling a glass of red wine on Sasha as he'd been heading for the door. He had responded with a flash of anger, and Intense Heather offered such abject apologies that the young musician burst into laughter and invited her to dinner. That had been the start.

So far, though, in every other parallel universe the Heathers had missed their chance, stumbling but catching the wine before it spilled, or losing Sasha before he walked out the door and never encountering him again. Heather had botched the opportunity entirely; when she mentally backtracked to the night in question, she realized that she had stayed home, unable to decide where to go.

Scar Heather sat down, picking up the conversation. "I'm flirting with Bruce, but I think he's just shy."

"Maybe I'll ask him out," said Gloomy, "but he'll probably say no."

"So what if he says no?" Intense responded. "You're not any worse off than if you don't ask at all. It's a no-brainer."

Heather found herself nodding. She had sensed the shy archaeologist's attraction for her, which he masked as appreciation for the successful work she'd done so far. Maybe she would push a little harder so that at least she'd have something to talk about with her counterparts the next time Intense bragged about her wild escapades with Sasha.

The smiling one who sat down was obviously Happily-Ever-After Heather, the one incarnation of all her parallel lives where circumstances had turned out perfect in every way. Two years before, most of the Heathers had been in a steady relationship with a computer programmer and part-time graphic designer named Perry. They'd fit together fairly well, but then Heather's sister Janni had been killed, and the tragedy had torn her apart. Withdrawing, she'd taken out her resentment on Perry, and the two of them had parted.

But circumstances were slightly different in the universe of Happily-Ever-After Heather. Janni had accidentally avoided becoming a random victim, and Happily-Ever-After had never faced the insurmountable stress in her relationship with Perry. Though they'd reached a crisis of personal goals and feelings, they had decided to work out their differences, investing in their bond instead of drawing apart. Perry and Happily-Ever-After had gotten married a year later, and now they had a fine home, both had good careers, and everything was perfect. The other Heathers halfway resented their counterpart, but most of all they envied her. . . .

When finally all of the alternate Heathers had their coffees and sat down at the table, Intense Heather unzipped her pack and withdrew her thinscreen. "Time to get down

to business. The portals will be back before you know it."
All eight of them looked at their watches with comical simultaneity.

Each Heather took out her carefully culled and organized database of archaeological information from her own universe. Instead of spending hours sifting through library records or digging out obscure references in journals, all the Heathers sat down for coffee and conversation. That way they could simply exchange all the files they had collated from their homes. In an hour of swapping and comparing records, the eight Heathers could achieve as many discoveries as if they had gone on eight separate timeline hunts.

This cooperative efficiency had made her quite a success in all her incarnations—at least all of the ones who showed up at the coffee shop. Heather's counterparts and their identical goals yielded a synergy that allowed each of them to deliver clue after clue to the endearingly appreciative Bruce Wanderlos. Most of the differences turned out to be of no interest to anyone, but occasionally they hit the jackpot.

And while their thinscreens were humming and exchanging, compiling and rejecting, Heather had a chance to listen to advice from her alternate selves. It was like having a sounding board better than a best friend, drawing upon common experience and shared hearts. The Heathers who had made bad decisions did their best to help those who had not yet encountered the risky situation.

At first, Heather had been somewhat hurt to discover that they'd labeled her Indecisive Heather, but the reasons were obvious even to herself and she couldn't fault them for it. She had come to depend on these conversations and personal strategy sessions. She rarely made up her own mind anymore, but hesitated too often, losing opportunities.

"I've got an idea," said Intense, slurping her double espresso. She targeted Gloomy. "You always say you missed your chance, that by sheer bad luck you're never in the right place at the right time. Believe me, half of it's your own problem because you don't take any chances—but here I'm offering you one. Switch with me. Go home to my universe and spend a day or two with Sasha."

Gloomy's eyes widened. "I couldn't do that. He's your—"

"And you think he'd be cheating on me if he slept with you? You *are* me. God, if I was the one who hadn't been laid in two years, I'd sure hope one of you might take pity on me."

"But . . . but how will I ever fool him? We don't have the same history. We look the same, but your personality's entirely—"

"You wouldn't have to fool him, Heather dear. He knows what I do for a living. In fact, he'd get a kick out of it, and you'd give me a rest. Frankly, I'm a bit sore, and I could do with a day or two of just sitting at home and reading a book. You've probably got the same unread novels on your shelf that I do."

The other Heathers immediately went into a detailed discussion about the morality and wisdom of this plan. Heather suspected many of them were secretly hoping for their own chance with Sasha.

Happily-Ever-After looked deeply uncomfortable. "Your lives are what you made them, every mistake, every decision. Why can't you be satisfied with the way things are? It's nice to compare notes with each other, but this is drastic."

"Sure," said Scar. "Listen to advice from the one who has a perfect life." Happily-Ever-After blushed as if ashamed of her own good fortune.

When all their databases had been exchanged, they finished their coffees and picked up the dishes. Heather was glad she didn't have to make the choice that Gloomy Heather faced. It would have taken her a month to make up her mind.

"All right," said Gloomy, "if I don't do this, you'll never let me complain again." She forced a wan smile. "I'll go back through your portal, you go back through mine." Gloomy and Intense shook hands like businessmen, then realized how absurd they looked and gave each other a simultaneous hug.

"Be careful, Sasha just might burn you out," Intense said.

"That'll be . . . quite a new experience for me," Gloomy answered.

They all split up. Heather shouldered her backpack and went to her own rendezvous point, where the discreet portal would shimmer through the air.

They would all meet again at another bistro in another parallel universe.

When she delivered her results to the technicians at Alternitech, Bruce Wanderlos was there waiting with a shy smile. While he skimmed the results, she went to the locker room to shower and change, getting back into decent clothes instead of the plain "don't notice me" outfit Alternitech asked its timeline hunters to wear.

Before she left for the day, though, the archaeologist met her outside the dressing room door. His eyes were shining, his face flushed, and he took a quick step toward her as if he wanted to give her a happy kiss. "You don't realize what you found there! There's a fleet of Greek warships sunk in a bay off the Anatolian Peninsula. They've been preserved in the deep, cold water. According to these papers, one of the archaeologists believes it was Agamemnon's fleet in the Trojan War!"

Heather recognized that such a discovery would make a name for Bruce. "Sounds like you've got your work cut out for you."

Bruce shook his head and drew a deep breath. "I don't know how I can ever thank you. I just wish—"

Impulsively, remembering her Intense and Happily-Ever-After counterparts, she said quickly before she could think about it too much, "Well, you could ask me out for a drink—or dinner, if you feel really grateful."

He seemed taken aback. "I didn't know that—I didn't think . . . are you sure it's all right if we mix business and socialization?"

Heather raised her eyebrows. "Bruce, if this is as big a discovery as you say, you won't need to hire my services any more."

"All right." He was delighted at his doubly unexpected good fortune.

She gave him her number and address, and they arranged a time. "Oh, and Bruce?" Heather called, giddy at her own good luck. "If this discovery is so significant, you better find someplace that doesn't just serve hamburgers."

"I . . . I'll make reservations."

"Just because a seafood chain has the word 'lobster' in its name doesn't mean it's a fancy restaurant," said Scar, but she looked more amused than disappointed.

Heather sat back and drank from her double mocha. "Well, I don't care. It was the nicest evening I've had in a long time."

"He took *me* to an Italian restaurant," said Silly Heather, who always had trouble opening up her real feelings and covered it all with a joke, even among her identical counterparts.

Happily-Ever-After just grinned. "I'm so pleased you finally made the decision to do it. Part of me wishes you'd try to patch things up with Perry, though, because we're so happy together."

"We know," groaned Intense.

"Perry's married again in my universe," said Heather. "I took too long—"

"He's only engaged in mine," said Scar.

Quiet Heather watched them all; she was one of the few who hadn't gotten up the nerve to nudge Bruce into a date, but she looked as if she might change her mind.

Intense seemed inordinately edgy and disturbed. All the doppelgangers were curious to hear the story of Gloomy's "perfectly licit" affair with the passionate Sasha . . . but Gloomy hadn't joined them today, or the previous two meetings.

"I'm sure it turned out all right," Heather said, sensing how deeply disturbed her normally gruff counterpart was.

"She probably just wants him for a few more days to get her fill," Scar suggested.

"Sasha can sometimes be a little . . . intense."

"You're a perfect match for him then," Silly said. Some of the other Heathers chuckled, but the Intense one did not.

"Bruce asked me out again," Heather announced, "on his own initiative this time."

"How long do you think I should wait until I sleep with him?" said another one.

"Are you kidding? He could barely manage a goodnight kiss."

"He's shy, not celibate," said Scar.

"Did you ask about his family?"

"Did you tell him about Janni?"

"He seemed very sad to hear it when I did."

"How serious is he about all this?"

"How serious am *I* about this? It's too soon to ask those questions."

"He's never been married, has he?"

"No. I asked him point blank."

"I wish he wouldn't hold his fork like that. Nobody ever taught him table manners."

"We had pizza, so I didn't get a chance to notice."

"Who cares about his table manners? It's his personality that counts, and Bruce is very nice."

Heather listened to the rapid-fire exchange of alternative dates that she could have had. It seemed as if she got to know Bruce Wanderlos better by hearing all the comparisons . . . but it was unfair. Did she really need these surrogate Heathers to live her life for her?

"You're all pathetic," said Intense. "Just listen to yourselves! I was always fairly strong and independent—and so are all of you. But now you sound like a bunch of airhead cheerleaders in a locker room."

"Excuse me," said Happily-Ever-After, "but you were insufferable yourself when you started seeing Sasha. I don't think I'm the only one who was tired of hearing about all your sex."

"Maybe you're just upset to be away from him," said Quiet Heather.

"Or maybe you're jealous because another one of us is with him," said Scar, "despite all of your assertions to the contrary."

Someone else came in to the bistro, and Intense looked up quickly, hoping that she would see her Gloomy counterpart return, but it was just a middle-aged man looking for a sandwich. Angry and frustrated, Intense grabbed her pack and took her thinscreen, though she hadn't finished exchanging files with all of her doppelgangers. She stormed out of the coffee shop while the other Heathers looked after her.

"Something's worse than she's admitting," said Heather. "Most of us would be worried in that situation, but not go ballistic."

Scar finished her coffee while Happily-Ever-After gathered their cups. "We still haven't settled how fast should we push this with Bruce. How far do we go?"

"We'll each have to decide that for ourselves," said Heather.

All of the others looked at her in surprise as if she had just told a joke.

On their second date Heather and Bruce went out to a foreign film with subtitles that Heather thought was supposed to impress her, though neither of them much enjoyed—or understood—the movie. Following the lead of what some of her counterparts had done, she decided to tell him about her sister Janni, showed him pictures. As she expected, Bruce was very understanding and compassionate without being maudlin.

Still, she felt odd every moment, a strange sense of déjà vu—as if she were stuck in an old rerun of "It's a Wonderful Life." Some people would have considered it an advantage to test out choices and decisions, then rewind and try again if they didn't work. Would Bruce himself think it was cheating, in a completely different sense from how he used someone else's archaeology work?

In an awkward yet sweet way, he asked her to come to

his apartment for coffee—she was getting tired of coffee, but she listened to his words, which he had obviously rehearsed in front of a mirror. She ended up staying for three hours, but the whole time they just sat on the sofa and talked. He didn't even try to kiss her until she was about to leave. Heather supposed that the next time she met her counterparts in the coffee shop, her doppelgangers would be full of alternate endings for this evening, some of them lurid, some of them embarrassing. But she liked the way her own had turned out, with or without coaching from her other selves. . . .

Thanks to Heather's results, Bruce now had more archaeological work than he could handle for years. Alternitech timeline hunters were expensive, and his grant money had nearly run out, so he finished his request for Heather's services, though he intended to keep seeing her on a more personal level.

On her last outing for the project, Heather went tentatively back to Mrs. Coffee, not sure if she even wanted to keep discussing their budding relationship with the other Heathers. Part of the excitement of romance was the spontaneity, the unpredictability, and she had an unfair advantage if she already knew a dozen possible ways that any evening might turn out.

Intense Heather's boyfriend Sasha seemed too unpredictable, a loose cannon with mood swings and fiery passion, while her own former relationship with Perry had been too sedate and comfortable. She didn't know how it was going to turn out with Bruce . . . and she wasn't sure she wanted to know. This wasn't being indecisive, as was her too-common flaw—it was being accepting.

Though the archaeology project was over, the Heathers would continue to meet in the coffee shop, discussing ways to increase their discoveries in alternate timelines. But Heather wasn't sure she was interested in talking about her personal life. Maybe she wanted to make her own choices for a change.

Today she was one of the last to arrive. Inside, it looked as if Intense was having a nervous breakdown. She shouted, "You don't understand! I'm terrified for her. I got her into this! I egged her into making her decision—and what if Sasha's hurt her?"

"He wouldn't hurt her," said one of the other Heathers, trying to be soothing.

"Oh, and you're the expert on his unstable personality? He's got problems. He flies into rages. He's supposed to take medication, but all the time the asshole convinces himself he doesn't need it."

"That doesn't sound like the man you've been talking about all along," said Scar.

Intense wrung her hands. "He's not like that usually. He can be sweet and romantic and passionate—but other times he just flies off the handle. I could sense he was getting impatient with me, said I was too domineering, that I was like a bulldozer. I thought maybe he'd want someone a bit more passive. I thought he'd *like* her. But sometimes being passive just provokes the abusive streak in him. What if he's killed her? My God!"

"You're overreacting, Heather."

"Am I? It's been five times, and she hasn't come back. And you know that I can't return to my own universe unless she comes through and opens the portal. There has to be an exchange. I can't just go get her."

"It was a decision that she made," Heather said, standing beside the crowded table.

Looking alarmed at the discord among the identical

women, the goateed barista stood close to the phone as if contemplating a call to 9-1-1.

Heather continued, looking at her counterparts. "You made up your mind. She made up her mind. We've all made up our minds—but we spend endless hours in here talking and discussing and gossiping. Dammit, my whole life has become a committee!"

"But what am I supposed to do about . . . her?" Intense said. She seemed to know something much more dangerous about Sasha than she had ever revealed them, especially Gloomy.

"Do whatever you decide, and then you'll have to live with it."

Seeing the group of Heathers in the coffee shop, she wondered how many other counterparts had already left the kaffeeklatsch, not wanting to hear about other lives or experience regrets for incorrect decisions. Of all the infinite universes, maybe only this handful of Heathers felt the need to commiserate with each other, share secrets and depend upon someone else.

She didn't even bother to remove her backpack. "I'd better be off doing my work. This isn't . . . what I want anymore. It's my life, after all, and I feel like I'm in a room full of dress rehearsals."

"Don't you want to wait and find out if the other Heather comes back?" said Intense. "Maybe she's all right, or maybe Sasha just kept her for an extra while."

"You know, I've decided it isn't relevant to me," she answered. "Because there are probably timelines where it happens every possible way. I need to focus on *my* life as a participant, not a spectator."

"Wait, you'll want to hear about what happened with Bruce last night," said Scar, raising her eyebrows. Several of the others leaned forward, eager as predators.

"What happened on your own date?" someone asked her before she could leave. "Weren't you supposed to go out with him again, too?"

But Heather turned away. "I'll just keep it to myself, for good or bad. Why should I live vicariously through all of you, when I can do it myself first-hand?"

From the set of troubled looks on their faces, Heather realized she had struck a nerve, that the thoughts had crossed most of their minds already. "Good luck," she said to herself and to all of them, then left the coffee shop behind.

Rough Draft

With Rebecca Moesta

After a decade during which he wrote and published nothing new, the fan letters dwindled to a few a year.

"Dear Mr. Coren, You're the best science fiction writer ever!"

"Dear Mr. Coren, Your book *Divergent Lines* changed my life. I felt as if you were speaking directly to me, and you helped me work through some major issues."

The entire experience, though great for the ego, had ultimately proved meaningless. Eventually he'd been forced to return the money for the second book advance, because he simply couldn't do it again. After enjoying a pleasant day in the sun, Mitchell Coren had retreated to his small apartment to live a normal life. The gleaming Nebula Award and the silver Hugo—both dusty now—were little more than knickknacks on the mantle of a fireplace that he never used.

Having convinced himself of the wisdom of J. D. Salinger's approach to authorial fame, Mitchell had squelched all thoughts of returning to writing. He immersed himself in a normal life with all its petty concerns.

Today, with an indifference born of long practice, Mitchell opened his bills and junk mail before finally tearing open the padded envelope that obviously contained a book. Another intrusion, no doubt. An annoying reminder of his old life. He still received advance reading copies from editors trying to wheedle a rare cover quote from him, rough draft manuscripts from aspiring authors who begged for comments or critiques, and books presented to him by new authors who had been inspired by his lone published novel.

Inside this envelope, however, he found his own name on the dust jacket of a novel he had never written.

INFERNITIES
Mitchell Coren
Multiple Award-winning Author of *Divergent Lines*

Whirling flakes of confusion compacted into a hard snowball in the pit of his stomach. "What the hell?"

His initial, and obvious, thought was that someone had stolen his name. But that didn't make sense. Though many editorial positions had changed in the decade since he'd published *Divergent Lines*, Mitchell was still well enough known in the insular science fiction community that somebody in the field would have noticed an imposter. Besides, how much could his byline be worth after all this time? It wasn't worth stealing.

Someone had tucked a folded sheet of paper between the book's front cover and the endpaper. He read it warily.

Dear Mr. Coren,

As a longtime fan of yours, I thought you'd appreciate seeing this novel I came across in a parallel universe.

I'm a timeline hunter by profession. Perhaps you've heard of Alternitech? Our company uses a proprietary technology to open gateways into alternate realities. My colleagues and I explore these parallel universes for breakthroughs or useful discrepancies that Alternitech can profitably exploit: medical and scientific advances, historical discoveries, artistic variations. My specialty is the creative arts.

I stumbled upon this book in an alternate timeline while searching for a new Mario Puzo. Since the science fiction market isn't nearly as large or profitable as the mainstream, I couldn't spend much time checking out its background, but a brief search showed that the "alternate" Mitchell Coren published a dozen or so short stories after *Divergent Lines*, then produced this second novel. I'm hoping Alternitech will want to arrange for its publication, but naturally I felt you should see it first.

> With deepest respect,
> Jeremy Cardiff

Mitchell stared at the letter with mistrust and growing irritation. He had heard of this company that searched alternate realities for everything from new Beatles records, to evidence of UFOs or Kennedy assassination conspiracies, to cures for obscure diseases. He could understand the more humanitarian objectives, but why *fiction?* What gave Alternitech the right to infringe on his life like this?

He opened to the dust jacket photo and saw that the picture did resemble him, though this other Mitchell Coren wore a different hairstyle and a cocky, self-assured grin. The bio mentioned that after completing *Infernities* he was "already at work on his next novel."

Oddly unsettled, Mitchell pushed the book away. Its very existence raised too many disturbing questions.

Three increasingly urgent phone calls to his former agent went unreturned. Since Mitchell had neither delivered anything new nor generated much income, his agent wasn't in a great hurry to attend to his so-called emergency. Even in the days when he'd briefly been a hot client, Mitchell had been relatively high-maintenance, needing encouragement and constant contact.

He decided to call his entertainment attorney instead. After all, Sheldon Freiburg charged by the hour and therefore had an incentive to get right on the matter.

"Mitch Coren! I haven't heard from you since the last ice age." Freiburg's voice was bluff and hearty on the telephone. "What on earth have you been doing? You dropped off the map."

"I've been working a real-world job, Sheldon. You know, regular paycheck, benefits . . . security?"

"Yeah, I've heard of those. Hopped off the old fame-and-fortune bandwagon, eh?"

"A modicum of fame, not a whole lot of fortune—as you well know."

Freiburg had handled the entertainment contracts for the two movie options on *Divergent Lines*. Mitchell had been young and naïve then, believing the Hollywood hype and enthusiasm. He'd been surrounded by smiling fast-talkers whose eager assertions of certain box-office appeal and guaranteed studio support were built on a foundation as strong as a soap bubble. After the attorney's fees and the agent's commission, the option money had been just enough to pay off his car, which was now ten years old.

"So, Mitchell," Freiburg said now, "people don't call me unless they have a situation—either good or bad—so let's hear it."

"Someone's trying to publish an unauthorized Mitchell Coren novel."

"You've actually done other work?" The lawyer sounded

surprised. "Something new? I thought you'd turned hermit on us. Did somebody steal your manuscript?"

"This is trickier than that. It isn't exactly a matter of stealing. This is a novel from a parallel universe, and Alternitech wants to get it published here." He explained the situation in full.

"Oh, that *is* tricky—but not unheard of. Listen, since it's Tuesday, I'll give you a special deal, a quick and inexpensive answer."

"Inexpensive? You've changed in the last ten years, Sheldon."

The lawyer chuckled. "How could I help it? The whole world has changed. But you're not going to like what I have to say."

Mitchell braced himself, clutching the receiver; thankfully, Freiburg could not see his tense expression.

"Precedents have been set in this area. In every dispute about the use of materials from alternate universes, Alternitech has come out the winner. I'm convinced the company spends as much money each year on their team of lawyers as they did developing their parallel universe gateway. You'd be wasting your money to try and block the publication. Compared to the rest of the entertainment industry, authors and books are minnows in an ocean. Even the Big Fish in the music and film industries haven't won a single case.

"Alternitech's timeline hunters bring back intellectual property that might conceivably belong to a counterpart in this universe. The first big case was when one of their music specialists, a guy named Jeremy Cardiff—"

"That's who sent me the novel."

"Great," Freiburg said, then continued, ignoring the interruption. "In Alternitech v the Carpenter Estate, Cardiff found several new albums by the Carpenters, in an alternate reality where Karen Carpenter never died of anorexia. The CDs sounded like the same old shit to me, but don't underestimate the huge amount of money generated by piped-in background music. The Carpenter Estate sued, citing copyright infringement and unlawful exploitation of a creative work.

"Alternitech countered that since Karen Carpenter was dead in this universe, she could not 'create' new works after the date of her death. They also argued using an old favorite of the pharmaceutical companies, that since Alternitech had made such a substantial investment developing their technology, they deserved to reap the benefits of its commercial exploitation.

"The ruling sided with the Carpenter Estate insofar as establishing a 'fair percentage' of profits that should go to the creator's counterpart in this reality—fifteen percent, I think it was. But since Alternitech's timeline hunters did all the work to obtain the property, kind of like salvage hunters on the high seas, they were granted full control of its use. Similar lawsuits have been raised by individual movie producers, screenwriters, directors, and even actors who resent the release of 'new films' starring them for which they never got paid. Like I said, in every case, they lose."

Mitchell remembered that one of the alternate Mel Gibson films had caused something of a stir, because the parallel-universe version of the actor had received an Academy Award for a role that this timeline's Gibson had turned down.

Freiburg continued. "When you get right down to it, Mitch, record companies and movie studios don't *want* the individual artists to win. Alternitech provides them with completely finished new work for a fraction of the cost or effort of making it themselves. Much less hassle, too. They just distribute the work through their normal channels and pay a standard percentage of artist's royalties directly to Alternitech. Then, if and only if the court orders it, Alternitech cuts a teeny weeny check to our own world's parallel artist or company or estate, and everyone is happy. Well, almost everyone."

"So you're saying I shouldn't even try, Sheldon? It's not . . . not *right!*"

"Mitch, if Paul McCartney can't win, then a mere sci-fi novelist doesn't stand a snowball's chance." He paused as if reconsidering. "On the other hand, Mitch my friend, I just thought of a factor that's ironically in your favor, if you really want to stop publication. There's a very real chance that Alternitech won't even bother with your little book. Look at your royalty statements. You're a science fiction writer ten years out of the public eye. Oh sure, there'd be a limited audience for a 'lost unpublished work' by Mitchell Coren . . . but it isn't exactly a Margaret Mitchell sequel to *Gone with the Wind*. If this Cardiff guy is a fan of yours, contact him and tell him how you feel. Who knows, he might do you a favor and pretend he never found it."

Mitchell didn't know whether to feel stung or take heart from the possibility.

Distracted and fretting, he polished the two awards on his mantel—something he hadn't done for the better part of a year. They looked quite impressive, he had to admit, and certainly gave him bragging rights. His occasional visitors asked about them, and he answered with feigned modesty. The awards seemed so irrelevant to his current life.

These days, Mitchell used his skills as a wordsmith in the unglamorous but stable profession of technical writing,

Kevin J. Anderson

producing essential documentation and annual reports for a manufacturing firm. Although it was a challenge to write compelling prose about new cereal box designs or recyclable plastic bottles, he was a master at slanting his text toward investors or consumers or environmental agencies, as needed.

Many of his coworkers—what the science fiction world called "mundanes"—were aspiring writers who never managed to finish or submit stories. Few of them knew about his past, however, since Mitchell rarely mentioned his novel.

As he rubbed a fingerprint off the Nebula's clear Lucite surface, looking at the suspended bits of metal shavings and semi-precious stones that formed a sparkling galaxy, he thought back to those brief, heady days. They were just memories now, but he wouldn't trade them for anything.

Divergent Lines had appeared with a splash like a giant water balloon. An excerpt of the novel had been published in *Analog* as the cover story and won that month's readers' poll. The novel itself had generated rave reviews and was immediately dubbed "a new classic" by critics and his fellow SF authors.

He had been welcomed as a hero at the World Science Fiction Convention. He'd always read science fiction, but had never attended a con before. The fans surprised him at panels, listening to everything he said. They lined up for his book signings in the autograph hall or followed him and asked embarrassingly earnest questions about details he himself had never considered.

When Mitchell went to the Hugo Awards ceremony, he found himself plunged into a sea of unreality as the emcee announced his name as the winner. Astonished and grinning, he stumbled up to the podium and held up his silver

88

rocket ship with mixed feelings of shock and giddy triumph.

The following spring, thanks to the continued buzz, *Divergent Lines* had been a shoo-in for the final Nebula ballot. New to the entire experience, Mitchell stood like a lost puppy in the lobby and the bar, surrounded by luminaries of the genre. He recognized their names from the covers of well-loved books, famous writers ranging from Grand Masters to prolific hacks, all of them legendary and, for the most part, *personable.*

He'd been in a daze. These Titans of science fiction talked to him as a peer, praised his novel. Mitchell found it unnerving, and he began to wonder how he could ever live up to their expectations. Did he deserve so much praise and success? What if his next work didn't measure up? Would he be exposed as a fraud and cast out of this distinguished circle of authors? How would he bear the humiliation?

His publisher paid for his Nebula banquet ticket, and Mitchell was treated as a celebrity at their table. With his stomach tied in knots, he could summon no appetite at all. In an agony of anticipation, he endured the drawn-out meal, the mandatory chit-chat, the interminable banquet speaker. By the time the awards finally began, plodding through each category as if in a calculated effort to increase his anxiety, Mitchell had convinced himself that he had no chance of winning. He was a newcomer. He had no track record. He had never played the politics of exchanging recommendations. He had not campaigned for the award. These writers couldn't possibly consider him a friend and certainly didn't owe him any favors.

And yet the name in the presenter's envelope said *Divergent Lines*. The Nebula seemed even more amazing than the Hugo, because this honor came from his *peers*, fellow professionals who supposedly knew good writing when they saw it. As Mitchell stood clutching the award, he imagined that someday, when he stood at the Pearly Gates and looked back on his entire life, this would be the high point. . . .

After that night, though, Mitchell Coren never wrote another word of fiction. He had left the science fiction community behind and let *Divergent Lines* stand as his sole legacy.

Even in his heyday, Mitchell had not spent much time with die-hard science fiction fans. Not because he didn't like them—he appreciated anyone who bought and loved his novel. But he didn't understand their intensity or their passions and usually ended up feeling outclassed when they wanted to talk shop.

He met Jeremy Cardiff at a quiet place called Mrs. Coffee, a small bistro with shaded outside tables where they could have a conversation in a pleasant atmosphere. Mitchell didn't know which of them was more nervous. He could see in the timeline hunter's eyes that Jeremy was a bona fide Fan.

"This is really an honor, Mr. Coren. I've always been an admirer of *Divergent Lines*, and now that I've read *Infernities*, there's no doubt in my mind that you're one of my all-time favorite authors. I felt so surprised and fortunate to have found the book." Jeremy, a youngish man with a thin face, long hair, and a neatly-trimmed brown beard, looked like a waif hoping for a pat on the head. His blue eyes were wide, his smile tentative.

Mitchell took a drink of coffee, then cleared his throat. "Well, Mr. Cardiff, that's what I'm here to talk to you about."

"Please, call me Jeremy." Then the younger man's face

fell as he interpreted Mitchell's reluctant tone.

Mitchell chose his words as carefully as he would have in preparing a viewgraph presentation for the board of the manufacturing company. He wasn't sure his reasons would make sense to anyone but himself. Though he knew he didn't exactly have a legal case, he might be able to play the celebrity card. Perhaps by asking a special favor from his number one fan, he could get what he needed. "I think you're perceptive enough to understand why I don't want the novel published here. It's not *my* book. Somebody else wrote it."

"No, Mr. Coren. You wrote it. Another version of you, maybe, but it was still your talent, your creativity. When I was in college, I read and reread *Divergent Lines* until my copy fell apart, and I've been waiting ten years for a new novel by the same author. When I found *Infernities*, I sent you the physical book I brought back through the portal, but I made a photocopy. I'm already on my second time through it. It's brilliant—full of intricate layers and nuances."

Mitchell desperately wanted to ask which book he thought was better. Dedicated readers like Jeremy were generally his toughest customers and his harshest critics and, because Mitchell didn't think a new novel could ever live up to their expectations, he had decided not to try.

"That man may have the same name and the same genetics as I do, but he grew up in a parallel universe with a different set of circumstances. He's not me. He obviously reached a different decision about his career. But I didn't write *Infernities*, and if you published it here in our universe, people would see it as my own work, no matter how many disclaimers you put on it."

"But it's good, sir. Have you read it?"

"No, I don't dare. It would seem almost . . . plagiaristic."

Kevin J. Anderson

As if clinging to hope, Jeremy said, "So . . . are you writing something of your own? Maybe a book that's similar to *Infernities*?"

"No. I'm not writing anything."

The young man looked at his coffee as if it were poison. He didn't seem angry at Mitchell's attitude, just deeply disappointed. "Then I don't understand. What made you stop writing? I mean, you got the royal treatment. People were lined up waiting for your next book. You had a contract to fulfill, didn't you?"

"Yes. And I . . . decided to return the advance."

"But why? It just doesn't make sense."

"Why? I'd already won the highest accolades in my field." Mitchell spoke softly, but his voice grew more intense. "Whether through brilliance or sheer dumb luck I muddled my way to the pinnacle of success my first time out of the starting gate. *Divergent Lines* was hailed as the best book of the year, won all the awards, got spectacular reviews in every periodical from *Publishers Weekly* and *Kirkus* to *Locus* and *Chronicle*. *Library Journal* called it an instant classic."

Mitchell sighed. "Don't you see? The weight of it all gets oppressive. Where could I possibly go from there? There's no place but down." An edge of bitterness sharpened his tone. "It's a very long way down. No matter how good it was, my second book—*Infernities* or whatever I might've called it—would never be good enough. The fans and the critics certainly aren't kind unless your sophomore effort is unbelievably spectacular.

"As it stands right now, I'll go down in history as the author of a great novel. But if I published twenty other books, regardless of how well-written they might be, I can tell you some of the review quotes already: 'A solid novel, but not as

92

inspired as *Divergent Lines*.' Or 'A fine effort, though it doesn't live up to the promise of its predecessor.' Or, worse yet, 'A disappointing follow-up to the author's first novel.' "

Jeremy frowned at what Mitchell was saying. "I think you're too hard on your fans, sir. We would have followed you. Even after ten years, most of us still want to read whatever you have to say."

"Maybe I don't have anything else to say," Mitchell said. "I can name author after author who falls into that category. Being successful is a Catch-22. If your first novel is a smash hit, an award winner and a critical success, it might mean your career has momentum and you're launched. On the other hand, it could mean your writing will never be good enough again. What should I have done—expanded *Divergent Lines* and written a couple of unnecessary sequels, so I could call it a trilogy? I could have licensed my universe, farmed it out to other authors, but that just didn't seem right to me. Either way, I would have been crucified by the fans and the critics."

"Just by the snobs," Jeremy said, "not by the *fans*. But you disappeared from fandom altogether. When's the last time you went to a science fiction convention?"

"The WorldCon where I got my Hugo was the first and last. I stopped reading *Locus* and *Chronicle* and *Ansible* after one of them ran an editorial about one-hit wonders that led off with 'What ever happened to Mitchell Coren?' " He looked at his coffee. "I didn't stand a chance of keeping up the momentum in my career. Fans and critics are too unpredictable. So I controlled the only part of the equation that I *could* control: I stopped writing fiction. My life is stable now that I've accepted the wisdom of anonymity. But if Alternitech publishes this apocryphal second novel that I didn't really write, then I'll be at the mercy of the public's expectations again. Please, don't do it."

Disappointment and resignation filled Jeremy's eyes as he unzipped his backpack and reached inside to withdraw a thick stack of photocopied pages. "Look, this is my only copy. What happens to it is not really supposed to be my decision. Alternitech owns proprietary rights to whatever I bring back through parallel universes. Still, no matter how much *I* loved this novel, I have to admit that this doesn't have the equivalent value to Alternitech of, say, an unknown collection of Sherlock Holmes stories by Arthur Conan Doyle or the Dean Koontz/Stephen King collaboration I uncovered once. I think people deserve to read it. I was going to have you autograph this for me." Jeremy slid the stack of papers across the table. "But now I guess you'd better keep it, so you'll know there aren't any other copies in existence. You decide what to do. It's your call, Mr. Coren. It's your book."

"I—" Mitchell started to speak, but found his voice choked with emotion. He took a long drink of his now-tepid coffee and started again. "Well . . . don't you want to keep it? You said you were reading it."

Jeremy shook his head. "If you know I have a copy, you'd always worry that someday I'd be tempted to post it on the Internet. It's better if you keep it."

The papers felt warm in Mitchell's hands. His vision blurred, and he took a moment to compose himself. "I . . . didn't expect this."

"I'm a musician myself, Mr. Coren. I write and record songs, but I haven't had much success so far. It was a minor consolation when I found that I did have a hit record in an alternate universe, but nothing here yet. I was the one who brought back the new music for that whole Karen Carpenter debacle, and I don't feel very good about it. As a musician, I thought Carpenter or her estate should have had some control over her own creative work, no matter which incarnation made the album. The same goes for you, sir. If you're uncomfortable about having *Infernities* published, then . . ." He shrugged.

"I can't tell you how much this means to me."

"I think I understand." Jeremy slurped his decaf cappuccino. "Besides, I'm your fan. I can't think of anything cooler than to know I am the only person in this entire universe who's read your new novel."

Dozens of the loose photocopy sheets wadded up under the fireplace grate made for good kindling. Mitchell rolled the remaining loose pages of twenty-pound bond into plump literary logs, rubber-banded them, and set them on the log holder above the crumpled pages. Then he fanned out the hardcover book and flattened it across the white paper logs. He stood back to observe the diminutive funeral pyre with a sense of uneasiness.

He should have felt relieved.

This potential source of humiliation or disruption would soon be dealt with. The book would no longer be in his life, could no longer irritate or goad him by its very existence. No fans would have a chance to either criticize or clamor for more. The chapter would be closed.

Yes, Mitchell was definitely relieved.

After he lit the match, he hesitated for a long, indecisive moment before finally touching the flame to the edge of one of the loose sheets. There. A burnt offering to a cruel muse.

As the fire caught, guilt gnawed at the ragged edges of his mind. There was something intrinsically criminal about burning a book, especially the only copies of a book. While this event would not go down in history with the sacking of the Library of Alexandria, it was still a loss to at least some tiny backwater of the literary sea—especially to the hopeful fans who had waited so long for any work by Mitchell Coren.

The flames grew higher, devouring the loose pages and curling the glossy dust jacket of *Infernities*. An interesting play on words, he thought. Infinity, Alternative, and Eternity all rolled together. Now he could add "Inferno" to the quadruple entendre. He wondered how it related to the story.

Didn't he owe it to himself at least to read his own work, to see what he could have done with his talent? *Infernities* was tangible proof that in some other reality his author-self had overcome the pressure and the expectations. But how? Didn't that mean that he, too, could do it?

No. He'd made the right decision. He thought with some satisfaction of the author photo blackening and blistering, cremating his cocksure successful doppelganger. The man had dared to risk his reputation, his spotless literary legacy, to write this second novel and offer it to an unpredictable reading public. He had dared. Had risked . . .

With a groan of annoyance and frustration Mitchell snatched the hardcover from the fire, dropped it to the floor, and stamped on it to put out the flames at the edges. He bent and picked up the singed novel that had disrupted his calm life.

As he picked up the blackened book, Mitchell's lips flickered in a smile. Though he still had no intention of publishing the novel, he would hold onto the book as a goad. Just to keep him honest. To remind himself of what could be.

He had his own ideas for new stories and novels, of

course. Every writer did. The ideas had never stopped coming, and he had jotted down notes during lunch hours at his tech-writing job. Some of the outlines were damn good, but he had been too afraid of failure to write the books, believing it better to let readers live with his mysterious seclusion than to risk them shaking their heads in disappointment.

Yet his alternate self had somehow shaken off the fear of failure. Therefore, it could be done. And that sincere, appreciative look he had seen in Jeremy Cardiff's eyes told Mitchell he still had an audience, no matter how small. . . .

Some authors were motivated to write strictly for the critics, for the kudos and awards. Others wanted the money and name recognition of sales, with big print runs and splashy publicity. Some wrote only for themselves, giving the finger to anyone else's expectations. But why had *he* become a writer?

Now there was a group to whom he owed something: his fans—the readers who understood what he was trying to do and who saw him as a human being with a talent that should not simply be thrown away. *Those* fans would enjoy whatever he wrote.

Certainly, a few of them went to the crazy fringe, seeing him as a guru with unparalleled insight into their particular problems. But most were just regular people. If he struck the right note, his pool of fans would be large; if he chose a path that was too esoteric, the numbers might dwindle. In either case, the readers still deserved his respect.

Mitchell looked at the charred copy of *Infernities* he held. He realized now that burning the novel was selfish. There were thousands (or maybe only dozens) of people like Jeremy Cardiff, who would have enjoyed this book if he allowed it to be published.

Setting the burned hardcover down, he opened the bottom file drawer of his desk where he kept the folder of notes and ideas that were just too good to throw away. If he was going to bury this cuckoo's egg of a book, then he was obligated to give the readers something in exchange.

Mitchell skimmed his outlines. He had forgotten how clever or thought-provoking many of them were. Had he intended to be an Emily Dickinson, locking his notes away in a box for someone else to find after he died? Not long ago, he had been tempted to burn these, too.

Now he would write some of them.

As he flipped through his notes, the ideas reached a critical mass, and Mitchell saw how he could combine concepts and characters. What might have been simple short story ideas now became enough material for a multi-layered novel. It wouldn't be just like *Divergent Lines*, but so what? It would still be good, still be worth writing.

He spread the papers out on his desk. He had an old, outdated laptop computer and plenty of time during his lunch hours. Some of the greatest works of literature had been completed a few pages at a time during lunch breaks. . . .

Mitchell glanced at the fireplace, where the fire had now died to a pile of orange embers. The photocopied novel was now nothing but ash.

On the mantel above, his Hugo and Nebula awards reflected the dull glow. He turned away from them and focused on his desk. *Divergent Lines* had been an unnecessary ball-and-chain to his creativity, along with all the other excuses he had made up over the past ten years. That was enough procrastination.

He looked at the charred but still readable hardcover of *Infernities*. First, before he started on any new book or short story, he had to write a letter.

"Dear Mr. Cardiff, let me make you a bargain." He proposed that if he had not produced any new novels or short stories in the next five years, then Jeremy had his blessing to publish *Infernities*, if only to reward the fans who had waited so long. He packaged the letter with the scorched book and mailed it to his "number one fan." Simply knowing the novel existed would be all the inspiration he really needed.

On the way back from the mailbox, he smiled to himself, convinced it would never be necessary for the other Mitchell Coren's book to be published here. He would take that risk for himself.

The expectations we place on our politicians seem impossible for any person to achieve. A candidate needs to be all things, know all walks of life, understand every segment of his constituency. How could one person achieve so much . . . without a little help?

Job Qualifications

Candidate Berthold Ossequin—the original—never made a move without being advised or cautioned by his army of pollsters, etiquette consultants, and style experts. Whether in public or in the privacy of his family estate, his every gesture and utterance was monitored. The avid media waited for Berthold to make any sort of mistake.

Elections would be held soon, and he must be absolutely perfect if he wanted to become the next Grand Chancellor of the United Cultures of Earth. According to surveys, he did have a slight lead over his opponent, though not enough to inspire complete confidence.

Berthold sat in an overstuffed chair that vibrated soothingly to calm him as he prepared to give a dramatic and insightful speech that his team had scripted for him. From rehearsing the speech before test audiences, the candidate knew where to modulate his voice and which points to emphasize in order to guarantee the strongest emotional impact.

Two young women, one at each hand, worked vigorously to trim his cuticles, file his nails, and give him that perfectly manicured appearance. A stylist worked with his bronze-brown hair and fixed every strand into place. Dieticians made careful recommendations about the foods Berthold should eat. Style experts met for at least an hour each evening to plan the candidate's wardrobe for the following day. No one could ever find fault with his appearance.

His stomach ached from eating too large and too rich a meal the night before, against the advice of his dieticians. He reminded himself to be careful with his facial expressions today, since a twinge of indigestion might show up as an inexplicable frown.

Berthold glanced up from the speech notes, looking at his chief advisor, who waited beside him. "How are the others coming, Mr. Rana?"

Rana nodded. "Precisely on schedule, sir. The others will be ready when they become necessary for your campaign."

The lash struck with a bite of electrical current that produced a fiery sting. Though the high-tech whip caused no actual harm, Berthold 12 felt as if his skin had been flayed. More misery, the same as the day before, and the day before that.

Fingernails cracked and bleeding, he stumbled under the heavy boulder he carried while the hot sun pounded down. He could smell rock dust and his own sweat, heard the impatient shouts of the guards and the groans of other slave-prisoners. His mind ached, and Berthold 12 drove back the myriad shouted questions that hammered through his head. Why was he here? What had he done? The injustice burned like acid within him. *Why do I deserve this?*

Up and down the winding jagged canyon, layered limestone walls crumbled like broken knives. Work teams moved sluggishly, carting loads of quarried stone. Berthold 12 knew that machinery existed to do this sort of work, robots and automated conveyers could have taken away the rock. But this labor site wasn't about efficiency; it was about misery and punishment.

When the electrical whip snapped again across his shoulder blades, Berthold 12 dropped the rock and collapsed to his knees. The guard's hover platform came closer, and the armored man loomed over him. Beneath the polarized helmet, Berthold 12 could see only the guard's chin and a smile that showed square white teeth. "I can keep whipping you all day if that's what you want, prisoner."

"Please! I'm working as hard as I can." His throat was raw, his body a living mass of aches. "I don't even know why I'm here! I don't remember anything . . . but this."

"Perhaps you committed the crime of amnesia." The guard chuckled at his joke, then threatened with the electrical whip again. "If your crime was bad enough that you blocked all memory of it from your head, then you probably don't want to remember."

Berthold 12 used his reserves of energy just to get back to his feet. He picked up the heavy limestone slab before the guard could lash him again. He could not recall any day that hadn't been this litany of labor and torture. He didn't know when this awful part of his life would end.

The greasy smells and comfortable bustle of the Retro Diner always made him feel at home. Berthold 6 stood by the heat lamps, adjusted his stained white apron, and pulled out a few guest checks. He quickly added up the totals while the short-order cook slopped extravagant nostalgic breakfasts onto warm plates and set them on a shelf. Low-carb pancakes and waffles, minimal-cholesterol eggs, reduced-fat bacon and sausage: Such dietary innovations had made the traditional American breakfast into something the trendy customers could once again consume with great gusto.

The Retro Diner, modeled after popular eating establishments of the mid-Twentieth Century, had silver and chrome fittings, stools and booths upholstered with red Naugahyde, table surfaces covered with speckled Formica. The menu featured re-creations of classic products. Many patrons got into the spirit by dressing up in old-fashioned costumes and smoking non-carcinogenic cigarettes. The place had a neighborly feel to it, a celebration of more innocent times. Berthold 6 felt right at home. He wouldn't have wanted any other job.

Carrying his loaded tray, Berthold 6 made a slight detour to snag the pot of coffee—weak, bitter, regular coffee, not one of the dramatically potent gourmet blends. "Here comes some morning cheer for you and your family, Eddie."

"Hey, Bert," said the jolly old man lounging back in his usual booth. "The waitresses around here are getting uglier every day."

"Yeah, but the waiters are certainly looking fine."

As the man grinned at the good-natured response, Berthold 6 delivered a stack of strawberry pancakes topped with a swirl of whipped cream, which looked like the eruption of a fruity volcano. He gave a cherry cola to the freckle-faced boy who sat next to his grandfather, refilled coffee cups around the room, then scooped dirty dishes from an unoccupied table into a bus tub.

Berthold 6 enjoyed working with regular folks. He liked serving people. He didn't earn much money, but enough to get by (though he wished some of his customers wouldn't *tip* like it was still 1953). He'd had a busy shift today, and tomorrow was his day off. Since he had no major plans, he thought he'd spend time with a few friends, talking, drinking beer, maybe watching sports or playing a game or two. Berthold 6 wasn't unduly stressed with the nonsense of unattainable goals or unrealistic ambitions. He was just an everyday guy, working an everyday job. A simple life.

"Order up!" the cook called with a clatter of dishes as he set the next breakfast under the heat lamps.

Before he was escorted off to a glamorous banquet, Candidate Berthold received Mr. Rana in his dressing chambers. The chief advisor brought documents for him to approve and sign. "This will take only a few moments, sir."

Berthold glanced down at the papers, shuffling from document to document. "Each one needs a signature?"

"Yes."

"Have they all been read for me?"

"Yes. And all necessary changes have been made."

"And do I agree with everything they say?"

"The statements are very much in line with your platform, sir." Rana formed a paternal smile. "You are, however, welcome to read any of them you like—in fact, I encourage it. The experience would be valuable for you."

Candidate Berthold gave a dismissive wave. "That won't be necessary. I'm already tired of the incessant paperwork, and I haven't even been elected yet." He laboriously began to sign each one. "I'll have plenty of time to learn after I get into office."

His head felt as if it would explode from so much information, but his passion for the material did not wane. His brain swelled with facts until all the bones of his skull— twenty-two bones in all, fourteen facial bones, eight cranial bones—seemed to pry apart.

For years Berthold 17 had been studying all aspects of medicine, from surgery to physical therapy to microbiology to anti-aging research. Even with proven teaching aids and somatic memorization devices, he struggled to remember the components of the human body and all the diseases and maladies that could afflict it.

He would be taking his exams in three days. His future depended on his performance during those vital hours.

Not that he had any doubts. He had been born for this. The prospect was daunting, but he always liked challenges. Upon first entering medical school, Berthold 17 made up his mind to become one of the best doctors ever. The higher the hurdles, the more effort he put into meeting them. He took great satisfaction in a reward that he'd *earned*. He had painted his own finish line and would never look back over his shoulder until he had crossed it. "Good enough" was not in his vocabulary.

Berthold 17 hit the books again, studying, studying. It would be a long night. . . .

Meanwhile, in another campus library in another state, Berthold 18 sat surrounded by legal tomes, equally convinced that he would pass the upcoming bar exam with flying colors.

They were all dying of Ebola-X.

Berthold 3 could do nothing to save the afflicted villagers, but he forced himself to remain at their sides and comfort the men, women, and children in their final hours. He prayed with them, he listened to them, he comforted them. Not being a doctor, he was unable to do anything else . . . and even the doctors couldn't do much.

Ebola-X, a particularly virulent strain of the hemorrhagic plague, had been genetically engineered by a brutal African warlord who, upon being deposed, had unleashed it among his own population. *As if their lives weren't already difficult enough,* Berthold 3 thought.

The villagers had impure drinking water, no electricity, no schools, no sanitation. Thanks to a persistent drought, almost certainly caused by the government and its short-sighted agricultural policies, the locals had lived on the edge of starvation for years. Immune systems and physical strength were at their nadir. When the Ebola-X arrived, it mowed down the village population as easily as if it were a jeep full of machine-gun-bearing soldiers. The thought of their situation tugged at his heartstrings. How could a person hold so much pain?

The hot and stifling hospital tent reeked with the stench of sweat, vomited blood, and death. Berthold 3 still heard every gasp, every moan, every death rattle. He sat quietly on a wooden stool, looking at the strained, pain-puckered face of a young mother. He read soothing passages aloud from the Bible, but he didn't think she could hear him or even understand the flowery English words. But he stayed with her anyway, changing the moist rag from her forehead, holding her shoulders when she needed to roll over and vomit.

The woman seemed to know she was dying. She had communicated with him about her three children, and Berthold 3 promised to look after them. He brushed her wiry hair, cooling her forehead again. He didn't have the heart to tell her that the children had died two days earlier.

Exhausted medics moved around him like zombies. They had too little medicine, certainly nothing effective against this epidemic. Berthold 3 tried to take as much busywork from the doctors as possible; he felt a calling to do his part, any part, so long as he helped these people. He had some first-aid training, but the bulk of his schooling had prepared him to be a missionary, not a medic. Perhaps if he'd known ahead of time, Berthold 3 would have learned more practical skills. Even so, he wouldn't have turned from this obligation. In his heart he wanted to be here, wishing only that he could ease their suffering more effectively.

The dying woman reached out, her hand extended upward as if trying to grasp the sky. Berthold 3 took it in his own hand, folding his palms around hers and pressing her clenched fist against his chest so that she could feel the beating of his heart. She breathed twice more, arched her back, and then died.

Berthold 3 said a calm prayer over her, then stood. He had no time to rest, no time to grieve. He dragged his wooden stool over to the cot of the next patient.

Red tape. Bureaucracy. Incomprehensible forms in triplicate. Revisions to revisions to procedures that had already been revised repeatedly.

Job security.

Berthold 10 could not pretend his job was interesting, nor could he console himself with the thought that it was necessary. But it was a career, and he was good at it. Few people were so careful or detail-oriented; some of his co-workers called him anal-retentive.

He sat in a small cubicle like thousands of others in this governmental office building for the United Cultures of Earth. Berthold 10 processed forms, input data, tracked regulations, and submitted comments and rebuttals to his counterparts in rival departments of the government in other cities around the world.

He was content to be sifting through paperwork in his own tiny cog in a single component of the sprawling wheels of government. It was good to have an understanding of how the details worked, instead of just the Big Picture, which the career politicians saw. Berthold 10 had no aspirations of running for office or being a great leader. He kept his sights on a shorter-term desire for an increase in pay grade. And he was sure to get it, with only a few more years of diligent service.

When the Urgent communiqué appeared in his IN box, Berthold 10 didn't at first pay special attention. Urgent matters went into a separate stack and he generally made an effort to take care of them first. But when he noticed that this message was addressed to him personally, from the office of the Candidate, he read it with puzzlement, then amazement.

He was summoned to the Candidate's mansion at a specified time and date. Berthold 10 looked around his drab cubicle at the never-changing piles of never-changing work. He didn't know what all this was about, and the letter did not explain. Official escorts would arrive to take him. He smiled. At last his life was about to become more interesting.

With Mr. Rana beside him to operate the apparatus, Candidate Berthold cradled the head of the final clone in his lap. The man still twitched and struggled—Berthold had forgotten which number this was—but the clutching fingers could not remove the electrodes and transmitters pasted onto his temples and forehead.

"I'm glad this is the last one," the Candidate said. "It's been an exhausting day."

One of the clones had struggled violently when the

guards brought him in, forcing them to break his forearm. The snapped ulna—ah, the medical knowledge was coming in useful already!—had been unforeseen, but not necessarily a bad thing. In his pampered life Candidate Berthold had never experienced a broken bone; now, after absorbing the clone's experience, he knew what it felt like.

Memories and thoughts continued to drain out of the last clone's mind like arterial blood spurting from a slashed throat. The candidate held his duplicate's shoulders, felt everything surge into his own brain. What a difficult and painful life this one had lived! But the experiences certainly built character, giving him a firm moral foundation and impeccable resolve. It would be an excellent addition to Berthold's repertoire. Each detail made him more electable.

Since worldwide leaders guided so many diverse people, the citizens of the United Cultures of Earth demanded more and more from their rulers. To win a worldwide election, a candidate needed to demonstrate empathy for a multitude of different tiers of voters, from all walks of life. He had to be both an outsider and an insider. He had to understand privilege, to grasp the overall landscape of the government as well as the minutiae of how the bureaucracy worked. He was expected to have a passion for helping people, a genuine heart for the common man, and a rapport with celebrities and captains of industry.

Such expectations were simply impossible for a single human being to meet. Fortunately, thanks to the mental parity of clones, men such as Berthold Ossequin—and quite certainly all of his opponents—could live many diverse lives in parallel. The clones were turned loose in various situations where they gathered real-life experiences that went far beyond anything Candidate Berthold could have learned from teachers or books. . . .

The last clone spasmed again, and his face fell completely slack, his mouth hung slightly open. His eyelids fluttered but remained closed. A few final, desperate thoughts trickled into Berthold's mind.

With a satisfied sigh, he peeled off the transmitter electrodes and motioned for the guards to carry away the limp body. All eighteen of the clones were now vegetables, empty husks wrung dry of every thought and experience. The comatose bodies would be quietly euthanized, and a newly enriched candidate would emerge for the final debates before the elections.

Berthold stood from his chair, completely well rounded now, full of vicarious memories, tragic events and pleasant recollections. The chief advisor looked into Berthold's eyes with obvious pride. "Are you ready, Mr. Candidate?"

Berthold smiled. "Yes. I have all the background I could possibly need to rule the world . . . though once I get into office, we may decide to continue my education in this manner. Are there more clones?"

"We can always make more, sir."

"There's no substitute for experience."

Berthold stretched his arms and took a deep breath, feeling like a true leader at last. He issued a sharp command to his staff. "Now, let's go win this election."

This is one of my early stories, full of ideas I had been playing with since high school, back when I wrote the first several drafts on an old Smith-Corona typewriter. After many iterations, I finally placed this novelette in one of the *New Destinies* anthologies, my first sale to Betsy Mitchell, who went on to edit at least a dozen of my novels.

Rest in Peace

Every shadowy corner hides a thousand assassins.

Prez Siroth stopped suddenly in the darkness just inside the crumbling catacombs. He narrowed his eyes. He sniffed the air, drawing in the earthy scent of shadows, the lingering smells that would attract rats.

The guards quickly stumbled to a halt to avoid running into Siroth, then backtracked to form a protective ring around him. In the dim torchlight, Siroth could see that their eyes had gone wide. "What is it, my Prez?" asked the captain of the guard.

With ice-blue eyes, Siroth gazed silently into the broken tunnels for a moment longer. Wispy long hair hung to his shoulders, untrimmed. Sacks of grain had been piled up against the collapsing walls to shore them up. In the older sections of the tunnels, worn and fragmented flagstones lined the floors . . . but the newly dug catacombs offered only hard-packed dirt, which might easily muffle the footsteps of someone in hiding.

"Light two more torches." Siroth turned to glare at the fat, dirty man leading them deeper into the tunnels. "And if *he* makes a single unexpected move—slit his throat."

Siroth's lips curved in a snarl/smile.

Rathsell, the fat man, tittered nervously. "You are too suspicious, my Prez."

"I have held my reign for *six years now*. You can never be too suspicious!"

"Nothing to fear from me, my Prez. Wait until you see what the children dug up. It's a great discovery!" Behind Rathsell's grin, Siroth could see the splotchy red of anxiety on the man's face.

"Children? I left *you* in charge of storing grain down here—"

"Oh yes, my Prez! But the children stay in here to kill the rats and to dig out more tunnels. You can be sure I gave them a sound beating when I learned they never told me about the vault they found. And then I came to you without delay!"

Siroth's voice was cold. "Why would you come to tell *me?*"

Caught off guard, Rathsell smeared his palms on his worn and dirty trousers. He wore no shirt to cover his folds of fat; a clean red barrette was clipped to his ear as an ornament. "I . . . um, well, my Prez, there are some who would pay great rewards for something like this . . ."

Siroth scowled. "What's so special about this vault?"

Fat Rathsell's eyes lit up, as if he was about to share the secrets of the universe. "It is from *Before!*"

"So are all the old buildings." The Prez sounded bored.

"But this vault is untouched!"

"If it isn't worth my while, I'm going to let Grull play with you."

A flicker of terror passed across the fat man's eyes, but he forced another smile. "It *will* be worth your while, my Prez."

Their footsteps suddenly became muffled as they passed from the last flagstones to the bare earth of the new tunnels. The shadows grew deeper.

"What can you possibly want with a reward? You already have more than you deserve here."

Siroth saw that fat Rathsell was struggling to put on his kindest face. "You may remember, my Prez, how ugly a woman my wife is, with three arms and all. With a nice reward, perhaps I can buy myself a prettier one. That's all I want with my humble life."

"Uh-huh," Siroth said.

Suddenly the Prez's heart twisted into knots, clenching and thumping as if choking on an air pocket. Pain shot through his chest, radiating like electrified wires from his sternum. He held his breath. He kept his face molded in a mask of self-control, showing nothing. Bloodwind roared in his ears; flecks of color tinged with black swirled behind his eyes. His mind began to pound, and he felt like he was rising, floating, swallowed up in a great maw more deadly than any assassin's knife. Siroth gritted his teeth as Rathsell led him onward, with the guards close behind. The Prez fought with himself not to stumble. He reached inside his tunic and massaged the long, lumpy scar in the center of his chest until the pain subsided.

Again? Already? he thought to himself. *I should have known a peasant's heart wouldn't last more than two years.*

The pain backed off again, momentarily tamed, and Siroth strode forward with a grim enthusiasm he hadn't felt in a long time. The undulating torchlight reflected off a metal door set into the left wall as they turned a corner. Rathsell made a show of opening the heavy door. The guards stood tense and silent. He gestured for Siroth to enter. "My Prez—?"

"No. You go first. Then three guards. Then I'll come. The rest of the guards will follow me."

Rathsell hastily agreed and entered the vault as pale light began to flow automatically from darkened plates along the interior walls. The guards uttered their astonishment as they followed. Siroth came next, trying to adjust his eyes to the light splashing on his face.

The Prez forcibly resisted expressing his awe. The glistening walls of the chamber were a polished white, cleaner than anything he had seen in his entire life. The faint, not-unpleasant smell of ammonia and chemicals floated just at the limits of perception, driving back the odors of dirt and mustiness from the catacombs. The floor of the chamber, though hard, somehow swallowed the sound of his footsteps as he walked farther into the room.

Most of the crowded floor space was taken up by eight oblong cases like crystalline coffins. Each contained a motionless human form. Siroth stepped cautiously among them, looking through transparent walls. The bodies inside seemed like wax sculptures, pale, not breathing . . . dead? For an indefinable reason, Siroth didn't think so.

The guards stood in silent awe, and Rathsell rubbed his hands together in delight. The fat man ran mumbling among the machines along one wall, closely inspecting a series of lights lazily pulsing on and off, as if he knew what he was doing. Siroth didn't like the look of Rathsell's confidence. Beside each of the coffins squatted a bulky control box that appeared to monitor the unmoving figure within.

One crystal coffin had been positioned slightly in front of the other seven, and Siroth moved slowly toward it, running his fingertips along the polished surface of the glass cases. The central human looked like a god come to Earth: his perfect face was capped with delicately styled black curls, and his physique was large and muscular, seeming to radiate power, even helpless as he was. The Prez rapped his knuckles on the glass in defiance, to show his own superiority.

"Do you like that one, my Prez?" Rathsell said. The fat man's eyes gleamed and his chins bobbed in a disgusting way. "I can make him speak to you. Watch—he can talk even while he's asleep!"

Intoxicated with his own good fortune, Rathsell rushed to a console under a blank patch on the wall opposite Siroth. Making certain the Prez was looking, Rathsell singled out a large green button surrounded by inward-pointing arrows; it simply cried out to be pushed, and Rathsell obliged.

Images began to form within the depths of the screen, rapidly crystallizing into a picture of the eight sleepers— awake now—standing together in spring-green jumpsuits and each bearing gleaming eyes and a blank smile. The picture made Siroth think of the old family photographs that scavengers sometimes burned in their hovels because the fumes made them feel lightheaded.

The godlike man with the dark hair stepped forward, looking out of the screen with black eyes as deep as the universe. The Prez stifled a shiver.

"Greetings, men of the future. If you have come to witness our awakening, we welcome you in peace and friendship. You will not remember us, for we are merely dreamers and have left no record of ourselves behind."

The leader smiled, pausing for a breath. The others smiled as well. "I am Draigen, and these seven others are with me: a surgeon, an artist, an agricultural engineer, an historian, a singer, a mathematician, a writer. We come from a troubled time, with many needs and many problems.

But we could see that this bureaucratic nemesis was dying at its core, strangled in its own red tape, lost within its own intricacies. Within a century, the serpent would have finished devouring itself. We had to *wait* until nothing would hinder us from doing what we had been called to do."

Siroth found the man's voice charismatic, dangerous. Draigen's words seemed laced with fever, and his dark eyes glistened. The other green-suited dreamers stood behind him as if in awe of their leader's vision.

"We collected our knowledge and all the tools we would need to reshape our world after the demise of bureaucracy—and came here to slumber for a hundred years. Now we shall help *you* to rebuild the world as it was meant to be, without opposition, without cruelty, with freedom and justice for all mankind!"

The tape finished, and the shining white wall absorbed the image. Siroth stood motionless, pondering, with a distasteful smile locked on his face.

He silently reached out to take a stainless-steel club from the nearest guard and hefted the heavy pipe in his hand. He stepped over to Draigen's case, looking down at the strangely impotent form of the dreamer. Siroth swung the pipe down, smashing the crystal coffin above the dark-haired dreamer's face.

The Prez smiled.

Siroth took a calculated breath before he went berserk, plunging from one case to the next, smashing them, swinging the club down to crush the monitor-computers, hurling the pipe like a spear through the screen at the far wall. He kicked at shards of crystal, dodging sparks and plunging through smoke.

The guards watched dispassionately. Fat Rathsell sobbed in horror, confusion, and genuine loss. He might have wanted to stop the Prez, but he dared not.

Panting, Siroth picked up the club again and casually handed it back to the guard. The rebellious pain behind his sternum returned, but he had more important things to attend to. He tried to ignore the pain, mentally and uselessly cursing his heart. But the pounding knives in his chest remained.

Siroth turned his cold eyes on Rathsell, motioning to the guards. "Take him away and execute him. For most vile treason!"

Rathsell's face blanched to a pasty white, as if his skin had just turned into gruel. The guards grabbed his arms and began to drag him out. The fat man struggled in disbelief and confusion, but his feet found no purchase on the polished white floor. The decorative red barrette dropped from his ear.

Siroth held up a hand. "But kill him *quickly*. That's his reward."

Rathsell made other sounds, but could form no coherent words.

In the shadows of the catacombs, haggard and dirt-encrusted children with eyes sunken from near starvation watched Rathsell's plight, and snickered.

Forgetting all else, Siroth stared down into the crystalline case containing Draigen's body. Tiny flecks of broken glass frosted the dreamer's brow like snowflakes, but otherwise the body was unharmed. The Prez reached out to touch Draigen's large, muscular arm, admiring the lean body. The mold for this one had been shattered long ago in the holocaust.

Rathsell's screams reverberated through the winding catacombs, then abruptly stopped.

The convulsive pain in Siroth's chest took a long time to

subside, but he managed to smile as he ran his fingernail on Draigen's motionless breastbone. "Such a helpful dreamer. I may be able to use you after all."

II

Deep in the Prez's chambers, the blind old man sat in front of a crackling fire, letting the warmth bathe his face. He heard one branch, somewhere near the back, settle heavily into the ash. The wood snapped and sputtered as it burned. It smelled a little green.

He felt a disturbance in the room, the barely noticed shifting of air currents. He tensed, trying to restrain his smile. "You sound weary, Siroth."

He heard the Prez slap his hand down on the tabletop in exasperation and defeat. "Dammit, Grull! How did you know it was me?"

"Your breathing is very distinctive. Look on the tabletop at the new device I designed."

The Prez looked at the scattered papers on the table. Grull stood up from the chair by the fire and unerringly found his way over to Siroth.

"See, the loops fit around the victim's fingers, toes, wrists and ankles, and are then attached to those wheels of varying sizes in such a way that merely by turning the wheels we can wrench every finger, every toe out of joint, one by one, until we have achieved the desired results."

Siroth nodded. "You still have trouble closing up your circles, Grull." He dropped the sketch back on the tabletop and went to sit in the old man's chair by the fire. The Prez cracked his knuckles as he watched the firelight. "What happened while I was gone?"

"Well, the fukkups staged another revolt, trying to break out of their pen and clamoring to be freed, again. They said they wanted to see you."

"And?"

"Three of them seemed to be the instigators. I had them strung upside down over the pens and then burned alive. The rest calmed down."

"Anything else?"

"Well, two men rode up, emissaries from Prez Claysus."

"That water-spined fairy!" Siroth snorted.

"Remember Praetoth, the architect who rebuilt your castle when it collapsed two years ago? You've still got him in the dungeons, you know. It seems the home of Prez Claysus has likewise fallen in on itself, and his emissaries are 'honorably requesting' that we should work together for the common good of all. Claysus wants to borrow our architect."

Siroth laughed. "That sounds exactly like him! Have you replied yet?"

Grull smiled broadly. "I tied the emissaries backwards on their horses with their own entrails, and sent them back."

"A straightforward enough answer."

Grull made his way back to the chair beside the fire, found that Siroth was already sitting in it, and scowled as he paced the room instead. "So what did Rathsell want?"

The Prez briefly explained about the vault from *Before,* the dreamers, and how he had destroyed the apparatus.

"A wise decision, my Prez. We don't want any empire-building dreamers from *Before* ruining all you've done. Everything in that vault should be burned."

"No." Grull detected a pensive note in Siroth's voice, though he could not see the expression on the other's face.

"I have saved them, especially their leader. I want his heart. And you can have his eyes."

Grull bit his breath back, stunned. Siroth rarely surprised him anymore.

"Doctor Sero has given me one new heart, but it is already dying. And now, with this godlike dreamer's heart . . . I will be *strong!* You should see him, Grull! He's perfect. Up until now you said you wouldn't have new eyes if they had to come from a peasant, or from a fukkup who had five or six extra eyes. But now it's *perfect!* You'll have your sight back, Grull. After sixty years."

The blind man sat in silence, thinking about sight and Siroth's not-quite-correct reasons as to why he had denied new eyes before. Grull had lost his sight during the holocaust, six decades before. He had never looked upon what *After* was like. He wasn't sure he wanted to.

III

The dark-haired dreamer lay on the surgical table, stretched out like a mannequin as Doctor Sero inspected him disdainfully. Rigor had shut Draigen's black eyes, trapping his Utopian visions beneath the thin lids. Later, before the body could begin to spoil, the doctor would have to cut those eyes out and preserve them for Grull.

Siroth turned his head and sat up on another surgical table beside Draigen's. "Are you about ready, Sero?"

The doctor looked up from his assortment of medical tools, staring with swollen, buglike eyes. "Yes, my Prez."

"And you *will* be successful?"

"I was successful the last time. You're a quick-healer, Prez Siroth. I explained it all to you before—the chromosome-scrambling viruses that filled the air after the holo-caust poisoned our gene pool. Most of the aberrations turned out like the fukkups, but what went wrong with them, went *right* with you. You know what happens when-ever you get injured." The doctor's voice betrayed his own lack of interest in the lecture, in the upcoming operation, and in the Prez himself.

"I've been practicing this operation for the past week. Out of ten tries, three have survived. All three were quick-healers."

Sero ran a finger along the scar on Siroth's bare chest, thinking how much it reminded him of an artist's signature on a masterpiece. His father had been a great surgeon from *Before* who had taught Sero from the books and implements found in the old buildings. But his father hadn't been good enough to heal himself of his own death wound. And now Sero had to discover all the lost surgical arts by hit-or-miss vivisection.

The Prez narrowed his eyes and reached out to snatch the doctor's fingers away from the old scar, holding them in a brutal grip with his clenched fist. "Grull will be here with my guards during the operation," he hissed.

"My father used to say a surgeon's hands are sacred things, never to be touched by another," Sero said almost offhandedly. "My dear Prez, if I saw you were about to die during this operation, I'd plunge a scalpel deep into my own throat, rather than let Grull touch me."

Siroth stiffened, and the doctor pushed him flat on the table. "But *relax,* my Prez. When you awaken, you'll have the heart of the biggest dreamer of all!"

His eyes took so long to focus.
An apparition stood in front of him, dressed in the

spring-green uniform of the dreamers. Draigen! No . . . one of the others on the tape, one who had lain sleeping at the far end of the vault. The dreamer's eyes were filled with tears and rage. "Why? *Why!*"

Siroth then saw Grull beside the dreamer, and he began to suspect that the apparition might be real after all.

"Guess who woke up," Grull said.

Siroth passed out again.

Grull took the arm of the seething dreamer, turning him away from the unconscious Prez. Blood still spattered the operating room, smeared into the wood with wet rags but not quite cleaned after the operation.

"Come along now. Let's have a chat." The blind man leaned heavily on the dreamer's arm, hoping to calm the other man. Grull guided him down a corridor where smoky torches had long ago replaced broken fluorescent lights.

"What's your name, dreamer? I am Grull."

The old torturer could not see the tears drying on the dreamer's cheeks, but he could feel the breath of the man's answer on his own face. "Aragon."

"How come you're still alive, Aragon, when none of your other companions woke up?"

"All our stations were monitored by delicate computer systems, with triple-nested backup functions. It's more of a surprise that no one else survived." Aragon took a deep breath, and Grull felt a faint shudder pass through the other's body. "My station was at the far end of the vault. Maybe your paranoid Prez had exhausted himself by then."

They said nothing more until they emerged into the open air from Siroth's great square castle that bore the crumbling words *First National Bank* across its façade. They walked through a courtyard and Aragon stopped short, but

Grull pulled him over to a stone bench in the sun. The stunned dreamer didn't resist.

The *First National Bank* castle rested at the top of a gentle hill, just high enough that the view stretched out to engulf the ruins of a city below. Streets had turned into lawns; roofs and walls had collapsed. An accidental forest of fast-growing, genetically engineered trees had grown up alongside the buildings.

The blind man let Aragon stare speechless down at the dismal panorama for long moments. The dreamer finally managed to choke out a whisper, sounding betrayed. "How long has it been?"

"Sixty years." He sat down on the cold stone seat and patted it, motioning the dreamer to join him. "I was too young to remember much about those few hours of madness when *Before* turned to *After*. Somebody screaming 'Get to the Shelter Get to the Shelter!' Something exploded in front of my face, spectacular, searing white fire, sort of a grand finale to my eyesight.

"I was eight years old. For a little while I lived on whatever I could find. Then a religious cult, 'the Apocalypse Now,' found me and took me in. They believed they had been chosen to rebuild the world exactly as God intended it to be, to the death of all nonbelievers. And here I was, a blind child who had miraculously survived the holocaust. Perfect prophet material."

He shrugged a little to himself, and had no way of knowing whether Aragon was paying attention. "But I never turned out to be what they wanted. I was smart enough to know I'd never make it alone, so I played along with them. The Apocalypse Now treated me with respect—they all died by the age of thirty from cancer or genetic defect, but I just kept getting older.

"The fukkups were being born then, every one of them with the wrong number of arms, legs, even heads. Something about the war, biological weapons rearranging everyone's genes. Most of the mutants were so messed up they died anyway, or the mothers would throw them away, or kill them—but some survived. At first they must have hidden in the ruins or in the burned-out forest, horrified of themselves and the others of their kind. But then they started banding together, venting their anger at the normals. You know, terrorizing the countryside, mutilating people to look like themselves.

"Of course, I had a distorted view of it all, living in the Apocalypse Now. But there were plenty of other hunter groups, or communes, or scavengers, and they all came together for defense under a new leader, the Prez. Prez Mecas, Siroth's father, managed to unite his realm with a few other Prezes and with the Apocalypse Now. Together, they managed to cut the marauding fukkups to pieces. Now we keep them all in a huge corral where they can rot on their feet for all we care. Sero uses them for his experiments, or Siroth plays with them on hunting games now and then. They've been made pretty much harmless."

Aragon didn't seem to know which expression to keep on his face. He sat silent, stunned, as if looking desperately for some way to survive his despair.

"After the fukkups were brought under control, the Prezes took to fighting among themselves—assholes, none of them had any *real* concept of leadership. Any given Prez might last a year or two before he was assassinated. Prez Mecas was a lousy dictator—didn't know how to hold people in fear of him, never listened to anyone's counsel because he was too busy with his own pleasure. He didn't know how to be careful.

"I had become Master Torturer of the Apocalypse Now. I went to his son Siroth because I knew I could train him to be a real Prez. We trapped Mecas in his chambers, tangling him in his own sheets, and fed him to the fukkups. Siroth didn't show any regret whatsoever. I knew he would make it, then. Love is one thing a Prez cannot have."

"A good leader should love his people above all else," Aragon muttered, but he seemed too stunned to begin an argument. "My God, the mess we left behind was the Golden Age of Mankind."

Grull frowned. "How can you possibly call *Before* a mess, compared to what we have now?"

"We still had plenty of problems. I kept finding perfect solutions to them—but people wouldn't *listen*. They said my solutions were 'wildly unrealistic' and that I should come down to the Real World. I never found their Real World—I found Draigen instead."

Grull detected bitterness in the dreamer's words, but they took a subtly different tone, as if Aragon were no longer speaking from his heart, but from a speech Draigen had given. He heard the dreamer stand up and shout toward the ruins at the bottom of the hill. "We understood things nobody else did. We could plan ahead. We could see the wisest things to say and do—but everyone was so bogged down with whether the books balanced, whether they would get the promotion, what kind of deodorant to use, what to cook for dinner . . . they never learned to understand life. We *understood* it!" He turned back to Grull, sitting motionless on the stone bench.

"I became an agricultural engineer, a damn good one, to solve the world's food shortage—and you know what? Nobody *wanted* me to! All the money spent to bring huge tractors, better seed and fertilizer to poor countries—and the

125

minute we turn our backs the savages let our shining tractors sit there unused while they go back out in the fields with their oxen and scratch plows, because 'that was the way their forefathers grew the crops.' Nobody seemed to remember that their forefathers died of malnutrition. They *wanted* to starve! How can a perfect solution work if people don't cooperate?"

"People, by nature, don't cooperate," Grull muttered.

"The seven of us under Draigen cooperated," Aragon said defensively. "All lonely revolutionaries, totally devoted to saving the world . . . but the world wasn't ready for us. Draigen had his dream. We were to make the world pure and good and right for all mankind. Why didn't anyone else want it that way? How can I carry on that great vision by myself?"

Grull directed his sightless eyes into the breeze. "Now do you understand why Prez Siroth could never let your group wake up?"

Aragon shuddered, as if suddenly remembering who Grull was. The old man let the dreamer sit in an uninterrupted, awkward silence, waiting for him to deal with his churning emotions. Aragon surprised the blind old man by sighing in apparent defeat.

"Your Prez has taken Draigen's heart. And now you're going to take his eyes. Isn't that enough?"

Grull found himself thinking back to the dim childhood memories he normally kept tightly locked away, answering a different question. "My mother had a large flower garden filled with roses and snapdragons. My father took me to the big city once . . . I can still feel how *tall* those shining buildings were." He fell silent for a moment, then. "Yes, I would like to see again. But I doubt Doctor Sero is capable of performing the transplant."

Aragon looked at him, raising his eyebrows. "Surely if this surgeon can transplant a heart, he can give you new eyes?"

"Siroth is a quick-healer. Sero could probably have *dropped* the heart into his chest and he would have survived. I am just a blind old man."

The dreamer smiled, and Grull could smell a strange excitement in Aragon's body scent. "Vesalius, the surgeon with our group, could have performed the operation easily. Too bad your Prez killed him. But we still have our medical knowledge in the vault, in a place even Siroth couldn't harm. That way we can be of *some* use to the world. Your Doctor Sero can study it.

"I want you to *see* what you've done to our Utopia."

IV

Aragon wandered, absorbing the immensity of *After* and feeling like a glass Christmas-tree bulb that had just been stepped on.

He went alone through the ruins, gazing at unrepaired buildings poised on the verge of collapse.

He went to the fukkup pen, where living lumps of twisted flesh screamed for their freedom, or at least an end to agony.

He returned to the smashed vault where all his dreams lay destroyed, and he wept.

The dreamer came to Siroth, now almost recovered from his surgery. "Prez Siroth, I have a few things I wish to say to you."

The Prez scowled with a "here it comes" expression on his face and sat up in his bed, waiting in silence. Aragon sighed, then sat down. "But they are hateful things, and better left unsaid. Hate destroys, and enough has been destroyed already. It is better if I just forgive you."

Siroth almost choked in surprise. "*Forgive?* You're a coward."

The dreamer looked at him for a long moment, holding the other's disturbed gaze. "It was the bravest thing I could have said."

Siroth tried to get out of bed. "I can still kill you, dreamer!"

"Then you are hopelessly lost." Aragon stood firm. Siroth looked uncomfortable. He ran his fingers through his silky-fine blond hair.

"Where's Grull?"

"He is with your Doctor Sero . . . receiving Draigen's eyes, remember?"

The Prez's face purpled with rage, and he swung himself out of bed. "What? He would leave my realm without someone in charge?"

"You were almost recovered."

"I need his counsel!"

"Think for yourself, Siroth."

The Prez sat back down on the bed, laughing darkly to himself. "And what do *you* want, dreamer? My lands? To be Prez yourself? Now's your perfect chance—Grull is gone, and I'm weaker than I should be. Go on, kill me! Make yourself Prez, and see how long you survive."

"No. With Draigen and the others gone, our dream is dead."

"Then what *do* you want?"

"I want you to change."

Aragon could see that had some effect on the other man, and he quickly continued. The Prez looked baffled, but not quite impatient. "Maybe I can make some small difference by myself. Have you ever walked out among the people? Actually *been* with them?"

"Too dangerous."

"How can you know what's going *on* out there?"

Siroth shrugged. "My guards report back."

Aragon sighed. "It isn't the same. Do you know that the old buildings are rotting, and another one collapses almost every other week? Do you know the horrors in that place where you keep the mutants corralled like so many animals? How they scream in agony, tear at each other, kill to eat the slop your guards throw at them, crying for freedom with even their dying breath!"

Visionary fire burned in the dreamer's eyes as his anger rose. "And the *people*, Siroth! Children *live* down in those filthy catacombs you found us in! Families starve because they cannot grow enough food. I have even seen evidence of cannibalism!"

"So what?"

"Don't you care?"

"No."

"Siroth, you must change!"

"My system works. I've been leader here for *six* years, with Grull's help. How would you change me?"

"Feel some compassion for the people you rule. They are your subjects—you should care for them!"

The Prez's voice was sour. "They don't care for me."

"If you were kind, and beneficial, seeing that their children are fed and educated, that their homes are repaired—Grull tells me you have a master architect in this castle, but you keep him under house-arrest! What good is he doing here?"

"I think you're retarded, and you understand nothing!

You want to make me into another jelly-spined Prez Claysus!" Then Siroth laughed. "I wish you had met my father, dreamer—then you wouldn't think I'm so bad!"

Aragon raised his eyebrows, trying another tactic. "In those six years, how many assassination attempts have been made on you? How many?"

"Too many to count. But I *survived*—that's all that matters."

Aragon continued to press. "Grull says that Claysus has held his lands for eight years now. How many attempts have been made on him?"

Siroth looked up, frowning. "None . . . but then I cannot be completely sure."

Aragon folded his arms in triumph. The Prez looked upset and stood up to pace the room, rubbing his hands together as if he were trying to get rid of something. "I'd rather trust what Grull has always told me."

"Grull showed you only *one* way—the only way he knows. But I'll teach you others, and I will make you change."

Siroth scowled, but refused to face the dreamer, continuing to stare into the fire. "*That* is exactly why I wanted to kill your group."

The wooden door smacked against the wall of the Prez's chambers as a guard burst into the room. "My Prez! The fukkups are going wild! It's bad this time. They already killed two guards, and they are smashing the fences in the corral!"

Siroth paled in alarm, and his eyes flickered from side to side as if searching for Grull. But only Aragon stood there, letting a trace of his self-satisfaction show through.

"*Try* it my way, Siroth, and I'll show you it can work! It's obvious Grull's solution has no effect."

"And if it doesn't work?" The Prez scowled.

Aragon nervously raised his head high, looking proud. "I'll stake my life on it!"

Siroth laughed in delight. "Now *that's* what I like to hear! All right then, come on—I want to watch this!"

Breathlessly, Aragon turned to grab the guard's arm and began to pull him toward the door. Siroth quickly dressed, flailing into a threadbare robe to cover the scars of his recent surgery.

The mutants silenced themselves with a hushed grumble as Prez Siroth arrived. They pushed closer to the spiked fence, leering, some drooling from mouths crowded with two tongues. And these were the ones that had survived birth.

Aragon could not force away his revulsion and broke out in a thin sweat as he pondered how Draigen would have dealt with such a situation. The Prez stood calmly, surrounded by his guards and looking around with his sharp cold eyes. He seemed curious and oddly satisfied, as if pleased that he could try a truly unexpected leadership tactic and possibly get rid of the dreamer at the same time.

Aragon swallowed and finally spoke. The fukkups quieted as his voice drew strength. "Who speaks for you? Do you have a leader?"

The mutants milled about, but did not answer. Then Aragon remembered what Grull had done to the leaders during the last insurrection.

"All right, then we speak to all of you. You are clearly dissatisfied here—Prez Siroth offers you an alternative." He took a breath and then spoke rapidly, anticipating that the Prez would stop him at any moment. "We will release you, give you your freedom—but you will have to *work*. Many of you have committed grave crimes against humanity, but we feel you have served your punishments. Up until now, we have used our own provisions to feed you—once freed, you will have to fend for yourselves. You will have to repair the old buildings for your homes. You will have to work the land, grow crops." He hesitated, thinking of the unfairness, but realizing Siroth would have to gain something other than a clear conscience from the bargain. "And we will let you keep *half* of your produce for yourselves."

The fukkups stood stunned for an instant. Siroth waited, glanced at his guards, and firmly believed the dreamer was sticking his head more firmly on the chopping block. The Prez picked up the speech as the mutants began to cheer. "*But*—this is a trial period for you. The fate of all your children depends on how you behave during the next few weeks." His voice was as hard and as sharp as a razor. "If *any* one of you harms a man, in *any* way, or does damage to property, or tries to flee—you will *all* be returned to this pen, never to be released again!"

Aragon spoke up quickly, shouting into the brief lull. "But you have nothing to fear if you're willing to work for your freedom. Isn't it better to work the land, produce food for everyone, than to rot here? Those are the terms—do you agree to all of them?"

Wild cheering almost deafened him as all the mutants clamored at once. He smiled at the Prez. "See, they're satisfied."

"You may very well have just sealed our doom. We still have to see if they'll keep their word." Then Siroth watched them with his darting eyes, and he let another smile steal across his face. "But just to make sure, I'm going to have you go live with them, without protection, for the first few weeks."

Siroth's smugness was squashed when Aragon calmly said, "All right."

V

Grull tried valiantly to be patient, commanding his fingers not to fidget. For days Doctor Sero had been cutting away his bandages, one by one; and now the old man could see grayish light behind his wrappings. To him, this was even worse than blindness, because now he knew his eyes might work.

The old man sat on the cold stone bench in the courtyard. The shadow of the *First National Bank* castle stretched out over him as the sun fell behind the building. He could sense Siroth beside him as Doctor Sero fumbled with the last bandages, removing one thread at a time. Impatiently, Grull slapped away the doctor's hand and ripped off the bandages himself.

After sixty years, he couldn't possibly have remembered what sight was like. Now even the blurred images shone with wonder as his aching mind tried to take in six decades' worth of light. The deepest shadows were blindingly bright. His thin but strong hands instinctively reached up to cover Draigen's eyes, *his* eyes now, but he drew them away, wanting to see more.

The forms and shapes slowly focused themselves, but he didn't know what he expected to see. He remembered only scattered visions from his childhood, the flower garden, the shining city with sky-scraping buildings of steel and glass. Grull blinked several times, and each time the world became clearer. Then he looked down upon the ruined city, the broken buildings, the weeds pushing up through crumbling streets and sidewalks.

The vision became indistinct again as his new eyes filled with water. Funny, he had never thought that simple tears would ruin anyone's eyesight. He blinked several times and tried to force his breathing to follow a slower rhythm. He had *never* guessed the effect would be this profound, and it embarrassed him.

Grull sat in silence for a long, long moment, and then turned to the man he recognized to be the Prez. "We really made a mess of things, didn't we?"

The guards looked askance at Aragon—dirt-smeared and clothed in the torn rags of his spring-green jumpsuit—but they moved aside to let him enter Prez Siroth's chamber. Two of the guards accompanied him, but Aragon smiled with self-satisfaction and ignored them.

Siroth looked up from the old-fashioned mousetrap he had been playing with on the table. Sunlight slanted in through the narrow and drafty windows of the chamber. "I'm surprised to see you still alive, dreamer. You didn't strike me as someone who could handle much hardship." He lifted the thin metal bar against the strong pull of the string, and let it fall shut with a loud snap against the wood. "You smell like shit."

"That's what I've been living in for the past week." Aragon looked tired, and hungry, but beatifically satisfied. The gleam of despair had faded from behind his eyes, to be replaced by the barest shadow of the visions that had haunted Draigen's eyes.

"I'm not a great leader who could have changed the world, like Draigen was. But I *am* an agricultural engineer! This is what I was trained for—to improve your godawful methods of farming. You don't have enough people to adequately work all the available land, and right now you split your fields in half, working one side and letting the other lie fallow for a year. With the mutants, I am showing them how to take the simple step of dividing the fields into thirds, plant grain on one third, legumes on another, and leave the last one fallow—just think of what a difference it can make! And there are efficient ways to use the fertilizers you have—just dumping manure all over the place isn't going to solve anything, you know. I can change that, too. Fewer people will starve."

Siroth pressed his fingertips together and turned to face Aragon. "And what do the fukkups have to say about all this? Have you been whipping them yourself? How do you expect them to obey?"

"When you treat them as human beings, Siroth, tell them the *reason* you're doing something and *show* them how it will help them—they work by their own free will. You can ask your own guards: in the first week, the mutants have not done a thing even your paranoid watchers could call dangerous.

"If you play this thing right, Siroth, your subjects will stop hating you. It's the difference between being a dictator and being a king."

Siroth raised the mousetrap again, let it snap down, almost catching his own finger. Dangerous. Playing with a dangerous toy, like this dreamer who was disrupting Siroth's philosophy by damnably proving an unconscionable theory, that the methods of leadership could still function the same way they did *Before*.

"I am impressed, dreamer. I'll admit that. I wish I could talk to Grull about this." But now Grull was gone as well, all because of this dreamer, and the other dreamer's eyes.

Cleaning, fixing, watching, polishing. Grull saw to it the *First National Bank* castle was repaired, loose stone replaced, new mortar added. He cleaned the interior. He removed all the weeds from the courtyard, and swept the

Kevin J. Anderson

flagstones at least once a day. He watched the fukkups as they tore down the fence surrounding their former pens and began to plow the land according to the guidelines Aragon had given them.

Siroth joined him, standing with folded arms and staring down the gentle hill at the remnants of the city below. Grull knew the Prez had come, but he waited for Siroth to speak first.

"Would you ever have believed the fukkups are actually keeping their agreement?" Siroth snorted a little, but to Grull it sounded somewhat forced. "They're working harder than any of our farmers. The food supply should be drastically increased from last year. I'll have to see to it that the children dig out more tunnels for storage."

Grull wanted to answer, but couldn't think of anything to say. He did notice that the stone benches could use a little more polish. And dust had begun to collect on the flagstones again. Siroth continued awkwardly. "The fukkups haven't even caused trouble, Grull. I hear they're building their own little village in the forest. Why would they build new homes when it's so much easier just to repair the old ones?"

Grull sighed and turned to look at him with Draigen's dark eyes, oddly set where the glassy blind ones had been. "That's good to hear, my Prez. But for some reason state matters don't interest me much any more."

The old man still had trouble correlating facial expressions with emotions, but he believed Siroth looked shocked by his comment. He tried to justify what he had said. "I'm an old man, Siroth. For sixty years I have meddled in political affairs, and now it's time to leave them to someone else. I might relax, and even enjoy my life for a change."

He found his broom and vigorously began sweeping out

136

the cracks in the flagstones.

"Grull," Siroth sounded almost concerned, "Aren't you getting a little carried away?"

The old man paused for a moment. "Nonsense. I didn't wait sixty years to see an ugly world." He replaced the broom and started to walk away, mentally dismissing the Prez.

"Where are you going now?"

"I think I want to plant a flower garden."

VI

The army of Prez Claysus arrived swiftly, and unexpectedly, with barely enough warning for Siroth to take even the simplest of defense measures. The castle gate was barred, the guards were mustered—but not much else could be done. Claysus's soldiers stood waiting on the long hill.

Furious, Siroth stood beside the dreamer on the balcony, glaring at the opposing army. He turned red in the face, and his fists clenched convulsively, as if he were desperate to strangle something other than his knuckles. "All these weeks I've been doing *kindhearted* things—" he almost spat the words, "and the wimp has been gathering up an army against me! Because of *you* I'm going to be defeated by a jelly-spined pansy!"

Aragon seemed confused, and Siroth felt a little satisfaction through his despair. "But you told me Claysus is a kind, gentle humanitarian—"

"He *is*, dammit! That's why I never expected this!"

Outside the castle, one man strode forward from the body of the army, Prez Claysus shouting so that Siroth could hear. "Prez Siroth! You are vile and inhuman—and I can no longer tolerate your foul ways! I will tear your castle apart brick by brick and take the architect by force! Then you'll atone for your hideous actions. It's going to take a lot to avenge the murder of my peaceful ambassadors!"

Claysus drew a weapon from his side, a kind of spiked club which looked too heavy for him to use. The other Prez held it out threateningly as his army fidgeted.

Aragon looked at Siroth. "What has he got against you? What 'ambassadors' is he talking about?"

The Prez sighed. "His castle collapsed about a month ago. He sent two ambassadors to ask if he could borrow my architect."

"And?"

"And Grull slit their bellies or something, then sent them back to Claysus still bleeding."

The dreamer's face suddenly turned greenish. "But they were *ambassadors!* They had diplomatic immunity!"

"Not in my lands they don't."

Aragon sat down weakly. "Siroth, you must change your ways!"

But the Prez unleashed his anger. "And these past weeks, if I *hadn't* changed my ways, if I *hadn't* been kind and nice and good, if I *hadn't* let my guard down—"

Siroth stopped abruptly, staring out the window as he caught a glimpse of something in the forest. His eyes widened; his jaw even dropped a little bit.

From out of the wood emerged dozens of horrible misrepresentations of the human form, each with the wrong number of arms or legs or heads—and they were armed with pitchforks, rakes, hoes, scythes, anything they could find.

"Dreamer," Siroth whispered, "I think you'd better see this."

The fukkups marched slowly out of the trees, determined and numerous enough to surround Prez Claysus's
startled troops. They did nothing, standing motionless, but
threatening nonetheless. One of them, a two-headed man
with one arm, cried out in a guttural voice that echoed
oddly from his twin throats. "We will fight to defend our
Prez!"

Siroth stood absolutely stunned, and his lips began to
work seconds before his voicebox did. "They're willing to
fight for me! For me!"

Aragon laughed in delight. "Of course they are! You
freed them. You showed them you *can* be kind, and they're
expressing their appreciation."

Prez Siroth stood speechless for a long moment,
watching the commotion in Claysus's ranks as the soldiers
realized what the mutants were doing. He began to chuckle
loudly. "Hah! Now I can crush him! With the fukkups and
my guards, we can wipe out Prez Pansy once and for all!"

Aragon leaped to his feet. "No! No, that's not the *point!*"
The Prez whirled in sudden rage again, looking as if the
dreamer had gone insane. "Look, Siroth, it doesn't matter if
you can defeat him or not! The point is you can do this
without fighting!"

The Prez's scowl became even more unpleasant; but
Aragon persisted. "Those mutants are standing up for you
because of how you've changed! If you're a *real* leader, you
won't have to resort to war."

"And how else am I supposed to get rid of Claysus?"

"You're the Prez. Solve it yourself, or else you've learned
nothing."

Siroth's forehead wrinkled as he thought, anxiously
looking around the room for someone to help him. "You
expect me to give up Praetoth willingly? After all this?"

"And that will atone for what you did to the ambassadors?"

"Yes!" Aragon stared at him relentlessly, until the Prez looked away. "No. I will also send along some of my men to help him rebuild."

"You could offer to supply some of the materials . . ." the dreamer suggested.

"Enough!" Siroth shouted, and Aragon decided not to press home the point. For a moment, he thought of Draigen's heart still beating after all, even in the chest of someone like Prez Siroth.

VII

Grull wandered in the courtyard, drifting gently through his vast flower garden. Everything had grown up tall and beautiful, in full bloom around the castle. He tended the flowers meticulously, pulling up a weed from between two brilliant orange snapdragons, humming to himself unconsciously.

He liked being alone. He knew Siroth was inside somewhere mediating a dispute between two mutants, but that didn't matter to him. Grull turned to look and noticed Aragon in the courtyard, sitting on one of the stone benches in his faded spring-green uniform, staring empty-eyed off into the distance. Grull followed the dreamer's line of sight, looking at the city and smiling faintly. Many of the buildings had been repaired and cleaned up, or torn down entirely. Grull decided he liked the encroaching forest after all. One of these days he was going to find a stream, and try fishing.

The old man bent down to inspect his rose bushes, and saw one bud just starting to bloom. He looked up at Aragon again, then at the city, then at the fukkups working the fields.

Grull snipped off the bloom and walked quietly over to Aragon, getting his attention. He extended the rose toward the dreamer's hand.

"This is for you."

Another very early story, originally written in a creative writing class, an "advanced fiction workshop" at the University of Wisconsin, Madison—where I first met my longtime friend and colleague, Kristine Kathryn Rusch. Our curmudgeonly professor made a habit of grousing about my penchant for writing science fiction (instead of plotless "my relationship is breaking up" creative-writing-class stories). The only problem was, I routinely came to class with another story sale to announce, while the rest of the students never managed to get published. Kris Rusch kept in touch, and we helped each other with our writing careers.

"Carrier" contains the seeds of many ideas I have since used in my *Seven Suns*, *Star Wars*, and *Dune* novels.

Carrier

In the dark shadows of the long-dead bridge, she found the captain's last log entry. Hesitantly, her fingers trembling with excitement, she punched the few buttons she had deciphered on the dusty control panel, feeding the log tape into her portable JR computer extension.

"Would you translate that for me please, Junior?"

"I will try, Mary Coven," answered the computer via the linkup with the main JR on Coven's ship.

"If you can do it, I'll let you call me just Mary."

"Thank you, Mary."

"Translate it *first*, Junior," she snapped, turning to look around the stiflingly small bridge of the derelict vessel, feeling the shadows push against her spacesuit.

On his first attempt to navigate the *Proud Mary*, Coven's

ship, Junior had almost run them into the ancient craft. The derelict was a series of cylinders strung together like a long train, each marked with a bold, glowing red triangle. An intact starship of the Population I race—the find of the millennium!

Coven had hastily suited-up and boarded the other ship, moving from compartment to compartment in awe, trying to figure out who would build a starship that seemed to be half sickbay, half morgue. Time had changed anything organic into a thin coating of dust; but the beautiful, desperate paintings that covered the walls stood undisturbed by the time that had passed since the artist had added his atoms to the dusty floor.

Magnificent alien landscapes swept across the ship's walls, somehow conveying that the artist knew he would never see home again. Coven blinked. She had murals like that on the walls of the *Proud Mary*—but this artist had stopped suddenly, in the middle of a painting. She briefly wondered why; but then she found the bridge, and excitement made her forget her concern.

A Population I ship. She grinned in amazement even though the craft was not as remarkable as imagination and rumor had made them out to be. The ancient race, built almost into demigods by wild stories and fantastic speculation, had completely vanished, leaving behind only tantalizing scraps of their dead civilization.

Earth, in its undying quest to gather knowledge, built what it called the Astro-Archaeology Foundation to assimilate those tiny fragments of Population I scattered so thinly about the explored portion of the Galaxy. When the artifacts came in too slowly to keep the Foundation busy, the "Star Search" was instigated, offering large sums of money to those people who might not otherwise look hard enough, when the only incentive was doing one's duty for all humanity.

Now, as she took in this ancient ship, Mary Coven could call herself the most successful of all the scavengers who had scoured space for any scrap that might be connected with Population I. She wondered how many people would kill to be where she was now.

"Hurry up, Junior!"

Coven had found a different artifact once before, a small plasticene scrap of an art object, half-buried in the wastes of a backwater planet. The plasticene had been painted with the tantalizing picture of a human-looking arm decorated with fine red lines.

With the generous reward she had received from the "Star Search" fund, Coven had bought herself a new JR computer, choosing one with a personality rather than the more efficient standard model. Hell, she could *fly* the ship herself; what she really needed was someone to talk to. It got lonely on some of those long flights. She just wished Junior wasn't so naïve at times.

"All finished, Mary."

"Well, play it then!"

A viewscreen on Junior's console lit up as an image of the Population I captain formed. He looked vaguely human, with grayish skin and a turned-up nose; but his face and arms were covered with livid red lines, searing into his body, eating him away. He trembled and spoke in a shaky tone. Junior's calm, artificial voice filled in the English equivalents, drowning out the captain's alien character.

"If you listen to this recording, I shed grief that you have ignored our clear warnings of the red three-corners. We are a plague ship! And if you have intruded into our environment, you too have the disease. Do not return to your origin!"

"Sorry, buddy, some of us are bright enough not to take off our spacesuits," Coven commented under her breath.

"We, the first victims, isolated ourselves at the outbreak of the plague, hoping to save our race—but we were too late. We are quarantined, and the pestilence burns through all worlds, killing off my people. They are all dying . . . dying . . ."

The screen flickered, then turned gray. "I have another very short clip tagged onto the end of this tape, Mary. Would you like to hear it?"

"Go ahead."

The captain's image appeared again, and this time the disease had ravaged him so that he could barely remain seated in his chair. "I have worked much thought into the possibility that a survivor might find our plague ship and re-birth the disease. I have made it so that this ship will self-destruct when the last of us dies. Oh . . . Untranslatable, Mary, but I believe it is an alien expletive. Why am I even recording this?"

The screen winked out. Coven looked around the haunting ship, admiring a few of the shadowy paintings in the pools of light spattered down the corridor. The thin, filmy dust, all that remained of the quarantined victims, showed her footprints clearly.

Junior spoke, breaking the silence. "I have found a small malfunction in the self-destruct sequence—but I have corrected it."

Coven froze. "What?"

"My programming specifically instructs that I correct malfunctions as I find them, Mary. You know that. I did not do anything wrong, did I?"

"Oh, Junior! How much time is left?"

"Thirty-two alien time units."

"Well, how long is an 'alien' time unit?"

"I will check through the main library. One moment, Mary . . ."

"No!" She grabbed the portable console and sprinted toward the airlock that connected to her ship. Her finger punched the hatch release, but it would not open.

The tinny voice of JR came through a speaker in the wall. "I can't let you through until you have been properly decontaminated, Mary."

"Junior! Let me in."

"It is standard procedure, Mary."

"Then get us out of here!"

"Mary, I can not fly the ship all by myself. I was just installed, and you haven't taught me everything yet."

"Then let me in, dammit."

"But, Mary—"

"If you don't open this stupid hatch we'll both be . . . terminated!"

"Well . . . all right, Mary."

Then JR grudgingly slid the airlock hatch into its recess, and Coven raced to the cockpit, leaping into her seat. Rapid acceleration slammed her back against the chair as *Proud Mary* lurched away from the doomed craft.

The Population I plague ship turned into a sun behind them, casting weird shadows through the viewscreens.

"All that knowledge . . ." Junior sighed.

"All that money," Coven moaned.

Mary Coven didn't look in mirrors much. Not that she was displeased with what she saw there—silver-brown hair, faint lines beginning to etch themselves around steely eyes—but she had no use for them. It wasn't until several days later that she noticed the red spiderweb of ruptured blood vessels beginning to trace its way along her cheeks, just like the captain of the Population I ship.

Her initial feeling of stricken helplessness lasted only a moment, as she stared at her reflection with a despairing outcry poised on her lips. Coven forced down the frantic thoughts blasting through her mind. Plague! She had the plague! She needed help, couldn't figure out the disease's cycle herself. She had to get back to Earth!

A cold chill crept through her as her composure returned. She didn't dare return to Earth. This disease had wiped out the entire Population I race. She just couldn't take the risk, vainly hoping that a cure could be found.

Coven made up her mind. She would go only within transmitting distance of Earth to tell them what had happened—she couldn't think of having *Proud Mary* placed on the list of missing ships—and to give them all the information she had taken from the Population I plague ship. Junior had at least gotten pictures of the ship, the log recordings, and a superficial gleaning from the library computer. She had contracted a deadly disease just to get that knowledge; someone may as well benefit from it.

Coven turned and looked wistfully at the murals covering her own walls, great vistas of the Alps, the Grand Canyon, Mount Rushmore, the Black Forest, a South American jungle—thinking of similar paintings on the Population I ship. She never thought they looked so beautiful.

"Junior," Coven spoke quietly to the ship, leaning back in her chair with a sigh, "Did I ever tell you why I left Earth?"

"No, Mary."

"I grew up in a dirty, ugly city filled with dirty, ugly people. And when I had fought my way out of the slums to see the real world, I found that the rest wasn't so pretty either, not what I thought it would be at all. So I left." Coven looked again at the old vistas of Earth. Things might have been different if her expectations hadn't been so high.

Over the next few days, Coven watched the red intaglio of plague creeping down her cheeks and neck, beginning to lace her arms. Her hands had developed a bothersome trembling which she could not control, and, at times, she found it increasingly difficult to breathe.

The Earth fell away from *Proud Mary* like a shed tear. Coven had stopped only long enough to tell the authorities that she wouldn't be coming back, and to transmit the data Junior had obtained on the Population I ship.

The Astro-Archaeology Foundation immediately named her the recipient of their most generous reward. Coven snapped into the transmitter, asking what in the world she was supposed to do with it.

"Shall we give it to your next of kin?" they had asked.

"If I had any next of kin, would I spend all my time out here alone?"

She listened to the confused pause. There had been someone once, but he had meant nothing to her. When he fell ill from some strange virus with a Latin name, she dragged him to the hospital, when everyone else would have left him to die in the alley, to rot and become compost for a new crop of garbage. Perhaps she should have left him; it would have saved the doctors the trouble of killing him. It was an accident, they said, we injected him with the wrong vaccine. It happened from time to time. They treated a lot of people and they couldn't be right every time. It was a good thing he had meant nothing to her. Coven was glad she could forget all about it.

The voice interrupted her thoughts, "Um . . . what shall

we do with your monetary compensation then?"

Coven thought of several things the stuffy bureaucrat could do with it, but answered, "Why don't you use it to make me a martyr? Build a statue and put it next to my memorial."

Where do you go to die?

A star named Meyer; a blood-red dwarf surrounded by a tight halo of rubble, scattered asteroids in nothing resembling an ecliptic. The faint star grew larger day by day, slowly becoming prominent across the rich field of stars ahead of the *Proud Mary*.

"Do you want to play another game of chess, Mary?"

"No, Junior."

"I promise I will not try so hard this time."

"I said *no*."

"But I'm bored, Mary."

"You can't be bored. You're a computer."

"Oh, well, you are bored, then."

Mary didn't answer.

The JR was silent for a few moments, then continued, "Do you know there is another ship following us, Mary?"

She snapped up, looking out the viewport, but could see nothing in the dizzying infinity of stars. "What?"

"It started to follow about a day after we left Earth, when you delivered your message."

Coven scowled. "Tell it to go away."

"It refuses to acknowledge."

"Well, what kind of ship is it?"

"Similar to ours, only slightly more efficient. We cannot outrun it—and it is slowly gaining on us."

"The pilot certainly doesn't want to go to Meyer. I've been there and, believe me, it's not the party spot of the Galaxy.

It's got some broken asteroids around it, and I'm hoping to find a comfortable one. But what does that idiot want?"

Silence fell on the ship as Junior paused, trying to communicate with the other ship. "He says he wants to dock."

Coven almost jumped, her arms shaking as the red lines burned their way down into her marrow. "Is he crazy? Tell him to kiss off, Junior."

Junior paused, as if uncomfortable. "But then he will be mad at me, Mary."

Coven pursed her lips, thinking. "All right, Junior. Check your charts and see if you can plot a roundabout route to Meyer. Now let me talk to that Burnhead following us, and when I signal, hit the brakes and change course. That should throw him off."

"Hit the brakes, Mary?"

"Decelerate rapidly. At the speed we're going, his ship will be out of range before he realizes we've made a complete fool of him."

Coven frowned smugly as the JR opened a direct comlink to the other ship. She refused to allow a visual linkup, waiting until Junior said the man on the other end was listening.

"Look, Space Cadet, I've got the *plague!* You don't want to see me. Everything I got from Population I has been sent to Earth. You're wasting your time. Now *leave me alone!*"

Coven signaled to one of Junior's optical sensors, then braced herself as *Proud Mary* lurched onto a new course. She watched as the following ship blazed past like a bullet to vanish instantly in the distance.

"Bye, bye, sucker."

Meyer loomed ahead of them like a drop of clotting blood. Junior analyzed the scattered clumps of asteroids, checking out some of the major ones, searching for a place for Coven to stay.

They entered the outer fringes of the distorted belt, passing into the thin forest of rocks. Junior's voice sounded anxious as he broke Coven's bleary silence in the cockpit.

"It is not my fault, Mary."

Coven looked up and tried to focus her eyes behind the pounding in her head. "What isn't your fault, Junior?"

"Our friend is back."

She stiffened, her fingers clenching convulsively in the grip of the advancing plague. *"How?"*

"He had a fairly good idea of where we were going, Mary."

"How close is he?"

"Still far from visual range, but he has definitely found us."

"Well, lose him again!"

"How, Mary?"

She drew in a deep breath. A muscle on her neck twitched violently. "All right, Junior, pay attention. I'm going to give you a lesson on how to get rid of a pain in the ass!"

"I have no bodily parts, Mary."

"Shut up and listen. Find a dense concentration of asteroids and shoot through them, placing them between us and his line of sight. Then alter course to find another tight cloud of rocks and do the same thing a couple of times until he has no way of knowing where we are."

Coven slumped in her chair, fighting to keep her vision straight. Over the days it had taken to finally reach Meyer, her arms had developed a perpetual trembling that occasionally turned into a seizure. Deep-seated headaches dug into her mind, and her vision blurred often. She had given up looking in the mirror, and tried not to notice the livid red tracery engraved into her arms. Junior now had almost complete control over the *Proud Mary,* and now Coven's conscience nagged at her for trusting the inexperienced JR to do stunt-flying in the asteroid field. But she certainly could not have done any better herself.

"Now what, Mary?" Junior repeated, and Coven realized she had passed out briefly. Junior had taken them through several passages of asteroids.

Coven's mind spun as she tried to remember what she had planned. "Okay, Junior. Now plot a typical orbit around one of those asteroids and inject us into it. Kill all the engines, and we'll drift in the arms of the Holy Laws of Physics for a while. He has no way of seeing that we're not just another rock, unless he comes into visual range of us. And the chances of that are . . ."

"Would you like me to calculate them, Mary?"

"No! Just get off my back!"

Proud Mary drifted in an elliptical orbit for a day and a half, undisturbed, slowly wheeling around the red star Meyer. Mary Coven passed through fits of violent trembling, throbbing headaches. And the broken scarlet lines seemed to sear deeper into her skin. She alternated periods of tranquilizers and stimulants, trying to decide which worked better.

Junior's insistent voice brought her out of a half-conscious state, slumped in the cockpit. Coven opened bleary eyes and fixed her gaze on the mural of the Badlands for a long moment before acknowledging.

"I think I have found a suitable asteroid for you, Mary."

"Give me some statistics."

"It is a sun-grazer of greater-than-average mass. It has a

temporary atmosphere like a comet now that it's near the star, mostly nitrogen and some oxygen. Mean surface temperature is thirteen degrees centigrade."

Coven nodded, focusing her attention. "A little chilly, but what can I expect?"

"It will be able to support you for a few months before it gets too close to the star. During perihelion, the entire surface will be molten."

Coven smiled grimly. "That's what I wanted. I don't want anybody else to come here and catch my little cold. Besides, it looks like I won't be needing a place for more than . . . a short while."

"Shall I take you there, Mary?"

"What are you waiting for?"

Dust settled around the *Proud Mary,* slowly clearing before the viewports; and Coven looked out at the asteroid she had chosen. She took the last four of her stimulants, found an oxygen mask, and told Junior she wanted to go outside.

"I must warn you, Mary, to take the proper precautions. You may become exposed to contaminated air."

Coven huffed. "Junior, haven't you been *listening?* I've already got the damned plague!"

The JR didn't answer, but instead slid open the first airlock hatch. Coven stepped inside the chamber and waited to be cycled through. The second hatch opened, and she stepped onto new soil.

Coven smiled ironically and spoke. "I hereby name you asteroid Quarantine."

The blood-red sheen of Meyer thickened the sky to a viscous purple, staining the lifeless scattered rocks in an eerie forest of shadows. The landscape was woven and broken, much like her, and she shivered in the chilly air. Then she decided to build a campfire as she had seen in some of the old pictures, and smiled with a burst of unwelcome nostalgia.

After convincing Junior to leave the double hatch of *Proud Mary* open, Coven collected a pile of combustibles and cleared a campsite within the cluster of rock pinnacles near the ship. Gritting her teeth to help control her trembling hands, she tried to light the pile of charts, cushions, and scrap paper, finally succeeding.

Coven leaned back against a cold rock, staring deep into the fire that was struggling to stay lit in the small oxygen content of the air. Brilliant points of light sparkled above her, other asteroids moving with Quarantine around the red dwarf. The dead asteroid was deeply silent. She couldn't even hear her own breathing.

A muffled sound came from inside the ship, as if Junior was calling to her, but Coven ignored it, trying to resist the clutches of unconsciousness that tugged at her. The stimulants weren't working.

A noise appeared off to her side, clear and unexpected in the thin air. She roused herself, then turned to look with reluctant, unfocusing eyes on a man, sealed completely behind the black visor of a full spacesuit. He stepped out of the shadows and walked towards her. Even here he had followed.

"Mary Coven."

Shock paralyzed her for an instant as she gagged on a quick gasp of air. Her limbs shuddered violently, but somewhere she found the strength to lurch to her feet and run. Her breath was almost gone and the cold, filtered air of Quarantine stabbed at her deteriorating lungs.

She danced across the broken, low-gravity surface, winding her way through mazes of fallen rocks. The man followed, but his bulky spacesuit slowed his pursuit. Coven pulled ahead, hoping she would lose him in the jumbled labyrinth of broken rock, wondering how he could possibly have found her, but then she realized how few asteroids around Meyer were capable of supporting life.

Coven quickly became exhausted. Her body shuddered, finding it almost impossible to breathe in the grip of the disease. She stumbled, falling to the rocky dust as both knees gave out simultaneously.

In the distance behind her she could hear the clank of the man's heavy boots as he crunched across the surface, following her. Desperately, she crawled into a shallow cave, hoping to hide in the shadows. Trembling, she fell against the far wall, shuddering with another seizure, her very marrow trying to crawl out of her bones.

He stood silhouetted in the cave opening, a bulky figure against the bloody sky. "You can't run away anymore, Mary."

She picked up a rock from the floor and threw it, trying to smash his black faceplate. But her trembling arm sent the stone flying off to the man's side.

"No violence now!" he snapped.

"Who are you? What do you want?"

"You have something from Population I. As a fellow scavenger, I want it."

"I told you, Burnhead, I gave everything to Earth! I have nothing left!"

"You have the plague," he answered quietly and moved toward her.

In Coven's shocked silence, he removed a medical kit from his suit and fumbled with a syringe in thickly-gloved hands. He grabbed her red-laced arm and jabbed the needle into her skin, beginning to draw blood.

"The 'Star Search' charter specifically states that they will pay substantially for *any* remnant of the Population I race. And this is the virus that destroyed them. What could be more important than that?"

He paused, looking into her wide, steely eyes from behind his opaque mask. "Think of how much we can learn about their physiology just by studying the disease that killed them off. Since you have declined your reward, I'm sure the Foundation will be much more generous with my own compensation."

Coven found her outrage was enough to let her shout at him. "You're crazy! What if the plague gets loose? It'll destroy the human race just like it wiped out Population I!"

The man filled a second vial of blood, poking her other arm when one artery seemed to run dry. "They'll take the proper precautions. Don't be such a pessimist."

"I grew up in the slums, Buddy-boy. I am, by definition, a pessimist."

The man didn't listen. He clipped the two vials of blood into his medical kit and carefully sterilized his equipment. "Thank you, Mary Coven."

She cried out after him. "You're botching up my entire sacrifice! I might as well have gone back to Earth and died in a comfortable hospital bed."

He turned his faceless helmet at her. "We all make bad judgments." And then he was gone.

Coven stayed in the cave a long time before she slowly got up on unsteady legs and began to stumble back to the *Proud Mary*. The doors were still wide open, and Junior's voice was incessantly calling her.

"Mary! Mary!"

She went haltingly inside, blood rushing painfully to her

head. She stopped the JR's excited chatter. "I know, Junior. He's already gone."

The computer paused as if waiting to spring a surprise. "But he'll be back."

She lifted her eyes to one of the speakers, frowning, then wincing as pain shot through her body. "What?"

"I thought you might like some company, rather than being alone on this asteroid. So, after he had left his ship, I contacted his computer—a primitive thing: no personality, able to do only its main functions, unable to stand up even to the weakest argument—and reprogrammed it. Shortly after takeoff, his computer will direct the thermal energy from his engines to the cockpit, quickly raising the temperature to about three hundred degrees centigrade."

Junior's voice seemed to hint that he took pride in his new understanding of human nature. "So, the pilot will decide he was much more comfortable here on Quarantine and he will come back to you, Mary."

Coven stared at the JR console, eyes wide. "Three *hundred* centigrade! Junior! He is a biological organism. At that temperature we . . . combust!"

A flicker of light caught her eye, and she looked up into the purplish sky to see a brilliant shooting star falling back to the asteroid.

"I'm sorry, Mary." Junior sounded crushed. "Did I do something wrong again?"

Coven absently rubbed her arm where the man had taken blood. Then she slowly forced a smile, wondering if Junior was truly as naïve as he seemed to be or—?

"No, Junior. You did just fine."

The late Jon Gustafson, writer and genre art appraiser, had an odd habit of challenging other authors to write a story that began "There were rats in the soufflé again." An unusual obsession, perhaps, but Jon did get enough stories to fill at least two anthologies. Here's what I did with the line . . .

Controlled Experiments

There were rats in the soufflé again.

Tricia screamed and dropped the plate as she withdrew it from the station's food-prep unit. Behind the metal walls of the circuitry, she heard clunks and sounds of the other rats stirring, scrambling, *coming at them.*

"Look out!" Captain Kennedy Brandt shouted, knocking her aside as he pointed his blaster at the unit, firing in one long, continuous stream of energy that sputtered and popped through the air. Metal shards spat out of the chamber along with globules of molten plastic. Sparks flew as slagged circuitry, plexiglass, and steel dripped down the cracks.

Rats screamed one last time as they regrouped, tried to fall back into formation, then died in smoking masses of fur and cooked flesh. Others deep behind the panel squealed from their injuries and fled. But they would find another way to get in. It was only a matter of time.

Outside the airlock of the one safe module on station SS-1, Tricia could hear the scrabbling of claws against the door, the scrape of metal. God, they were using *tools* again!

Tricia regained her composure and looked at the ruined

food-prep unit and wide-eyed Captain Brandt staring down at the depleted blaster in his hand. "Great, Captain. That was your last blaster charge. Now what are we going to do when they finally do break in?"

"They're not going to break in!" he shouted, his voice husky with panic.

Behind them, low to the floor, Tricia heard a slow chuckle from the only other survivor aboard the orbital research station. Dr. Sonnya Lyov, with her Amazon build and long gray-blond hair, looked out of place curled up like a terrified baby, drawing her knees up to her chin. "They'll get smarter and smarter," she said. "It'll never end. They'll find a way to get us."

The captain whirled toward Tricia defensively, misdirecting his helplessness. "You said you purged the life-support systems!"

"I did, and the food channels, too. I dumped hard vacuum into all the ducts." She shook her head. "But you know how smart the rats are. They must have rerouted everything to protect themselves." Tricia sat back down again, gasping, trying to stop from hyperventilating. "Now we don't even have a food-prep unit. Thanks, Captain."

Kennedy Brandt whirled at her, wild-eyed. "The rescue shuttle will be here in a few hours! We won't need any more food."

Sonnya Lyov moaned and covered her eyes. "The rats will get us before then. There'll be no rescue shuttle."

Tricia lunged to her feet, screaming at the doctor. "Lihue's message did get through! It was acknowledged! Just shut up."

The first officer on SS-1, Kai Lihue—now dead—had run bellowing out into the corridor as Captain Brandt covered him. When the airlock door to their module had opened, rats screamed and scattered, white fur flying as Lihue charged. His muscular Hawaiian frame looked enormous compared to the scurrying super-intelligent rats.

"Good luck," Tricia had whispered after him.

The last she saw of Lihue was him ducking around a corner as the rats regrouped to mount a defense. Scattered along the corridor she had noticed tiny pieces of metal, electronics, pointed objects—*weapons*. The rats had been building bizarre, rodent-sized weapons.

She saw sparks flying, minuscule projectiles. The rats were shooting at Lihue! He stumbled, but kept running, firing his own weapon and making blackened holes on the walls as bolts of energy *spanged* off the metal plates.

Captain Brandt had sealed the door immediately behind his first officer.

Through the station intercom, they heard Lihue reach one of the other separable modules. He had locked himself in, panting, then blasted the few rats he found tinkering there. He had managed to reconfigure the transmission antennas that the rats had sabotaged, then began broadcasting to unsuspecting Earth below, telling their story and begging for an emergency rescue before they were forced to set off the station's automatic self-destruct.

Just as Lihue began to repeat his message, the rats outside had somehow figured out how to blow the explosive bolts. They jettisoned Lihue's module from the main core of the station, sending it adrift in orbit. It would likely have crashed flaming through Earth's atmosphere—but the rats couldn't wait for that. They managed to reconfigure SS-1's solar-power mirrors, focusing the concentrated energy onto the side of Lihue's drifting module, breaching its containment.

Over the radio, they could hear the first officer's screams

fade into a hissing rush of vacuum.

The rats had done it out of revenge and their own scientific curiosity. That was all they seemed to want.

Now, Sonnya Lyov struggled with her long legs and muscular arms, trying to stand up, but it seemed too difficult a task for her. She slumped back into her corner. "Everything we do, everything we try and fail, teaches them more and more. They keep learning." She grinned. "That was what they were designed to do."

"Then we'd better not fail anymore. Right, Captain?" Tricia said.

Brandt swung around with his dead blaster ready to fire, as if that would help anything. Tricia finally snatched the weapon out of his hand and tossed it clattering to the deck.

Station SS-1 had been designed as an orbital isolation lab for genetics research, but after a decade it had been adapted for nanotechnology research. Well-known investigator and Nobel Prize winner Dr. Sonnya Lyov was trying to increase human mental abilities by developing cellular machines to fit inside the brain, acting as vast warehouses that could organize information, store countless encyclopedias of facts where they could never be forgotten.

After a year of final prototyping, Dr. Lyov and her assistant Billy Donatelli had tested it out on their dozens of captive lab rats to see if they could master mazes better, run through them faster. And did they ever!

After only two days, the results were remarkable. Somehow, the rats could communicate with each other the correct routes. Those watching above in the cages would help direct the test rat through the maze, offering a bird's-eye view.

Excitement ran high. Several live newsnet interviews

from orbit astonished the scientific world.

Until, one sleep period, the rats escaped from their cages. Every one of them. When Lyov and Donatelli came into the lab the following morning, they found the cages sprung open with tiny ladders dangling down from the high shelves. Melted spots on the metal sides glimmered beside tiny contraptions that could only be miniature welding tools put together out of lab junk, hooked into the station's primary power supply.

And the rats had all vanished. Lyov had kept it secret for half a day, searching the modules while Lihue, Tricia, and Captain Brandt smiled patronizingly at the oddball scientists.

That night, during their year-anniversary celebration meal in the mess, Tricia had called up soufflé from the food-prep database. All of the crew had gathered for the meal. When she pulled it out of the chamber, the dish was infested. The rats had been trying to rig an explosive into the food package.

Another check showed that the rats had broken into the food stores and stockpiled everything for their own uses. Billy Donatelli found that the rats had also removed the access panels to several of the station's computer terminals. The rats had tapped into SS-1's entire database, downloading every scrap of knowledge stored in the master computer.

And they kept learning. . . .

That night, while Billy Donatelli worked alone in the lab, the rats caught him.

They vivisected him.

The following morning, Sonnya Lyov found her assistant's body and various organs strewn throughout the module. Body parts had been locked in empty cages. Tiny clawed footprints, smeared in the plentiful blood, skittered along the stools, the tables. Small pawprints marked the keys on the computer terminal. A brief message had been typed onto the screen.

"WE KNOW WHAT YOU HAVE DONE TO RATS FOR CENTURIES IN THE NAME OF SCIENCE. NOW WE HAVE DISCOVERED HOW ENJOYABLE SCIENTIFIC RESEARCH CAN BE. WE WILL CONTINUE OUR OWN SERIES OF EXPERIMENTS."

Now, only the three survivors remained, trapped in a single module with the doors barricaded and no way out. They continued to hear scratching at the door and tiny hissing noises. The rats were experimenting with more gadgets.

Suddenly a large hollow *thump* reverberated through the station. Dr. Lyov whimpered. Captain Brandt dove for his empty blaster on the floor. "What is it?" he cried. "What is it!"

Tricia gripped the metal stem of a mounted chair as the station rocked. "I think they've blown another one of the detachable modules. Just like Lihue's."

Captain Brandt scratched his square jaw. "I don't know why they haven't just jettisoned us, if they're so anxious."

"That wouldn't be any fun for them!" Dr. Lyov said, then started giggling again. "They're observing our reactions under stress."

Station SS-1 had begun to spin crazily, knocked into an off-center axis that made their module wobble with each rotation. Out of the tiny porthole, Tricia couldn't see Earth. The stars of the Galaxy spun overhead.

Outside the metal door, the murderous rats kept trying to get inside. . . .

The "incoming message" indicator chimed, startling Tricia, Dr. Lyov, and Captain Brandt. The light blinked again. Tricia rushed to the message pad and pushed RECEIVE. Capital letters spilled across the screen.

"RESCUE SHUTTLE *ACHILLES* APPROACHING STATION SS-1. UNABLE TO REACH YOU ON VOICE BAND. ESTIMATED ARRIVAL, 25 MINUTES. WILL DOCK AT YOUR MODULE'S AIRLOCK. PLEASE ALLOW ACCESS."

"We're saved!" Captain Brandt shouted.

"ACKNOWLEDGED," Tricia typed. "All right, now we just wait." She pushed aside sweaty strands of hair.

The metal plate below the main bulkhead door felt warm. The rats must be trying to burn through. She heard skittering noises, as if the rats were redoubling their efforts. Tricia clenched her hands together.

Before fifteen minutes had passed, they heard the *clunk* of something heavy striking the walls of SS-1 on the outside. The message terminal chimed again.

"RESCUE SHUTTLE *ACHILLES* RENDEZVOUS SUCCESSFUL. ASTRONAUT TROY IN YOUR AIRLOCK IN 5 MINUTES."

"We're going to make it!" Captain Brandt shouted. Even Sonnya Lyov crawled to her feet.

Tricia heard the rats on the other side of the door renew their scrabbling. They had only a few minutes left.

The lights on the outer airlock blinked on, indicating that someone had opened the external hatch. The colors turned from red to amber.

Captain Brandt pounded on the door, as if to communicate his desperation. The rescuer knocked back once, signaling. Dr. Lyov stood up to wait by the airlock door, taller than either Brandt or Tricia.

Tricia felt ready to break down now and allow herself to feel the panic. She looked out the porthole again to take one last look at the wheeling stars overhead—and she saw shards of metal, wreckage of structural supports, white ceramic heat tiles. "What?"

Captain Brandt opened the inner airlock door, allowing the astronaut to enter. The rescuer took two slow steps forward. Captain Brandt ran to grasp the hand of his savior.

But something wasn't right. Tricia turned to look at the newcomer. "That's one of *our* suits!" She saw the markings of SS-1 and the station logo plain as day on the helmet, on the breast. "That suit's from one of our EVA lockers!"

Out of the corner of her eye she saw more wreckage drift past the porthole. It was the twisted remains of a destroyed shuttle. The real rescue shuttle. Then a human body drifted across her field of view.

The shuttle had never rendezvoused. The rats had destroyed it somehow, perhaps by knocking one of the detachable modules right into its path as it approached. They had been faking the transmissions.

At the airlock, Dr. Lyov started laughing hysterically one last time as the faceplate of the rescuer's suit burst open, revealing five rat-pilots sitting in tiny command chairs hauling joysticks rigged to pulleys and gears mounted inside the suit, making it walk, making it raise its arms, making it move toward them.

Other compartments of the suit split open, and more rats boiled out holding tiny guns, projectile launchers, possibly poison-laced needles.

Tricia shrank back against the wall and thought about the shuttle *Achilles*, the astronaut *Troy*. "We fell for that old trick again," she thought. "Maybe we're no smarter than rats after all."

Captain Brandt fell down trying to *clonk* the rats with his dead blaster. Dr. Lyov offered no resistance whatsoever.

As the rats swarmed toward her, firing paralyzing needles into her arms and legs, Tricia wondered exactly what type of experiments the rats intended to perform on them.

When my friend Janet Berliner joined with famous illusionist David Copperfield to put together an anthology of stories about magic, Arthur C. Clarke's famous quote immediately came to mind. How else can you do a science fiction story about *magic?*

TechnoMagic

"Any sufficiently advanced technology is indistinguishable from magic."

—Arthur C. Clarke

"Twenty-seven years for a rescue ship? You've got to be kidding! What am I supposed to do on this planet in the meantime? How am I—"

—Taurindo Alpha Prime,
last transmission from scout vessel
before crashing in the Nevada desert
(loosely translated)

The first garish posters had said *The Great Taurindo!*—some over-enthusiastic publicist's idea, not mine—but my fame grew so rapidly that within a few years the marquees in the Las Vegas amphitheaters shouted my name in letters even taller than I was. (And I am slightly greater in height than the average Earthling, though I look just like one of them.)

The evening's crowd was sprawled out at various tables, more than could comfortably fit in the room, thanks to the outrageous ticket prices people were willing to pay to see me perform. The rich ones sat in the best seats, drinking expensive cocktails, while busloads of budget tour groups crammed together at the long tables, jabbering their schemes for how to win at the nickel slots.

Everyone fell silent as the show began. I cracked my knuckles in the shadows at the edge of the stage, waiting, making sure my smile looked right. Many species in the Galaxy believe the flashing of one's teeth to be a threatening gesture, but on Earth it's considered friendly. Just another of the odd details about them.

The master of ceremonies announced me as the "World's! Greatest! Magician!" Sometimes I'm called a magician, other times an "illusionist"—neither of which is truly accurate, since what I do is not magic nor illusion, but the real thing . . . courtesy of my planet's highly advanced technology. None of the spectators knew that, though.

The broad stage reminded me of when I had taken my oral exam before the xeno-sociology degree committee back on the homeworld. I strode out and took my bow as I introduced the evening's first spectacle.

"Remember the old saw about the woman being cut in half in a box?" I said. The audience chuckles. No one from my planet would have understood the reference, but this was a hoary old trick performed *ad nauseam* by Earth magicians. Simple enough to master, but I had added a new twist. "Tonight I'll show you a *new saw*, a very large saw in fact." I smiled again.

The lights flashed. Hot white beams reflected from the highly polished, stainless-steel teeth of the giant chainsaw blade that would slice me in two before their very eyes.

The audience loved the show so far—my lovely assistants were wearing even skimpier outfits than usual.

"I won't hide in a box, I won't use mirrors or distractions. I will lie on this table in plain sight, and this chainsaw will cut me in half—*as you watch!* You'll see it all, every second of it."

The music built. The lights dimmed.

I stepped back into the artificially deep shadows at the back of the stage, and then I sent my perfect clone forward out into the brilliant light. He was an identical match for my body, cell for cell, although his brain was completely blank. It was all the vapid simulacrum could do to stagger across the stage and lie down on the table under the motionless chainsaw.

The beautiful assistants strapped him down, and he didn't resist, instinctively smiling out at the audience like an idiot. All clones smile. It's a secret they seem to share in their brainlessness.

The eyes of all the men in the audience were trying to catch a glimpse of just a bit more through my assistants' scanty uniforms and paid little attention to the mechanics of the actual trick. Others were trying to figure out what the gimmick was—while some few, the blessed ones, remained happy enough just to be entertained.

The music swelled loud and dramatic. The chainsaw blade spun up with a loud roar that built to a threatening whine, like a dentist's drill for King Kong.

The lighting technicians slipped a thick red gel over the spotlights, bathing the stage in an ominous crimson glow, as the deadly blade began to descend, rattling as the chain teeth whipped around and around in a circle. The clone lay twitching on the table, bound by the restraints and staring with uncomprehending eyes up at the sharp spinning blade about to rip him to shreds.

That's show biz, as they say.

Timing was everything now, and I had to depend on my crew. They knew what they were supposed to do.

The chainsaw slammed down, ripping through the clone's ribcage and sparking on the steel tabletop. Blood flew in a bright arc—one of the more picturesque ones, I thought. The clone let out a shriek of instinctive pain that was abruptly cut off . . . then all the lights went out for an instant to be replaced by only a single faint spotlight on the retracting chainsaw blade still slowly spinning, dripping blood.

The audience swelled with thin screams. I wondered how many of them would faint this time, though I had done this trick many times and they must have *known* there would be no accident. Not this time. Not any time.

I could have kept the lights up, of course, since this was all real. I could have shown the audience the gory, anatomically correct mess on the table. But that would have gone beyond the bounds of good clean entertainment. Instead, the glimpse of the bloodied saw and the clone's genuine scream was all they needed to know.

As the lights dropped to black, the automatic nanocritters—microscopic destructive robots—began the busy-work of taking my clone apart cell by cell, dissolving him into a simple protein mass in the space of less than a minute. And when the entire body was denatured, the liquid obediently seeped into drains in the table (placed there ostensibly for spilled blood). I would use the protein mass to grow a clone for another performance.

The lights came up again with enough flash and dazzle to temporarily blind the audience, and there I stood in the middle of the stage, intact and smiling, taking my bow to thunderous applause—as always.

Outside the bright lights of the casino, I melted into the crowd, where I could study the way humans interact. I've never gotten tired of it, even after so many years.

On the sidewalk at a street corner, where impatient pedestrians waited for DON'T WALK to change to WALK, I saw an aspiring magician walking among the people, pestering them, showing off to the best of his ability. Doing card tricks, pulling colored scarves from his sleeves—amateurish stuff, but I stopped in mid-stride with a warm glow of nostalgia. Perhaps he hoped for some sort of special attention as he stood overshadowed by the huge marquee for *The Great Taurindo!*

I watched him for a while. This struggling magician with stars in his eyes and the reckless hope for fame reminded me of one of the first Earthlings I had ever met. . . .

Just before my burned-out scout ship crashed out on this planet's desert wastelands, I was able to salvage only a few things from the hulk. After transmitting my distress call and pinpointing my position for the eventual rescue ship, I hurried away from the ship as the self-destruct nanocritters began to turn the hull and engines to indefinable dust.

Swallowing hard, I hiked across the rocky scrub in the general direction of the large city I had spotted just before impact.

Because of my profession studying alien cultures, I had been through the "first contact" routine numerous times before, and this one went off without a hitch. But as I ambled through the streets of Las Vegas, trying to fit in while staring wide-eyed around me, I came upon a street magician. He had a battered cardboard box open on the sidewalk, in which had been scattered bits of paper and round metal (obviously the monetary currency in use).

The magician extended a deck of playing cards to passers-by, asking them to select a card, whose identity he would then guess. In another trick he hid a bright red ball under one of three bowls, rapidly shuffled them around, then asked someone to find it—and invariably they guessed wrong.

At first, I suspected these humans had telepathic powers, but as I watched I soon realized this was not the case. The magician was merely fooling his audience with sleight of hand. And people were tossing him money for it.

I watched him for some time, but since I had no local currency to give for the performance, I wandered away.

I began to think that I could do such stunts, only better—given my superior technology. Among the few items I had snagged from the ship before its quiet self-destruct was the wonderful Central Autonomic Molecular Device—a complex whirlwind computer, synthesizer, and nanotechnology processor. I called it the "gizmo," ignoring the pretentious technical terminology that I didn't understand anyway. The machine was far beyond my level of education and training—I was a xeno-sociologist and observer, not an engineer. The palm-sized gizmo *worked*, and that was all I needed to know during my exile here.

I was stuck on Earth for twenty-seven years, and I would have to make something of myself in the meantime. And magic fascinated these people.

As I assimilated into this culture I came upon an interesting observation called Clarke's Law. It said that "Any sufficiently advanced technology is indistinguishable from magic." The postulate had been derived by a visionary who also developed the concept for this planet's geosynchronous communication satellites, had popularized the idea for the space elevator as an alternative to expendable launch vehicles, and had also written the story for an amusing film called *2001: A Space Odyssey*, which I enjoyed very much. (I wonder if Mr. Clarke's awe of alien intelligences might have been so great if he'd had the pleasure of meeting the bovine slugs of Merricus or endured the screeching carrion ballets of Vulpine Five, however.)

Clarke's postulate about technology and magic gave me an idea. With the gizmo to serve me, I simply had to learn what sort of magic the Earthlings wanted to see and how to make a good show out of it.

Showmanship proved to be the hardest part. Simply displaying an endless string of miracles would not be enough. (Besides, Central Authority back home would have been very annoyed if I accidentally started a new religion on Earth.)

I watched Earth's best performers, astonishing magicians and illusionists, trying to learn the secret to a good show. At times I was confounded, wondering if these showmen somehow had access to contraband extraterrestrial technology themselves. It didn't matter—I knew my gizmo was superior to anything they might have. I could do better.

It took me a long time to understand their attitude toward entertainment—but once I did, it became a key to grasping the human psyche. While Earthlings are endlessly curious and easily perplexed, these people honestly didn't want to know *how* a magic trick was performed. They might claim so, and half mean it, but they would rather be intrigued and amazed. They'd be outraged if every magician went on their endless talk shows and explained all the secrets.

That would squash the thrill for them, the *magic*.

One of my simplest tricks (and therefore one of my favorites) was transporting myself instantaneously from one part of the arena to another. It was a trivial teleportation gimmick—but with the appropriate buildup, the music, the lights, the smoke and mirrors, the gorgeous assistants, and pounding drums, it became an amazing feat. Other Earth magicians had done similar acts, some with people, some with animals—but no one did it with my method (so far as I know).

After selecting a volunteer from the audience—a fidgety young man with too-short pants and a sweat-stained polyester shirt—I climbed into a vertical metal box at the back of my stage, holding the lid open. An identical box stood at the far end of the seats, a good distance away, containing my unwitting volunteer. The young man stood inside the box as if it were a coffin, looking out and wanting to shrink away from the sudden attention.

The assistants sealed the door of his box. The young man's eyes were bugging out and his throat bobbed as he gulped.

Waving from the stage, I closed the door on my box, activating the instantaneous teleportation circuit in the gizmo strapped to my waist.

Less than a second later, I emerged intact in the opposite booth, while assistants opened the box on the stage, allowing the wide-eyed volunteer to stumble out, gawking in amazement and completely at a loss as to how he had traveled a hundred meters in an instant. He rubbed his still-tingling skin and blinked into the bright lights and the applause. He grinned like a clone.

My promoters and agents (*these* people are true aliens, even among Earthlings) kept insisting that I do bigger and more daring stunts—and I obliged, attempting to surpass even the greatest illusions ever performed by master magicians. Though some of the spectacles required more power, my precious gizmo had a century-and-a-half useful lifespan, according to its warranty. I trusted the engineers from my planet. They knew what they were doing.

Most outrageous trick: I made the Empire State Building vanish at midnight, right under floodlights and helicopters and in front of the slack-jawed faces of the gathered crowd.

In the blind instant when the spotlights shut off, I touched the gizmo at my waist to *disintegrate* the entire skyscraper, all 102 stories (plus television tower). When the lights came back up again, only shaven foundations remained of one of the tallest buildings on this planet. A few disconcerting sparks flickered up from severed electrical cables, nothing more.

I sincerely hoped the publicists had evacuated the building as they'd promised.

Once the cheers and applause began to subside, we dropped the lights again and I re-integrated the building, according to its molecular pattern stored in the gizmo's computer. Simple enough, when you think about it, given a little bit of engineering know-how . . . or at least a machine that can do it all for you.

Then I made my big mistake.

It was a trick I had done dozens of times, and it had never proved difficult before. Overconfident, I let my guard down, forgetting how truly alien these Earthlings are, how they panic when there isn't the least bit of danger. I "screwed up," to use their own quaint phrase.

For the finale of my act I had taken to *flying*—my trademark performance, as it were. I strapped an auxiliary antigravity pack to my chest just below the gizmo itself, using it to levitate and flit about the stage.

As always, it gave the Earthlings an added thrill to see a randomly chosen audience member fly along with me.

(Showmanship, showmanship!) This evening I had picked out a pretty young blonde with a good figure, gleaming smile, and giggly personality—audiences responded best to sexy volunteers, though the anti-grav belt could have lifted even one of the hefty matriarchs who sat sipping wine coolers and killing time before they got back to the slot machines.

"Are you ready to fly?" I asked the young lady, raising my rich voice for the audience. Her eyes were as large as those of the mantis people that had nearly devoured me on Karnak Delta. Her name was Tiffany, naturally.

I held her trembling hand as the assistants came out with hoops, swooping them around me to prove that I had no wires attached to my body, no flying harness (just the gizmo and a small anti-grav generator). Tiffany saw the tests and she saw my face and then looked around. Standing right beside me, she knew better than anyone else that this was no trick.

I held her snugly around the waist like Superman and Lois Lane, and we lifted off, drifting above the stage. I should have noticed her growing uneasiness. We were skewered by the blazing spotlights that tracked our every movement, drifting back and forth. Tiffany was stunned—but her amazement lasted only a moment.

When I soared out over the audience and the tables, alas, it proved too much for her. She became hysterical to get down, struggling in my grasp so that I had to clutch her just to keep her from plummeting to the stage.

"Stop it!" I whispered, but she didn't hear me. The audience was too busy shouting their *ooohs!* and *aaaahs!* I whisked us back over the stage. The flying routine was the climactic end to my show, and I wanted to milk it for as long as possible—but I couldn't swoop around and do my typical stunts with a writhing, panic-stricken human in my arms!

Tiffany clutched my shirt, her long fingernails scratching my chest, grabbing for anything to hold on to. Her hands snatched the thin strap that bound the gizmo to my waist. The strap snapped.

The gizmo fell thirty feet down to the hard stage.

I heard a *clunk*, then a broken *tinkle*. The audience muttered, wondering if they had caught me at something. The spotlights weren't on the stage floor where my woefully damaged device lay, so I covered the gaffe quickly by shouting, "Tiffany, calm down! I think your teeth just fell out."

This brought a chuckle as I lowered us to the far end of the stage with the last trickle of reserve power in the anti-grav belt. I felt sick inside, but "the show must go on," so I took my bows and said my goodnights, letting Tiffany return to her giggling friends. She would probably tell them how much fun it had been.

When the lights went down, I dashed across the stage to retrieve the debris and hurried back to my dressing room, where I refused all visitors for the rest of the night. . . .

I stared down in dismay at the broken innards of the gizmo, the convoluted circuits, the delicately imprinted control paths and microchips far beyond any technology Earth has ever created. The warranty wouldn't do me any good now.

As I said before, I am a xeno-sociologist, not an engineer. I stared down at my ruined miracle-working machine and thought again of Clarke's Law. The electronic paths and schematics meant absolutely nothing to me. The high-tech gizmo might as well have been magic.

I knew this would be my last night of performing.

Without the gizmo the Great Taurindo was nothing, unless I learned how to do magic the hard way. . . .

So the years passed. I had amassed a considerable fortune during my years as a star, and I was able to continue living comfortably, though I never set foot on the stage again. I became something of a legend, the reclusive master illusionist who had suddenly quit performing and would tell no one why. I gave no interviews. Numerous books were written about me and my reasons, offering wild speculations, though none so preposterous as the truth.

In the privacy of my home, I continued to practice a few tricks for my own entertainment. I became quite proficient, actually, but nothing good enough to meet the expectations of those who had seen me perform before.

When at last the twenty-seven years had passed, and I received the signal from the rescue ship, I felt an overwhelming joy . . . as well as a not-inconsiderable sadness at leaving this interesting backwater planet.

I rushed into the desert to the pickup point, abandoning my home and all my possessions at the darkest hour of night—my sudden disappearance would only increase the mystique about me—and ran to meet the ship.

The pilot and crew were in a great hurry. A Cultural Inspector from Central Authority hustled me off to my seat in the passenger compartment, and we roared back out through Earth's atmosphere. Finally, when we had reached our hypercruise speed, the Cultural Inspector came to debrief me—and I had been waiting for her.

"So, Taurindo Alpha Prime," she said, "you have spent many years on this planet. Tell me what you have learned of their culture."

I smiled. "I can do better than that—I can show you."

From a pocket in my jumpsuit I withdrew a standard deck, shuffled with a dazzling flourish and a snapping blur of sound, then fanned and extended them toward her.

"Pick a card," I said, "any card."

Time travel and its associated paradoxes have caused numerous headaches (and generated numerous story ideas) for generations of science fiction writers. Just imagine the legal troubles all of those paradoxes might cause.

Paradox & Greenblatt, Attorneys at Law

You might say our little firm specializes in contradictions. In a few years Aaron Greenblatt and I are sure to be millionaire visionaries overloaded with cases, but right now our field of law is still in its infancy. We've carved out a new niche, and people are already starting to find us.

Since we can't afford a receptionist (not yet), Aaron took the call. But because he was up to his nostrils in a corporate lawsuit—a client suing Time Travel Expeditions for refusing to let him go to the late Cretaceous on a dinosaur hunt—he passed the case to me.

"Line One for you, Marty," he said as I came out of the lav, wiping my hands. "New case on the hook. Simple attempted murder, I think. Guy sounds frantic."

"They all sound frantic." I pursed my lips. "Is time travel involved?"

He nodded, and I knew there would be nothing "simple" about the case. Fortunately, temporal complications are right up our firm's alley. We're forward-thinkers, my partner and I—*and* backward-thinkers, when it's effective. That's why people call us when nobody else knows what the hell to do.

I picked up the phone and punched the solitary blinking light. "Marty Paramus here. How can I help you?"

The man talked a mile a minute in a thin, squeaky voice; even if he hadn't been panicked, it probably would have sounded unpleasant. "All I did was try to stop him from buying her some deep-fried artichoke hearts. How could that be construed as attempted murder? They can't pin anything on me, can they? Why would they think I was trying to kill anybody?"

"Maybe you'd better tell me, Mr. . . . uh?"

"Hendergast. Lionel Hendergast. And I read the terms of the contract very carefully before we went back in time. It didn't say anything about deep-fried artichoke hearts."

I sighed. "What was your location, Mr. Hendergast?"

"Santa Cruz Boardwalk. The place with all the rides and the arcade games. They have concession stands and—"

"Sure, but *when* was this?"

"Umm, two days ago."

I hate having to pry all the obvious information out of a client. "Not in your time. I mean in *real* time."

"Oh, um, fifty-two years ago."

"Ah." I made a noise that hinted at a deeper understanding than I really had, yet. "One of those nostalgic life-was-better-back-then tours."

Now he sounded defensive. "Nothing illegal about them, Mr. Paramus. They're perfectly legitimate."

"So you said. But someone must think you broke the rules, or you wouldn't have been arrested. Was this person allergic to artichoke hearts or something?"

"No, not at all. And it wasn't the artichoke hearts. I was just trying to prevent him from buying them for her. I didn't want the two of them to meet."

A light bulb winked on inside my head. "Oh, one of those."

"Altering history" cases were my bread and butter.

* * * * *

The jail's attorney-client meeting room wasn't much better than a cell. The cinderblock walls were covered with a hardened slime of seafoam-green paint. The chairs around the table creaked, and veritable stalactites of petrified chewing gum adorned the table's underside. Since prisoners weren't allowed to chew gum, their lawyers must have been responsible for this mess. Some attorneys give the whole field a bad name.

Lionel Hendergast was in his mid-twenties, but looked at least a decade older than that. His too-round face, set atop a long and skinny neck, reminded me of a smiling jack-o-lantern balanced on a stalk. His long-fingered hands fidgeted. He looked toward me as if I were a superhero swooping in to the rescue.

"I need to understand exactly what you've done, Mr. Hendergast. Tell me the truth, and don't hold back anything. No bullshit. We have attorney-client privilege here, and I need to know what I'm working with."

"I'm innocent."

I rolled my eyes. "Listen, Mr. Hendergast—Lionel—my job is to get you off the hook for the crime of which you're accused. Let's save the declarations of innocence for the judge, okay? Now, start from the beginning."

He swallowed, took a deep breath, then said, "I took a trip back in time to the Santa Cruz Beach Boardwalk to 1973, as I said. You can get the brochure from the time-travel company I used. There's nothing wrong with it, absolutely not."

"And why did you want to go to Santa Cruz?"

He shrugged unconvincingly. "The old carousel, the carnival rides, the games where you throw a ball and knock down bottles. And then there's the beach, cotton candy, churros, hot dogs, giant pretzels."

"And artichoke hearts," I prodded.

Lionel swiveled nervously in his chair, which made a protesting creak. "Deep-fried artichoke hearts are sort of a specialty there. A woman nearing the front of the line had dropped her wallet on the ground not ten feet away, but she didn't know it yet. In a few minutes, she was going to order deep-fried artichoke hearts—and when she discovered she had no money to pay, the man behind her in line would step up like a knight in shining armor, pay for her artichoke hearts, and help her search for her wallet. They'd find it, and then go out to dinner. The rest is history."

"And you seem to know the details of this history quite well. What exactly were you going to do?"

"Well, I found the woman's wallet, on purpose, so I could give it back to her. Nothing illegal in that, is there?"

I nodded, already frowning. "Thereby preventing the man behind her from doing a good deed, stopping them from going to dinner, and"—I held my hands out—"accomplishing what?"

"If they didn't meet, then they wouldn't get married. And if they didn't get married, then they wouldn't have a son who is the true spawn of all evil."

"The Damien defense doesn't hold up in court, you know. I can cite several precedents."

"But if I had succeeded, who would have known? There would've been no crime because nothing would have happened. How can they accuse me of anything?"

"Because recorded history is admissible in a court of law," I said. "So by attempting to keep these two people from meeting, you were effectively trying to commit a murder by preventing someone from being born."

"If, if, if!" Hendergast looked much more agitated now.

"But I didn't do it, so how can they hold me?"

The legal system has never been good at adapting to rapid change. Law tends to be reactive instead of proactive. When new technology changes the face of the world, the last people to deal with it—right behind senior citizens and vested union workers—are judges and the law. Remember copyright suits in the early days of the Internet, when the uses and abuses of intellectual property zoomed ahead of the lawmakers like an Indy 500 racecar passing an Amish horse cart?

Now, in an era of time-travel tourism, with the often-contradictory restrictions the companies impose upon themselves, legal problems have been springing up like wildflowers in a manure field. Aaron Greenblatt and I formed our partnership to go after these cases. We are, in effect, creating major precedents with every case we take, win or lose.

Where was a person like Lionel Hendergast to turn? Everyone is entitled to legal representation. He didn't entirely understand the charges against him, and I was fairly certain that the judge wouldn't know what to do either. Judges dislike being forced to make up their minds from scratch, instead of finding a sufficiently similar case from which they can copy what their predecessors have done.

"Do you ever sit back and play the 'what if?' game, Mr. Paramus?" Lionel asked, startling me. "If a certain event had changed, how would your life be different? If your parents hadn't gotten divorced, your dad might not have killed himself, your mom might not have married some abusive truck driver and moved off to Nevada where she won't return your calls or even give you her correct street address? That sort of thing?"

I looked at him. Now we might finally be getting somewhere. "I've seen *It's a Wonderful Life*. Four times, in fact, including the alternate-ending version. I'm very familiar with 'What if.' Who were you trying to kill and what was the result you hoped to achieve?"

"I wasn't trying to *kill* anyone," he insisted.

From the frightened little-boy expression on Lionel's round face, I could see he wasn't a violent man. He could never have taken a gun to someone or cut the brake cables on his victim's car. He wouldn't even have had the stomach to pay a professional hit man. No, he had wanted to achieve his goal in a way that would let him sleep at night.

"The man was Delano R. Franklin," he said. "You won't find a more vile and despicable man on the face of this Earth."

I didn't want to argue with my client, though I could have pointed out some pretty likely candidates for the vile-and-despicable championship. "Much as it may pain me to say this, Lionel, being unpleasant isn't against the law."

"My parents were happily married, a long time ago. My dad had a good job. He owned a furniture store. And my mom was a receptionist in a car dealership—a dealership owned by Mr. Franklin. We had a nice home in the suburbs. I was supposed to get a puppy that Christmas."

"How old were you?"

"Four."

"And you remember all these details?"

He wouldn't look at me. "Not really, but I've heard about it a thousand times. My parents couldn't stop arguing about that day my dad took time off in the afternoon. He decided to surprise my mother over at the car dealership by bringing her a dozen long-stemmed roses."

"How romantic," I said.

"At the car dealership they take a late lunch hour so they

can take care of the customer rush between noon and one. When my dad couldn't find anyone at the reception counter, he went to the back room and opened the door— only to find my mom flat on the desk with her skirt hiked up to her hips, legs wrapped around Franklin's neck, and him pumping away into her."

It wasn't the first time I had heard this sort of story. "I can see how that would ruin a marriage."

"My dad went nuts. He tried to attack Franklin and as a result, ended up in jail with charges of assault. Franklin had most of our local officials in his pocket—small town. At first my mom insisted that Franklin threatened to fire her if she didn't have sex with him. In the resulting scandal, she changed her story, saying that the affair had gone on for a while, that Franklin wanted to marry her. My parents split up, but as soon as the divorce was final, the creep wanted nothing to do with her. He kicked my mom out. She had no job, and by that time my dad had lost his furniture store."

"Sounds like a mess. So what happened to little Lionel?"

"We lived in Seaside, California—that's not far from Santa Cruz and Monterey. My dad got drunk one day and drove too fast along Highway 1."

I'd been there. "Some spectacular cliffs and tight curves on that stretch of highway."

Miserably, Lionel nodded. "The road curved, and my dad went straight. Suicide was suspected, but nobody ever proved it. Then, one day my mom just packed up, dropped me off at foster care, and left. Said she hated me because I was just like my father. I lived in six different homes until I was sixteen and old enough to emancipate myself."

I tried to sound sympathetic. "Not a very happy child-hood."

"Meanwhile, Delano R. Franklin did quite well with his

car dealership. In fact, he opened three more. He married some bimbo, divorced her when she got wrinkles, then married another one. Never had kids, but I think his wives were young enough to be his daughters."

I wanted to cut the rant short. "All right, but what does this have to do with deep-fried artichoke hearts?"

Tears started running down his cheeks. "I remembered my mother yelling at Franklin once. He had wooed her by telling romantic stories, describing how his own parents met. The man who would be Franklin's father came to the rescue, helped find a lady's wallet at the artichoke stand, took her out to eat . . . and eventually spawned this inkblot on the human race, a uniting of sperm and egg that any compassionate God would have prevented!"

I paced around the table, locking my hands behind my back. "So you figured that if you kept Franklin's biological mother and father from meeting, he would never have been born, your parents' marriage would have remained happy, and your life would have been wonderful."

"That's about it, Mr. Paramus. But Franklin had someone watching me, so I got caught."

"Watching you? How could he possibly have suspected such an absurd thing?"

"Because I, uh . . ." Lionel blushed. "I told him. I couldn't help myself. I wanted the scumbag to know he was about to be removed from existence."

I groaned. In this business, the only thing worse than a hardened criminal is an unconscionably stupid client.

"You have to get me out of here, Mr. Paramus!" Given the circumstances, an unreasonable demand. "That holding cell is a nightmare. It smells. There's no privacy even for the toilet, and they took blood samples to test me for HIV and other diseases. They drew my blood! That means other people in the cell must have those terrible diseases. What if I—"

"It's just standard procedure, Lionel." I snapped my briefcase shut. "Let me work on this and see what I can come up with. I'll try to get you bail. I'll talk to Mr. Franklin and his attorney on the off chance I can get them to drop the charges."

It was certainly a long shot, but I wanted to give poor Lionel something to cling to.

I set up a meeting in the "boardroom" of the dumpy offices Aaron and I shared. I doubted I could impress Delano Franklin, but maybe I could convince him it wasn't worth the trouble to press charges. Lionel Hendergast had almost no money, and when I learned who Franklin had hired for his own counsel to go after civil damages, I knew that money—or at least showmanship—would be a primary factor in this case.

If you look in the dictionary next to the definition of the word "shyster," you'll find a picture of Kosimo Arkulian. He was overweight, with thinning steel-gray hair in a greasy combover that fooled nobody. He wore too many rings, too many gold chains and a too-large gold watch, and he spoke too loudly. You've seen Arkulian on television with his boisterous ads, flashing his jewelry and his smile, treating everyone with a hangnail of a complaint as the next big millionaire in the lawsuit sweepstakes.

When Arkulian sat down beside his client, I could tell it was going to be a testosterone war between those two men. Both were accustomed to being in charge.

I gave my most pleasant smile. "Can I offer you coffee or a soda?"

"No, thank you," Franklin said.

"This isn't a social call," Arkulian answered in a brusque tone.

"There's always time for good manners." I looked at the clock on the wall. It was 1:00. "How about Scotch, then?" I had to get Franklin to take something. "Or a bourbon? I have a very good bourbon, Booker's." From my research, I knew Franklin was quite fond of both.

"If your bourbon's expensive, I'll have one of those," he said.

Arkulian shot him a glance. "I wouldn't advise it—"

"I'm not going to get sloshed," Franklin said. "Besides, I see a genuine irony in soaking this guy for a good expensive drink."

Arkulian grinned. "Then I'll have one, too."

I had been careful to wash everything in our kitchenette before the meeting started. I quickly poured three glasses of fine bourbon, neat, and handed one to Franklin and one to Arkulian. The third I placed in front of me in a comradely gesture, though I barely sipped from it. I had a feeling I'd need to keep my wits sharp.

Franklin looked like a distinguished late-middle-aged businessman gone bad. If groomed well, he could have fit comfortably into any high-society function, but he had let himself grow a beer gut. His clothes were garish, something he no doubt thought younger women found attractive. The ladies probably laughed at him until they found out how much money he had; then they played along but still laughed at him behind his back.

I tried my best gambit, pumping up the sob story, practicing how it would sound before a jury, although it was unlikely this case would ever go to trial. The law was too uncertain, the convolutions and intangibilities of time paradox too difficult for the average person to grasp.

"None of this has any bearing on what your client tried to do to my client," Arkulian said. "Sure, the poor kid had a troubled life. His mother had an affair with my client some twenty-six years ago, which led to the breakup of his parents' marriage. Boo-hoo. As if that story doesn't reflect half of the American public."

Maybe your half, I thought, but kept a tight smile on my face.

"Mr. Hendergast attempted to murder my client. It's as simple as—"

Impatient with letting his lawyer do all the talking, Franklin interrupted. "Wait a minute. This is far worse than just attempted murder." As if he needed the fortification of liquid courage to face what had almost happened, Franklin grabbed his tumbler of bourbon, and took a long drink. He set the glass down, and I could see the smear his lips had made on the edge. "If Lionel Hendergast had gunned me down in the parking lot of one of my car dealerships, he might have killed me, yes, but my legacy would have been left behind—my car dealerships, my friends . . ."

"Your ex-wives," I pointed out.

"Some of them remember me fondly." He didn't even blush.

Arkulian picked up the story. "You see, what Mr. Hendergast was attempting to do would have erased my client entirely from existence. He would have obliterated the man named Delano R. Franklin from the universe, leaving no memory of him. Nothing he ever accomplished in this life would have remained. Complete annihilation. An unspeakably heinous crime! And if Mr. Hendergast had succeeded, it would have been the perfect crime, too. No one would ever have known what he did, since there would have been no evidence, no body, no victim."

I had heard my share of "perfect crime" stories, and I had to admit, this ranked right up there with the best. I didn't offer them another drink. "What exactly is it you want from my client?"

"I want him to go to jail," Franklin said. "I want him to be locked up so that I don't have to worry every morning that he's going to sneak back on another time-travel expedition and try again to erase my existence."

Arkulian smiled and folded his fingers. I couldn't imagine how he could fit them together with all those rings on his knuckles. "I'm guessing the publicity on this case will give a remarkable boost to my business—and don't expect me to believe you haven't thought of the same thing, Mr. Paramus."

He was right, of course. I shrugged. "Publicity is free, after all, and TV ads are a bit out of my price range." Ambulance chasing seemed to be paying off quite well for Arkulian. I couldn't resist taking a small jab at him. "How much *do* ten of those rings cost?"

Miffed, Arkulian stood up. "If there's nothing else, Paramus? We'll see you in court."

I let the two men show themselves out, staying behind in the boardroom. When they were gone, I took a clean handkerchief, carefully lifted the near-empty bourbon glass Franklin had used, and made sure there were sufficient saliva traces on the rim. This was all I'd need.

Predictably, a media frenzy surrounded the case. Arkulian held a large press conference in which he grandstanded, accusing me of leaking the story in order to get publicity. Within an hour I had a press conference of my own, accusing him of the same. Both of us received plenty of coverage, and neither of us ever admitted to making a few discreet phone calls and tipping reporters off.

Lionel put his complete trust in me, which always sparks that uncomfortable paternal feeling. But I hadn't been kidding when I told him the law is still murky in these sorts of cases. Nobody had any idea which way it would go, and even my "ace in the hole" was a long shot. I still hadn't got the lab results back.

For the preliminary hearing, we were assigned an ancient female judge, the Honorable Bernadette Maddox. I was uneasy about her age: In my experience, elderly judges don't deal well with the second- and third-order implications of rapidly changing technologies. I'd rather have had the youngest, most computer-savvy person on the bench.

I still held out some hope that Bernadette Maddox was a sweet old lady, and the sob-story aspect would work on her. Not a chance.

"Mr. Arkulian!" she roared from the bench in a battleaxe voice, before he had even finished his pompous remark. "You will sit down, shut up, and let me run this show." I looked over at my rival with a twinge of sympathy. So much for the nice old lady bit. "And you will remove that disgusting cheap jewelry in my courtroom unless you have an appointment with Time-Travel Expeditions to go back to the days of disco."

"Your Honor, my personal appearance has no bearing on—"

"You will remove the jewelry because it hurts my eyes. I can't even see your client through the glare from all those rings."

Cowed, Arkulian left the room. A nervous Lionel sat at the bench next to me, whispering, "Was that a good sign?"

"It wasn't so much a sign—more like a demonstration. The judge is only showing him who's boss. And let me warn you ahead of time, she's going to feel she needs to even the score and scold me as well at some point. Expect it and try not to get too upset."

"What are we going to do, Mr. Paramus?" He sounded so miserable. I felt sorry for this kid who had lost his parents, his Norman Rockwell childhood, and a lifetime of happiness, all because of Delano R. Franklin.

I had dug into Franklin's background, perhaps even more than Lionel had. There was no question in my mind that the world would be a better place if Franklin had never been born. He had left a decades-long trail of ex-wives and shady business dealings behind him. His primary legacy was a handful of auto dealerships, but since he had no heirs and couldn't keep employees around long enough to put them in positions of authority and responsibility, no one would take over the car lots upon his death, and they'd probably be liquidated. Even without Lionel's time-travel help, Franklin would vanish.

Since we were the defendants, we sat back and listened as a now-unadorned Arkulian outlined the civil part of the case, explaining time-travel paradoxes in painstaking detail, using examples culled not from any law library but from classic science fiction stories. He was long-winded and explained too much to the judge, treating her as if she were incapable of grasping the classic grandfather paradox.

I kept checking my watch as I mentally rehearsed my opening statement. The courier should have been here by now. I would have preferred hard facts to fast talking, but I could proceed either way. As Arkulian rambled on and on, even Franklin looked bored.

Finally it was my turn. I hoped the judge would stall just to give me a few more minutes, but she puckered her wrinkled lips and leaned over like a hawk from the bench. "Now then, Mr. Paramus, let's hear what you have to say. I trust you can be more succinct—or at least more interesting—than Mr. Arkulian."

I stood up and cleared my throat. Still no sign of my delivery person, and I really wanted to know which direction to go. Either my ace in the hole was a high trump or a discard. With a sigh, I reached into my briefcase and pulled out a carefully prepared document. "Your Honor, I wish I did not have to do this, but would it be possible to request a brief continuance? I have not yet received an important piece of evidence that has a strong bearing on this case."

Lionel looked over at me, surprised. "What evidence?"

"A continuance?" the judge said with a snort. "I've been sitting here all morning, Mr. Paramus! You could have said this at the very beginning. How long are you asking for?" I was about to get my scolding, and Judge Maddox was clearly primed to let loose with even more venom than she had inflicted on Arkulian.

Suddenly the large doors were flung open at the back of the courtroom. The bailiff tried to stop a man from entering, but my partner Aaron Greenblatt sidestepped him. He marched in, waving a document in his left hand. "Excuse me, your Honor. Please pardon the interruption."

I stifled a laugh. It was a real Perry Mason moment. I suspected Aaron had always wanted to do that.

My partner's face was stoic; I hated the way he covered his emotions. He could have at least grinned or frowned to give me an inkling of what he held in his hands.

Judge Maddox lifted her gavel, looking more inclined to hit Aaron in the head with it than to rap her bench.

I blurted, "Your Honor, I withdraw my request for a continuance—so long as my associate can hand me that paper." I turned, not waiting for her answer as Aaron handed the lab results to me. He finally broke into a grin as I scanned the numbers and the comparison charts.

With a huge sigh of relief, I turned back to the bench. "Your Honor, in light of recent developments I request that the attempted murder charges against my client be dropped."

Arkulian growled, "What are you playing at, Paramus?"

"I'll ask the questions here, Mr. Arkulian," the judge said, rapping her gavel for good measure. "Well then—what are you playing at, Mr. Paramus?"

Bernadette Maddox already knew the sordid Peyton Place story of the ruined marriage, the broken family, the miserable life Lionel Hendergast had lived because of Franklin's actions.

"Your Honor, the prosecution's client was not entirely forthcoming about how long his affair with my client's mother lasted. If I might recap: when Lionel Hendergast was four years old, his father discovered Mr. Franklin and my client's mother *in flagrante delecto,* which triggered the chain of events leading to the crime of which my client is accused."

"And?" Judge Maddox said, drawing out the word.

"In fact, the affair had gone on for at least five years previous." I fluttered the sheet of lab data. "I have here the results of DNA tests comparing the blood sample my client gave to the county jail with samples I obtained from Mr. Franklin."

I smiled sweetly at them. Franklin appeared confused. Arkulian was outraged, realizing I had probably tested the saliva left behind on his drinking glass—an old trick.

"These results prove conclusively that the father of Lionel Hendergast is not the man he always believed, but rather Mr. Delano R. Franklin."

Lionel's eyes fairly popped out of their sockets. The judge sat up, suddenly much more interested. Both Arkulian and Franklin bellowed angrily as if in competition with each other until finally Arkulian stood up in a huff, reacting in the way he had seen too many lawyers react on TV shows. "I object! This has no bearing—"

"This has total bearing," I said.

Lionel looked as if he might faint, slide off the chair, and land on the courtroom floor. I put a steadying hand on his shoulder. He looked over at the prosecutor's table, and his two words came out in a squeak. "My father?"

I forged ahead. "The prosecution has interpreted this crime entirely wrong, your Honor. My client is accused of going back in time with the intent of preventing Mr. Franklin from ever being born. But if he had done that, then Lionel Hendergast would've erased *himself* from existence as well. He would have wiped out his own father, thereby ensuring that he himself could never be born."

I smiled. The judge seemed to be considering my line of reasoning. After all, Arkulian had prepped her in excruciating detail about grandfather paradoxes and the like.

"Therefore, instead of attempted murder, my client is guilty, at best, of attempted *suicide*—for which I recommend he be remanded for therapy and treatment, not incarceration."

"This is preposterous!" Arkulian yelled. "Even if Mr. Hendergast *had* accidentally erased himself, his original intention was to do the same to my client. His own death would merely have been incidental to his stated objective. The primary target of his malicious actions was still Delano Franklin."

With a sigh of infinite patience, I looked witheringly at Arkulian, then turned back to the judge. "Again, my esteemed colleague is mistaken."

The judge was actually listening now, fascinated by the implications. I had mapped out the strategy until it made my own head spin.

"My client is accused of *attempted* murder. However, based on these lab results, such an action would be temporally impossible." I waited a beat. "If Mr. Hendergast had actually succeeded in what the prosecution alleges was his intent, then he himself would never have been born. In which case, he could never have gone back in time to prevent Mr. Franklin's parents from meeting. How can my client be charged with attempting a crime that is fundamentally impossible to commit?"

"This is outrageous! Why not debate how many angels can dance on a pinhead?" Arkulian said.

I shrugged in the prosecutor's direction. "It's a standard time-travel paradox, your Honor. As Mr. Arkulian explained to the court so exhaustively."

Lionel was still staring in wonder over at the prosecutor's table. "Daddy?"

The judge rapped her gavel loudly. "I'm announcing a recess for at least two hours—so I can take some aspirin and give it time to work."

When the judge finally dismissed all charges against Lionel, I was relatively sure Arkulian wouldn't take it to appeal. The hardest part was explaining the convoluted matter to journalists afterward, so they could report it accurately; in the end, it proved too intricate for most of the wire services.

Aaron and I celebrated by going out for a fine dinner. We compared notes on cases, and he got me up to speed on his time-travel dinosaur-hunting lawsuit. I came back to the office late at night by myself—after all, that's where I kept the best bourbon—and saw the light blinking on the answering machine. Multiple messages. Four more cases waiting, none of them simple. Some actually sounded like they would be fun. Certainly precedent-setting.

Oddly, after the fallout, Lionel actually reconciled with his biological father. Months later, when I drove past one of Franklin's car dealerships, I saw a crew replacing the big sign with a new one: FRANKLIN & SON.

Funny how things turn out. Sometimes people just need a second chance, even when they aren't looking for it.

Some writers like to keep their ideas close to their chest, as if superstitious that the Muse will abandon them if they divulge any secrets. I, on the other hand, love to brainstorm and bounce crazy ideas back and forth with someone who also has a hyperactive imagination. In my career, I have taken on many projects with a coauthor. As of this writing I have written seven novels with Brian Herbert, eight with Doug Beason, two with Kristine Kathryn Rusch, one with John Betancourt, one with Dean Koontz . . . and close to thirty with my wife, Rebecca Moesta.

Obviously, something's working there. This story takes the collaboration concept about as far as we could imagine . . .

Collaborators

With Rebecca Moesta

Tara held the second cable in her hand as she crept behind her husband in the dim light of the den; but he was already jacked in, impervious to all distractions.

Chandler lay slouched back in his battered college-salvage chair like a marionette with severed strings, his face slack, eyes REMing behind the translucent sheaths of his lids as he wrestled with his commissioned VR art. From his sighs, fidgety spasms, and general restlessness, she could tell he was blocked again.

Chandler always kept his art to himself, reluctant to talk about it until he finished, even when she offered herself as a sounding board for ideas. But this time Tara would surprise him—or piss him off. Either way, she hoped Chandler would get out from under the creative block that had been smothering him. If she could just help him get over the hump . . .

Without his knowledge, Tara had installed the black-market splitter behind the wall plate. Now she could jack into the same data stream and help him directly, a true meeting of minds.

She stared at the viper-prongs of the cable in her hand, then mounted it in the socket at the base of her skull. Still moving quietly, she pried off the wall plate and squinted to see the bright silver end of the splitter's input port, a shunt piggybacked onto the main cable. She had never used a splitter before, never even *seen* one. But Fizzwilly had promised it would work.

Chandler's fingers twitched on the worn maroon fabric of the overstuffed chair, as if searching for something to clench.

By jacking in, Tara could see what was bugging him, help him work through the problem. She had purchased the illegal device from her former friend Fizzwilly, who was technically still on the run. It was still prototype hardware, he said, not completely certified, but that didn't mean the splitter wasn't useful. She decided to take the risk, if only to get closer to her husband.

Chandler, unaware of her presence in the dim work-room, continued breathing fast and shallow, butterfly wings in his lungs. His eyes looked sunken, lost in a nest of shadows, and his milky skin seemed paler than usual. His red-gold hair hung lank over the interface cable. In her mind, Tara caught a glimpse of what he would look like as an unhappy middle-aged man.

Before marrying Chandler two years before, Tara had spent plenty of time jacked into virtual environments. Her friends, "the wrong crowd," had sharpened their claws by rerouting legal shipments to illegal chop-shops, altering financial transactions out to many decimal places. Tara had held herself on the fringe, amusing herself by diddling with her own grades and records at the Virtual University, not because she was unable to complete the classes herself, but because she was impatient to begin doing the "real stuff." She'd had her heart set on a career as an architect or an archaeologist, not as an electronic scam artist.

But when the heat came down and they all got caught, Tara had been stripped of her degree, barred from ever working as anything higher than a grunt at a sprawling architectural firm, and denied all access to genuine archaeological sites; the others stumbled into jail, and Fizzwilly became a fugitive.

Chandler had saved her, dragged her back onto the straight-and-narrow; and now, with her own future as an architect slammed shut in her face, Tara felt like an outsider watching Chandler's career explode as he created virtual worlds for purchase by anyone rich enough to own a simulation chamber.

But Tara still knew how to find Fizzwilly, and he had gotten the splitter for her. No questions asked.

Right now Chandler needed her. She plugged the second cable into the splitter.

With a sigh, she felt herself being dragged down, vanishing with a virtual echo into a whirlpool where Chandler was working. She would join him in his mind, in his imaginary universe.

In Chandler's world the rain fell, the flowers bloomed, and exotic birds preened their iridescent plumage.

There, and yet not there, Tara's ghost image stared at

his Eden. Sapphire-winged butterflies danced above brilliant orchids. The trees seemed ready to collapse from the weight of foliage so bright and rich it looked lacquered. Droplets of dew sparkled in the sunlight that penetrated the canopy. The sounds of insects and birds and unseen small animals rustling through the underbrush made the silence deeper. Everything seemed perfect, a paradise.

Tara felt like an intruder.

Chandler's image stood staring up a tall tree, fingering a thick, ropy vine. He appeared to be deep in thought, perplexed.

"So . . . when exactly is the deadline?" she asked, hoping not to startle him too much.

Chandler whirled, dissolving into static at the edges, then snapping back to focus. "Tara! What are you doing here? How—?"

She pressed her lips together as she worked up her nerve. Chandler had always called that her most endearing expression.

"A splitter. Don't ask where I got it. I just thought you needed a fresh point of view." She looked away, then crossed her arms over her small breasts. "Let me help, Chandler. I want to do work that *means something* again!"

Chandler stood frozen in his rain forest, as if trying to put together pieces of an invisible puzzle. "But splitters—"

"They're perfectly safe," she said, tossing her black hair over her shoulder in an impatient gesture. "Let's not go on about it, okay? When is your deadline?"

Chandler took a moment to collect his thoughts. Always before, he had created his own work, done his best job, and then looked for a company to purchase his virtual environment for their holo chambers. But this time he had taken an assignment, following a client's guidelines rather than his own imagination. Constrained and worried about producing to someone else's specifications, he had stalled.

"The office complex already has the holo rec room constructed for their execs. Occupancy in less than three weeks. If I'm going to make a reputation—"

"Keep your reputation," Tara said.

"—as a reliable professional instead of a flaky VR *artiste*," he waggled his fingers, "I've got to deliver as promised. But I want it to be spectacular, not just serviceable. This could be my big break."

Her ghost went to stand next to his, looking at the details of the thick rain forest. "Then let me help you," she said again. "I might be able to offer a few suggestions. I can take some of the burden." She raised her eyebrows. "Why don't you show me around?"

Chandler gave her the full virtual tour. He started talking about his work, gradually opening up as he pointed at tall weeds, birds, colorful beetles, exotic fungi. She ducked as a bright red macaw swooped low overhead.

"It's good—I can't deny that," he said. "But it's missing something, and I can't figure it. More birds? Different flowers? Right now it's pretty high on the 'So What?' factor. I even tried putting traces of a big fire in the distance to evoke a sense of impending loss and suspense, but you can't see the smoke unless you go up to canopy level, and that's an advanced option."

With his fingertip he selected a cluster of white starlike flowers and moved them to a different location near a weathered old rock. "I've got all the details right, accurate down to the individual leaves. And I'm planning to add the other sensory modules: a light warm breeze, dampness in the air, various scents. It's correct by every measure I can make—but something indefinable just doesn't work."

Tara chose her words carefully, speaking one step behind the thoughts forming in her head. "Let me check out my first impression. The part that makes the Eden myth so poignant is not the paradise itself, but paradise *lost*." Her image gestured at the jungle. "This is too perfect. It needs . . . pathos."

She reached up to call down the virtual image palette, linking to her old archaeology databases and selected a few images to place in the midst of Chandler's jungle. The old boulder transformed into a moss-covered idol, worn half-smooth by centuries of wind and rain.

"Step back," she said, and they zoomed out to observe a larger part of the rain forest. Crumbling ziggurats appeared, tall Mayan pyramids hulking in the jungle, the Temple of the Jaguar, remnants of Tiahuanaco. Vines covered immense carved blocks of dark-gray lava stone while animals and birds nested in the cracks. She included no people, only the mysterious relics of a lost and fallen society.

"The mighty have fallen," she said. "Nature conquers all with the passage of time. Think of that poem 'Ozymandias'—nothing left of the great conqueror except for a weathered old statue in the middle of the desert. It's a sense of loss that tugs at your heart strings." She stopped speaking, self-conscious, turning to look at him. "So what do you think? Are you mad at me?"

"No, I'm not mad." His face beamed, no longer a reflection of inexorable middle age, but a return to the boyish exuberance that had drawn her to him a few years ago. "You found the missing ingredient."

Standing together atop an ancient temple, their ghost images looked out across the lush rainforest.

With the success of Chandler's "Lost Rainforest" virtual

ecosystem, clients offered him bigger commissions. Tara watched his confidence building, but he kept searching for the best follow-up assignment.

Chandler had always been driven, focused on his creations to the exclusion of the rest of the world, including her. Though they had been dating while she was messing around with Fizzwilly and friends in the network, Chandler had remained oblivious to her other activities, accepting her as just another student. After her troubles with the other hackers, he had been an anchor for her, staying by her. He had refused to let Tara give up in despair at the loss of her degree.

For two years Chandler kept telling her that she would work her way up in an architectural firm, that her talent would open doors for her even with the stain on her record. For him, she tolerated an uninteresting job as an underling for a large firm designing nuevo deco special-interest malls, though it had no future she could see.

But she wanted more, a task she could buy into with the same enthusiasm that came so naturally to Chandler. She wanted to share his passion, to sweat blood and enjoy it. . . .

Tara spent the morning jacked in, walking through 3-D wireframe displays of design modifications before submitting them to the review board. Dull work. While waiting for Chandler to come home from his luncheon meeting, Tara had cracked open the sliding balcony door, and a breeze drifted in, curling the vertical blinds.

She disconnected when Chandler came home, draping both wrists over his shoulders and tilting her face up to kiss him. She tasted curry and onions, spicy Indian food. A good sign, she thought; the Bengal Dawn café was expensive, not a restaurant chosen casually by disinterested clients.

Tara could tell by the excitement on his face that he had already made up his mind.

"It's the Grand Canyon," Chandler blurted. "They want me to recreate the Grand Canyon in 'all its grandeur.' Not the *real* canyon, but an idealized and enhanced version, the way it should be. All the strata, all the terrain. And it's big, very big. Not just a slice of rainforest."

Tara tried to share his excitement but did not quite understand. "How can you improve on the Grand Canyon?" she asked. "Isn't the real thing spectacular enough?"

He shook his head, slipped his net-access plaque onto the synthetic marble countertop so he could gesture with his hands. "If they wanted the real thing, they could just set up some beam-splitters and a hologram generator and be done with it. They could even massage out the rimside resorts and the roads and the tourists to make it look pristine.

"They want me to use the real canyon as a foundation, but pump up the grandeur, make it so even the stodgiest urban cynic will gasp in awe at Nature's majesty. It's been six years since I hiked down into the canyon, and my own memories are rose-tinted with time. *That's* the way I want to portray it."

Chandler held out his hand, tentatively withdrew it in hesitation, then squeezed her own. "Hey, would it be all right if you helped me again? From Day One this time. We can brainstorm with the splitter . . . you can help me shape the project before I blunder down blind alleys."

Tara felt as if she had been blindsided, but she leaped at the chance. "Sounds better than checking design mods. But I've never been to the Grand Canyon. Is that going to be a problem?"

"*I* have," he said, shaking his head, and gestured to the den, where the splitter hid behind the wall socket. "And I'll share all the images with you. I can do a direct feed."

Tara grabbed his hand and pulled him toward the workroom before he could change his mind. "Okay, Chandler, take me to the Grand Canyon."

In the den workroom, they both affixed cables to their sockets, joined by the splitter. Tara leaned back, closing her dark eyes and letting a numbing swirl of images flood across to her: stark corkscrewing mesas sliced out by erosion, scrub brush, incredible sunsets like pastel fingerpaintings across a huge sky, roiling clumps of thunderheads, close-up strata in ocher and tan and green-gray and vermilion, the muddy violence of the Colorado River, and finally a crisp night full of stars—like the universe crammed into the narrow alley of sky visible up through the canyon's towering walls.

Her mind simply received the data; over the next day or so she would assimilate it, sort it out, and make sense of Chandler's memories.

"There," he said, disconnecting. "You know everything you need to see about the Grand Canyon."

She sighed and smiled and blinked her eyes as the brilliant images continued to whirl across her forebrain. "It's almost like I went with you."

That night as she dreamed, Tara's mind continued to shuffle the memories, unlocking more than Chandler had intended. She heard the crunch of leather hiking boots on the sun-baked trail, felt sweat prickle on her/his hairy arms, saw another woman close by, smiling and panting, sharing swigs from a lukewarm canteen as they paused under a shaded overhang, sleeping naked on top of their zipped-together sleeping bag, making love under the narrow alley of night sky framed by the canyon's towering walls. . . .

Tara sat up abruptly, clammy sweat filming her skin. Beside her Chandler slept wound in a single sheet, the blanket tossed aside. "You went with Celine!" she said.

He jerked awake, blinking his eyes rapidly to focus. He scratched the jack socket at the back of his head. "What?" he said, rubbed his eyes, and looked at her. "What did you say?"

"You went with *Celine* to the Grand Canyon," Tara repeated. "I dreamed it. It must have been tagged to the memories you shared with me. I got the whole experience, not just the edited version you handed over."

Chandler's expression rippled with concern, but not about the same thing. "There must have been some backwash in the transfer. Maybe the splitter—"

"You slept with her!" Tara said, startling herself with her anger. "You told me you were just friends, that she was an 'old college acquaintance' of yours. We've had her over for dinner half a dozen times and you never told me you two were screwing each other!"

Chandler kneaded a lump of the sheets, as if afraid to touch her. "Celine and I *are* just friends. We were only lovers for a week, during that trip, and it didn't work out between us. That was a year before you and I started seeing each other. What does it matter now?"

Tara kept her voice low. "It wouldn't matter, if you had told me. The fact that you kept it a secret means a hell of a lot."

He blinked at her in the wash of street light filtering through the blinds. His face passed through a sequence of emotions from confusion to stunned anger that reminded her uncomfortably of how he had looked when she had been charged with altering her Virtual University files. "I'm not the only one who's ever kept secrets," he said.

Tara looked away, stung. "Touché." Chandler squeezed her shoulder, and she was torn between the desire to mollify him and the desire to knock his hand away.

Tara sighed and tried to find words for her emotions. "All right, Chandler. So we've peeked at each other's skeletons in the closet. We're even. But no more secrets, okay? We're married. We exchanged vows, combined our lives, promised to share everything. I don't like secrets. I want to be part of what you're doing."

He climbed out of bed, standing naked in the dim yellowish reflection. "Okay, mea culpa. No more secrets. We share and share alike. Genuine partners, collaborators." With slow, smooth motions, Chandler eased the straps of the sweat-soaked teddy off her shoulders and slid it down her body.

When they made love, tentatively at first, salving the sore spots between them, all Tara could think about was the splitter in the other room . . . and how it would feel to share bodies while sharing the same mind.

Chandler licensed "The Grandest Canyon" to more than a dozen office complexes. His hazel eyes gleamed as he swept Tara toward the door of their apartment. "Kimba's Steak House tonight," he said, "for a celebration."

For the past two years, they had made a habit of feasting on rich red meat once a month, whether they could afford it or not. Tara enjoyed their special meals, the evenings away from his work, though sometimes their budget had allowed them only a small filet to divide between them. Splitting a steak with Chandler was doubly difficult, since he insisted on eating his meat bloody rare, and she preferred hers medium well; as a result, they settled for medium, leaving neither particularly satisfied.

But tonight they were celebrating, and they would each have the meal of their choice. Tara sucked on a cholesterol-suppressant lozenge and handed one to Chandler as they boarded the transit tube and rode to the steak house.

Chandler talked with her about possibilities as he strode along the sidewalk to Kimba's. He gestured with his hands, walking straighter, more confidently. Tara thought of him slumped in his maroon chair not so long ago, jacked-in and blocked for ideas—she liked the change in him.

They passed through the artificial bamboo gates of Kimba's, next to the stuffed white lion mascot. The receptionist keyed up their reservations and led them to a narrow booth in the back near one of the shimmering fake fireplaces, under the stuffed head of an artificial ibex. Gaudy Zulu shields and long spears hung on the walls, and a soundtrack of throbbing drums and squawking birds came from microspeakers buried in the potted plants.

They called up the familiar menu on the datapad set into the end of the table, punching in their selections. He picked a large Porterhouse, she chose a filet mignon. It felt extravagant to select what they *wanted*, rather than what they could afford.

Chandler hunched over the lacquered table, resting his elbows on it as he reached out to her. "I want to show you something," he said. He dipped a hand into his shirt pocket to pull out a deck of newly imprinted plastic wafers, business cards with a magnetic strip containing autodialer information. She recognized the basic logo, but he peeled off one of the wafers and slid it across the table to her.

"I changed the company name from *Chandler Damon, Worldbuilder*, to *Worldbuilders, Inc.* I put your name on the ID strip, too."

He grinned at her, his pale, freckled face looking ruddier

in the cast-off light from the imitation fire. She held the plastic card in her hands, rolling the edges against her fingertips, as if afraid they might turn into razors. "You put my name on it?"

Chandler shrugged. "Well, you're going to be a part of it from now on, aren't you? Especially considering the new contract I got offered today—something really spectacular. We're reconstructing ancient Egypt, an interactive diorama environment displaying the creation of the pyramids and the great sphinx. It'll go in one of the top recreational floors in the financial center towers."

"You mean I can quit my other job?"

He shrugged, as if not sure how she would take the news. "Well, you keep telling me how much you hate it."

Before she could find a way to express her delight, the server placed their meals in front of them. Chandler sliced into his dripping red Porterhouse, eyeing the meat as if he were a predator. Tara talked with her mouth full, tugging out details of the Egypt project as she let the excitement wash over her.

The filet was delicious, perfectly cooked, but she had already received a far greater treat than the steak could ever be.

A hot sun baked the desert along the Nile. A simulated sky shimmered with the heat, refracted blue glinting off airbrush-smooth sands. Holographic slaves clad in dusty loincloths and rimed with sweat and mud constructed the monumental pyramids as Tara and Chandler worked at constructing the rest of the program.

Chandler's ghost image stood up a level on the pyramid adding details to the animated work crews. The slaves hauled enormous limestone blocks into place, sliding the chunks along mud-slick tree trunks. Chandler looked ridiculous in his guise as a slave driver: arms crossed at his bare chest, legs spread apart, bright white linen wrapped around his waist. He had added a dark Egyptian cast to his normally pale, freckled skin. His red-gold hair hid under a headdress. His lips pressed together as he concentrated, an expression she had not seen him wear before.

He stared down at the work gangs roped together, sweating as they maneuvered their loads up ramps. Working with a palette grid he pulled out of the air, he adjusted their expressions and routines, altering the dirt and details of their rags.

Tara's ghost image walked up one of the slick ramps and clambered across a network of palm-trunk scaffolding to inspect the architectural details. Playing the game, she had dressed her image in the gaudy garb of a Pharaoh's wife, her eyes black and greasy from a layer of kohl, her neck burdened with a necklace of gold and lapis lazuli, her knuckles adorned with scarab rings.

"Hey Chandler!" she said, raising her voice. Automatically the synthesized sounds of rumbling stone, cracking whips, and shouts of pain damped and faded into the background. "Do we have a revised estimate of the completion date? We're ahead of schedule, aren't we?"

Chandler's image nodded from the other side of the pyramid. His headdress wagged in the bright sun. "I want to emphasize the immensity of this construction, yet leave the impression that it's perpetually in progress. A metaphor for life: constantly building—and no matter how large it gets, you're never actually done. Like La Sagrada Familia, Gaudi's cathedral in Barcelona."

Somehow Tara knew instantly what he meant, though she could not recall ever having heard of the architect

Gaudi before. Deep in virtual Egypt, Tara had gotten better at interpreting mental messages from Chandler. They built upon each other's ideas.

The pyramids had gone up with amazing rapidity, with details as sharp as a new icepick. The work was not merely interesting, it was *good*. She could see things with a more artistic eye now, Chandler's eyes.

She turned her kohl-smeared eyes toward the work crews. In her years of knowing him, she had never felt so close to Chandler, had never felt so close to *anyone*. It was an immense relief, and something she had always wanted. She didn't want the project to end.

The sharp knife in Chandler's hand slashed down, dicing bok choy, Chinese eggplant, and celery on the wet cutting board. He chattered with Tara, distracted by his own excitement.

In the hot wok, vegetables sizzled with the pungent smell of onions and garlic in sesame oil. On the tile counter beside the wok, soft sweaty masses of turkey breast glistened like damp skin.

"I've already got future projects lined up," Chandler said. "The pyramids were really a breakthrough, and my agent is searching for commissions appropriate to my—to *our* talents."

"Good," Tara said, watching from the comfortable stool as he washed another jewel-purple eggplant under the tap and brought it glittering over to the cutting board where he chopped at it with short, stuttering strokes.

She felt free now, with open doors ahead of her again since she had scraped away her unchallenging architectural work, like mud off her shoe. Chandler didn't care about the mistakes in her past; he let her be herself and help him.

Chandler paused in his cutting, scooped the chunks of turkey and vegetables into the hissing hot oil, then reached for a green bell pepper. "I already told my agent that you and I would be taking projects jointly from now on."

She grinned at him. Chandler glanced at her with a shy smile as he automatically brought the blade down again, slicing his index finger.

"Damn!" he cried, dropping the knife and looking at the blood welling from the gash. "Not again! This is the same finger I cut last year. I'll probably need another three stitches."

Tara sprang to her feet, rushing around the counter to help him, but she froze halfway. "Chandler—*I* cut my finger last year, not you."

He held his cut under the cold running water and looked at her in confusion. She lifted her right hand, extending her index finger to show him the thin white line of her scar.

Chandler turned pale. "That was you? But the memory in my head was so clear!" He removed his hand from the water, wrapped a dishrag around the cut and pressed hard.

Tara went to the medicine cabinet to get gauze and tape. Her mind buzzed. More backwash from the splitter?

She brought the medical supplies, and though her hands looked steady, she was shaking inside. "Maybe we should . . . back off a little," she suggested. "Stop jacking together so often."

Chandler seemed preoccupied as he wrapped his cut. His lips pressed together as he concentrated in an expression she found endearing. For a moment he seemed convinced, but then his expression changed, like plaster-of-Paris setting in a mold, growing sharper and harder.

"Let's think about it," Chandler said. "We've got a lot of opportunities, and we don't need to rush into anything."

* * * * *

Tara returned alone to Kimba's Steak House. Chandler was off at a luncheon banquet to receive an award for his "Lost Rainforest" environment, but she wanted some time alone, treading water in a vague ocean of dissatisfaction. Perhaps she had picked up some of her husband's need for solitude.

Or perhaps she was just depressed because she had learned that Fizzwilly had finally been caught, the last of her group of hacker friends. Her only remaining connection to that past existence had been severed. Tara decided she didn't really want to go visit Fizzwilly and commiserate with him.

Preoccupied, she found a table surrounded by the kitsch safari atmosphere. She sat under a stuffed zebra head this time, looking up at its placid face, striped black and white, as if a black horse and a white horse had somehow merged imperfectly. It reminded her of Chandler and herself.

Resting her chin in her hand, she keyed in her order and stared at the gaudy decor, wondering if any of it was real, or if it had all been manufactured as props. She decided she didn't care: with as much time as she spent jacked in with Chandler to a virtual universe, reality had earned a different meaning for her.

Waiting for her food, Tara pondered how her life had changed, admitting how much more involved she was with Chandler now, an inextricable part of his work. Tara had dreamed about this . . . but she wasn't sure this was what she had had in mind. She had grown together with him, but at the cost of part of herself.

The server interrupted her reverie by bringing her meal. She cut into it with her steak knife, but stopped short when she saw blood pooling on the plate. She turned to the menu pad and called up her order, staring at the words she had keyed in. She looked at her steak again.

The Porterhouse was grayish on the outside, and a rich, cold red at the center.

"—and then we'll stop," Chandler said, his eyes pleading.

As Tara looked at him, she caught an image of the gaunt, middle-aged man again, riddled with self-doubt and the fear that he would be unable to complete the job he had taken on. "Just help me finish this one," he said. "You'll enjoy it. I promise."

Tara turned away, uneasy and afraid to meet his eyes. "Tell me again what's wrong," she said.

Over the past week or so, she had refused to jack in at all. Spooked by the growing evidence of the crumbling barrier between their personalities, she had decided to back off, worried about the danger of using the prototype splitter.

"I don't know what's wrong with it!" Chandler lashed out on the verge of panic. His eyes glittered in a silent plea. She had never seen him look so helpless. "It's missing something at the heart. Without your help it's only a shell. I'm falling flat on my face."

He reached out in desperation and clung to her hand. He hadn't done that in a long time. "Please?"

As the refusal died in her throat, Tara realized how drastically their needs had changed, as if they had swapped insecurities. Chandler needed to become more a part of her, and she retreated, trying to build barriers and maintain her own soul.

But as she looked at him grasping her hand and silently begging, she saw the man who had stood beside her when her bright future had been stripped from her, who had let her share in his growing success and giving her a new chance. She saw him redefining his company to include her, asking her to become his partner in everything.

"All right," she said. "We'll make this one our masterpiece, a final flash of glory. Then we'll stop. You'll be on your own from now on."

"Sure," Chandler said with obvious relief. "It's for a whole shopping mall. It'll be really big."

Tara went to the wall jacks, wondering why he would think that the size of the implementation had anything to do with her decision to help him.

She carefully mounted the viper fangs of the jack cable into the socket in the back of her head. Rushing and fumbling with his own socket, Chandler linked up. They plugged into the splitter, and both swam down into the virtual world.

He took her to Mount Olympus.

Chandler had chosen the assignment to pique her interest, since in her student days she had traveled through virtual Greece, visited the ruins of the Parthenon, the Acropolis, statues of Apollo and Athena.

Tara looked around under the bleached-bright sky of Chandler's land of the gods. Mount Olympus towered, reaching to the clouds, where Zeus and the other gods dwelled, working their mischief by playing games with mortal lives.

Tara's image had entered the world at the foot of the great volcano. On grassy hills stood weathered, half-fallen remains of Greek architecture, a random mix of Doric, Ionic, and Corinthian columns, small temples and larger structures scattered in no particular order, as if Chandler had captured their images from a mixed-bag database and pasted them to the slopes as the impulse struck him.

Black obelisks of volcanic rock thrust out at the base of the mountain. Steam and sulfurous fumes curled from fissures, and a blistering glow rose from a large opening, accompanied by loud sounds of clanging metal, a sighing forge, and someone massive stirring.

She saw no image of Chandler waiting for her. They had both jacked in, but he had gone to a different place. As Tara listened to the grunting, clanging sounds in the fire-filled cave, she knew where to find him, where he wanted her to go. He was playing some sort of game with her.

She stepped inside what she guessed would be the forge of Hephaestus. The sharp-edged cave walls reflected the burning-hot light rising from a river of incandescent lava that flowed, rumbled, growled through the chamber.

On a flat rock in the midst of the lava stood the incarnation of Chandler—Hephaestus himself—his head a mass of wiry black hair matted with perspiration, a voluminous beard, eyebrows like feathers from a bird of prey, a face lumpy and ugly. He wore only a soot-stained loincloth. Sweat trickled down his bronzed and muscular frame. One of his feet was crushed and shriveled; Tara remembered the myth of an angered Zeus hurling Hephaestus from the top of Mount Olympus.

He withdrew a sharp metal object from the lava—the glowing tip of a new trident for Poseidon. He looked up, his eyes flashing reflections from the fiery, molten rock. "How do you like it?" Chandler asked. His familiar voice sounded strange issuing from the vocal cords of a massive Greek god.

Tara glanced down at herself to see her body a sculptured model of absolute beauty, pure alabaster, clad in sparkling white flowing robes. She felt luxurious tresses of

218

hair draped between her shoulders. She rolled her eyes at the irony of being too lovely to touch—cool and aloof, unreachable. "Am I supposed to be playing Aphrodite to your Hephaestus?"

"You're my wife, aren't you?" Chandler asked with an eloquent shrug. He began to hammer the smoking trident on an enormous, misshapen anvil; the sledge blows sent thunder reverberating through the grotto.

She indicated the cave, the forge. "Well, the exterior of Mount Olympus needs work, but you've surpassed yourself here."

Chandler looked at her longingly, his large green-tan eyes glowing beneath the bristling brows. "That isn't why I wanted to bring you here," he said. He laid down the trident and stepped down into the flowing lava as if wading across a stream.

"In here, metaphor becomes reality—or whatever reality can become." The molten rock rippled around his naked thighs as he took another limping step on his deformed leg and sank up to his waist. "I need you Tara," he said, holding out a grime-blackened hand. "I've become a part of you, I've become addicted to you. And I can't do my work without you inside me."

Tara felt alarm well up inside her. "What in the world are you talking about?"

"I think you know. Come into the fire with me," he said. "Together we have unlimited potential. You must know it. Merge with me, once and for all. All or nothing. No secrets. Remember what you said? We exchanged vows, combined our lives. We're supposed to be partners." He dropped his voice. "We can share everything, down to the smallest thoughts. We'll both be in each other's head: a complete synthesis."

He took another halting step forward, stretching his

hand toward her, imploringly.

"Oh, Chandler, I wanted to be closer to you," she said, "not to *become* you."

Chandler shook his head. "You won't become me. *We'll* become *us*." Swirling thoughts screamed for her attention, but Chandler kept talking. "We won't even need the jacks anymore. We can do it ourselves. Our minds have already started growing together. We've intertwined. I'm in you, and you're in me."

She tried to respond, but found no words. Wouldn't it be wonderful to have constant mutual support, shoring up each other's weaknesses, never to be alone, always a part of a team? She thought of herself, and wondered how much she really had to lose.

Tara found her own hand lifting toward his as she stood on the brink of the fiery river, gazing at him, knowing she was the image of perfect beauty, fragile yet enduring. And he stood in the lava, powerful, a symbol of unending labor in all its grimy ugliness.

Her hand hovered in the air as the molten rock continued to bubble and hiss. She longed to join with her husband, but she knew that one personality would ultimately prove stronger. For now, Chandler could stand unharmed in the purging fire—but eventually one or the other of them would be consumed.

As Chandler touched her fingers, Tara viciously jacked out.

With an abrupt motion, like a drowned woman gasping back to life, Tara wrenched the end of the jack cable from the illegal splitter in the wall.

Reeling and disoriented, she suddenly found herself back in her mundane den, where Chandler still sat on the floor beside his old maroon chair, his face slack, his mind lost on Mount Olympus. Tara threw the jack cable down with a sharp gasp, as if it had stung her. She looked at it lying on the floor like a disembodied tentacle, and uncontrollable shudders wracked her body.

She never wanted to go back into the same data stream with Chandler. She had no boundaries left, and neither did he. They would keep merging, averaging. She had to get rid of the temptation—before Chandler could talk her out of it.

Tara dug behind the wall plate, routed Chandler over to the main network access, and disconnected the splitter. The clunky-looking gadget made of plastic and wire snapped like cracking knuckles as she ground it under her heel. The prototype had not been made for durability. She tossed the pieces into the kitchen incinerator and came back to stare at her husband.

Crouched in a lotus position, Chandler remained unaware of her presence. His eyes REMed back and forth; his red-gold hair hung limply over the interface cable. She wondered if he was grieving in the forge of Hephaestus.

They were already intermingled. Their minds had touched and shared and come away with pieces of each other. But from this point on they would no longer be on the same path; partners, yes, but not two people averaged together. From here, she and Chandler could move on parallel life roads, or they could diverge—but they would not be stepping in the same footsteps.

She could be part of him, and apart from him. The best of both worlds, if he would settle for that.

Tara's eyes filled with tears as she stared at Chandler, who now seemed separated from her by an impenetrable wall. When she called his name, he didn't answer, and so she reached out and caressed his hair instead.

Most of my work with Doug Beason is set fairly close to home, somewhere between the territories staked out by Tom Clancy and Michael Crichton. In this novelette, we ventured into full-fledged far-future science fiction. Some of the ideas and situations here seem ripe for further exploration.

Prisons

With Doug Beason

I am still called the Warden. The prisoners consider it an ironic jest.

Barely a meter square, the forcewalls form the boundaries of my holographic body. Once this felt like a throne, an isolated position from which I could control the workings of Bastille. Now, though, I must look out and watch my former prisoners laughing at me.

This projection has been an image of authority to them. Since living on this prison world was too great a punishment to inflict upon any real warden or guards, my Artificial Personality was entrusted to watch over this compound. I am based on a real person—a great man, I think—a proud man with many accomplishments. But I have failed here.

Amu led the prisoners in their revolt; he convinced them that Bastille is a self-sufficient planet after all their forced terraforming work for the Federation. They have survived all Federation attempts to reoccupy the world, keeping the invaders out with the same systems once intended to keep the prisoners in. Besides the prisoners, I am the only one left.

Once, I ran the environmental systems here, the production accounting, the resources inventory. I monitored the automated digging and processing machinery outside. I controlled the fleet of tiny piranha interceptors in orbit that would destroy any ship trying to escape. But now I am powerless.

Amu's lover Theowane comes to taunt me every day, to gloat over her triumph. She paces up and down the corridor outside the forcewalls. To me, she is flaunting her freedom to go where she wishes. I do not think it is unintentional.

At the time of the revolt, Theowane used her computer skills to introduce a worm program that rewrote the control links around my Personality, leaving me isolated and helpless. If I attempt to regain control, the worm will delete my existence. I feel as if I have a knife at my throat, and I am too afraid to act.

At moments such as this, I can appreciate the sophistication of my Personality, which allows me to feel the full range of human emotions.

It allows me to hate Theowane and what she has done to me.

Theowane makes herself smile, but the Warden refuses to look at her. It annoys her when he broods like this.

"I am busy," he says.

Leaving him to dwell on his fate, Theowane crosses to the panorama window. Huge, remotely driven excavators and haulers churn the ground, rearing up, crunching rock and digesting it for usable minerals. *At least,* she thinks, *Bastille's resources are put to our own use, not exported for someone else.*

Lavender streaks mottle the indigo sky, blotting out all but the brightest stars. A dime-sized glare shows the distant sun, too far away to heat the planet to any comfortable temperature; but overhead, dominating the sky, rides the cinnamon-colored moon Antoinette, so close to Bastille and so nearly the same size that it keeps the planet heated by tidal flexing.

On some of the nearby rocks, patches of algae and lichen have taken hold. These have been genetically engineered to survive in Bastille's environment, to begin the long-term conversion of the surface, of the atmosphere. On a human timescale, though, they are making little progress.

Farther below, Theowane sees the oily surface of the deadly sea, where clumps of the *ubermindist* weed drift. A few floating harvesters ride the waves, but the corrosive water and the sulfuric-acid vapor in the air cause too much damage to send them out often. That does not matter, since they no longer need the drug as a bargaining chip. Amu has refused to continue exporting *ubermindist* extract, despite a black market clamoring for it.

Theowane finds it bitterly ironic that she and so many others sentenced here for drug crimes had been forced by the Federation to process *ubermindist*. The Federation supports its own black market trade, keeping the drug illegal and selling it at the same time. After taking over the prison planet, Amu cut off the supply, using the piranha interceptors to destroy an outgoing robot ship laden with *ubermindist*. The Federation has gone without their precious addictive drug since the prison revolt.

When the intruder alarms suddenly kick in, they take Theowane by surprise. She whirls and places both hands on her hips. Her close-cropped reddish hair remains perfectly in place.

"What is it?" she demands of the Warden.

He is required to answer. "One ship, unidentified, has

just snapped out of hyperspace. It is on approach." The Warden's image straightens as he speaks, lifting his head and reciting the words in an inflectionless voice.

"Activate the piranha swarm," she says.

The Warden turns to her. "Let me contact the ship first. We must see who they are."

"No!" Bastille has been quarantined by the rest of the Federation. Any approaching ship can only mean trouble.

Shortly after the prison revolt, the Praesidentrix had tried to negotiate with Bastille. Then she sent laughable threats by subspace radio, demanding that Amu surrender under threat of "severe punishment." The threats grew more strident over the weeks, then months.

Finally, after the sudden death of her consort in some unrelated accident, the Praesidentrix became brutal and unforgiving. The man's death had apparently shocked her to the core. The negotiator turned dictator against the upstart prisoners.

She sent an armada of warships to retake Bastille. Theowane had been astonished, not thinking this hellhole worth such a massed effort. Amu had turned loose the defenses of the prison planet. The piranha swarm—so effective at keeping the prisoners trapped inside—proved just as efficient at keeping the armada out. The piranhas destroyed twelve gunships that attempted to make a landing; two others fled to high orbit, then out through the hyperspace node.

But Amu is certain that the Praesidentrix, especially in her grieving, unstable state, will never give up so easily.

"Piranha defenses armed and unleashed," the Warden says.

Five of the fingerprint-smeared screens beside the Warden's projection tank crackle and wink on. Viewing through the eyes of the closest piranha interceptors, Theowane sees different views of the approaching ship, sleek yet clunky-looking, a paradox of smooth angles and bulky protuberances.

"Incoming audio," the Warden says. "Transmission locked. Video in phase and verified."

The largest screen swirls, belches static, then congeals into a garish projection of the ship's command chamber. The captain falls out of focus, sitting too close to the bridge projection cameras.

"—in peace, for PEACE, we bring our message of happiness and hope to Bastille. We come to help. We come to offer you the answers."

Theowane recognizes the metallic embroidered chasuble on the captain's shoulders, the pseudo-robe uniforms of the other crew visible in the background. She snorts at the acronym.

PEACE—Passive Earth Assembly for Cosmic Enlightenment, a devout group that combines quantum physics and Eastern philosophy into, from what Theowane has heard, an incomprehensible but pleasant-sounding mishmash of ideas. It has appealed to many dissatisfied scientists, ones who gave up trying to understand the universe. PEACE has grown because of their willingness to settle raw worlds, places with such great hardship that no one in his right mind would live there voluntarily.

Theowane sees it already: upon hearing of the prisoners' revolt, some PEACE ship conveniently located on a hyperspace path to Bastille has rushed here, hoping to convert the prisoners, to gain a foothold on the new world and claim it for their own. They must hope the Praesidentrix will not retaliate.

"Allow me to stop the piranhas," the Warden says. "This is not an attack."

"Summon Amu," she says. "But do not call off the defense." Theowane lowers her voice. "This could be as great a threat as anything the Praesidentrix might send."

She hunkers close to the screens and watches the lumbering PEACE ship against a background of stars. The deadly pinpoints of piranha interceptors hurtle toward it on a collision course.

The First Secretary enlarges the display on his terminal so he can read it better with his weakened eyesight. Across from him, the Praesidentrix sits ramrod straight in her chair.

She waits, a scowl chiseled into her face. The Praesidentrix looks as if she has aged a decade since the death of her consort, but still she insists on keeping her family matters and all details of her personal life private.

The way her policies have suddenly changed, though, tells the First Secretary just how much she had loved the man.

The First Secretary avoids her cold gaze as he calls up his figures. "Here it is," he says. "I want you to know that your attempts to retake Bastille have already cost half of what we have invested in Bastille itself. On the diagram here,"—he punches a section on the keypad—"you'll see that we have thirteen equivalent planets in the initial stages of terraforming, most of them under development by the penal service, two by private corporations. Several dozen more have gone beyond that stage and now have their first generation of colonists."

Overhead, the Praesidentrix chooses the skylight panels to project a sweeping ochre-colored sky from a desert planet. The vastness overwhelms the First Secretary. His skin is pale and soft from living under domes and inside prefabricated buildings all his life. He doesn't like outside; he prefers the cozy, sheltered environment of the catacombs and offices. He is a born bureaucrat.

"So?" the Praesidentrix asks.

The First Secretary flinches. "So is it worth continuing?" *Especially,* he thinks, *with more important things to worry about, such as raising the welfare dole, or gearing up for the next election six years from now.*

"Yes, it's worth continuing," she says without hesitating, then changes the subject. Her dark eyes stare up at the artificial desert sky. "Have you learned how one prisoner managed to take over the Warden system? He has a very shrewd Simulated Personality—how did they bypass him? I thought computer criminals were never assigned to self-sufficient penal colonies for just that reason."

The First Secretary shrugs, thinks about going through an entire chain of who was to blame for what, but then decides that this is not what the Praesidentrix wants. "That's the problem with computer criminals. Theowane was caught and convicted on charges of drug smuggling although all of her prior criminal activity seems to have involved computer espionage and embezzlement."

"Why was this not noticed? Aren't the records clear?"

"No," the First Secretary says, raising his voice a bit. "She . . . altered them all. We didn't know her background."

"Nobody checked?"

"Nobody could!" The First Secretary draws a deep breath to calm himself. "But I think you are following a false trail, Madame. Theowane only implemented the takeover on Bastille. Amu is the mind behind all this. He's the one who convinced the prisoners to revolt. He's the one who refuses to negotiate."

She turns, making sure she holds his gaze. "I have already set a plan in motion that will take care of him once and for all. And it will get Bastille back for us." The Praesidentrix leans back in her purple chair as it tries to conform to her body. Her gray-threaded hair spreads out behind her. *She was a beautiful woman once,* the First Secretary thinks. The rumors have not died about her dead consort. . . .

The First Secretary makes a petulant scowl. "It's obvious you don't trust me with your plans, Madame. But will you at least explain to me why you are doing this? It goes beyond reason and financial responsibility." He purses his lips. "Is it because the prisoners are in the *ubermindist* loop? I find that hard to believe. It's just another illegal drug. Cutting off the supply will upset a few addicts—"

"More than that!"

"And cause some unrest," he continues, "as well as some reshuffling on the black market, but they'll adjust. Within a few years we'll have an equivalent drug from some other place, perhaps even a synthetic. Why is Bastille so important to you?"

The coldness in her gaze is worse than anything he could have imagined from her two months before.

"The *ubermindist* is only one reason," the Praesidentrix says. "The other is revenge."

I feel as if I am watching my own hand plunge a sword into the chest of a helpless victim. The piranha interceptors are part of me, controlled by my external systems—but I cannot stop them now. Theowane has given the order.

I watch through the eyes of five interceptors as they home in for the kill, using their propellant to increase velocity toward impact. With their kinetic energy, they will destroy the vessel.

I receive alarm signals from the PEACE ship, but I ignore them, am forced to watch the target grow and grow as the first interceptor collides with a section amidships. I see the hull plate, pitted with micrometeor scars, swell up, huge, and then wink out a fraction of a second before the interceptor crashes, rupturing the hull and exposing the inner environment to space.

Another interceptor smashes just below the bridge. I hear a transmitted outcry from the captain, begging us to stop the attack. Two more interceptors strike, one a glancing blow alongside the hull; the shrapnel tears open a wider gash. The PEACE ship continues its own destruction as air pressure bursts through the breaches in the hull, as moisture freezes and glass shatters. The fifth interceptor strikes the chemical fuel tanks, and the entire ship erupts in a tiny nova.

From the debris, a small target streaks away. I recognize it as a single escape pod. I detect one life form aboard. Of all the people on the ship . . . only one.

The escape pod descends, but then my own reflexes betray me as another interceptor also detects the pod, aligns its tracking, and streaks after it. Both enter the atmosphere of Bastille.

Now Amu arrives in the control center. I can tell he is upset by his expression, by his elevated body temperature. His head is shaved smooth, but his generous silvery beard, and eyebrows, and eyes give him a charismatic appearance. He is raising his voice to Theowane, but I cannot pay attention to their conversation.

The PEACE escape pod heats up, leaving an orange trail behind it as it burrows deeper into the atmosphere. It seems to have evasive capabilities, and it knows the piranha is behind it.

The interceptor also picks up speed, bearing down on the escape pod. But their velocities are so well matched that the piranha causes no damage when it bumps its target.

A few moments later, the interceptor—with no shielding to protect it from a screaming entry into the atmosphere— breaks into flying chunks of molten slag.

Amu seems mollified when Theowane explains to him that the intruder was a PEACE ship. I know Amu wants nothing to do with religious fanatics; he has had enough of them in his past.

I pinpoint the splashdown target for the escape pod. Without waiting for an order, I dispatch one of the floating *ubermindist* harvesters across the oceans of Bastille. No matter how great a hold Theowane has over my Simulated Personality, she can do nothing against my life-preservation overrides, except when the security of the colony is at stake.

Ostensibly to allow it greater speed, but actually just out of spite, I tell the harvester to dump its cargo of *ubermindist* before it churns off across the sea to reach the pod.

Amu stands in the holding bay of the cliffside tunnels. His bald head glistens in the glare of glowtablets recessed in the ceiling. His eyes flash.

A second rinse sprays the outside of the escape pod. Black streaks stain the hull from its burning descent, but the craft appears otherwise undamaged. After its dunking in the corrosive seas, Amu waits for purified water to purge the acidity.

Theowane follows him into the chamber. Amu listens to the last trickles of water coming out of the spray heads; drips run through a grate on the floor where the rinse water will be detoxified and reused.

For the hours it has taken the floating harvester to retrieve the escape pod, Amu has waited in silence with Theowane. He keeps his anger toward her in check.

Sensing his displeasure, she twice tries to divert his thoughts. Normally he would acquiesce just to please her. She has been his lover since before the revolt. But he doesn't like her making such important decisions on her own. It sets a bad example for the rest of the prisoners.

On the other hand, Amu knows that Theowane tried to keep Bastille free of the PEACE ships. And he approves.

Both of Amu's parents had been involved in a violent, fanatical sect and had raised him under their repressive teachings, grooming him to be a propagator of the faith. He had absorbed their training, but eventually his own wishes had broken through. He fled, later to use those same charismatic and mob-focusing skills to whip up a workers' revolt on his home planet. If the revolt had succeeded, Amu would have been called a king, a savior. But instead Amu had ended up here, on Bastille.

He wants nothing more to do with religious fanatics. Now this one PEACE survivor presents him with an unpleasant problem.

Theowane runs her fingers over the access controls. "Ready," she says. She keeps her voice low and her eyes averted.

Amu stands to his full height in front of the escape pod. "Open it."

As the hatch cracks, a hiss of air floods in, equalizing the two pressures. Then comes a cough, then sputtering, annoying words. A young boy wrestles himself into a sitting position and snaps his arms out, flexing them and shaking his cramped hands. "What took you so long? You're as bad as PEACE."

Theowane steps back. Amu blinks, but remains in place.

The boy is thin, with dark shadows around his eyes. His body appears bruised, his hands raw, as if he has been trying to claw his way out of the escape pod.

Amu can't stop himself from bursting out with a loud laugh. The boy whirls to him, outraged, but after a brief pause he too cracks a grin that contains immense relief and exhaustion. With this one response, he proves to Amu that he is no PEACE convert.

"Why didn't you let yourself out?" Theowane asks. "Isn't there an emergency release inside?"

The boy turns a look of scorn to her. "I know what's in the air on Bastille, and in the water. I couldn't see where I was. It might be bad to be cramped in this coffin for hours—but it would be plenty worse to take a shower in sulfuric acid." He pauses for just a moment. "And speaking of showers, can I get out of here and take one?"

After the boy has cleaned and rested himself, Amu summons him for dinner. The other prisoners on Bastille have expressed their curiosity, but they will have to wait until Amu decides to make a statement.

"Dybathia," the boy says when Amu asks his name. "I know it sounds noble and high-born. My parents had high expectations of me." He stops just long enough for Amu to absorb that, but not long enough for him to ask any further questions.

"I ran away from home," Dybathia says. "It took me a week to make it to the spaceport. When I got there, I slipped onto the first open ship and hid in their cargo bay. I didn't care where it was going, and I didn't plan to show myself until we were on our way into hyperspace. I figured anyplace was better than home, right?" He snickers.

"It turned out to be a PEACE ship. They wouldn't let

me off. They kept me around, constantly quoting tracts at me, trying to make me convert. Do my eyes look glazed? Am I brain-damaged?"

Amu allows a smile to form, but he does not answer.

Dybathia says, "They shut off their servo-maintenance drones and made me do the cleaning, scrubbing down decks and walls with a solvent that should have been labeled as toxic waste. Look at my hands! The captain said monotonous work allows one to clear the mind and become at peace with the universe."

Theowane breaks into the conversation, "Why were you the only one who got to an escape pod?" Amu looks up at her sharply, but she doesn't withdraw the question.

Dybathia shrugs. "I was the only one who bothered. The rest of them just sat there and accepted their fate."

This rings so true with Amu from his memories of his parents that he finds himself nodding.

Dybathia looks at the mind-scanning apparatus; this will be the most dangerous moment for him. The device is left over from the first days of Bastille, when human supervisory crews had established the colony. That month had been the only time when non-prisoners and prisoners cohabited the planet; as a precaution they had used intensive search devices and mental scanners, which had remained unused since those other humans had turned Bastille over to the Warden.

"You do understand why we have to do this?" Amu asks.

Dybathia sees more concern on the face of the leader than he expects. This is going better than he had hoped. "Yes, I understand perfectly." He flicks his gaze toward Theowane, then back to Amu. "It's because she's paranoid."

Theowane bristles, as he expects her to. She makes each word of her answer clipped and hard. "Your story is too convenient. How do we know you're not an . . . assassin? What if you've been drugged or hypnotized? We can't know what the Praesidentrix might do."

Knowing it is imperative for him to allay their suspicions, Dybathia submits to an intensive physical search that scans every square centimeter of his body, probes all orifices, uses a sonogram to detect any subcutaneous needles, poison-gas capsules, perhaps a timed-release biological plague.

They find nothing, because there is nothing to find.

"The psyche assessor won't hurt you," Amu says. "Just stick your head within its receiving range."

"How does it work?" Dybathia asks. He frowns skeptically. "How do I know this isn't one of those machines to condition prisoners? I don't want to end up like a PEACE convert."

"Explain it to him, Theowane." Amu smiles at her, as if he knows how it will rankle her.

Theowane blows air from her lips. "Everyone has a basic mental pattern, like a normal position that can never change. However, certain training—brainwashing, you'd call it—can superimpose another set of reactions on top of it. If you've been brainwashed or specially trained to do anything to Amu, or Bastille, it will show up here." She adjusts her apparatus.

Dybathia rolls his eyes. Amu smiles at that. Dybathia knows he is easing past the leader's defenses. "Let's just get this over with."

Without a word, the boy leans into the psyche assessor's range. Theowane makes no other comment as she works with the apparatus and takes her reading. She asks him a series of questions designed to break down mind-blanking techniques.

Dybathia answers them all without resisting.

Finally, Theowane shrugs. "It's clear," she says. "No one's been messing with his mind. He has no special training. He hasn't been brainwashed."

"I could have saved you trouble if you had just listened to me in the first place."

Amu claps a hand on the boy's shoulder. "I'll let you know when I've thought of a suitable way for Theowane to apologize."

When the survivor of the PEACE ship comes through with Theowane and Amu, I receive the unmistakable impression of tourist and tourguides. No, that is not quite correct . . . more like a visiting dignitary being shown points of interest.

Inside the forcewalls I watch them. True, I have a million different eyes around Bastille, optics to observe through, from monitoring cameras around the corridors, to the remote sensors of automatic digging machines. But my real eyes are here.

Purposely, I think, Amu ignores me as he brings the boy down the corridor. He points to the auxiliary control systems, explaining them with deceptive ease, making them sound simpler than they are. The three keep their backs pointedly turned and walk to the viewing window, outside of which the diggers continue their relentless excavations. The sky swirls with dark, oily colors over the hostile sea.

"It's going to be generations before anybody can bask under the Bastille sun, but at least it is now ours," Amu says, then lowers his voice. "And we aren't going to give it back when this world becomes habitable."

"Is it going to be worth the wait?" the boy asks, pushing his face close to the thick glass. I flick my concentration to one of the digger machines outside, looking through a different set of eyes, but the coarse optics and the glass distort the boy's face through the window.

Amu shrugs and rubs a hand on his silvery beard. "Theowane spends hours down here staring out the window. Actually, I think she just likes to taunt the Warden."

Finally, they turn toward me. I am too familiar with Theowane's close-cropped reddish hair and her narrow, hard eyes. Amu carries much more capacity within him—an extraordinary person, with charisma and intelligence and compassion that allows him to do virtually anything he wants to. But he has chosen a path that society deems unacceptable.

The boy is the last to turn away from the sprawling view. He looks at me directly. I see him.

I know him.

He has counted on me recognizing him.

Instantly, I flash through a handful of buried newsclips, quick photographs shaded by the promise of anonymity, but it is enough. It augments my suspicions. I can remember few details of the person on whom I myself have been based, but some things are impossible to erase.

I remember.

I wonder what he is up to. Why is he here, and what am I supposed to do about it?

The three visitors say no word to me as they continue their tour. I am left with the absolute conviction that the fate of Bastille, and perhaps the Praesidentrix's Federation depends upon me recognizing this boy, understanding what he wants, and acting accordingly.

I can no longer avoid the risk to myself. I must save my son.

Amu sits across from Dybathia for another meal. The boy fascinates him. He reminds Amu of himself as a young boy, or what Amu wanted to be—scrappy, irreverent, and intelligent.

Amu serves the two plates himself. Prisoners in the kitchen have prepared a tough pancake-like dish from cultured algae and protein synthesizers. They are trying to develop a pseudo-steak, but they are several years from perfecting it. No matter. Amu is used to it and it is, after all, nutritious. What more can they ask for, with their limited supplies?

"It's tough. You might need to use your knife to cut it," he says. Dybathia frowns at the crude knife in his hand, but Amu continues. "It is easy to get mush from the hydroponics tunnels, but we keep striving for something with a firm texture. It's only been in the last month or two that we've been able to have something tough enough to cut."

Dybathia works at the food on his plate. "I was looking at the knife." The blunt instrument is barely serviceable.

Amu smiles; it is the "winning" smile he uses when making converts to his various causes. "A holdover from prison life."

"That was long ago," Dybathia says.

"Yes, and things have changed now."

Dybathia lifts an eyebrow.

"We're here alone, with no non-prisoners for us to worry about. Knives are no longer any threat. And the Warden is nicely contained. But we like to remember what we are and where we are. We manufacture these knives, and they serve the purpose." Amu lowers his voice. "Maybe if the meat gets a little more meat-like, we'll need better ones."

Amu looks across the table at Dybathia. The boy seems fascinated with everything about Bastille, and Amu waits for him to ask the obvious question. But over several days it has not been forthcoming. Finally Amu breaks down and answers it anyway. "I grew up on New Kansas and left my parents, and their religious sect—" he burns inside, thinking of the PEACE converts.

Dybathia smiles. Amu dims the lights, bathing the room in a softer glow. It is storytime.

"New Kansas was a young planet, the soil somewhat unstable. We had planted grassland across entire continents. Wheat, alfalfa and prairie grass, with some used as rangeland for imported animals. But three-quarters of what we grew, the landholders exported offplanet. They were a handful of people who had financed the first colony ships and therefore claimed to own all of New Kansas. We were forbidden to leave our holdings.

"But I had learned how to whip my followers into a frenzy of religious devotion. We fought for our freedom. The colonists had come to New Kansas to start a fresh life. They felt that the Federation owed them at least a chance at autonomy. I knew how to galvanize them.

"They burned their fields. The fires swept across the plains for dozens of kilometers, pouring smoke into the sky that you could see from landholding to landholding. The others rose up."

Amu speaks with a sense of wonder, paying little attention to the boy. "My people were ready to die for me. Can you imagine that? Holding people so much in the palm of your hand—" Amu extends his fist across the table, opening it so that Dybathia can see the calluses from his hard life— "they were ready to *die* for me. And we almost succeeded."

Amu lowers his eyes and pushes his plate away from him. "Almost."

"I've had enough," Dybathia says. He has eaten most of his pseudo-steak, but Amu stares at the wall, seeing in his memories the visions of burning grass and the bodies of his followers after the landholders had called in Federation reinforcements.

He doesn't notice as Dybathia stands and slips toward the door. "I'm going to sleep," the boy says. "I'll see you in the morning."

Amu nods and blinks his eyes. But they are filled with water and sting as if from smoke.

Theowane enters the control center alone. She moves with precise steps, as if stalking. She wants to know what is going on. She will catch the Warden. She will get the information together, and then she will take it to Amu.

The holographic Warden looks at her from his glass-walled cage. His expression remains dubious, fearful, with a layer of contempt. Theowane says nothing as she casually walks over to the panorama window. She gazes across the blasted ground. Though the diggers continue to reform the landscape, she never sees any actual improvement.

Theowane stares for a few moments longer, then turns to meet the Warden's eyes. "You pride yourself so much in having human emotions and human reactions, Warden, but you're naive. You don't know how to hide things from other people. I can read your reactions as clearly as if they were spelled out on a screen."

The Warden blinks at her. "I do not understand."

"I caught you yesterday."

He extends his hands forward until the image fuzzes near the edge of the forcewalls. "What do you mean?"

"The boy," Theowane says. "You recognized him. It was painfully obvious. You know who he is. You know why he's here—and it isn't because of that crazy story he told us. Explain it to me now."

The Warden hesitates a moment, then hardens his face into a stoic mask. "I don't know what you are talking about."

Theowane raises her eyebrows. She reaches out and caresses the control panel. "I can turn the worm loose and delete you." That doesn't seem to frighten the Warden; she has used the same threat too many times before.

"Then you will lose whatever information you imagine I have."

"Perhaps I can find some way to make you feel pain," she says.

The Warden shrugs. "I am not afraid anymore."

In all her taunting, Theowane has taught the Warden as much about herself as she has learned from him. He knows exactly how to infuriate her.

"I'll inform Amu," she says, trying to regain her composure. "That will stifle whatever plans you are hatching."

Theowane straightens away from the window and sees the Warden turn his head, flicking his glance to look outside. Sensing something, hearing a muffled sound too close, she whirls around—

The giant automatic digger rears up and plunges through the glass. With its great scooping and digging gears churning, it claws out the poured-stone and insulation, ripping girders and breaching the wall.

Theowane stumbles back, sucking in a breath to scream as the deadly, acid-drenched air of Bastille rushes inside.

"You're quiet today," Amu says as he leads the boy down into one of the lower levels. Smells of oil, dirt, and stale air fill the tunnels.

"Introspective," Dybathia corrects. He thinks that word will better disarm Amu. He has not thought his silence and uneasiness would be so noticeable, but then he remembers that Amu is a master at studying other people.

"Ah, introspective is it?" Amu's lips curl in amusement.

"I have been through a lot in the last few days."

Amu accepts this and continues leading him down to where the corridors widen into larger chambers hewn from the rock. Amu spends hours showing him distillation ponds that remove the alkaloid poisons from the seawater. Like a proud father, Amu demonstrates the rows of plants growing under garish artificial sunlight, piped in and intensified through optical-fiber arrays stretching through the rock to surface collectors.

Other prisoners work at their tasks and seem to move more quickly when Amu watches them. Dybathia wonders how they can consider this to be so different from working under another kind of master.

Amu continues to talk about his grand vision, how they have made their colony self-sufficient. It has been difficult at first without supply ships from the Federation, but they have overcome those obstacles and now have everything they did before—except their prison.

Then Amu speaks in a dreamier voice, explaining about the terraforming activities, how he has switched the diggers to mining materials useful for their own survival, rather than supplying *ubermindist* offplanet. The floater harvesters are spreading algae and Earth plankton that have been tailored to Bastille's environment. They are resculpting the atmosphere of the planet, making it a place where humans will one day be able to walk outside and in peace. Amu's long-term goals and his naive sense of wonder disgust

Dybathia, but he keeps his feelings hidden. The boy will know when the time has come.

Amu says something he thinks is funny. Dybathia isn't paying attention, but automatically snorts in response. Amu nods, approvingly.

When alarm klaxons belch out and echo in the tunnel, the noise startles Dybathia, even though he has been expecting it.

My life-preservation overrides force me to close the airlock on the other end of the corridor to keep Bastille air from penetrating farther into the complex. I do not resist the impulse. I know it will trap Theowane inside.

She sprawls on the floor, trying to crawl forward. The floor is smooth and slippery, and she cannot get enough purchase to move herself. Her eyes are wide with horror. Her lips turn brown, then purplish as she gasps, and the sulfuric acid eats out her lungs. I force myself to watch, for all the times she has watched me.

The digging machine, sensing that it has been led astray, stops clawing and churning, then uses its scanners to reorient itself. The big vehicle clanks and drops clods of dirt and shattered rock as it backs outside.

Theowane croaks words. "Open—open door!"

"Sorry, Theowane. That would endanger the colony."

Before, I was afraid of the worm, which forbade me to do anything against Theowane and the other prisoners. But the worm, though deadly, is not intuitive and is unable to extrapolate the consequences of my actions. I will take the risk, for my son. I can do much damage, while doing nothing overt.

I have used an old sensor-loop taken from the archives of the digging machines' daily logs. Broadcasting this sensor-loop along with an override signal to one nearby digger, I made the machine think it saw a different landscape, where the route of choice led it directly through the viewing window.

The chamber has filled with Bastille's air, and I begin to see static discharges as the corrosive atmosphere eats into the microchips, the layers that form the computer's brain, my Simulated Personality—and the worm.

But the auxiliary computer core lies deep and unreachable below the lower levels. Bastille's acid atmosphere will destroy the main system here, where the worm has been added, but within a fraction of a second my own backup in the auxiliary computer will kick in. I should lose consciousness for only an instant before I am recreated.

My only wonder is whether the other Me will be me after all, or only a Simulated Personality that thinks it is.

Theowane lies dead but twitching on the floor, sprawled out in front of me. Blotches cover her skin. It is difficult for me to see anything now, with the images growing distorted and fuzzy, breaking up. I feel no pain, only a sense of displacement.

In the last moment, even the forcewalls seem to be gone. I have conquered the worm.

Dybathia watches Amu closely as the alarms sound. The leader stiffens and looks around. The other prisoners run to stations. Amu claps his hands and bellows orders at them. His face looks concerned: he doesn't understand what is happening.

Dybathia gives him no time to understand.

Amu bends down to him. "We've got to get you to a safe place. I don't know what's going on—"

In that moment, Dybathia brings up the prison knife

taken from Amu's table, pushing all the wiry strength of his body behind it. He drives the dull point under Amu's chin, tilting it sideways, and slashes across his throat. He has only one chance. He has no special training. Only his heritage.

Blood sprays out. Amu grunts, falling to his knees and backward. Scarlet spatters the silver of his beard, and the whites of his eyes grow red from burst capillaries. He reaches out with a hand, but Dybathia dances back, holding the dripping knife in his hand.

Amu's expression is complete shock shadowed with pain and confusion. He tries to talk, but only gurgles come out.

Dybathia kneels and hisses. "How? Is that what you're trying to say? *How?* Are you amazed because your psyche assessor detected no brainwashing? You forgot to consider that maybe I wasn't brainwashed, that maybe I *wanted* to do this because I hate you so much. I am free to act. I have no special training."

The light fades behind Amu's eyes, but the confusion seems as great. Dybathia continues. "My father was a great man, an important man—a fleet commander. He became an *ubermindist* addict, and that was a great secret. Does that mean I am not supposed to love him? That I wasn't supposed to try to help him? Do you know what happens when an *ubermindist* addict is cut off from his supply?"

Dybathia kneels beside the dying man to make sure his words come clear. "The withdrawal fried my father's nerves. He lost all muscle control. He went into a constant seizure for eight days—his mind took that long to burn out. He went blind from the hemorrhages. His body was snapped and broken by his own convulsions. You caused that, Amu. You did that to him, and now I did this to you. My choice. My revenge."

But Amu is already dead. Dybathia does not know how

much he understood at the last. The only sound Dybathia hears is his own breathing, a monotonous wheeze that fills his ears. The boy stands without moving as several other prisoners shout and come running toward him.

Inside her office, the Praesidentrix has chosen a honey-colored sky with a brilliant white sun overhead. She finds it soothing. For the first time in ages, she feels like smiling.

The First Secretary stands at the doorway, interrupting her reverie. "You asked to see me, Madame?"

She turns to him. For a moment he wears a fearful expression, as if he thinks she has caught him at something. She nods to make him feel at ease. "I've just received word from the Warden on Bastille. We have two gunships in orbit and all prisoners are now subdued. Amu and Theowane are both dead."

The First Secretary takes a step backward in astonishment. He looks for someplace to sit down, but the Praesidentrix has no other chairs in her office. "But how?" He raises his voice. "How?"

"I placed an operative on Bastille. A . . . young man."

"An operative? But I thought Amu had equipment to detect any training alterations."

The Praesidentrix pulls her lips tight. "The young man's father died from *ubermindist* withdrawal after the prison takeover. I believed he had sufficient motivation to kill Amu. He was free to act."

The First Secretary sputters and keeps looking for a place to sit. "But how did you know? What did you do?"

"He acted as a catalyst to spur the Warden into taking a more drastic action than he was likely to take on his own, with nothing else at stake. Remember, we built the Warden's Artificial Personality. I knew exactly how he would react to certain pressures." She waves a hand, anxious to get rid of the First Secretary so she can use the subspace radio again. "I just thought you'd like to know. You're dismissed."

He stumbles backward, unable to find words. He stops and turns back to the Praesidentrix, but she closes the door on him. The subspace projection chimes, announcing an incoming transmission. She sighs with a pride and contentedness she has not felt in quite some time. He has called her even before she could contact him.

The Warden's image appears in front of her like a painful memory. It is as she remembers her consort when he was a dashing and brave commander, streaking through hyperspace nodes and knitting the Federation together with his strength.

The Warden is only a simulation, though, intangible and far away. But that would not be much different from their original romance, with her consort flitting off through the Galaxy for three-quarters of the year while she held the reins of government at home. She had rarely held him anyway; but they had spoken often through the private subspace link.

They greet each other in the same breath and then the widowed Praesidentrix begins catching up on all the things she has wanted to say to him, repeating all the things she did tell him while he writhed in delirium from his withdrawal, while she had concocted a false story about his fatal "accident" in order to avert a scandal.

But first she must say how proud she is of their son.

Greg Benford and I spent many months extrapolating a possible epic future of Siberia, with geopolitical forces in conflict, resources in question, and colonization of the last great frontier on Earth. As an offshoot of these plans, we came up with a grand scheme for cloning mammoths—an idea that's not so far-fetched. In fact, several research teams are currently at work on the concept, as it is described in the following novella. And radical protest groups are already up in arms, writing scathing letters to the San Francisco Chronicle, science magazines, and other venues. Even some of the museum curators and scientists we talked to as research for this story reacted with knee-jerk resistance, fearing the very idea of bringing back an extinct species—even if that species was wiped out not by any natural process but due to the efforts of mankind.

"Mammoth Dawn" is only the prologue to a projected novel, if we can find an interested publisher. Unfortunately, the reality of this concept is sweeping down upon us with the speed of a stampeding woolly herd. There may be real mammoths among us before the novel is published.

Mammoth Dawn

With Gregory Benford

If only the protesters' intellect matched their verbal cleverness, Alex thought, the Helyx Corporation wouldn't have any problems at the front gate.

It's Not Nice to Fool with Mother Nature! said one of the waving signs displayed on a securitycam window projected on the surface of his desk. The usual. Alex Pierce had stopped trying to understand the Evos' odd point of view, had ceased even being bemused by their antics. He had a company to run.

He relegated the securitycam image to the background and brought more important documents forward. Datascreens and e-mail lists cluttered his table-sized desktop screen as much as memos and paper messages had once done.

Earlier that morning he'd woken up in Miami with a hangover. He'd downed three drinks too many at yet another fancy fund-raiser dinner—this one to preempt birth defects through parental genetic screening. Before midday he had choppered back to the main lab administration offices in rural Montana. For a worldwide corporation, business hours lasted all day long, and it was always time for the boss to get back to work.

His wife Susan had stayed home on the ranch. She disliked black-tie functions like the one in Miami, though she could be devastating in a cocktail dress, the barest breath of jewels implying wealth far better than gaudiness did. But too often the diplomats and VIPs treated Alex as the only important face in the room, and Susan as the gorgeous trophy wife rather than a talented scientist in her own right. She hated the attitude, and Alex had made appropriate excuses for her.

But Susan's real reason was that she wanted to stay with her mammoths.

As his company had grown from a fledgling startup with one biotech product—a symbiotic microorganism that could fend off strange *E. coli* in the human digestive system—to a corporate leviathan that spent most of its resources just figuring out how to receive and manage the enormous profits, Alex had learned to multi-process. While taking care of corporate details, answering vidmessages, and delegating responsibilities, a calm and meditative part of his mind was anticipating an evening of campfires and peace with his wife, out near the herd. . . .

"We got another fence-jumper," Ralph Duncan said on the secure phone, interrupting a dozen separate trains of thought and delivering a problem of his own. "Got him cold."

Alex's autosecretary instantly knew this was important, captured the call and transferred the Security man's weathered image to the upper corner of the desk. "Remember that li'l hint we got on the acoustics? Tracked him in the woods up along the eastern ridgeline. Ambitious bastard."

Alex was glad to be interrupted from pharmaceutical statistics, Third World traveler health records—dull, even if they did point to continued success. "Another Evo type?"

"They don't carry some kinda ideology tag, Boss, but you can bet he was trying to get a look at the mammoths. Should I tell the sheriff?"

"No, he'll just process the guy, slap him on the wrist, and let him back out to cause more mischief." Alex rubbed his fingers over thin lips. "Usually only the hardcore ones try to get past the fences. How's he outfitted?"

"Pretty fancy. Overnight gear, one of those microbags for sleepin', videocam with closeup fittings. Five kilometers inside the fence, easy. No question about boundaries and jurisdictions." Ralph snorted.

By now, the questions came automatically to Alex. The ranch often had intruders. "No weapon?"

"Nope. Except for tryin' to run at first, gave us no trouble."

As he dealt with the conversation, Alex finished some

routine computer work, forwarded several inquiries to Susan's mailbox, bumped a set of interview questions to his PR squad (who knew all the right answers anyway), and keyed out, using his thumbprint to secure. At no point did Ralph ever notice that he didn't have Alex's full attention.

"If you ask me, this guy wanted to be caught. Claims he knows you professionally." Ralph's sun-grizzled face showed just a hint of amusement. "His ID says Geoffrey Kinsman."

Now Alex paid attention. "Damn! I think I know him. Spelled with a G?"

"Yep."

"What's a good biologist doing with that bunch of Luddites?"

"Says he'll talk only to you, Boss."

Alex shut down the other operations in the office, signaling all his staff distributed around the world that he was not presently available. "Bring him to the Hospital, not here."

Ralph had an intuitive sense of Alex's moods, born of a decade's close collaboration. But now the Security man seemed surprised. "Show and tell, Boss? For one of those clowns?"

"The Evos are always more afraid of what they imagine than what they actually see." He put on a pair of spex and tested the uplink as he headed out of the office, his boots clomping down the varnished wooden stairs, and out onto the plank porch. "Stall him for five, Ralph. Give me time to profile him."

When Helyx had purchased an isolated chunk of northern Montana, Alex kept the original ranch buildings, letting them fade and weather from bleached white to an ash gray like raw silver. The primary genetics labs were in the old pine-log barn, which Susan had dubbed the Pleistocene Hospital.

"Full database search," he subvocalized into the spex as he walked. "Summarize relevant information on Dr. Geoffrey Kinsman. Reference point: He was in my lab around fifteen years ago. Apply context filters."

With a big drive-in bay and concealed windows, the hospital barn looked like an equipment garage. Inside, the crisp antiseptic air mixed with the moist organic odors of feathers and fur, droppings and feed—a contrast to the smelly oil drums just outside on the loading dock.

Lounging in his jeans against the split rail that bounded the old barn, Alex read a data summary that scrolled across the spex. All he needed to know about Geoffrey Kinsman: a man with just a bit too much clout and education to dismiss as simply a misled Luddite, as Alex had always considered the Evos to be.

For years, Kinsman had associated with political activism, starting with *Ruckus Society* training camps, where bright-eyed kids learned street protest tactics. His molecular biology research had produced over a hundred papers, recently with an angle toward genetics and species preservation. Another "clean genes" guy. Unarmed, a routine lab type, Kinsman did not seem dangerous. Maybe that didn't include the threat of being bored to death.

Alex bit his lip in annoyance. He wished they had a network of sympathetic locals who would warn Helyx before a guy got this far in. He had endured the backwoods suspicions, had expected them because he'd grown up just over the Idaho border. For the first few years, the locals had given him a narrow-eyed appraisal. In fact, for a while an ugly rumor had spread that he was here to recruit locals as organ donors for sinister Helyx experiments.

But when his staff offered only day work and some well-paid farmhand jobs, the people were disappointed—until the area economy picked up and kept growing. Within a year Alex Pierce could walk into any bar and get his beer paid for, because Helyx Ranch pumped in a goodly share of the county's revenue.

Alex pursed his lips, pondering. A lot of the locals might agree with the protesters' views, even help them out a little. A bitter truth—he hadn't won the war of ideas even here, in home country. He knew these people, shared many of their gut responses. But he had not lived in their world, really lived in it, for a good long while. Ralph was the real thing— and looked it in his rough pants and boots as he came through the door with his captive.

The man walking next to him was a dapper, compact item, fresh from an upscale outfitter: olive green Gore-Tex jacket, trim all-weather leggings, a big hiker's watch with a Global Positioning readout. He looked as out of place as a chicken in church. A bit heavier than Alex remembered, but the tight mouth was the same.

Geoffrey Kinsman's voice was as hard and flat as a stove lid. "Dr. Pierce." East Coast accent, mid-Atlantic state. He held out a hand, and Alex ignored it. "You don't remember me?"

"I remember. Just read the data squirt about you, Dr. Kinsman. All the good stuff." He decided to have some fun with him. "You seem to have strayed a bit out of your way."

"Might as well admit the obvious," Ralph growled, playing the tough cop. "You wanted to create some disturbance—give the Feds a pretext to come in here."

Kinsman glanced at the old security chief as if he were some kind of lab specimen. "You overestimate my powers."

"That's just what you did at that animal experimentation facility outside Topeka, five years ago," Alex said. It sometimes put these people off balance if you could demonstrate up front that you knew all about them.

But Kinsman didn't even blink. "That was coincidence."

Ralph snorted, and Alex grinned. Kinsman was not going to be any trouble, he judged; he didn't even have a cover story. "We'll be fine, Ralph. Thank you." As the Security man turned to leave, Alex scowled back at Kinsman. "So why, exactly, was it so important to break through my fences and trespass on my private property?"

The man allowed himself a small, dry chuckle, but his eyes were a brittle gray, like chips of slate, as he said, "To talk some sense into you. I consider that constructive, not destructive."

"Sense? Those people at the South Gate have an excuse: they're ignorant. But we worked together, so I thought—"

"You didn't think twice about me when you published that paper, the one on mammoth genes."

"Right, you did some of the preliminary scans on the gene lines. A grad student for two years, then left."

Kinsman took on a self-righteous air. "I disagreed with the work, once I understood what you were doing."

"So what was your gripe? Was it because I 'didn't think twice' about you?"

"Neither of you even asked if I wanted my name on that paper."

Alex shook his head. "You were doing straightforward stuff. Not original. Sorry if we didn't acknowledge you—" He couldn't even remember for sure.

"Oh, there was a paragraph at the end, thanking me and a dozen others, sure."

Alex smiled slightly. "You wanted to be on the paper. Is that what this is about?"

"No, damn it!" But Kinsman's flushed face belied his words. "I just thought you'd listen to me because I was a lab grunt for you once. Maybe your money has insulated you from the arguments against this entire—"

Alex held up a hand, quick and decisive. "Already heard them. Before I took you on as a grad student, I had invented most of the arguments. Or my wife had. But we thought it through. Decided for ourselves."

Kinsman blinked, looking taken aback at Alex's bluntness. He must have had plenty of time to rehearse this confrontation while backpacking across Helyx wilderness property, Alex mused, but a lot of emotion churned in his face. There had been plenty of grad students in Alex's lab then, most of them doing routine tasks to get experience. Somehow this one had left little impression on him. But clearly that old, simple paper had been a big deal to Kinsman. Students normally didn't get their names on technical papers unless they did something creative, but Kinsman had apparently taken that irritating grain of sand and turned it into this pearl of a grudge. Alex had never been really good at judging people, but his years leading a stupendously successful company had sharpened what little skill he naturally had.

Nothing brings enemies out of the woodwork more effectively than success.

"Okay, let me talk some sense into *you*." Alex gestured toward the old oaks that towered near the barn and the ranch buildings. The immense, gnarled trees were majestic and stately—and full of birds. "Look over there, Dr. Kinsman. Beautiful birds, graceful. You should see them fly at sunset, like a cloud." Even without squinting, he could pick out a dozen nests in the branches, and the constant shifting, cooing, fluttering made the branches tremble.

"I didn't come here to look at birds, *Dr.* Pierce." He spat out the title.

Alex turned to him sharply. "You should. Once they blackened the skies, billions of them in North America when Columbus landed. But it was in their nature to nest in huge colonies, only in big stands of oaks or beeches, which made them easy prey. Over the centuries settlers cut down the oaks and beeches for firewood and lumber, or just to clear farmland. Hunters shot millions of those birds, usually for sport, though they shipped the carcasses to the cities by the barrelful."

Kinsman looked impatient, then startled. "Those are—"

"Passenger pigeons lay only one egg each spring. They couldn't possibly reproduce faster than they were slaughtered. It was genocide, pure and simple, *Dr.* Kinsman, perpetrated by human beings. The last passenger pigeon died in 1914 in the Cincinnati Zoo, and the species was extinct in a historical blink of an eye. Until Helyx brought them back." Alex couldn't keep the happy pride out of his voice.

Kinsman, though, looked disgusted to the point of being ill. "Extinction is Nature's way, Pierce—for whatever reason. You can congratulate yourself for the hubris of your genetic breakthroughs, but can you honestly say the world is a better place because you have brought back a . . . pigeon?" He waved dismissively toward the oaks. As if at a signal, several of the birds took flight, ruby-throated, with lovely gray body feathers and long pointed tails. "Your means are dangerous, and your ends are utterly inconsequential. Pigeons!" The fire in Kinsman's eyes made Alex reconsider the wisdom of having sent his security chief away so quickly. "You're a bigshot businessman—what possible market can there be for passenger pigeons. For zoos? Pets? *Meat?*"

"Market talk is what I feed the Board, but that doesn't even start to explain why I'm here." He allowed a small, self-deprecating smile. "I didn't want to go down in history as Dr. Diarrhea." Alex turned from the split-rail fence. "Come have a look. Maybe we can use a crowbar to open your mind."

Inside, the lab was a mix of cool high-tech surfaces and ancient woods, the barn's past never wholly banished. Consoles and elaborate digital diagnostics stood next to old feed cabinets, still useful for storage. High spotlights gave the scene an evenly lighted patina and crisp, conditioned air fought the old horsy smells and new disinfectants. Chrome countertops sat next to wooden fences and thick wire-mesh cages.

"Not many people get to see this, Dr. Kinsman," Alex said.

"Not many people should."

Why do I try? he thought. *If Kinsman wasn't a colleague . . .*

Inside a shoulder-high pen stood two gawky-looking birds like giant chickens with stretched necks. They had mottled brown feathers, lizard-like feet, and towered nearly ten feet tall.

"This is our first mating pair of moas, a New Zealand bird that went extinct sometime in the 1600s." Elated notes crept into Alex's voice, but he saw no wonder in Kinsman's eyes. "We're currently in our third-generation retrograde development of the Tasmanian tiger, too. But the lack of a close sibling-species as well as general difficulties in dealing with the marsupial gestation process has caused some delays."

He glanced toward the set of thick doors and reinforced windows at the back of the Pleistocene Hospital. Kinsman looked suspiciously at the closed-off rooms . . . but Alex didn't think the man was ready for that sight yet. "Other resurrected animals," he explained with an offhanded comment. "Look, I don't have time to show you everything. It's obvious you're more interested in proselytizing than in science."

A rotund bird higher than a man's knee waddled across the floor, looking comical, its black beak blunt and ugly, its eyes innocent. Two stubby wings betrayed the flightless nature of the bird, which moved at a rapid, though ungainly clip. A tufted curlicue of feathers poked up like a pigtail from its rear. The bird prodded around in corners, pecked at imaginary insects, as if it had forgotten where its food dish was.

This time Kinsman stared. "*Dodos*, too?" The dapper man leaned forward and took out his pen, pointing it at Alex as if it were a symphony conductor's baton. "Where will you stop, Pierce? Do you intend to bring back smallpox as well? Or any number of vermin the world is better off without? Have you no respect for the natural order?"

Alex picked up the ungainly bird and carried it squawking to a bowl of grain. The dodo immediately forgot its annoyance and began to gobble the corn. "These birds lived quite nicely on the island of Mauritius until European sailors came and killed them for food. That wasn't so bad, but the sailors also let loose dogs, rats, and hogs, which ate the dodo's eggs. It took only a century or two for the entire species to be wiped out." He scratched the feathers on the turkey-sized bird. "What, exactly, is *natural* about that?"

Kinsman directed a condescending look at Alex Pierce—who captained a gigantic corporation, who had developed a cure for the digestive misery of billions—as if he were an ill-educated child. "You can't possibly predict the long-term consequences of your tampering. Forced breeding, gene-selection, wombs implanted with embryos they were never meant to carry. Why must you *push* things so much?"

"Because I don't have time to waste," Alex said mildly. "Evolution can meander all it likes. We have calendars."

Kinsman sniffed, clicked his pen twice in a nervous gesture. "Mankind is part of the natural order, Pierce, the dominant species on Earth, while other species failed along the way."

"Sometimes with a little help from us. What's wrong with rectifying that?"

Kinsman tossed his pen onto a cluttered desk and actually clasped his hands together in a melodramatic beseeching gesture. "What makes extinction caused by human interference so different from extinction due to, say, a huge asteroid impact? Will you try to bring back dinosaurs next?" He scoffed. "Or woolly *mammoths?* I've heard what you have back in your valleys."

Alex maintained a noncommittal expression. "Rumors."

"Satellite photos."

Alex didn't respond, trying to hide his surprise that Kinsman and his protesters could have gotten such high-resolution images from the Feds.

Kinsman pressed his advantage. "I want to see them, Pierce."

Blocked from view by a thick stand of Ponderosa pines, the corral had once been used for breaking horses. But Helyx had reinforced the fences, added motion detectors and voltage zappers, and made the barricades much taller. As needed.

Inside the enclosure, Susan studied two of the first-generation hybrids, giving each one a standard monthly physical exam. Maybe Kinsman would be satisfied with this.

When she saw her husband pass through the double

gate, Susan's face lit up. They had spoken via earlink after he'd arrived back from Miami, but both of them had been too absorbed with ranch duties to see each other before now. They would have plenty of time tonight, camping out under the stars, back where no one could find them. . . .

Susan rang the old notes in him with a little breath, a flash of a smile. He had called those eyes "molasses brown" because when he looked into them he felt stuck and never wanted to look away. High cheekbones, luxuriant brown hair, a delicious set of curves artfully set off in a blue blouse atop trim black jeans. She greeted Alex with a broad smile, but when she saw Kinsman follow him into the corral, she immediately adopted a more businesslike expression.

"Susan, this is Geoffrey Kinsman. Remember, he was a grad student back—"

"Oh yes. And now a member of our loyal opposition." Her voice was neutral, neither friendly nor antagonistic.

"I came to see your mammoths. I didn't know whether I could believe the appalling—"

Susan immediately clued in with just a glance at her husband. "Actually, these are 'mammophants.' Just a first-generation hybrid, still far from being an actual mammoth, Mr. Kinsman."

"Please, it's *Doctor* Kinsman. I got my degree at—"

"This one is Short Stuff," she continued without the slightest hesitation and stepped close to the oldest of the mixed-breeds, a docile gray-haired beast with rumpled skin and big eyes, a trunk shortened to a few feet, and no tail. "We used mammoth DNA from Siberia, inserted it into a female elephant's egg, and let the mother bring the baby to term with a lot of uterine monitoring."

Playfully, Susan reached up and slapped Short Stuff's rump, and the tall beast ambled a few feet, then stopped to munch from a pile of sage-green hay piled near a corrugated water trough. "And she's a sweetie."

Alex knew the details, had lived with them for a decade. Short Stuff was not a pure mammoth because she had spent twenty-two months in an Asian elephant's womb, sharing the chemical and hormonal bath evolved for elephants alone. But the womb had proved similar enough to a mammoth's, or the hybrid would have spontaneously aborted.

"We're learning the hard way that there's a critical conversation between the genes and the womb," Susan said. "Call it feminine knowledge. So we're still working to get the right dialog between the mammoth genes and the wombs of each new generation."

Indeed, Short Stuff's womb had turned out to be a much better approximation, and using the sperm of the first male, Middle Man, their offspring was even closer.

"You can sure see the original elephant genes showing through." Susan lifted Short Stuff's leathery left ear, as big as a blanket. "No woolly mammoth had this large an ear. It would lose too much heat in an Ice Age climate. Most of Short Stuff's body was designed for the tropics—she's got a hide that stands up under strong sun. Still, you can see the beginnings of hair, an extra coat to keep her warm. A step in the right direction."

She talked faster as Kinsman's frowning displeasure became more obvious. Susan moved to the other big animal in the corral, the first hybrid male. He snorted, curled his trunk, but she fearlessly thrust a hand into the sparse pelt beneath the massive mouth to reveal stubby, gray-brown shafts. "See Middle Man's tusks? Pretty short for now, but they'll grow longer than any elephant's."

Susan rubbed her hands along Middle Man's midsection, eliciting a pleased sort of grunt.

Kinsman ground his teeth—the first time Alex had ever seen anyone do that, outside of movies. "And what is the point of this nonsense animal? The pure species died out long ago, and your interbreeding process creates only a succession of polyglot monstrosities."

Susan gave him her patented I-don't-suffer-fools-gladly expression. "Exactly. Did you think species just jumped in one shot to a completely different form? That's why it's called *evolution*."

Kinsman eyed the two hairy elephants in the corral. "Evolution didn't make these forms—"

"Right. We did," Susan shot back. "Unlike evolution, we have a goal. Short Stuff and Middle Man are investments for the next generation."

Alex smiled; his wife was a better debater than he could ever be. And she wasn't giving away anything technical, either, trying to swamp Kinsman with pizzazz. He did not need to know how far the plan had already progressed.

Mammoth DNA was a heritage that belonged to all humanity—paid for with private money, part of the fortune Alex had earned as "Dr. Diarrhea." Early on, before he'd learned to keep quiet about Helyx's activities here, he and Susan had published a joint paper—the one Kinsman had done some routine lab work on—showing that the difference between elephants and mammoths was only a few dozen critical loci. The media speculation *that* provoked taught them to keep their work quiet. Every journalist could see the potential, write a quick deep-think piece. But making the project happen was a career.

"You frighten me," Kinsman said, looking from Susan to Alex. "Both of you. Our environment is a vast and complicated system that adapts to changes through delicate checks and balances. Dodos and passenger pigeons and moas—

and, yes, mammoths—were removed from Earth's equation long ago, and your meddling may well throw everything out of balance again."

"That's an awfully sophisticated argument for a bunch of protesters who usually can't come up with anything more pithy than 'It's not nice to fool with Mother Nature.' "

Kinsman dismissed his cohorts down at the South Gate. "They're just afraid of genetic engineering on general principles. They don't need any deeper argument than that."

"No, I don't suppose they do. People like that have always used their ignorance as a weapon." *And often it turned to violence.*

Kinsman backed toward the gate, as if afraid to get any closer to the gentle hybrids. "Your work is immoral, even aside from the ethical issues. Introducing a big grazer into lands that cows and sheep have already depleted is sure to have a major impact on the environment."

"Helyx's track record speaks for itself. We're concerned about the environment—and it isn't just corporate bullshit either," Alex said with a sigh. Whatever hope he had harbored that a real biologist would be open to rational ideas faded as Kinsman's sour scowl deepened.

As a last shot, the man said, "You have to know that a lot of us in this world think what you're doing here is, at the very least, ugly." He flicked a disapproving glance at the furry mammophants wandering around the enclosure.

Alex could tell the discussion was over, and he knew Susan was already close to losing her cool. "I could tell you things—*ugly* things—that'd make your ears curl up in self defense."

He remembered news images dating all the way back to the late Twentieth Century: Eco-terrorists burning fields of modified rice that would have grown in the alkaline soil and brackish water of the poorest Third World countries. Or ripping up experimental plantings of frost-resistant straw-berries, like children throwing a tantrum. Later, assassi-nating a researcher who was developing a protozoan symbiote that would have enabled starving populations to break down cellulose and digest some forms of grass.

And if they were caught afterward, the violent protesters always seemed smug and self-justified! Thick-headed fools . . .

All of those things would have helped the human popula-tion, fed millions, improved the quality of life worldwide. And yet the rowdy rabble felt they were in a better position to decide what was best for the world than all the blue-ribbon panels of experts and all the United Nations com-mittees. Yes, indeed, they sure seemed to have the best in-terests of humanity uppermost in their minds.

He pointedly nudged Kinsman through the gates of the corral before Susan could lash out at him, then used the di-rect-connect uplink in his spex to summon Ralph and a Se-curity escort. "It's time for you to go. You've had your say . . . I just wish you'd had your 'listen.' "

When they emerged from the dense pines around the corral, Ralph was already there to take him away.

It wasn't until later that Alex discovered Kinsman had left his pen behind inside the Pleistocene Hospital. Rather than hurrying to give it back to the educated Luddite—was that an oxymoron?—he tossed it into a desk drawer in dis-gust. He had better things to look forward to that evening.

Alex rode his strong black gelding uphill, stretching him-self and enjoying the zest of at last getting away from the of-fice, far away, with Susan and the young ranch hand Cassie Worth. Clement Valley was about as deep in the wilderness as he could go and still remain on his vast acreage.

After the irksome arguments and corporate busyness of the afternoon, this was heaven. He had spurned the convenience of using a company jeep; taking the horses felt more natural, more *real*. As the dense alders and ponderosa pines closed around the narrowing four-wheel-drive road, they rapidly left the log-cabin lab buildings and the Pleistocene Hospital behind.

Cassie, the spunky and at times incredibly earnest young ranch hand, urged her horse into a trot ahead, anxious to get to the high overlook into the next valley. The young woman's long chestnut hair had been quickly woven into a thick practical braid that dangled beneath her white cowboy hat. Her face still retained a splash of youthful freckles, and her clear blue eyes held a fresh sense of wonder.

With good reason, he thought, *since she has seen miracles.*

But Alex and Susan did not hurry. Feeling anticipation build, they rode side by side, smelling the creaking saddles, the sweating horses, and the sweet sun-warmed pine sap. It had been a long time since they'd been so calm, though young Cassie's presence would dampen any amorous impulses in the sleeping bags out by the campfire. No matter; it was good just to be together.

While Susan watched approvingly, he had made a brave show of switching off his pager, but within half an hour the cloying weight of corporate responsibility forced him to turn it back on. When Susan wasn't looking, of course . . .

Horse Valley was more lush now than it had been for millennia. Using Helyx profits, Alex had started this ranch by channeling mountain streams into the headlands above, so that his experts could use the moisture to grow the sedges that normally flourished only in tundra. Reflections of aspen shimmered in mirror puddles of water as he headed up the slope, relishing the crisp air. Purple poets always talked about the "forest primeval" and Alex couldn't get the phrase out of his mind. *That's how this is supposed to be.*

In low-lying swampy areas beside the path, giant ferns like horned and scaly monkeys' tails curled up, flourishing next to fluted flat-leaved hyacinth—ancient plants that had not grown naturally since the last ice age. As they rode past, he sniffed the mulchy smell, wondering if the resurrected plants were edible, if there might be a high-end niche market for, say, Jurassic Salads. . . .

"Majestica is looking ready to deliver," Cassie called over her shoulder, slowing her mare so her two bosses could catch up. "I've gotten close enough three times in the last week to take readings, but Bullwinkle doesn't like it."

Alex smiled. "They trust you, Cassie." Forget the scientists and the so-called professional handlers; this young woman had a better knack with the big beasts than anyone else on the ranch.

Susan drew a deep, satisfied breath. "It'll be our first pureblood, after fifteen years."

"Think of it as an anniversary present," he said. "Without your grandiose dreams I would have spent all my research money on a cure for flatulence." The three horses splashed across a stream, climbing steadily now.

Susan laughed. "I still think you deserve the Nobel Prize."

"Relieving the world's diarrhea problems through genetic engineering makes one fabulously rich, but earns no professional respect whatsoever."

Behind them, the view was stunning, a full mile of untouched wilderness. It felt odd to know that he owned very nearly everything within view, even from the highest vantage. Only in Montana was there enough land to tackle the really big projects that made his wife happy.

"After this, Alex, nobody will even bother remembering all the little things you did in your reckless youth."

Impatient with the two romantics, and smiling with anticipation, Cassie led them toward the top of the ridge. All around the valley, thick pine and aspen forests covered the hills. Cassie slowed her horse as they entered a rank of thoroughly stripped trees that showed long scraped gouges in the bark.

Susan was amazed, and concerned. "They're foraging all the way up here? They shouldn't be wandering so far afield." She urged her gray mare into the great field of sedges and sages so carefully arranged by innumerable days of gardening.

Cassie cocked her hat back with a wry smile. "Do you want to be the one to tell them where they can and can't go, Ma'am?"

Alex made a mental note to see about putting a few sonic "discouragers" up here. He couldn't imagine what would happen if a stray happened to wander down the valley to within view of the protesters at the gate. Then he'd have to deal with the local sheriff, the Feds, a dozen regulatory agencies, and a host of tabloids. . . .

As they emerged from the aspens, the girl's sweeping arm drew Alex's attention to the grassy lowland in the bowl of the valley. "See, they always come together at dusk. It's the best time to watch."

Their horses standing close together, the three of them looked down onto Clement Valley in the last light of afternoon. Susan could barely tear her dark eyes from the sight below, but she gave her husband a loving glance that said, *We did this, you and I.*

Alex stood transfixed by the slowly moving shapes before him. His company had been right to keep the media resolutely away from the valley, and here was the proof. You had to see the woolly mammoths for yourself.

Whenever he had a fresh glance at the herd, the beasts seemed like sailing ships. There was a stately glide to their passage as the great russet vessels crossed the flatness, each beast moving as though before steady winds. Only slowly did the mammoths tack and turn, ponderous yet inevitable.

As if Cassie had trained them to recognize her, the nearest behemoth raised its head and let out a long, soaring salute. The next took up the sound, and the next, and soon nearly three dozen massive beasts joined in the trumpeting call.

Alex felt an eerie shiver travel down the length of his spine. The strange, echoing song reached even deeper into his primal core, building in layer after layer, delving into bass notes seldom heard outside the cathedrals of Europe. Even when the haunting chorus faded into the soft sigh of a breeze among the shadowed pines, the three human interlopers remained still, afraid to move as if they had been the ones transported through time, not the mammoths.

"Humans haven't heard that call in ten thousand years," Susan said as she leaned over to kiss him. He was too overwhelmed to say anything at all.

With Cassie in the lead, sitting high on her roan mare, Alex and Susan rode down toward the mammoths in the last light of afternoon. The herd was accustomed to horses, and especially to the smell of the young ranch hand who tended them. Raised entirely without predators, the mammoths were unwary. Though his gelding seemed a bit skittish,

Alex did not feel threatened as he approached the magnificent woolly behemoths.

The sedge grasses were tall and resilient, grazed short and trampled flat especially around the muck of watering holes. Playing the Helyx CEO, Alex noted that at the grassy margins the cottonwood branches and even bitterbrush were being browsed down to nubs. He would have to speak to the tenders about keeping the food supply going so the animals didn't wander into the stands of trees bounding the meadows. Soon, the herd would outgrow this valley.

He made a mental note to look into buying even more land, maybe expanding the huge Helyx Ranch into adjacent valleys. The politics of doing that would be far worse than the economics; the perpetual gang of Evo demonstrators at the South Gate would grow, joined by garden-variety environmentalists. Folks around here didn't look much to the future—or to the distant past, either, it seemed—and they didn't like change. . . .

With the approach of the horses, the mammoths snorted and stirred. Bullwinkle, the big leader of the herd, hung his shaggy head and lowered long tusks as he gazed at the others. The mixed-bag of hairy elephants had a range of body types, each generation only a few years separated from the previous, and each one significantly woollier than either of the two hybrid mammophants Alex had allowed Geoffrey Kinsman to see.

Cassie halted her mare beside a tree completely stripped of leaves and half of its bark. "Best to tie up our horses here." She dismounted with the springy grace of a gymnast. "I prefer to walk among them."

"Aren't you afraid of getting stepped on?" Susan asked.

The ranch hand flipped her braid back between her

shoulderblades and adjusted her hat. "No, Ma'am. But I'm afraid for the horses."

The few stands of valley grass darkened to jade as the sun settled on the distant blue mountains. A nighthawk flitted with thin cries above the willows of a narrow creek that meandered through the meadow. Alex's eyes followed the hawk up toward the peaks that towered against a hard cobalt sky already dotted with the fires of far suns. The light would fade fast, dark scarcely an hour away.

A perfect night to camp.

Cassie started ahead, glancing over her shoulder and resisting the impulse to leave the other two behind. Alex remembered when he had been that impatient, and that young—not so long ago. Though this entire project had sprung from his wife's dream decades ago, Cassie Worth was the unrelenting factotum who supercharged the Helyx staff and never seemed to sleep. She ran down innumerable practical details about exotic animal husbandry, and she figured out the answers for herself when no alleged "expert" had a clue.

Alex reflected as he watched the young woman move swiftly through the herd. To think that she had just applied to Helyx out of the blue. No advanced degrees, just solid experience at UC Davis, a farm upbringing, and an ache to bring back to the world something long gone. Alex had noted more common sense in Cassie than in half of his own VPs and Division Heads. And she had a real rapport with the animals.

"Come on you guys, I want to show them off, but I'll need to get us back up on the slope where I can set up camp for the night . . . or did you change your minds again?" She turned her clear blue eyes to Alex—did he see a girlish crush there? He was abashedly reminded that he had canceled their plans three previous times for the usual "business reasons."

"Nothing's more important tonight." Alex reached over to stroke Susan's shoulder. "My wife and I are going to sleep out under the stars."

"Where I can hear my mammoths snore," Susan added.

They moved among the gigantic but gentle animals; it seemed to Alex as if he had wandered into a truck stop filled with living, hairy semis. The heavy air was laden with smells like hot oiled leather, old upholstery, musk and fur—stronger than the closeness of bison or penned cattle. But it was a wild musk, from thick and wiry hair grown to protect the beasts from the cold of an Ice Age.

Alex felt giddy.

It was a pure joy to watch Cassie in her element, like a child at a petting zoo. She led them from one large bulk to the next. Alex had never before seen so many of the beasts together in the valley. In a single glance he could see that each successive generation had fewer of the humped backs of African elephants. Instead, the younger hybrids' backs sloped down, the rich cinnamon-colored pelts thickened, and the males' tusks grew.

Closer and closer.

Cassie reached beneath the coat of the nearest hybrid and pulled up the coarse guard hair to reveal silky red under-wool. "It's so good now we should be able to leave them out all through next winter."

"Even in Montana's worst?" Alex asked, trying not to sound as if he was just protecting his investment.

"They'll love it," Susan said, smiling at the young woman.

"And they're getting interested in mating with each other now!" Cassie said, then lowered her voice as if embarrassed. "I follow them on the vidcams, and they really go at it. Just frisky play, so far. After all, they haven't reached adolescence yet. But the males are starting to herd the females—another sure sign."

Susan said softly, "We can't actually let them mate, though."

Cassie cried, "Why not? Just think—no more egg transfers, no sperm-sucking games to play." Her face wrinkled in disgust, and Alex didn't want to imagine the details of the mammophant sperm-harvesting operations.

Susan put an arm around Cassie. "We're careful with their genes. Select for mammoth aspects, weed out the elephant ones. Unchecked mating would scramble all that."

Cassie looked stricken. Plainly this had been her big announcement.

"But you're right," Susan hastily added. "Just like in nature. Desire is the only sure diagnostic." She gave her husband a quick, sultry glance. His breath caught. "These animals know, right down in their hearts—which by the way are bigger than a human head, bigger even than Alex's!—that they are worth making more of."

He hugged her. "And so we'll make more." *Some people buy diamonds for their wives . . . I clone mammoths.*

Cassie made quick jabs at nearby shapes, showing off as she quickly recited the names of the other hybrids. "Those two are Rachel and Napoleon—the shorter ones are always the worst—and Angel Pie."

Alex was amazed she could identify the individual herd members so easily. The Helyx geneticists had used five to ten elephants for each step of the process, because it took twelve years for any one of the hybrids to mature to fertility. And some interbreeding attempts spontaneously aborted, Nature's editing.

Cassie led them unerringly to a huffing female, her big eyes casting a calm gaze down at the small humans. Long breaths steamed in the cooling air as dew condensed on the rocks and trampled grass. "Here, Majestica is at term and already showing signs of labor. Everything's normal, as far as I can tell. She's been in labor for about a week already."

"I can't imagine being in labor for a week," Susan said.

And the big female's gestation period had already taken nearly two years. "Mammoths and elephants aren't in much of a hurry about these things," Alex said.

Actually, the gestation period had varied with each hybrid generation, as the offspring approached pure mammoth stock. According to her continuing researches into the original genome, using numerous fourth-order projections with hypercomputers inside the pine-walled stable building, Susan was convinced that the mammoth gestation time in the Pleistocene would have been longer than a modern elephant's twenty-two months. One of the earlier female hybrids, Alexandria, had carried her baby for twenty-three months.

"We're converging toward the mammoth pattern in the ancient wild, I bet," Susan said.

Alex smiled wryly. Given her anxious attention to all aspects of the projects, his wife probably would have preferred to keep the pregnant Majestica in a separate corral back at the Pleistocene Hospital, with a whole bank of real-time blood-test gear, round-the-clock technicians, and a full array of instrumentation and diagnostics surrounding her pregnant bulk.

However, these creatures needed to bear their young naturally, in the wild, and Cassie Worth had seen more live births among ranch stock than any of Helyx's experts. She was ready.

But no one alive had ever seen the birth of a real woolly mammoth.

The smoke of green branches and dry wood wafted up from the campfire, crackling with a pungent, sweet bitterness. Alex breathed deeply, smelling the heady primal scent. Hidden in the gathering darkness, insects and night birds set up a simmering background music that seemed to come from a different time altogether.

Below them in the valley, under the light of the waxing moon and a billion stars in transparent Montana air, the herd of elephant-mammoth hybrids settled down for the night. Many of the big dark shapes still moved about restlessly. While some slept like mounds of dirt near the watering hole, others paced around, munching on sedge grass. Eerily, some of the mammoths on the fringe looked as if they were keeping watch.

Cassie busied herself, happy to be out camping, much more comfortable here within sight of her mammoths than up around the administration buildings. She never tried to understand the protesters, preferring to ignore them by staying far from the gate. "People always find something to complain about, especially when somebody else is successful," she had said once.

The young woman had outdone herself with the fire, the bedrolls, the childishly simple dinner of hot dogs roasted on twigs over the flames, a speckled blue-enamel coffee pot hung over the coals. All they needed was marshmallows (and Alex wouldn't have been surprised if Cassie had them stashed in her saddlebags). A perfect evening, in every detail.

Helyx could have provided the most sophisticated camp equipment, thermal chargers for foodpacks, heated sleeping bags and damp-resistant tents. Alex could have assigned workers to set up comfort-weave tents, groom the clearing, erect tables, string lanterns, even prepare a gourmet meal.

But this was better, much better.

"When do we start singing Kum-bay-ya?" Alex said with a grin to his wife.

"I have a strummerpack," she answered, calling his bluff.

Alex's implanted pager tingled, and he recognized the source. He reached up, touching a contact point. "What's the trouble, Ralph?"

Susan frowned at him, mouthed the words, *I thought you turned that off?*

"Can't figure, Boss." His usually casual voice now sounded pinched with concern. "We're getting pinged by microwaves. Somebody's interrogating a passive receiver. Must be located somewhere around the ranch buildings."

"Not one of ours?"

"No chance. Just a simple incoming pulse from some airplane, flying pretty high. Don't think anybody could get much from that, maybe just a location marker. The pulse could be hitting some tiny receiver that shoots it back with a li'l information attached, I'd guess. Not powerful enough for us to track down where it is, though."

"Probably some new gear brought in by the demonstrators at the gate," Alex suggested. He didn't need a new technical puzzle to ruin his jealously planned evening.

"Could be, Boss. Those Evo types have plenty to spend on new toys."

"Keep on it." He disengaged the pagerlink, saw both Cassie and Susan staring at him with concern. He made a placating gesture but didn't volunteer any details. The ranch hand would assume it was yet another corporate emergency such as had canceled their first three outings; Susan, though, could read his expression much better. Her molasses-brown eyes trapped him again, looking like bottomless wells in the smoky campfire shadows.

He leaned against Susan as they both stared into the throbbing orange and yellow embers. Their clothes smelled of sweat mixed with the musk of mammoths. Alex preferred this sharp but resonant aroma to the infrequent, expensive perfumes his wife felt obligated to wear at ecological fundraisers—like the recent one she'd skipped in Miami.

Under the stars, Alex helped with the bedding down chores, glad for the chance to get his hands dirty rather than just pound on a computer keyboard all day. It felt good, and safe, to be out here, "just like a real person."

The crackling wood made him think of the prehistoric hunters, Cro-Magnon warriors who had tracked herds like this using spears and pits and cliffs to kill the giant animals for food, fur, and ivory.

Like the restored bison on the Great Plains, Susan's dream-experiment might turn out to be so wildly successful that large numbers of these once-extinct creatures could roam the open Montana range. They might wander north into Saskatchewan and Alberta, heading up toward the subarctic regions for which their huge bodies were designed.

He had been so focused on working one generation after another, converging toward a full-blood woolly mammoth, that he had not let his mind wander far into future possibilities.

"Maybe one day we'll have a large herd of mammoths that breed true and reproduce in the wild." He ran fingers over Susan's hair, recalling Kinsman's concern (one of his few legitimate ones) about the impact a sizable group of such huge grazers would have on the landscape and environment. What if they had to thin the herd? "Can you imagine if we had enough of them that we could even sponsor a good old-fashioned mammoth hunt?"

Cassie, very protective of the animals, glared across the fire at him. "What! Use guns on my mammoths?" She had been working here only two years, but the mammoths were *hers.* "Not unless you play fair." The girl's firm lips curled into a devilish grin on her freckled face. "Dress your big-game hunters in furs, then send them out with stone axes and sapling spears. Pleistocene rules. I don't think you'd get many takers."

"Not me," Susan said. "Not for all the testosterone in the world."

Alex returned a noncommittal smile. He did not argue, but he knew both women were wrong. Over the years, he had encountered any number of too rich, too bored, dot-com millionaires or genetics patent holders—people who had delusions of immortality and an overblown sense of necessary machismo.

Even with Pleistocene rules, Alex knew he could find plenty of takers. . . .

As he bedded down next to Susan, the moon continued to rise, spilling silver light. Even here, as isolated as one could be in the continental U.S., he felt as if he were under a spotlight. He couldn't sleep, and he knew Susan was awake and thinking beside him.

Below, the mammoths sounded restless. Snuffles and loud snorts rippled through the big animals. Most of them seemed awake. On the other side of the fire, young Cassie sat alone, her knees drawn up to her chin as she stared down into the valley, reflecting the animals' uneasiness.

Alex couldn't imagine what possible threats or predators

could worry the gigantic prehistoric beasts this deep within ranch property. "Are they like this every night?"

Impishly, Cassie raised her eyebrows. "I *do* have quarters of my own back in the complex, Dr. Pierce. Sleeping outdoors is a treat for me, too."

A bright meteor streaked overhead, low and horizontal, like a rocket on the Fourth of July. It came over the line of trees on the ridge, flying hot, traveling with a speed and deadly accuracy that surpassed any shooting star.

Make a wish . . .

Susan was already on her feet, leaping out of the blankets on the damp ground. "It's heading toward the lab complex!"

The trail of fire faded into orange against midnight blue, and the incandescent arrow struck the valley behind them with a bright flash. The main Helyx compound. A muffled *whump*.

As Alex lurched to his feet, the implanted pager tingled again. "Boss, we've been hit down here. Somebody sent in a mini-cruise, I'd say. Hit the pines close to the Hospital . . . still trying to assess the damage."

"A mini-what?" Alex subvocalized, and his words went back to Ralph.

"Backpack-sized cruise missile, Boss. Short-range, with a nose full of high explosive. A man can carry one a fair way, then launch it from a rack."

Susan was already racing for her horse while Alex paused to get an update. "I'm going there!" she shouted and swung herself up bareback. "Short Stuff and Middle Man are still in the corral."

"Wait! You can't do anything—"

"Just work things out with Ralph," she called over her shoulder, then raced her horse down the four-wheel-drive road and disappeared into the shadowed trees. He had never seen her ride like that before.

Reacting on instinct, Cassie was at their supply packs. She withdrew the two shotguns she had carried with them, ostensibly for protection against coyotes or bears.

Alex didn't need to think hard about who might have done such a thing. "Kinsman was a decoy," he said to Ralph. "Him and his supposedly reasonable discussion, he was just a plant to get inside. But how could they target the hospital in the dark and from so far away?"

"I'm willing to bet they targeted this place with those microwave echoes I keep hearing. If Kinsman planted some sort of passive echo locator—"

"His pen! Damn, I didn't even think! He left it on purpose. They could have targeted from that. I'm packing up Cassie, and we'll be right down there."

Before Alex could switch off, the Security chief said, "Wait—that's gunfire. Jesus, those bastards are coming in from the South Gate!" Ralph's voice strayed for a moment as he barked orders to a security crew, who scrambled in response. "The Hospital's in flames, Boss. We're sending people in to try and rescue the animals."

"Keep yourself safe," Alex barked. "Susan's already on her way." He thought of the two adult mammophants in the corral, the wonderful dodos and moas, all the exotic and frightening animals he kept in the solid-wall pens in the back of the Hospital. And all of his people. He prayed his wife would be safer down there with Ralph and his crew than up here. "We're coming in—"

Another thin patter of popgun shots rang out. Alex thought he was getting Ralph's background noise until Cassie cried, "Just below us!"

"Ralph, we've got intruders up here, too."

"Clement Valley! Jesus, do you want me to send a—"

"You just do your job there. And watch Susan's back, dammit."

He shut down his link and studied the shadowy trees. Another few shots, yes, nearby. One of the mammoths bellowed in surprise, or perhaps pain, sounding like a squeaky cannon.

"Hey!" Cassie tossed Alex one of the shotguns, and he caught it instinctively. The weapon felt hard and cold and strange in his hand. She looked at him with an anguished face. "Maybe that missile hitting the Hospital was just to get our forces away—so they could come up here and kill my mammoths." She swung herself up onto her already frightened mare and bent low, snatching the tether rope. "I'm going down to the herd."

The gunshots came faster as she rode hard down into the valley.

"Wait!" Alex called after her—pointlessly—then got his butt in gear.

He mounted his own gelding and followed her into the darkness. Here he was, the head of a gigantic international corporation—and his wife and a young girl had both jumped into action while he stood around and talked to himself.

The horses were already uneasy with the smell of the mammoths, and the pattering gunfire spooked his mount even more. He caught up to the young ranch hand as she tried to see down into the darkness. "You leave the mammoths alone!"

"Quiet!" he urged, fearing the shadowy attackers might target Cassie instead of the animals.

Sharp, flat shots from their left.

Alex saw dim shapes running, stalking closer, as if intimidated by coming so close to the prehistoric beasts. Simple rifles would have little effect on a woolly mammoth, he thought—just before another round of muffled percussive bangs.

A few seconds, then distant explosions came from the open valley floor.

"Grenade launchers."

"You bastards!" Cassie screamed.

"Hush! They don't know we're up here." He and the young ranch hand were still on a slope above the trees, a hundred meters from the open grassland. They urged their horses closer. It was quiet for a moment, a deathly stillness.

The mammoths churned about, grunting, drawing closer like covered wagons circling against a Comanche attack. Amazingly, acting on instinct, the bigger bulls formed outer ranks, clearly to protect the rest of the herd. The alpha male, Bullwinkle, with its huge tusks and russet fur, snorted and moved forward like a locomotive, looking for an enemy.

No sign of the shadowy figures, but the fringe forests offered plenty of cover.

Alex knew that Cassie's first thought was for Majestica, the pregnant female about to give birth to the first pure mammoth. They rode toward her, and Alex prayed the beasts could tell the difference between friendly humans and deadly ones.

Abruptly, scarlet fireballs burst a hundred meters away . . . and another right on top of them. One of the wild grenades struck Majestica between the shoulders, and the impact knocked even the giant female battleship flat to the ground, her upper body cratered with ragged, flashburn wounds.

Cassie screamed. She threw herself off her horse and raced to the fallen pregnant female.

Alex waved his shotgun around, then took a few high potshots, hoping the retaliatory gunfire would at least stall the attackers, send them scrambling for cover. But it was a pitiful gesture at this range. None of the terrorists came out of the tree line.

Gunshots rang out and ineffectual bullets peppered the mammoth-elephant hybrids, sending them trumpeting into a frenzy. Some charged, stopped, trumpeted. But the big male Bullwinkle thundered into the night, toward the attackers hiding in the trees.

Alex dismounted and came up beside a determined but weeping Cassie. His heart wrenched, knowing they had all been betrayed. The young woman impatiently swiped tears from her eyes and got to work. "Damn, Dr. Pierce—I don't have the equipment for this!"

Back in the forest, startled shouts turned to shrieks. Alex could well imagine the giant bull trampling the bastards into paste on the ground. Bullwinkle hooted, a powerful bellow that brought more shrill screams. A grenade burst near the beast, then the big mammoth was into the trees, smashing branches, splintering trunks, following the panicked outcries.

More screams. He did not think further about what Bullwinkle was doing. He could see only the pregnant mammoth's blood shining dark and wet in the moonlight. "Don't worry. I'll help," he said to Cassie. Corporate CEO bullshit, but it seemed to be what she needed to hear. He knelt beside her, trying to anticipate what the young woman was trying to do. She worked with utter concentration, adrenaline, and desperation, staving off panic.

As he tore off his shirt and wadded it up into a large pad—nowhere near enough, he saw, as he pressed it into the gaping wound—he heard a faint sound and looked around. Other mammoth hybrids bellowed, but the gunfire had halted for the moment. Bullwinkle's work?

The whispery sound of feet in the sedge grasses came nearer. Cassie didn't notice it. Bare-chested, Alex backed away from the dying animal, leaving his shirt to soak up a gusher of blood. He smelled gunpowder and meat. "They're coming back," he said. Grabbing his shotgun from the trampled ground, he moved as quietly as he could around Majestica's massive bulk.

"Keep them the hell away from my mammoths," Cassie said, her voice thin. She didn't even look up from Majestica.

Alex jacked a shell into the shotgun, hoping the flat clack-click sound would be enough of a deterrent. *Never.* Halfway around the heaving beast, he crouched down, looking across the moonlit expanse.

He cursed himself as much as the fanatics. He had underestimated their dedication, dismissing them entirely. He had scoffed at their mindset, never giving them credit for a zeal that would push them beyond theoretical protests. How could they be so *vehement?* There was a long, precarious bridge between waving signs and launching missiles, but Kinsman and his Evos had crossed it.

He'd considered the Luddites to be quaint, backward, even silly. Now they had proved deadly. Causes had always attracted violent crusaders whose actions seemed inexplicably extreme to most people—pro-lifers shooting abortion doctors, environmentalists "protecting the Arizona desert" by setting fire to luxury homes. Could any ends justify such means?

The Evo crusaders came out of the trees, hunched over as they emerged from the protective shadows. They were competent enough, moving quickly, not talking. But Alex saw the reflection of their eyes as they covered the last twenty meters. Three that he could see, two headed directly this way, weapons ready . . . thinking they had already won.

He raised the shotgun and a lot of thoughts ran through his mind. It was easy enough to think you could shoot at an enemy, someone with a grease-blackened face and cradling a grenade launcher, pistol strapped at his waist. But when it was a kid of maybe twenty . . .

The kid raised an arm to his comrades, who immediately squatted and aimed—at Majestica. And Cassie! They knew their target. They knew exactly what they intended to shoot.

And Alex had no time left for doubt. Executives, he often said to others, were people who could make decisions on time. Well, here was one. He shot the kid with a spray of pellets. He hit him in the legs, but square on.

Alex did not let himself hear the screaming as he jacked the next shell in, sighted on a man who had half-risen to his feet and was swinging a long-barreled weapon toward Alex. "Cassie, get down!" he yelled, then sighted and squeezed off the round. The feel of the gun was as natural as when he'd potted away at clay pigeons on weekends, long ago.

Now the third Evo, a woman—but she was already running away. He let the terrorist take three more strides to be sure she was out of lethal range. The blast of pellets against her shoulders and backpack did not knock her down, but she cried out, and ran even faster in a headlong stagger back toward the trees.

The first kid was yelling, rolling around with his bloody-hamburger legs drawn up to his chest. The second man lay still; Alex didn't even know where he'd hit the terrorist. The woman made it to the trees, where Bullwinkle was still crashing around. Alex kept down—the Evos had plenty of distance weapons, and would be looking toward the source of his shots.

"Dr. Pierce! I need your help here!" Cassie sounded closer to panic than he had ever heard her.

Slinging the shotgun low, ready to spin around and open fire again into the night, Alex scrambled back around the dying Majestica.

Susan rode hard, and her horse was hot, its mouth foaming as she careened down the bumpy jeep road. She could see the darkness of trees and night blended with probing beams of hard white surveillance lights ahead.

She and Alex had always talked about beefing up security in an apron covering the entire approach from the South Gate. When the protesters had settled in, they'd brought their own lights, as well as coolers of food and drink, so they could squat down and begin chants and drum beating in a general disruptive "people power" party. They kept it up until the early hours, youthful idealism uniting with the universal instinct to party. Annoying, certainly, and frustrating—but nothing to be taken seriously.

That had been their biggest mistake.

Occasionally, those little protests had only been a distraction, a cover for one or two Evos to slip past the fencing and guard stations in the dark. Once inside, though, they had no good idea which targets to go for, what vandalism to accomplish. Inept commandos, they generally blundered into staff housing or maintenance sheds, which had been deliberately disguised to look like laboratories and stables.

But now, the log-fronted Pleistocene Hospital was on fire. They had struck directly to the heart of the retrograde evolution project.

"Damn you," she said. "Damn you all." She kicked her horse, riding harder.

The tall pines surrounding the corral had become torches in the night, crackling resinous flames. From inside the high, reinforced fences she heard a roar, an indescribable screaming cry that sounded like nothing human. Short Stuff and Middle Man, the first two mammophant hybrids, were still in there, far from the safety of the rest of their herd . . . brought back to the ranch buildings for regular health monitoring.

Susan dismounted from her gray mare before the horse had even come to a stop. She hit the ground running and, frightened by the noise and the smoke, the exhausted mare trotted away in confusion. The fire from the Ponderosa pines had already descended to the corral fence. Susan slammed through the gate, calling out to the two oldest mammophants.

Middle Man had backed to the far corner, away from the burning trees, away from the light. The big male trumpeted a sound like anguish, obviously frightened and confused. He bled from several wounds in his thick hide, but the injuries seemed relatively minor. Susan didn't even stop to consider whether Middle Man might charge her.

In the center of the trampled enclosure lay Short Stuff, collapsed to the ground like a defeated calf in a rodeo spectacle. High-powered gunshots had blasted both of her forelegs, ripping gouges in muscle and bone until the female hybrid had crashed. Short Stuff chuffed and hooted as she struggled on the grass, her legs bloody and useless appendages.

In shock, revulsion, and helplessness, Susan swayed backward, grabbed for the corral fence to support herself, but missed. Watery-kneed, she sank down, and froze, utterly unable to do anything. Short Stuff trumpeted again in unspeakable pain.

Ralph Duncan strode into the corral, swinging his head from side to side, taking in details. His eyes had always looked world-wise, as if they'd already seen everything, but now his face had a disgusted horror. "God damn! God *damn!*"

He strode forward like an avenger, holding the powerful rifle at his side. Susan made a strangled sound, and he whirled, ready to shoot, but when he recognized her, his expression instantly changed. "Miz Pierce!"

Short Stuff let out another hollow, trumpeting call. Ralph's expression hardened, and he turned away from Susan, ignoring her. Without hesitation, he marched up to the writhing, wounded mammophant, pushed the barrel of his rifle up against the base of Short Stuff's massive skull, and pulled the trigger. The hybrid groaned and slumped. Ralph shot her again, then turned back to Susan. His face was ruddy and murderous. "God damn it!"

Shaking, Susan pushed back to her feet, then grabbed the corral fence and vomited. More shouts and gunshots came from the main lab complex. Through the fence and the trees she could see flames shooting from the admin building. She coughed and spat. "How many are there? What—"

He took her arm and led her out the gate. "Middle Man's fine for now. I've got security troops split between defending the ranch and trying to fight the fires." He touched his earpiece, listened, then shouted, "Dammit, don't wait for the sheriff! Just move on it!"

Susan heard the distant patter of gunfire, military-style commands, and the frenzied shouts of shadowy attackers. They could have broken through the fences anywhere. Were these the same protesters that had innocuously waved their signs and posed for the TV cameras? Could it all have been a feint, a ploy to let Helyx security believe the Evos were in-effectual whiners and bored activists in search of a cause . . . when all the while they were planning this brutal strike as soon as they could get a man inside?

She saw birds fluttering in the trees, the passenger pigeons disturbed from their nests in the big oaks. "I'm going to the Hospital!" She heard sounds that could only be giant moas squawking in panic. "Ralph, get those fires put out!"

As she ran toward the Hospital, Ralph yelled louder into his voice pickup. On one side of the main admin building, a few men had set up a hose and were spraying the yellow flames on the log walls, but fiery fingers already crept along the roof.

Susan didn't give a damn about the computers and office furniture inside. She ran toward the Hospital itself where all the retrograde hybrids were kept, her life's work, the maturing ambassadors of species long extinct. Why would anybody want to harm them?

Probably the same people who break into cancer-research centers and "liberate" all the experimental animals, she thought. *I guess they don't see the contradiction.*

Out in the Hospital yard, she saw tall, ostrich-like moas set free from their cages, wandering around in terrified confusion. Brown feathers ruffled, serpentine necks swiveling about, horny beaks open with hissing squawks, they kicked up dirt with lizard-like feet and pecked at any person who came close. Ungainly dodos scrambled about like overgrown, drunken chickens, honking in fright. Susan heard other animals scream and yowl from within the Hospital itself. Smoke oozed through several broken windows, growing thicker, blacker.

Just then a man with a prim face and dapper-looking clothes stepped across the porch holding a revolver in his hand. Geoffrey Kinsman. Like a grim executioner, he pointed at the dodos and methodically shot them all, moving from one to the next to the next.

Though armed with nothing but her anger, Susan raced toward him. Other protesters ran past Kinsman into the lab building, not willing to simply let the fire do its work.

Kinsman turned toward the closest frightened moa, putting three bullets through its long neck. The giant bird toppled like a fallen tree. Not even pausing to reflect on his handiwork, the man stalked toward the smashed-open door of the Hospital and vanished inside.

Susan screamed in outrage, but Kinsman didn't even notice her.

After stepping over the shattered carcasses of the magnificent lost birds, she barged into the main laboratory. Evos were overturning desks, smashing computers, dumping animal feed on the floor in a wild frenzy, like capering cannibals celebrating the arrival of a boatload of missionaries. These crusaders had no organization, no plan, just chaos.

Dressed in her jeans and camping clothes, Susan entered the lab, smelling the fire and spilled chemicals, the blood and nose-tingling gunsmoke.

In the harsh, stinging smoke she saw Geoffrey Kinsman, proud slayer of helpless dodos and moas, trotting from cage to cage, shooting every creature inside. Fast, methodical, intent.

Susan's eyes burned with disgust. Ducking through the smoky light, she went to the cages on the other side, past lab furniture, desks, equipment racks. She threw open cage doors and coops, chasing the dodos, moas, and other hybrids out, giving them a chance. Squawking and hissing, the marvelous creatures ran, fleeing the fire, fleeing the gunshots.

There, dammit! The chaos grew. Shouting and gunshots echoed from outside. She heard a shrill whistle, a bullhorn. A helicopter circling.

Grinning, a blond-haired, clean-shaven man ran past her holding a long shovel, battering file cabinets, smashing beakers, computer screens, even ceramic coffee cups. He took a swipe at a waddling dodo, missed, and Susan grabbed the shovel handle, wrenching it out of his grip.

The man shrugged, then toppled a heavy laser-ROM storage rack, scattering the prismatic platters like Christmas ornaments. He snatched up a crowbar some other protester had dropped.

From nearby came the sound of a window smashing. More strangers ran in through the Hospital door, carrying weapons.

When his pistol was empty, Kinsman took a repeater assault rifle from one of the Evos, checked that it was loaded. Then he looked up and saw Susan. Recognized her.

"Damn you!" she said, raising the shovel as if it was a match for his rifle.

Behind her, the reckless blond Evo grabbed the closed doors of the larger pens at the back of the laboratory. The barricaded, reinforced rooms.

Kinsman hesitated with his rifle, smug with self-justification. "This has to be done."

With a deft twist the blond Evo pried open the lock. He must have expected nothing more than another awkward-looking bird. He held his crowbar loosely in one hand, as if ready to bash a few more animals.

And a saber-tooth cat lunged out at him, already maddened by the fire and the noise.

The big panther's front fangs gleamed, as long as scimitars. It reared up to embrace the man and with a throaty growl it bore him down, muscles moving like liquid beneath its mottled, long-furred coat. The Evo screamed as the panther/sabre-tooth hybrid tore open his chest, raising long curved fangs and plunging once, twice, three times.

Susan managed to shout "No!"—just as a panicked Kinsman opened fire.

On the sedge grass, trampled and bloodstained, Cassie leaned over the gasping, quivering hulk of the fallen Majestica. The female almost-mammoth panted and shuddered, her body core ripped open by the grenades.

"She's dying." Cassie looked up at Alex, her eyes wide and pleading, as if somehow this important corporate executive could do something.

"Yeah," he said uselessly.

She seemed to be in a daze, saw the shotgun slung low in his hand. "You shot at the Evos?"

"Forget them."

Majestica's body heaved and clenched and trembled in spasmodic labor—dying, but also following a biological imperative. Alex heard a snorting and pounding sound and held up his shotgun, ready to defend them against a continued Evo attack—but he saw only the huge head and long curved tusks of the angry Bullwinkle. The large mammoth stomped on the ground, thrashed his shortened trunk.

In the stark, silvery moonlight Alex saw a few flecks of black blood peppering the shaggy fur, minor wounds from gunshots. He had expected to see the bull's long ivory spears coated with gore, his front feet splattered with the blood of crushed humans. But Alex heard the Evos still screaming and crashing away into the night as they fled up the valley.

The bull mammoth had let them live. Bullwinkle could easily have trampled everyone into the ground. Instead, he had just driven them off and turned back to come here. At the moment, Alex himself didn't feel so civilized.

Lumbering close to Majestica, the shaggy bull sniffed, quested with his hairy trunk. Bullwinkle watched with round, wise eyes as Cassie felt the pregnant female's heaving belly, her hands exploring the quivering muscle and tough hide.

She drew her long hunting knife.

The other hybrids milled about nearby, circling and snorting, some trumpeting their pain, all clearly agitated. One of the youngest hybrids waded out to the middle of the muddy watering hole and raised its trunk high as it honked into the night.

The Evos had gone away, their destruction accomplished, leaving pain in their wake. *Making their savage point.* Alex knew he should call Ralph and his security men, bring them out here in Helyx choppers to run the terrorists into the ground, apprehend them and haul them off for Federal prosecution.

But as he knelt beside a blood-streaked Cassie, he didn't feel that was important enough right now.

The pregnant female had closed her intelligent eyes in wrinkles of dark skin, blinking only occasionally. Majestica's breath was slow and deep, a bass-noted wheezing, accompanied by a bubbly wet sound of blood and air oozing from large holes in her massive torso.

Majestica's pelt gleamed, glossy and moist. A heavy musk mixed with the metallic sourness of blood rose from the laboring mountain. The female's pelvis was tilted, her womb clenching as she used the last of her energies to squeeze.

A charge of tension permeated the air, a slow silent sense of gathering energies . . . of time contracting down to a completion.

Cassie pressed her hand against the distended belly. The abdominal muscles shuddered, but Majestica was clearly dying in the moonlight. Even Alex could see that. She wouldn't last long enough to give birth, and the purebred infant woolly mammoth would die inside the womb.

He knew that young Cassie had needed to sacrifice mother animals before, delivering their young by Caesarean. It was a part of ranch life when there were a lot of animals to herd and tend. In her hesitation now, he read that Cassie didn't know if her muscles and her resolve and her knife edge would be up to the task she now faced.

Ralph's hoarse voice chirped in Alex's ear, with words so devastating that Alex could spare no attention for what the young ranch hand was about to do. "Boss, you'd better get back here." The old security chief paused, as if gathering courage. "It's Susan. Get back here now."

Cassie barely looked up as Alex ran to his horse.

Sobbing, she raised her long knife high, hesitated, then plunged it deep.

When Alex rode up to the main Helyx complex, two of the ranch buildings were engulfed in flame. Fire crackled and roared, clean woodsmoke mixed with the foul stench of burning electrical wires, chemicals, and plastics.

He called for Ralph, then he saw the security men dragging bodies out onto the lawn in front of the Pleistocene Hospital. His stomach lurched.

Alex had underestimated the Evos completely, the intensity of their gut-level resistance to what he was doing. And Kinsman himself, a former colleague, was someone who should have known better. Alex had rolled his eyes at the silly signs, foolishly dismissed the objections of people he considered Luddites. "It's not nice to fool with Mother Nature."

Recreating the mammoths had aroused such a passion, such a sense of wonder in his wife—but he had never considered that it might engender equal and opposite emotions in her detractors.

He called for Ralph again, but his voice broke as he stumbled across the yard. The rangy old man jogged up to him, feverish, his leathery face fallen in despair. He threw himself on Alex, both arms around his shoulders. Alex went weak with dread.

"Where is she?" he croaked, but he could tell from the stiffness in the security chief's muscles that he was already too late. "Where is she!"

Ralph staggered back. Without a word he walked with Alex toward the burning Pleistocene Hospital. In the acrid yellow glow, a few surviving animals ran about in panic. Passenger pigeons squawked from the oak trees. Others fluttered across the night sky, escaped from burning nests. Bloody mounds of feathers on the grass marked the slaughtered dodos and moas. *Extinct again.*

He took a few steps, choked on acrid smoke, turned.

Susan lay outside on the ground where Ralph had carried her. She had a crumpled, broken look, he thought abstractedly. That was when the fog began to wrap itself around him, dulling the clamor, shrouding the world in a ghostlike slowness. He shook his head, but the fog remained. His field of view telescoped away and he staggered. He reached out to steady himself on a beam and his hand felt nothing. Sour air rasped into his lungs. The iron taste of blood told him he had bitten his tongue. And the soft fingers of fog thickened.

The feathers of ancient birds fluttered around her like a halo, catching the glow of hot white security spotlights. Her flannel shirt had soaked up the crimson blood. She lay, waxen, lifeless. He did not count the gunshot wounds.

In the background he barely heard Ralph's security men shouting. Ranch workers, in shock and keeping themselves moving with forced activity, braved the inferno of the lab to rescue a few remaining experimental animals from their cages. To salvage some of the records. To preserve cellular specimens. Sometime in the distant future, he would probably thank them.

None of that mattered now.

He tried to take two steps toward Susan, but his muscles disobeyed. His knees buckled, weak and watery. Alex collapsed, sitting on the rough ground. Close enough to see her, but she would never again be close enough to touch.

An empty man rode back out to Clement Valley. The cool night air brushed at his face, but he did not feel it. The east brimmed with a pale glow but he did not see it. The soft fog fingers were still there in his head. He shook it.

He found Cassie, her shirt and braided hair and jeans soaked with dark wetness. When he saw the blood, he had a sudden fear that she too had been shot. But she got up on unsteady legs, looking utterly exhausted in the beam of his flashlight.

Then Alex saw the small creature, like a newborn elephant but covered with matted wet fur. It stood already. About the size of a riding lawnmower. The baby mammoth moved on wobbly legs slick with its mother's fluids—aware and healthy. Somber eyes accepted him in a mute communion.

Alex drew a deep breath. A mammoth, the first purebred ambassador from that extinct species, arriving on this night of smoke and blood.

He felt a trickle of amazement through his shell of despair. Though its mother had been murdered by attackers, this fourth-generation offspring had been successfully delivered alive.

In spite of all this. Thanks to Cassie.

"It's a start," she said. Her large, wonder-filled eyes stared at Alex as he touched the thick reddish fur on the young mammoth's sturdy shoulders. He knew he should tell her about Susan, but he wasn't ready to deal with the questions . . . or the sympathy. He couldn't think of anything to say.

"I want to name him Adam," she continued. "Seems appropriate."

The rest of the herd huddled together in the naked night, while Bullwinkle stood near Majestica's carcass. He twitched his trunk, snorting steam plumes in the waning moonlight. Alex imagined the big bull was as anguished at losing his mate as he himself was over Susan. He heard a low, guttural note in its sighs and wheezes that had not been there before.

He turned away. Shared grief was little comfort.

The big animals clustered together, calmer now, as light seeped into the valley. Tall, powerful, magnificent. Back from extinction. Distantly, hollowly, a part of Alex thought that the throwback Evos were a portion of humanity that might be better off extinct. Not these creatures. Not these strong and wonderful miracles that his wife had brought forth from dreams.

Alex stood among the herd and looked at young Cassie, seeing her resolve undampened. She was saying something but he could not hear, somehow.

In Susan's memory, he promised himself that he would carry on this project. Even though he might have to move to the ends of the Earth, where he and the mammoths could be safe . . .

Somehow.

Adam tottered off toward the herd. It waddled in the grass, lit by thin rays of sun, bleached of all color. Bullwinkle saw the small moving thing and sent a blaring trumpet salute. The herd answered with a chorus of bellows and huffs.

In this moment Alex felt his own life slip into insignificance, one more mote beneath the hard stars. One more member of a newcomer species, a mere vessel. His best work lay forever in the past now, but he could still make some difference.

The fog around him cleared, just a bit, letting in the glow of the east. Susan could live only through these creatures, through her work. He would have to speak and care and fight for his wife's memory, too, and for all of her legacy, living and dead.

Clouds were moving in, he noticed absently. It was a shrouded dawn, though it could turn bright.

FANTASY

Sure, I have a degree in Physics and Astronomy, which lends itself to my science fiction interests. However, my minor in college was Russian History, so I also enjoy a great fascination for history and myths. I like to explore blank parts on the map of the imagination, places still marked as "Here Be Monsters."

"Sea Wind" was inspired by the album and eponymous song "Point of Know Return" by *Kansas*, one of my favorite progressive rock bands. After its initial publication, the magazine's compositor came up to me at a convention to tell me that she had cried while typesetting the story. (I didn't ask how often her job drove her to tears.)

Sea Wind

The man had everyone's attention now. He shouted into the milling, familiar chaos surrounding the harbor, forcefully waving the stump of his right hand.

"I have been sent here by the captain of the *Sea Wind*, a three-masted lateener now lying at anchor in your beautiful harbor of Lisbon!" His voice was hoarse and gravelly, as if from too much shouting in his life. Somehow, he had set up a small podium on the wharf, flanked by two burly seamen in fine sailing clothes. Many merchants and workers, wrapped in their own business, flowed around the barely noticed obstacle, but others stopped to listen.

"The captain bids me to tell you that the *Sea Wind* is now taking on crewmembers for a voyage of discovery. We need twenty brave young men, and we will pay well."

Francis, my older brother, pulled me with him as he pushed through the loose crowd, weaving our way closer to the podium, our own task forgotten as he heard the man's speech. I held two newly mended iron hoops in my hand; our father needed them for a barrel he was making in his cooper shop. I tried to tell Francis, but he impatiently made me hold my words. Only a few people were actually listening to the man.

"Where are you sailing?" someone asked.

The man with the stump turned toward the question. "We shall sail westward to the newly discovered island of Madeira, a paradise with jungles, flowers and fruits, and birds the colors of jewels; and then we shall sail southward along the coast of Africa. Our own Prince Henry had commanded us to discover the world—"

"*Prince Henry* himself commissioned your ship?" Francis cried.

The man smiled uncomfortably, turning to gaze down at him. "He has given *all* men the task of exploring the seas, boy. Not two years ago, Prince Henry's own Squire Eannes successfully rounded Cape Bojador in Africa—what was once thought to be Hell itself where men are black as charcoal because they stand so close to the sun, and the ground is a burning lake of sand! Eannes brought back tales of vast lands farther south—and the *Sea Wind* will go *beyond!* To lands of untold riches—pearls as big as your fist, more gold than our ship can carry!"

His words were laced with fever, and he looked directly at Francis, pointing with the raw pink end of his stump.

"Do you remember the stories of the great Marco Polo? Of the riches and exotic lands he visited, of the adventures he had? Would you like to see lands never before beheld by the eyes of Christian men? Would you like to sail with us on the *Sea Wind?*"

Francis's eyes were glittering, and I was uncomfortable. I reached up to tug on his sleeve, but he began to speak. "How long—" he stammered. "How long do I have to decide?"

"The *Sea Wind* will set sail in four days; but we intend to gather the crew today. Are you interested, boy? Can you write your name?"

"Of course!"

I don't know which question he was answering. I was afraid for him, but Francis looked so sure of himself. One of the sailors handed him a stained piece of paper and a quill. Francis refused to meet my gaze and carefully wrote his name. Grandfather had shown him how to write it—Grandfather's name was Francis, too—but he couldn't show me how to write my name. He had never seen what "Stefan" looked like.

The man from the *Sea Wind* smiled at my brother and rested his stump on the wood of the podium as if to say he would have shaken Francis's hand had he been able.

The iron barrel hoops in my hand were getting heavy.

Father turned back to his work, away from Francis, seeming to quell his anger. His voice was gruff. "You can't go. You are my oldest son. I need you here." He began to arrange the staves for the barrel.

Francis wouldn't allow his dreams to be broken so easily. "Stefan knows how to do the work as well as I do—he can carry on! I *am* going, Father. This is what I want to do. I'm old enough now." He paused, still waiting for Father to look at him. "Don't make me run away from home."

Father let the staves fall together with a flat clatter and stood up. He looked tired. "How long?" He drew a deep breath, looking down at the barrel and then at me as if I were part of a conspiracy. "How long will you be gone?"

Francis seemed to fight back a smile. "We'll sail as far as we can down the coast of Africa, maybe to India! I'll bring back more riches than we've ever had! Probably within a year."

Father wasn't as angry as I had thought he would be; he seemed resigned to the fact, as if he had been expecting this to come any day now.

"Well, if you're going to be gone for a year, then you'd better at least help me finish this barrel."

"Look at her!" Francis breathed, staring at the *Sea Wind* lying at anchor in the harbor. We sat on the wharf as the late afternoon sun turned golden, the waves brushing against the docks. The air was heavy with screaming gulls and the moist, salty scent of the sea.

Lisbon, the city that looks like a staircase, stumbled downward from the surrounding hills in successive layers into the Tagus River which spilled into the ocean, forming a calm, sheltered harbor at its mouth.

The *Sea Wind* rocked gently in the sleepy water, giving us a peek at the line of scum and barnacles crusted below the waterline. She was a magnificent ship, one of the largest in the harbor—seventy feet from bow to stern, and could comfortably hold thirty men on a long voyage.

She had three raked masts, fitted with wide triangular lateen sails rippling in the wind, brushing against the spiderweb of rigging which entwined the ship. The *Sea Wind*'s hull was carvel built, as were most of the ships in the harbor, the planks fastened flat against the skeleton, and she was also finely decorated as an exploring ship should be to bear the pride of Prince Henry the Navigator throughout the oceans. The railing was painted gold as was the stem, and the sails were emblazoned with a brilliant scarlet design.

Francis sat in awe, staring at the ship he would call home for the next year, but I could see that wonder blinded his eyes. As I watched the *Sea Wind*, I knew Francis didn't notice that the gold paint on the railing was peeling and scarred by the graffiti carved there by other sailors. The ship creaked more than it should have in the gentle wash of waves, and the wood looked as if it might have shipworm. I squinted my eyes against the sun, and I could make out that the sails had been patched several times, and the thick layers of barnacles showed that the *Sea Wind* had been in the water a long time. The wind seemed to pick up slightly, and the ship creaked loudly.

"Francis," I breathed, frowning, "What if you don't come back?"

"I'll come back."

"But you'll be out on the ocean, alone! Everyone knows of the sea monsters just waiting to prey on sailing ships! And you might sail off the edge of the world! Francis! You're going where nobody has sailed before—what if the *Sea Wind* goes over the edge!"

Francis turned away from the ship, looking at me, his face grim; but I could see the fear behind his eyes.

"Stefan, somebody has to go. Somebody has to show the way. I talked to some of the other seamen—the *Sea Wind* has sailed south once before, but they thought they could never make it past Cape Bojador. They told me terrible stories of the bleak desert that pokes its finger into the sea, making the water dirty brown with suspended sand, and so shallow that the keel scrapes the bottom twenty miles offshore. And they told me of barren cliffs of sandstone, naked, without even a weed growing on them as the sun burns down to bake the rock.

"That was the end of the world, or so they thought. So *we* thought! Until Squire Eannes rounded the Cape, and came back to say there was more of Africa beyond, and more, and more! It was the end of the world before—and now it's perhaps a gateway to India! Somebody's got to go—you know that.

"You were always content with the excitement of Lisbon, with helping Father make his barrels, but you know I've always wanted to go to sea, how I've stared at the ships, heard the sailors' stories. I *have* to go. I don't have any choice."

Francis looked at me, and even though less than a year separated us in age, he seemed infinitely older than me.

"I'll miss you, Francis."

"I'll miss you, too."

One candle in the corner was guttering badly, flashing shadows like moths around the room, randomly switching the patches of light and darkness. It was night, and the candle would be extinguished soon anyway. Francis wanted to be in bed early, for the next morning he would be departing on the *Sea Wind*—but I didn't see how he could sleep this night of all nights. I knew I would be lying awake myself.

Our baby brother Matthew had already been tucked into his basket of straw, supposedly to sleep; but he could sense the tension in the air and his bright eyes watched us as our family sat together in uncomfortable silence.

Father brooded by himself, not looking at Francis—I honestly didn't know if he approved or disapproved, if he were angry or sad.

Mother sat staring at Francis, staring as if she needed to say something but found it impossible to speak. Her fingers played nervously with a loose thread in her faded dress. Her dark hair was drawn back into a braid which was becoming undone, rampant hairs protruding wildly to shine in the uncertain candlelight; her dark eyes glistened from a coating of what might have been tears.

"Francis . . ." her voice was uncertain. "We love you."

The expression on his face showed that he didn't know how to reply. On the other side of the room, baby Matthew stood up on his straw and began bouncing up and down, shouting in his tiny voice.

"How long until I'm old enough? I want to go on a ship too! I want to go with Francis!" he bubbled, and Mother ran to him; she sounded as if she were crying.

After a long moment of uncertainty, Francis looked up and Grandfather, his namesake, met his gaze. Grandfather was seated in his chair, the one he rarely left except when he helped Father in the cooper shop. He was not yet too old to work.

"Francis," Grandfather spoke softly so that Francis was forced to come sit beside him in order to hear his words. I followed my brother.

"Francis . . . you have talked with the other sailors? You know what awaits you . . . out there?"

As a boy, Grandfather had almost embarked on a voyage similar to the one Francis would begin in the morning. But, before the ship had even left the harbor, he had tangled his hand in one of the winch ropes, crushing it, so that he was forced to return home without seeing the sea as he had hoped. Perhaps he looked at Francis with envy because my brother had a chance to complete the voyage he had never been able to go on.

"I've heard the stories," Francis answered. "Of the abyss at the edge of the world where horrible creatures wait to devour unfortunate sailors, and of the great sea serpents and sirens and—"

"And the Kraken? Have you been warned of the Kraken?" The look on Grandfather's face said that he was not going to tell the story, whether he had heard it or not.

Francis remained silent for a moment. "The Kraken . . ." he breathed, looking up into the shadows where the walls met the ceiling. "When you are out there, and the sea turns dark, and the sky turns darker—you'll know. You'll know when the Kraken has come. He is veiled in storms—and when the wind whistles through your rigging and tears at the sails, when the water foams and seethes—you'll know."

Grandfather pushed his face closer to Francis's eyes, "And when the black tentacles thick as your mainmast rise out of the water to wrap around your ship and *crush* it as if it were straw—and when the Kraken drags you under, *screaming,* to feed his children—you'll know. And you won't ever return, Francis, but your bones will keep him company far beneath the sea, alone forever—for the Kraken can never die."

Francis looked nervously around the room.

"And we will wait for you here, a year, maybe two; and we will know what has become of you, Francis . . ."

"Oh, Francis!" I gasped, drawing a breath which was cold with shadows. The candlelight seemed to be dimmer than before.

A different light came into Grandfather's eyes. "But I know that no stories can change your mind. When that sea wind blows, calls you to her—you must follow it, you must go to the sea. I know. There is no other way."

Francis smiled. "You understand." He looked at Father, then back at the old man. "You understand."

It was lonely without Francis.

He had left the morning before, looking both excited and afraid as the *Sea Wind* set her sail, tacking into the wind, and drifted out of the harbor toward the sea. Francis had always been by me, ever since I could remember, to keep boredom away, to talk to.

And now I was alone.

The room was dark, and the air was hot and thick with moisture, scented by the wood Father was soaking for his barrels. Light rain trickled against the side of the house, runneling down the white plaster. Faint echoes of thunder rumbled in the distance.

Francis was gone.

Baby Matthew was crying off in the corner, frightened by the storm. I heard Mother comforting him, whispering into his tiny ear. "It's just rain, little Matthew. The storm won't hurt you—it's far away. The storm is far, far out at sea."

The storm was out at sea.

My straw bed was damp from moisture, and I knew I would waste my time trying to sleep for a while yet. Silently, I crept to the window and placed the canvas curtain, cut from an old sail, behind my head, peering out into the night. A mist of ricocheting raindrops glistened on my face.

The cobblestoned streets were wet, reflecting the distant flashes of lightning. The other buildings, every one of them a white box with narrow windows decked with flowers, sat in a frozen tumble scattered down the steep levels of the city in jerky steps toward the harbor.

I could barely make out the dark water of the harbor, and I certainly couldn't see the ocean; but the storm was out there, and so was Francis.

Is the sea dark now, Francis, and the sky filled with storm clouds even darker? Is the wind singing through the rigging, tearing at the sails? Is the water white foam boiling against the side of the ship, crashing on the deck? Is that roar of thunder your cry for help?

I could picture him standing at the rail, his knuckles white and his fingers gripping onto the peeling gold carvings scarred by the graffiti, trying to hold himself steady against the screaming wind and crashing waves, peering down into the dark sea, white with terror and waiting for the black tentacles of the Kraken to reach up and smash the *Sea Wind.*

Francis!

Will you ever return to us?

Days later I found myself walking alone on the beach; I had come far from the harbor. As if the storm had never been, the sun beat down to strike away my sweat.

The greatest loneliness was past now, and I was learning to be Stefan, instead of "Francis's brother." Father had begun teaching me what needed to be done to be a cooper; and already I was becoming more independent. Perhaps, when Francis came back I would even be ready to embark on a voyage of my own.

But I would wait a year for my brother. I would wait to hear his stories, what perils he had survived. Mother was already seeking out sailors to see if they had any news of the *Sea Wind* and when it would return. But I could be patient and wait for Francis, though I would miss him.

The sun glared on the water, but I shaded my eyes to see a dark shape floating toward the beach, a piece of driftwood. I watched it bob along for a few moments and finally, when patience deserted me, I waded out to retrieve it.

I stood with warm water lapping about my waist, soaking into my coarse shirt; and I looked at the wood.

It was a piece of wreckage, part of a ship, probably the splintered remnant of a rail. I turned it over, but in my heart I already knew.

Peeling gold paint . . . scratched and obscured by sailors' graffiti.

The ocean made soft rushing noises, and I stared at the rail for a long time. Many ships were the same, many ships could have shed that piece of wood—but my mind had no doubt.

Mother would continue to wait, day after day, for some word, watching for the *Sea Wind* to return. How long will you wait, Mother?

I let the driftwood slip back into the water and I pushed it away from shore. I knew I wouldn't tell her.

I turned and walked back toward the beach, washing the flecks of gold paint from my hands.

When we were first dating, Rebecca diligently read most of my stories. After she'd finished quite a few, she gave me a near-impossible challenge: "I want you to write a story that has a happy ending for once."

This was her Valentine's Day present.

Frog Kiss

He had gotten used to it by now. The frog tasted cold and slimy against his lips, with a taste like brackish water, mud, and old compost. But Keric gave it a dutiful smack on its mouth, hoping that it wouldn't suddenly turn in to the fat old king, who had also been enchanted, along with several more desirable members of the royal family.

But the frog just looked at him, squirmed, and then urinated on Keric's palm. Nothing. Again. He took a dab of red pigment from his pouch, smeared it on the frog's head, and then tossed the creature through the trees and marsh grass. He listened to it plop in another pool. Another one tried and failed.

Around him, the sounds of thousands of frogs croaked in the dense swamp, loud enough to drown out the whine of mosquitoes, the constant dripping of water, and the occasional belch of a crocodile.

Sweat and dirty water ran in streaks from his brown hair, down his cheeks, and avoided the frog slime around his mouth. He had caught and tested more than three dozen frogs already, but it would be years before he could find them all—and that was only if any members of the frog-cursed royal family remained alive in the deep swamps. A crocodile splashed somewhere out in the network of cypress roots and branches. Somehow Keric couldn't imagine the brittle old Queen Mother deigning to eat flies, not even if they were served to her by someone else.

When the evil wizard Cosimor had taken over the kingdom less than a year before, he had followed the traditional path of sorcerous usurpers by capturing the entire royal family and transforming them into frogs and then turning them loose in the sprawling, infected swamps of Dermith.

Cosimor had intended to tax the kingdom to its death, drive the subjects into slavery, and generally keep himself amused. But less than three weeks later the wizard had died choking on a fish bone—no vengeful curse, that; simply poor cooking. Now the kingdom had been left without any rulers, not even the incompetent but somehow endearing royal family.

Keric, who lived in a hut on the fringes of the Dermith swamps, trapping muskrats and selling the fur in the noisy walled town, had decided to try to find the royal family in its exile, free at least one of them with a kiss, and then count on his reward. A palace of his own, perhaps? Gold coins stacked as high as an oak tree? Fine clothes. He pulled on his dripping, mud-soaked rags. Yes, fine clothes first. And then perhaps the hand of one of the princesses in marriage?

He spat drying slime away from his lips. But first he had to catch the right frog—and they all looked alike!

He slumped down on a rotting log covered with Spanish moss, then looked across at the piled undergrowth to see a bloated old bullfrog sitting under a drooping fern. Plainly visible on the frog's back were three equally spaced dark blotches, just like the supposed birthmark carried by every member of the royal family! Was this the old king, then? The fat duchess, the king's sister? It didn't matter to Keric—the frog sat right in front of his eyes. It had always taken him too long to see what was right in front of his face.

He didn't want to hesitate too long. Keric shifted his body forward and then lunged, splaying out his mud-caked fingers. He skidded through a spiderweb, needle-thin fronds, and dead leaves, but the bullfrog squirted away from him. He scrambled and grabbed again.

He didn't see the girl until she leapt out from the bushes in front of the bullfrog, opened up the mouth of a large squirming sack, and swept the frog inside. The bullfrog made a croak of alarm, but then the girl spun the sack shut. "Got him!" she said, giggling. Then she sprinted away through the underbrush, leaving only disturbed willow branches dangling behind her.

"Hey!" Keric shouted and jumped to his feet. He ran after her, flinging branches out of the way. He splashed through puddles of standing water, squished on sodden grass islands, and ducked his head in buzzing clouds of mosquitoes. All around, the other frogs continued their songs. "That one was mine!"

"Not anymore!" He heard her voice from the side, in a different direction from where she had disappeared. He looked in time to see her running barefoot down a path only she could see. Barefoot!

Keric ran after her. He found himself panting and sweating. He had grown up in and around these swamps. He considered himself an exceptional woodsman in even the deepest parts of the morass. He could outrun and out-hunt anyone he had ever known. But this girl kept going at a pace he could not hope to match. He stumbled, he missed solid footing, he splashed scummy water all over himself.

"Wait!" he shouted. He heard only the crocodiles growling.

"If you'd look over here, you'd have a better chance of seeing me!" She laughed again.

He whirled to see her across a mucky pool, not twenty feet from him. Without thinking—since he was wet and filthy anyway—he left the path and charged across the way. "Give me my frog!"

Keric tried to run with both feet, but each step became more difficult as the ooze sucked at his boots. He had to get the bullfrog with the three spots. He *knew* it was somebody from the royal family. The girl probably didn't know what she had. Maybe she wanted to eat it!

He sloshed onward, but before he had gone halfway across the pool, he felt the muck dragging him down. He sank to his waist, but found he could not take another step. He continued to submerge in the ooze. "Oh no!"

From the spreading cypress tree over his head, he heard the girl's voice. "You should be more careful out here in the swamps. Plenty of dangerous things out here. Crocodiles, water moccasin snakes, milt spiders bigger than your hand, poison plants." Keric looked up to see her sitting on one of the branches, holding onto the frog sack with one hand and munching on a dripping fruit in the other. "But you really have to watch out for that quicksand. That's especially bad."

"Would you help me out of this?" He looked at her. He had sunk up to his armpits and felt the cold muck seeping into his pores. The mud crept to the tops of his shoulders. Keric had to lift his head to keep his chin out of the ooze. "Um, please?"

"I don't know. You were chasing me." She finished her fruit and tossed the pit down. It splashed beside him.

"I'll tell you what you've got in that sack of yours."

"It's frogs."

"No, if you'll just let me kiss one of them I'll show you something magic!" He had to talk rapidly now. The quicksand had reached his lips.

"Oh, you mean *that!* Sure, I've got the whole royal family here." She reached in and pulled out another frog, this one sleek and small. It also had the three identical splotches. "You don't think you were the only one to get the idea for finding the frogs in the swamp, do you?"

Actually, Keric *had* thought he was the only one to think of that. Once again, the obvious was staring him in the face.

"But you were going about it all wrong," the girl continued. "You kept trying to kiss them out here in the swamp. Now tell me, just what would you have done if the frail and arthritic Queen Mother had appeared? Or one of the dainty princesses who would squeal at the sight of a beetle? How would you get them back? Makes more sense to me just to carry the frogs in a sack, go back to town, and then change them all back. Reward would still be the same, maybe more for saving them the journey."

Keric had to lean his head back to keep his nose and mouth above the surface. "Will you please help me now, and give me advice later!"

She shrugged. "You haven't asked me the right question yet."

"What is the question?"

"Ask me what my name is! I'm not going to risk my life to rescue a total stranger."

"What's your name? Tell me quick!"

"I am Raffin. Pleased to meet you." She paused. "And what's your name?"

"I'm Keric! Help!"

She tossed a vine down that struck near his face. Keric grabbed at it, clawing at the slick surface of the vine with his mucky hands. But he managed to haul himself forward, toward the near edge of the pool of quicksand. He heaved himself out onto the soggy ground and shivered. He had lost his left boot, but he had no intention of going back to get it.

When he looked up at the tree, Raffin was gone.

After dark, when Keric remained cold and clammy but unable to light a fire, he saw an orange light flickering through the tangled branches. He followed it to Raffin's fire, then crept close to where he could see.

She sat humming to herself and holding four sticks splayed in the flames. Little strips of meat had been skewered on the wood and sizzled in the light. The bound bundle of royal frogs sat beside her. "Come closer and sit down, Keric. You're making enough noise at being quiet."

Angry, Keric came out of his hiding place and strode with confidence into her firelight. Finally, he sighed and shook his head. "I thought I was good in the swamps, moving silently, always knowing my way. I can't believe I am being so clumsy around you."

Raffin shrugged. "You *are* good. The best I've seen. But I'm better."

Her long pale hair must once have been blond but now had taken on the color of fallen leaves and dry grass. Her eyes looked startling blue within the camouflage of her appearance. Raffin had washed most of the grime from her face, arms, and hands before preparing her food.

Keric didn't want to imagine what he looked like himself.

Raffin took one of the sticks out of the fire and blew on

the sizzling strips of meat. "Frog legs, filleted." At his shocked expression, she laughed. "No, just normal frogs. Don't worry. Would you like some?"

Keric swallowed. "I haven't eaten anything all day."

"Say please."

"Please. Uh, I mean, Raffin, may I please have some?"

"Of course. You're my guest. I saved your life. Do you think I'd refuse a simple request like that?"

He took the stick she offered and ate the crispy meat right off the bark so he wouldn't have to touch it with his dirty fingers. "What are you doing out here all alone in the swamps?"

"I live out here. Don't worry, I can take care of myself."

Keric could believe that. He guessed she was only a couple years older than himself.

"But I don't mind company once in a while." Suddenly, Raffin appeared shy to him. "Just listen to those night sounds, the frogs and the humming insects. Why would anyone want to live in the town?"

Keric frowned and ate the last piece of meat. "Then why are you trying so hard to get the royal frogs?"

"Because you are. I've been watching you for days. It's been fun. Besides, I have dreams of getting a prince of my own."

They talked for much longer after that, but Keric could get no better explanation from her. He felt the weariness from the day sapping his strength, making him drowsy. He interrupted what she was saying. "Raffin, I am going to sleep."

He saw her smile as he let his eyes drift shut. "Make yourself at home."

When Keric cracked his eyes open again an hour later, his body screamed at him just to keep sleeping. But he couldn't. He had something much more important to do.

Raffin had stayed beside the fire, which now burned low and smoky, still driving the mosquitoes away. She lay curled up on the ground, her cheek pillowed on her scrawny arms. She looked very peaceful and vulnerable. Keric frowned, but then thought of palaces and princesses and fine clothes.

The fire popped as two logs sagged, and Keric used the noise to cover his own movements as he crept to his feet. She had left the sack containing the royal family sitting unguarded on the other side of the camp. He shook his head, wondering why she had made it so easy for him.

He picked up the sack and slipped out of the firelight, starting to run as soon as he got out under the moonlit trees.

"Keric!" she shouted behind him.

He stopped trying to be silent. The marsh grass whipped around him as he picked up speed. Willow branches snapped at his eyes. He kept splashing in puddles or flailing his hands at large, flapping night insects.

"Keric, come back!"

He didn't answer her, but started to chuckle. He could make it out of the swamp to his hut. He would go immediately into the walled town and kiss all the frogs, even the old Queen Mother, and bring them back before Raffin could find him.

He used all his forest skills to weave his path. He couldn't hear her following, but then he doubted if he would. She was too good for that.

Keric looked behind him as he ran, seeking some sign of her. Raffin impressed him with her knowledge of the swamps. She might be able to teach him many things. He decided he would share his royal reward with her anyway, once he got it, but for now he wanted to succeed on his own, to impress her that his own survival abilities weren't so trivial either.

He tripped on the tail of the first crocodile and could not stop himself until he had stumbled into a cluster of the beasts. Once again, he had been looking in the wrong place and missed what was right in front of him.

The crocodiles hissed and belched at him. Keric cried out. He could count at least seven of them, startled out of their torpor and suddenly confronted with something worth eating. An old bull scuttled toward him, looking as large as a warship. It opened its mouth so wide that Keric felt he could have walked inside without ducking his head.

He turned and searched for a way out. Hissing and snapping their enormous jaws, the crocodiles moved in. The old bull lunged. Keric leaped back, caught his heel on the long body of one of the smaller reptiles, and sprawled backward. Even the smaller crocodile chomped at him. Keric dropped his sack of royal frogs.

He scrambled to his hands and knees, looking for an escape. The moonlight made everything dim and confusing. He thought he saw a flashing orange light behind a sketchy web of cypress roots, but he concentrated only on the nightmare of wide, fang-filled jaws.

Raffin appeared and struck the snout of the nearest crocodile with her roaring torch. "Get away from him!" The beast hissed and grunted as it lurched backward. Keric blinked in amazement. In her other hand, Raffin held a pointed stick that she jabbed at the remaining crocodiles.

The beasts backed away. The enormous bull stood his ground and let out a deep growl from somewhere at the bottom of his abdomen.

Keric crawled to his feet, too stunned and frightened to be much help.

Raffin faced the bull's charge and shoved her torch at her attacker. The crocodile hissed and snapped at her, but she was quick with the end of her torch, touching the burning end to the soft tissue inside the reptilian mouth. Keric heard the sizzle of burning meat.

With a defeated roar, the bull backed away and then, in a final gesture of frustration and spite, he lashed out with his long snout and snapped up the tied sack of royal frogs. The frogs made a combined sound like someone stepping on a goose. The giant crocodile crunched down with his jaws, chomped again, then swallowed. After a satisfied grunt, the crocodile crawled out of the clearing and splashed into the water.

"I told you to be careful out in the swamps," Raffin scolded Keric. "Do I have to watch out for you all the time?"

Keric sat stunned. "They're all gone! In one gulp, the whole royal family!" He shook his head. "I never meant for that to happen."

Raffin took hold of his hand and pulled him to his feet. "The kingdom will do fine without them. They weren't particularly worth rescuing." She stared at him, but he continued to sulk. "Hey, it was fun while it lasted."

"No, I meant my reward. The gold, the fine clothes, the palace—"

"And what would you do with all that stuff?" She looked at him, then tugged at his old, mud-caked tunic. "Fine clothes? Are you seeking what you really want, or just what you think you're *supposed* to want? What other people tell you to want isn't always right for you."

Keric lowered his head, sighed deeply. He looked at

himself and realized she was right. "If I had a palace, I suppose I'd just track mud in it all the time."

Raffin giggled. "It's not so bad out here, you know."

"But what about my princess?"

Raffin flicked her hair behind her shoulders and looked angry for a moment, then spoke in a very shy voice. "You could stay in the swamps." She paused. "With me."

Keric looked up at her and listened to the frogs and the night insects. One of these days he was going to learn to notice the things right in front of him.

The first story I ever sold (for a whopping $12.50) was to the small-press magazine *Space & Time*. I was a Senior in high school. "Luck of the Draw" was about a group of itinerant knights drawing straws to see who would slay the dragon and win the hand of the princess. I liked the idea enough that when I was asked to contribute to an anthology, *The Ultimate Dragon*, I rewrote the old story from scratch.

Short Straws

Yes, a dragon was terrorizing the land, so the king had offered his daughter in marriage to any brave knight who slew the foul beast. Same old story. I was new to the band of warriors, but the others had heard it all before. This time, though, the logistics caused a problem.

"We could split a *cash* reward," said Oldahn, the battle-scarred old veteran who served as our leader. "But who gets the princess?"

The four of us sat around the fire, procrastinating. Though I was still wide-eyed to be part of the group—they had needed a new cook and errand runner—I'd already noticed that the adventurers liked to talk about peril a lot more than actually doing something about it. I was their apprentice, and I wanted for us to go out and fight, a team of mercenaries, warriors—but that didn't seem to be the way of going about it.

We knew where the dragon's lair was, having investigated every foul-smelling, bone-cluttered cave in the kingdom. But we still hadn't figured out what to do with the princess, assuming we succeeded in slaying the dragon. It didn't seem a practical sort of reward.

Reegas looked up with a half-cocked grin. "We could just take turns with her!"

Oldahn sighed. "One does not treat a princess the way you treat one of your hussies, Reegas."

Reegas scowled, scratching the stubble on his chin. "She's no different from Sarna at the inn—except I'll wager Sarna's better than your rustin' princess at all the important things!"

"She is the daughter of our sovereign, Reegas. Now show some respect."

"Yeah sure, she's sacred and pure . . . Bloodrust, Oldahn, now you're sounding like *him*." Reegas shot a disgusted glance at Alsaf, the puritan.

Alsaf plainly took no offense at the insult. He rolled up the king's written decree, torn from the meeting post in the town square, and stuffed it under his belt, since he was the only one of us who could read. Alsaf methodically began polishing the end of his staff on the fabric of his black cloak. He preferred to fight with his staff and his faith in God, but he also kept a sword at hand in case both the others failed. Firelight splashed across the silver crucifix at his throat.

Reegas spat something unrecognizable into the dark forest behind him. Gray-bearded Oldahn chewed his meat slowly, swallowing even the fat and gristle without a word, mindful of worse rations he had lived through. He wore an elaborately-studded leather jerkin that had protected him in scores of battles; his sword was notched, but clean and free of rust.

I sat closest to the campfire, nursing a battered pot containing the last of the stew, letting my own meat cook long enough to resemble something edible. "Uh," I said, desperately wanting to show them I could be a useful member of their band. "Why don't we just draw straws to see who goes to kill the dragon?"

Alsaf, Oldahn, and Reegas all stared as if the newcomer wasn't supposed to come up with a feasible suggestion.

"Rustin' good idea, Kendell," Reegas said. Alsaf nodded.

Oldahn looked at all three of us. "Agreed, then. Luck of the draw."

I scrabbled over to my bedding and searched through it to find suitable lots. I still preferred to sleep on a pile of straw rather than the forest floor. The straw was prickly and infested with vermin, but it reminded me of the warm bed I had left behind when running away from my home. The straw was preferable to the cold, hard dirt—at least until I got hardened to the mercenary life.

I took four straws, broke one in half so that all could see, then handed them to Oldahn. The big veteran covered them in a scarred hand to hide the short straw, and motioned for me to draw first.

Tentatively, I reached out, unable to decide whether I wanted the honor of battling the dragon. Sure, being wed to a princess would be nice, but I had barely begun my swordfighting lessons, and according to stories I had heard, dragons were vicious opponents. But I wanted to be a warrior instead of a shepherd's son, and a warrior faced whatever challenges he encountered.

I snatched a straw from Oldahn's grasp, and could tell from the others' expressions even before I glanced downward that I had drawn a long one.

Alsaf came forward, holding his staff in his right hand as he reached out to Oldahn's fist. He paused for a long moment, then pulled a straw forth. His black cloak blocked my view, but he turned with a strangled expression on his face, looking as if God had deserted him. The short straw fell to the ground as he gripped his silver crucifix. "But, my faith—I must remain chaste! I cannot marry a princess."

Reegas clapped the puritan on the back. "I'm sure you can work something out."

Alsaf was pale as he shifted his weight to rest heavily on his staff. He nodded as if trying to convince himself. "Yes, my purpose is to destroy evil in all its manifestations. A divine hand has guided my selection, and I will serve His purpose." Alsaf's eyes glinted with a fanatical fury as he strode to the edge of the camp.

"Take care, and good luck," said Oldahn.

Alsaf whirled to face the three of us, holding his staff in a battle-ready stance. "I shall be protected by my unquenchable faith. My staff will send the demon back to the fires of Hell!" He looked at the skeptical expressions on our faces, then changed the tone of his voice. "I shall return."

"Is that a promise?" Reegas asked, and for once his sarcasm was weak.

"I give you my word." The puritan turned to stride into the deep stillness of the forest night, crunching through the underbrush.

It was the only promise Alsaf ever broke.

"For our honor, we must continue." Oldahn held three straws in his hand, thrusting them forward. "Come, Reegas. Draw first."

Reegas cursed under his breath and reached out to grab a straw without even pausing for thought. A broad grin split his face. He held a long straw.

I came forward, looking intently at the two straws, two

chances. One would pit me against a scaly, fire-breathing demon, and the other would give me a reprieve. Knowing that the dragon had already defeated one warrior, I decided the princess wasn't so desirable after all. Alsaf had seemed so strong, so confident, so determined. I hesitated, hoping the puritan would return at the last possible moment. . . .

But he didn't, and I picked a straw. It was long.

Oldahn stared at the short straw remaining in his hand. Cold battle-lust boiled in his eyes. "Very well, I have a dragon to slay, a death to avenge, and a princess to win. I had thought it too late in my life to settle down in marriage—but I will adapt. My brave exploits should be sung by minstrels all across the kingdom."

"Our kingdom doesn't have any minstrels, Oldahn," I pointed out.

The old warrior sighed. "I should have volunteered to go first anyway. I am the leader of our band."

"Our band?" Reegas said, sulking in his crusty old chain mail shirt. "Rust, Oldahn—with you gone we aren't much of a band any more."

Oldahn patted his heavy broadsword and walked stiffly across the camp. It was a beautiful day, and the sun broke through in scattered patches of green light. Oldahn looked around as if for one last time. He turned to walk away, calling back to us just before he vanished into the tangled distance, "Don't be so sure I won't be coming back."

By nightfall, we were sure.

The campfire was lonely with only Reegas and me sitting by it. Oldahn had fallen, and the fact that he was the best warrior in our group (old mercenaries are, by definition, good warriors) didn't improve our confidence. I could hardly believe the great fighter I had revered so much had been *slain*. It wasn't supposed to be this way.

I looked at Reegas fidgeting in his battered chain mail. "Well, Reegas, do you want to wait until morning, or draw straws now?"

"Rust! Let's get it over with," he said. His eyes were bloodshot. "This better be one hell of a princess."

I picked up two straws, one long, the other short. I held them out to Reegas, and he spat into the fire before looking at me. I masked my expression with some effort. Reegas reached forward and pulled the short straw.

"Bloodrust and battlerot!" he howled, jerking at the ends of the straw as if trying to stretch it longer. He crumpled it in his grip and threw it into the fire, then sank into a squat by my cookpots. "Aww, Kendell—now I can't teach you some things! I meant to take you over to the inn one night where you would—"

I looked at him with a half smile, raising an eyebrow. "Reegas, do you think Sarna takes no other customers besides yourself?"

Wonder and shock lit up his craggy face. "You? . . . Rust!" Reegas laughed loudly, a nervous blustering laugh. He clapped me on the back with perverse pride. "I won't feel sorry for you anymore, Kendell." He drew his sword and leaped into the air, slashing at a branch overhead. "But I'm gonna get that rustin' princess for myself. Maybe royalty knows a few tricks the common hussies don't."

He turned with a new excitement, dancing out of camp, waving farewell.

Alone by the campfire, I waited the long hours as the dusk collapsed into darkness. The forest filled with the noisy silence of a wild night. As the stars began to shine, I lay on the cold ground with my head propped against the rough bark of an old oak. I gave up sleeping on straw in fear that I would have dreams of dark scales and death.

The branches above me looked like the black framework of a broken lattice supporting the stars. The mockingly pleasant fire and the empty campsite made me feel intensely lonely; and for the first time I felt the true pain of my friends' losses. I had wanted to be one of them, and now they were all gone.

I remembered some of the stories they had told me, but I hadn't quite fit in with the rest of the band yet. I was a novice, I hadn't yet fought battles with them, hadn't helped them in any way. And now Alsaf and Oldahn were gone, and Reegas had a good chance of joining them. . . .

Since the time I had talked my way into accompanying the band, nothing much had happened. Until the dragon came, that is.

Of course, if I had known my first adventure would involve a battle with a large reptilian terror, I might have endured my dull old life a little longer. My father was a shepherd, spending so much time out with his flocks that he had begun to look like one of his sheep. Imagine watching thirty animals eat grass hour after hour! My mother was a weaver, spending every day hunched over her loom, hurling her shuttle back and forth, watching the threads line themselves up one at a time. She even walked with a jerky back and forth motion, as if bouncing to the beat of a flying shuttle.

Me, I'd just as soon be out fighting bandits, dispatching troublesome wolves, or chasing the odd sorcerer away under the grave risk of having an indelible curse hurled at me. That's excitement—but slaying a dragon is going a bit too far!

I couldn't sleep and lay waiting, listening to the night

sounds. At every rustle of leaves I jumped, peering in to the shadows, hoping it might be Reegas returning, or Oldahn, or even Alsaf.

But no one came.

Finally, at dawn, I threw the last long straw on the dirt and ground it under my heel. I had only ever used my sword to cut up meat for the cook fires. I was alone. No one watched me, or pressured me, or insisted that I too go out and challenge the dragon. I could have just crept back home, helped my father tend sheep, helped my mother with her weaving. But somehow that kind of life seemed worse than facing a dragon.

I stared at the blade of my sword, thinking of my comrades. Alsaf and Oldahn and Reegas had been my friends, and I was the only one who could avenge them. Only I remained of the entire mercenary band. I had been with Oldahn long enough, heard his tales of glory, seen how the group worked together as a team. I couldn't just let the dragon have its victory.

Muttering a few curses I had picked up from Reegas, I left the dead campfire behind and set off through the forest.

The forest floor was impervious to the sunshine that dribbled through the woven leaves. A loud breeze rushed through the topmost branches, but left me untouched. I knew the boulder-strewn wilderness well, and my woodlore had grown more skillful since my initiation into the band. While we had no serious adventures to occupy ourselves, there was still hunting to be done.

My anxiety tripled as I crested a final hill and started down into a rocky dell that sheltered the dragon's den, a broken shadow in the rock surrounded on all sides by shattered boulders and dead foliage. The lump in my throat felt larger than any dragon could ever be. The wind had disappeared, and even the birds were silent. A terrible stench wafted up, smelling faintly like something Reegas might have cooked.

I crept forward, drawing my sword, wondering why the ground was shaking and then I saw that it was only my knees. Panic flooded my senses—or had my senses left me? Me? Against a dragon? A big scaly thing with bad breath and an awful prejudice against armed warriors?

The boulders offered some protection as I danced from one to another, moving closer to the dragon's lair. Fumes snaked out of the cave, stinging my eyes and clogging my throat, tempting me to choke and give away my presence. I could hear sounds of muffled breathing like the belching of a blacksmith's furnace.

I slid around a slime-slick rock to the threshold of the cave. I froze, an outcry trapped in my throat as I found the shattered ends of Alsaf's staff, splintered and tossed aside among torn shreds of black fabric. I swallowed and went on.

A few steps deeper into the den I tripped on the bloody remnants of Oldahn's studded leather jerkin. His bent and blackened sword lay discarded among bloody fragments of crunched bone.

On the very boundary of where sunlight dared to go, I found Reegas's rusty chain mail, chewed to a new luster and spat out.

A scream welled up as fast as my guts did, but terror can do amazing things for self-control. If I screamed, the dragon would know I had come, the latest in a series of tender victims.

But now, upon seeing with utmost certainty the fates of my comrades, my fellow warriors, anger and lust for vengeance poured forth, almost, *almost* overwhelming my terror. The end result was an angered persistence tempered with extreme caution.

Leg muscles tense to the point of snapping, I tiptoed into the cave where I stood silhouetted against the frightened wall of daylight. The suffocating darkness of the dragon's lair folded around me. I didn't think I would ever see the sun again.

The air was thick and damp, polluted with a sickening stench. Piles of yellowed skulls lay stacked against one wall like ivory trophies. I didn't see any of the expected mounds of gold and jewels from the dragon's hoard. Pickings must have been slim in the kingdom.

I went ahead until the patch of sunlight seemed beyond running distance. My jerkin felt clammy, sticking to my cold sweat. I found it hard to breathe. I had gone in too far. My sword felt like a heavy, ineffective toy in my hand.

I could sense the lurking presence of the dragon, watching me from the shadows. I could hear its breathing like the wind of an angry storm, but could not pinpoint its location. I turned in slow circles, losing all orientation in the dimness. I thought I saw two lamp-like eyes, but the stench filled my nostrils, my throat. It gagged me, forcing me to gasp for air, but that only made me gulp down more of the smell. I sneezed.

—and the dragon attacked!

Suddenly I found myself confronted with a battering ram of fury, blackish green scales draped over a bloated mass of flesh lurching forward. Acid saliva drooled off fangs like spears, spattering in sizzling pools on the floor.

I struck blindly at the eyes, the rending claws, the reptilian armor. The monster let out a hideous cry, seething forward, fat and sluggish to corner me against a lichen-covered wall. My stomach turned to ice, and I knew how Alsaf,

Oldahn, and Reegas must have felt as they faced their death—

Let me digress a moment.

Dragons are not exactly the best fed of all creatures living in the wild. Despite their size and power, and the riches they hoard (but who can eat gold?), these creatures find very little to devour, especially in a relatively small kingdom like our own, where most people live protected within the city walls. Barely once a week does a typical dragon manage to steal a squalling baby from its crib, or strike down an old crone gathering herbs in the woods. Rarer still does a dragon come across a flaxen-haired virgin (a favorite) wandering through the forest.

Hard times had come upon this particular dragon. Only impending starvation had driven it to increase its attacks on the peasantry, forcing the king to offer his daughter as a reward to rid the land of the beast. The future must have looked bleak for the dragon.

But then, unexpectedly, a feast beyond its wildest dreams! This dragon had greedily devoured three full-grown warriors in half as many days, swallowing whole the bodies of Alsaf, Oldahn, and Reegas.

And so, when the dragon lunged at me in the cave, it was so *bloated* and overstuffed that it could barely drag its bulk forward, like a snake which has gorged itself on a whole rabbit. Its bleary yellow eyes blinked sleepily, and it seemed to have lost heart in battling warriors. But it snarled forward out of old habit, barely able to stagger toward me. . . .

I won't, by any stretch of the imagination, claim that killing the brute was easy. The scales were tougher than any chain mail I could imagine, and the dragon didn't particularly want its head cut off—but I was bent on avenging my

friends and winning myself a princess. If I could just accomplish this one thing, I could call myself a warrior. I
would never have to prove myself again.

Alsaf, Oldahn, and Reegas had already done much of the
work for me, dealing vicious blows to the reptilian hide. But
I still can't begin to express my exhaustion when the
dragon's head finally rolled among the cracked bones in its
lair. I slumped to the floor of the cave, panting, without the
energy to drag myself back out to fresh air.

After I had rested a long time, I stood up stiffly and
looked down at the dead monster, sighing. I had won myself a princess. I had avenged my comrades.

But perhaps the best reward was that I could now call
myself a real warrior, a dragon-slayer. I imagined I could
think of a few ways to make the story more impressive by
the time I actually met my bride-to-be.

The monster's head was heavy, and it was a long walk to
the castle.

When I was asked to write a werewolf story, I didn't see any reason not to do a funny one! I've always been a fan of the old monster movies, and for this tale I drew upon my years of diligently studying *Famous Monsters of Filmland* magazine.

Special Makeup

The second camera operator ran to fetch the clapboard. Someone else called out, "Quiet on the set! Hey everybody, shut up!" Three of the extras coughed at the same time.

"*Wolfman in Casablanca*, Scene 23. Are we ready for Scene 23?" The second camera operator held the clapboard ready.

"Ahem." The director, Rino Derwell, puffed on his long cigarette in an ivory cigarette holder, just like all famous directors were supposed to have. "I'd like to start today's shooting sometime *today!* Is that too much to ask? Where the hell is Lance?"

The boom man swiveled his microphone around; the extras on the nightclub set fidgeted in their places. The cameraman slurped a cold cup of coffee, making a noise like a vacuum cleaner in a bathtub.

"Um, Lance is still, um, getting his makeup on," the script supervisor said.

"Christ! Can somebody find me a way to shoot this picture without the star? He was supposed to be done half an hour ago. Go tell Zoltan to hurry up—this is a horror picture, not the Mona Lisa." Derwell mumbled how glad he was that the gypsy makeup man would be leaving in a day or two, and they could get someone else who didn't consider himself such a perfectionist. The director's assistant dashed away, stumbling off the soundstage and tripping on loose wires.

Around them, the set showed an exotic nightclub, with white fake-adobe walls, potted tropical plants, and Arabic-looking squiggles on the pottery. The piano in the center of the stage, just in front of the bar, sat empty under the spotlight, waiting for the movie's star, Lance Chandler. The sound stage sweltered in the summer heat. The large standup fans had to be shut off before shooting; and the ceiling fans—nightclub props—stirred the cloud of cigarette smoke overhead into a gray whirlpool, making the extras cough even when they were supposed to keep silent.

Rino Derwell looked again at his gold wristwatch. He had bought it cheap from a man in an alley, but Derwell's pride would not allow him to admit he had been swindled even after it had promptly stopped working. Derwell didn't need it to tell him he was already well behind schedule, over budget, and out of patience.

It was going to take all day just to shoot a few seconds of finished footage. "God, I hate these transformation sequences. Why does the audience need to *see* everything? Have they no imagination?" he muttered. "Maybe I should just do romance pictures? At least nobody wants to see everything *there!*"

"Oh, God! Please no! Not again! Not *NOW!!!*" Lance couldn't see the look of horror he hoped would show on his face.

"You must stop fidgeting, Mr. Lance. This will go much faster." Zoltan stepped back, large makeup brush in hand, inspecting his work. His heavy eastern European accent slurred out his words.

"Well I've got to practice my lines. This blasted makeup takes so blasted long that I forget my blasted lines by the time it comes to shoot. Was I supposed to say 'Don't let it happen *here!*' in that scene? Hand me the script."

"No, Mr. Lance. That line comes much later—it follows 'Oh no! I'm transforming!' " Zoltan smeared shadow under Lance's eyes. This would be just the first step in the transformation, but he still had to increase the highlights. Veins stood out on Zoltan's gnarled hands, but his fingers were rock steady with the fine detail.

"How do you know my lines?"

"You may call it gypsy intuition, Mr. Lance—or it may be because you have been saying them every morning before makeup for a week now. They have burned into my brain like a gypsy curse."

Lance glared at the wizened old man in his pale blue shirt and color-spattered smock. Zoltan's leathery fingers had a real instinct for makeup, for changing the appearance of any actor. But his craft took hours.

Lance Chandler had enough confidence in his own screen presence to carry any picture, regardless of how silly the makeup made him look. His square jaw, fine physique, and clean-cut appearance made him the perfect model of the all-American hero. Now, during the War against Germany and Japan, the U.S. needed its strong heroes to keep up morale. Besides, making propaganda pictures fulfilled his patriotic duties without requiring him to go somewhere and risk getting shot. Red-corn-syrup blood and bullet blanks were about all the real violence he wanted to experience.

Lance took special pride in his performance in *Tarzan*

Versus the Third Reich. Though he had few lines in the film, the animal rage on his face and his oiled and straining body had been enough to topple an entire regiment of Hitler's finest, including one of Rommel's desert vehicles. (Exactly why one of Rommel's desert vehicles had shown up in the middle of Africa's deepest jungles was a question only the scriptwriter could have answered.)

Craig Corwyn, U-Boat Smasher, to be released next month as the start of a new series, might make Lance a household name. Those stories centered on brave Craig Corwyn, who had a penchant for leaping off the deck of his Allied destroyer and swimming down to sink Nazi submarines with his bare hands, usually by opening the underwater hatches or just plucking out the rivets in the hull.

But none of those movies would compare to *Wolfman in Casablanca.* Bogart would be forgotten in a week. The timing for this picture was just perfect; it had an emotional content Lance had not been able to bring into his earlier efforts. The country was just waiting for a new hero, strong and manly, with a dash of animal unpredictability and a heart of gold (not to mention unwavering in Allied sympathies).

The story concerned a troubled but patriotic werewolf—him, Lance Chandler—who in his wanderings has found himself in German-occupied Casablanca. There he causes what havoc he can for the enemy, and he also meets Brigitte, a beautiful French resistance fighter vacationing in Morocco. Brigitte turns out to be a werewolf herself, Lance's true love. Even in the script, the final scene as the two of them howl on the rooftops above a conflagration of Nazi tanks and ruined artillery sent shivers down Lance's spine. If he could pull off this performance, Hitler himself would tremble in his sheets.

Zoltan added spirit gum to Lance's cheeks and forehead, humming as he worked. "You will please stop perspiring, Mr. Lance. I require a dry surface for this fine hair."

Lance slumped in the chair. Zoltan reminded him of the wicked old gypsy man in the movie, the one who had cursed his character to become a werewolf in the first place. "This blasted transformation sequence is going to take all day again, isn't it? And I don't even get to *act* after the first second or so! Lie still, add more hair, shoot a few frames, lie still, add more hair, shoot a few more frames. And it's so hot in the soundstage. The spirit gum burns and ruins my complexion. The fumes sting my eyes. The fake hair itches."

He twisted his face into the practiced look of horror again. "Oh, God! Please no! Not again! Um . . . oh yeah—don't let it happen here!" Lance paused, then scowled. "Blast, that wasn't right. Would you hurry up, Zoltan! I'm already losing my lines. And I'm really tired of you dragging your feet—get moving!"

Zoltan tossed the makeup brush with a loud clink into its glass jar of solvent. He put his gnarled hands on his hips and glared at Lance. The smoldering gypsy fury in his dark eyes looked worse than anything Lance had seen on a movie villain's face.

"I lose my patience with you, Mr. Lance! It is gone! Poof! Now I must take a short cut. A special trick that only I know. It will take a minute, and it will make you a star forevermore! I guarantee that. You will no longer suffer my efforts—and I need not suffer you! The people at the new Frankenstein picture over on Lot 17 would appreciate my work, no doubt."

Lance blinked, amazed at the old gypsy's anger but ready to jump at any chance that would get him out of the makeup trailer sooner. He heard only the words "it will make you a star. I guarantee that."

"Well, do it then, Zoltan! I've got work to do. The great Lon Chaney never had to put up with all these delays. He did all his own makeup. My audiences are waiting to see the new meaning I can bring to the portrayal of the werewolf."

"You will never disappoint them, Mr. Lance."

Without further reply, Zoltan yanked at the fine hair he had already applied. "You no longer need this." Lance yowled as the patches came free of his skin. "That is a very good sound you make, Mr. Lance. Very much like a werewolf."

Lance growled at him.

Zoltan rummaged in a cardboard box in the corner of his cramped trailer, pulled out a dirty Mason jar, and unscrewed its rusty lid. Inside, a brown oily liquid swirled all by itself, spinning green flecks in internal currents. The old man stuck his fingers into the goop and brought them out dripping.

"What is—whoa, that smells like—" Lance tried to shrink away, but Zoltan slapped the goop onto his cheek and smeared it around.

"You cannot possibly know what this smells like, Mr. Lance, because you have no idea what I used to make it. You probably do not wish to know—then you would be even more upset at having it rubbed all over your face."

Zoltan reached into the jar again and brought out another handful, which he wiped across Lance's forehead. "Ugh! Did you get that from the lot cafeteria?" Lance felt his skin tingle, as if the liquid had begun to eat its way inside. "Ow! My complexion!"

"If it gives you pimples, you can always call them character marks, Mr. Lance. Every good actor has them."

Zoltan pulled his hand away. Lance saw that the old man's fingers were clean. "Finished. It has all absorbed right in." He screwed the cover of the jar back on and replaced it in the cardboard box.

Lance grabbed a small mirror, expecting to find his (soon-to-be) well-known expression covered with ugly brown, but he could see no sign of the makeup at all. "What happened to it? It still stinks."

"It is special makeup. It will work when it needs to."

The door flew open, and the red-faced director's assistant stood panting. "Lance, Mr. Derwell wants you on the set right now! Pronto! We've got to start shooting."

Zoltan nudged his shoulder. "I am finished with you, Mr. Lance."

Lance stood up, trying not to look perplexed so that Zoltan could have a laugh at his expense. "But I don't see any—"

The old gypsy wore a wicked grin on his lips. "You need not worry about it. I believe your expression is, 'Knock 'em dead.' "

Lance sat down at the nightclub piano and cracked his knuckles. The extras and other stars took their positions. Above the soundstage, he could hear men on the catwalks, positioning cool blue gels over the lights to simulate the full moon.

"*Now* are you ready, Lance?" the director said, fitting another cigarette into his ivory holder. "Or do you think maybe we should just take a coffee break for an hour or so?"

"That's not necessary, Mr. Derwell. I'm ready. Just give the word, see?" He growled for good measure.

"Places everyone!"

Lance ran his fingers over the piano keyboard, "tickling

the old ivories," as real piano players called it. No sound came out. Lance couldn't play a note, of course, so the prop men had cut all the piano wires, holding the instrument in merciful silence no matter how enthusiastically Lance might bang on it. They would add the beautiful piano melody to the soundtrack during post-production.

"*Wolfman in Casablanca*, Scene 23, Take One." The clapboard cracked.

"Action!" Derwell called.

The klieg lights came on, pouring hot white illumination on the set. Lance stiffened at the piano, then began to hum and pretend to plink on the keys.

In this scene, the werewolf has taken a job as a piano player in a nightclub, where he has met Brigitte, the vacationing French resistance fighter. While playing "As Time Goes By," Lance's character looks up to see the full moon shining down through the nightclub's skylight. To keep from having to interrupt filming, Derwell had planned to shoot Lance from the back only as he played the piano, not showing his face until after he had supposedly started to transform. But now Lance didn't appear to wear any makeup at all—he wondered what would happen when Derwell noticed, but he plunged into the performance nevertheless. That would be Zoltan's problem, not his.

At the appropriate point, Lance froze at the keyboard, forcing his fingers to tremble as he stared at them. On the soundtrack, the music would stop in mid-note. The false moonlight shone down on him. Lance formed his face into his best expression of abject horror.

"Oh, God! Please no! Not again! Don't let it happen *HERE!!!*" Lance clutched his chest, slid sideways, and did a graceful but dramatic topple off the piano bench.

On cue, one of the extras screamed. The bartender

dropped a glass, which shattered on the tiles.

On the floor, Lance couldn't stop writhing. His own body felt as if it were being turned inside out. He had really learned how to bury himself in the role! His face and hands itched, burned. His fingers curled and clenched. It felt terrific. It felt *real* to him. He let out a moaning scream—and it took him a moment to realize it wasn't part of the act.

Off behind the cameras, Lance could see Rino Derwell jumping up and down with delight, jerking both his thumbs up in silent admiration for Lance's performance. "Cut!"

Lance tried to lie still. They would need to add the next layer of hair and makeup. Zoltan would come in and paste one of the latex appliances onto his eyebrows, darken his nails with shoe polish.

But Lance felt his own nails sharpening, curling into claws. Hair sprouted from the backs of his hands. His cheeks tingled and burned. His ears felt sharp and stretched, protruding from the back of his head. His face tightened and elongated; his mouth filled with fangs.

"No, wait!" Derwell shouted at the cameraman. "Keep rolling! Keep rolling!"

"Look at that!" the director's assistant said.

Lance tried to say something, but he could only growl. His body tightened and felt ready to explode with anger. He found it difficult to concentrate, but some part of his mind knew what he had to do. After all, he had read the script.

Leaping up from the nightclub dance floor, Lance strained until his clothes ripped under his bulging lupine muscles. With a roar and a spray of saliva from his fang-filled jaws, he smashed the piano bench prop into kindling, knocking it aside.

Four of the extras screamed, even without their cues.

Lance heaved the giant, mute piano and smashed it onto its side. The severed piano wires jangled like a rasping old woman trying to sing. The bartender stood up and brought out a gun, firing four times in succession, but they were only theatrical blanks, and not silver blanks either. Lance knocked the gun aside, grabbed the bartender's arm, and hurled him across the stage, where he landed in a perfect stunt man's roll.

Lance Chandler stood under the klieg lights, in the pool of blue gel filtering through the skylight simulating the full moon. He bayed a beautiful wolf howl as everyone fled screaming from the stage.

"Cut! Cut! Lance, that's magnificent!" Derwell clapped his hands.

The klieg lights faded, leaving the wreckage under the normal room illumination. Lance felt all the energy drain out of him. His face rippled and contracted, his ears shrank back to normal. His throat remained sore from the long howl, but the fangs had vanished from his mouth. He brushed his hands to his cheeks, but found that all the abnormal hair had melted away.

Derwell ran onto the set and clapped him on the back. "That was *incredible!* Oscar-quality stuff!"

Old Zoltan stood at the edge of the set, smiling. His dark eyes glittered. Derwell turned to the gypsy and applauded him as well. "Marvelous, Zoltan! I can't believe it. How in the world did you do that?"

Zoltan shrugged, but his toothless grin grew wider. "Special makeup," he said. "Gypsy secret. I am pleased it worked out." He turned and shuffled toward the soundstage exit.

"Do you really think that was Oscar quality?" Lance asked.

★ ★ ★ ★ ★

The other actors treated Lance with a sort of awe, though a few tended to avoid him. The actress playing Brigitte kept fixing her eyes on him, raising her eyebrows in a suggestive expression. Derwell, having shot a perfect take of the transformation scene he had thought would require more than a day, ordered the set crew to repair the were-wolf-caused damage so they could shoot the big love scene, as a reward to everyone.

Zoltan said nothing to Lance as he added a heavy coat of pancake and sprayed his hair into place. Lance didn't know how the gypsy had worked the transformation, but he knew when not to ask questions. Derwell had said his performance was Oscar quality! He just grinned to himself and looked forward to the kissing scene with Brigitte. Lance always tried to make sure the kissing scenes required several takes. He enjoyed his work, and so (no doubt) did his female co-stars.

Zoltan added an extra-thick layer of dark-red lipstick to Brigitte's mouth, then applied a special wax sealing coat so that it wouldn't smear during the on-screen passion.

"All right you two," Derwell said, sitting back in his director's chair, "start gazing at each other and getting starry-eyed. Places everyone!"

Zoltan packed up his kit and left the soundstage. He said good-bye to the director, but Derwell waved him away in distraction.

Lance stared into Brigitte's eyes, then wiggled his eyebrows in what he hoped would be an irresistible invitation. He had few lines in this scene, only some low grunting and a mumbled "Yes, my love" during the kiss.

Brigitte gazed back at him, batting her eyelashes, melting him with her deep brown irises.

"*Wolfman in Casablanca,* Scene 39, Take One."

Lance took a deep breath so he could make the kiss last longer.

"Action!" The klieg lights came on.

In silence, he and Brigitte gawked at each other. Romantic music would be playing on the soundtrack. They leaned closer to each other. She shuddered with her barely contained emotion. After an indrawn breath, she spoke in a sultry, sexy French accent. "You are the type of man I need. You are my soul mate. Kiss me. I want you to kiss me."

He bent toward her. "Yes, my love."

His joints felt as if they had turned to ice water. His skin burned and tingled. He kissed her, pulling her close, feeling his passion rise to an uncontrollable pitch.

Brigitte jerked away. "Ow! Lance, you bit me!" She touched a spot of blood on her lip.

He felt his hands curl into claws, the nails turn hard and black. Hair began to sprout all over his body. He tried to stop the transformation, but he didn't know how. He stumbled backward. "Oh, God! Please no! Not again!"

"No, Lance—that's not your line!" Brigitte whispered to him.

His muscles bulged; his face stretched out into a long, sharp muzzle. His throat gurgled and growled. He looked around for something to smash. Brigitte screamed, though it wasn't in the script. Tossing her aside, Lance uprooted one of the ornamental palms and hurled the clay pot to the other side of the stage.

"Cut!" the director called. "What the hell is going on here? It's just a simple scene!"

The klieg lights dimmed again. Lance felt the werewolf within him dissolving away, leaving him sweating and shaking and standing in clothes that had torn in several embarrassing places.

"Oh Lance, quit screwing around!" Derwell said. "Go to wardrobe and get some new clothes, for Christ's sake! Somebody, get a new plant and clean up that mess. Get First Aid to fix Brigitte's lip here. Come on, people!" Derwell shook his head. "Why did I ever turn down that job to make Army training films?"

Lance skipped going to wardrobe and went to Zoltan's makeup trailer instead. He didn't know how he was going to discuss this with the gypsy, but if all else failed he could just knock the old man flat with a good roundhouse punch, in the style of Craig Corwyn, U-Boat Smasher.

When he pounded on the flimsy door, though, it swung open by itself. A small sign hung by a string from the doorknob. In Zoltan's scrawling handwriting, it said "FARE-WELL, MY COMPANIONS. TIME TO MOVE ON. GYPSY BLOOD CALLS."

Lance stepped inside. "All right, Zoltan. I know you're in here!"

But he knew no such thing, and the cramped trailer proved to be empty indeed. Many of the bottles had been removed from the shelves, the brushes, the latex prosthetics all packed and taken. Zoltan had also carried away the old cardboard box from the corner, the one containing the jar of special makeup for Lance.

In the makeup chair, Lance found a single sheet of paper that had been left for him. He picked it up and stared down at it, moving his lips as he read.

"Mr. Lance,
"My homemade concoction may eventually wear off,

as soon as you learn a little more patience. Or it may not. I cannot tell. I have always been afraid to use my special makeup, until I met you.

"Do not try to find me. I have gone with the crew of Frankenstein of the Farmlands to shoot on location in Iowa. I will be gone for some time. Director Derwell asked me to leave, to save him time and money. Worry not, though, Mr. Lance. You no longer need any makeup from me.

"I promised you would become a star. Now, every time the glow of the klieg lights strikes your face, you will transform into a werewolf. You will doubtless be in every single werewolf movie produced from now on. How can they refuse?

"P.S., You should hope that werewolves are not just a passing fad! You know how fickle audiences can be."

Lance Chandler crumpled the note, then straightened it again so he could tear it into shreds, but he didn't need any werewolf anger to snarl this time.

He stared around the empty makeup trailer, feeling his career shatter around him. There would be no more Tarzan roles, no thrilling adventures of Craig Corwyn. His hopes, his dreams were ruined, and his cry of anguish sounded like a mournful wolf's howl.

"I've been typecast!"

Just in case you've started to think that all of my fantasy stories are light and humorous . . .

After studying the history of Japan, the fall of the last samurai, the opening of Japan to western influences, and then the early history of filmmaking, I added the ingredients into this story. "Redmond's Private Screening" was published in German translation several years before it appeared in English because most magazines considered it too gruesome. Even though it's been toned down some, I still consider it one of my favorite creepy stories.

Redmond's Private Screening

Sharper than any barber's straight razor, the edge of the samurai blade nicked the skin, drew blood. The director hissed in surprise, frowning at his cut finger, then laughed at himself. "How'd you like to slice *that* across your belly, Mikey?"

As his assistant Michael Kendai watched, Redmond held the blade up to the bright California sunlight that streamed into the makeshift studio through open windows and a cobwebbed skylight. "The katana is real, sir, a century old. More than just a prop."

"Forged in 1811, eh?" He didn't sound impressed. "It's just a sword."

Outside, the muffled sounds of motorcar traffic echoed along the dirt streets. One of the rattling vehicles backfired, and someone shouted obscenities in coarse Italian. Horses clopped by, pulling a late-morning milk cart. In his tiny warehouse studio, Michael knew that Redmond never no-

349

ticed any outside distractions. He was too caught up in finding interesting things to shoot with his motion-picture camera, and he would never believe the doomsayers who claimed that nickelodeon audiences were tired of seeing marvels on celluloid film.

"Where did you get this samurai Taka-what's-his-name?" Redmond spoke as if the young Japanese man and his elderly parents weren't already right there beside him. The immigrants spoke no English, remained apart from the conversation; but they knew full well the business matters being discussed. "And how did you talk him into doing Harry Carry in front of the motion picture camera?"

Michael folded his hands together, frowned at Redmond's unkempt appearance, mussed red-brown hair, and pungent cologne. He gave the director a look that plainly said *Not many people try my patience, but you are one of them.* "Akira Takahashi came to me of his own free will and volunteered his performance of *hara-kiri*."

He looked around the small back-room studio, not eager to begin, but they would lose the best sunlight soon. The glass cyclopean eye of his hand-cranked movie camera stood watching the young samurai. A spare camera (which didn't work anyway) leaned against a corner.

Takahashi sat in bright robes, cross-legged on the white blanket he had spread out for him on top of the sour sawdust. His pate had been shaved in the traditional fashion, his straight black hair gathered in a ponytail at his neck. The old father, holding a worn, nicked sword of his own, squatted stony-faced beside his son, staring straight ahead. Only the wrinkled mother showed fear and anger, flashing tears at Redmond.

Michael explained, "Mr. Takahashi wishes to book steamer passage back to Japan for his parents, and he can

350

think of no other way to raise the money. He considers it a fair exchange."

Redmond laughed nervously. His face had too many freckles, his skin was too pasty, his personality too slippery. "A lot of people are trying to get into this new movie business, but not usually by killing themselves on film." He sheathed the blade and handed the slim katana back.

Michael frowned at how low he himself had fallen, how disappointed the spirits of his own dead family must be. "Most directors do not wish to photograph such a spectacle either, and most patrons do not wish to see the result. But there are exceptions everywhere." He gave Redmond a cold stare. "You and I know how to find them."

The director raised his chin, pontificating. "Fifteen years ago, people flocked to nickelodeons to see a man sneeze, to watch a waterfall or a running horse. Today, we've got to give them something more for their money, eh?"

"I'm sure we do."

With a deaf ear for his assistant's sarcasm, Redmond strutted around the floor, looking at the natural light, at the position of the white blanket, but Michael had already set everything up perfectly. The three Japanese followed the director with their eyes, like animals in a cage.

"If they liked it so much in Japan, why'd they come to Hollywood in the first place, eh?" Redmond whispered, as if he didn't want the family to hear.

Michael drew a deep breath. "Many well-to-do samurai families were ruined in the overthrow of the last Shogun in 1868. Akira's father tried to earn a living in the new Japanese National Army, but he could not tolerate the army's lack of traditional honor. His eldest son, Akira's brother, entered the Japanese navy and was killed five years ago in the Russo-Japanese War. Akira and his parents then fled to

America, but they found no opportunities here. Now they are destitute and wish only to go home to die."

"Well, we'll help them out then, eh?" Redmond removed a folded piece of paper from his trouser pocket. "I drew up a simple contract for Mr. Samurai. Get him to sign it, and we can start shooting." He looked critically at the slanting daylight in the studio. "Read it to him, if you like."

Michael glanced over the contract; it looked as if Redmond had done the typing himself. He formally presented the samurai with his sword, then spoke rapidly in Japanese, explaining the contract and its purpose. The young man drew himself up, glared at Redmond, and answered Michael sharply.

"He doesn't understand the need for a contract." Michael turned to Redmond. "He asks if you are questioning his honor, if you doubt he will do as he has promised."

"What?" Redmond was oblivious to nuances. "The contract's for his protection, not mine."

Michael relayed the information. The old mother spoke quickly, while her son stared down at the curved sword in its sheath. "They ask why they should not trust you. Are you not an honorable man?"

Redmond made an exasperated sound. "Mikey, just explain to them I need to have it in writing that he's fully aware of what he's doing, that he offered his services willingly, and that I did not seek him out. What does he care anyway, eh? He's going to be dead."

Michael considered for a moment, then spoke in Japanese again. "I told him it was our custom to require such agreements. They have a great respect for customs and traditions." Finally, Takahashi took the contract and signed.

Redmond rolled his eyes and tucked the signed paper into his pocket. He clapped his hands for attention. "Okay, let's get this show on the road."

Michael took up his position behind the tripod, checking the lens, making sure the celluloid reel was loaded properly. Due to the questionable legality of his projects, Redmond involved as few people in the productions as possible. Michael had become accustomed to cranking the camera himself.

Sunlight poured through the flyspecked skylight, flooding the blanket spread on the floor. Akira Takahashi blinked in the glare. The handle of the katana looked like molten silver. Redmond didn't have to tell anyone what to do.

The old mother moved out of the light to where she could watch. The elder Takahashi drew himself taller, holding his own sword in one hand. He waited just behind and to the right of his son.

"Mikey, what's the old guy doing with a sword?" Redmond asked.

"He is the *kaishaku*." Michael paused just long enough to emphasize how little Redmond understood about what was going to take place. "During *hara-kiri*, a samurai is permitted to have a close friend stand beside him. Once he has succeeded in cutting open his belly, the friend is allowed to strike off his head, releasing him from the terrible pain."

Redmond's eyes widened. "You mean the old man is going to chop off—oh, fantastic! You didn't tell me that before."

Michael scowled, then erased the expression. By participating in this heinous act, he felt as if he was betraying the Takahashi family—but he was giving them what they wanted. Even with his rationalizations, he disgusted himself.

Michael looked through the camera and signaled to

Takahashi that everything was ready. The young samurai held the gazes of his parents for a long moment then he took up the sword. Michael began to turn the crank, recording every second on the clicking ribbon of film.

Takahashi pulled the katana from its sheath, never taking his eyes from the steel. The traditional samurai sword had been crafted by one of the finest Zen swordmakers, displaying an edge that consisted of half a million layers of folded steel, so sharp it seemed to slice rays of sunlight.

Takahashi took a white cloth from his father and wrapped it around the blade close to the hilt, leaving five inches of naked metal. He placed the wrapped katana on the blanket in front of him so he could proceed without taking his eyes from it. He never blinked while he undid the sash of his ceremonial robe, baring his chest. His stomach muscles were firm and tense.

Maintaining an even, smooth motion, Michael turned the camera crank as queasiness built within him. If a blade had plunged into his own belly, a swarm of butterflies would have emerged. . . .

Takahashi stared into space. Moving by itself, his hand picked up the katana again, flipped it around so that its point rested against his abdomen. Michael saw the smallest of tremors in his throat, as if he were trying not to swallow.

For long moments he did not breathe. Everything stopped, like a still from a motion picture. The father stood like a statue behind his son, sword raised and waiting. The ancient mother stared wide-eyed, but made no sound.

Redmond fidgeted. "What's he waiting for?"

"Shut up, Redmond."

Takahashi uttered an animal sound and thrust five inches of the blade into the left side of his abdomen. He made an astonished, coughing sound. He sat rigid, frozen again.

Crimson soaked into his bright robe, dribbled onto his leg. Spasms flickered across his face, betraying the pain. Takahashi's hands became slippery with blood, but he managed to keep his grip on the handle.

He used both hands against the back of the blade to push the cutting edge across his stomach in a gash that grew wider like a grotesque smile. His face turned gray and wet, and his breathing had no rhythm at all.

Michael continued to turn the camera crank. Redmond stared, silent with awe and fascination.

Takahashi's body shuddered as the blade cut below his navel. He gave another, weaker cry and wrenched the blade the rest of the way across.

Michael's world turned red and fuzzy. Black things swam in his stomach and his eyes; sweat trickled down his forehead. His knees turned to water, but at least he didn't topple the camera. Redmond saw him faint, muttered a curse, and pushed him out of the way. He began cranking the camera himself.

Takahashi's body convulsed as if he were trying to vomit, and intestines spilled out into his lap like gray, white, and red eels. His eyes pushed away their glassy bleariness and widened upon seeing all that had been kept neatly inside of him. He made a gurgling sound.

"Seppuku!" the old man cried and brought down his sword, striking off his son's head. The dead samurai collapsed into a heap of blood and mismatched flesh. The old man fell to his knees.

"Perfect!" Redmond said and stopped filming.

Two days later, Michael found Redmond waiting for him in a booth at the back of the café, adding too much sugar to his mug of coffee. Michael felt bone-weary and ragged. "The funeral pyre was very difficult to arrange, Redmond."

The director scowled up from his plate of fried eggs. "I don't care how hard it was, Mikey, you're not getting any more money for it. We've got a written agreement."

Michael let out a disgusted sigh as he sat down. "I was merely stating a fact." Seeing Michael's Japanese features, the waiter ignored him.

Redmond stirred his coffee, oblivious to how his spoon clanged against the mug. He whistled for the waiter to bring coffee for Michael. "So why did you go to all that trouble, if it was so difficult? That part wasn't written into the contract."

The waiter brought a silver pot over, then left scowling when Michael ordered tea instead. Michael leaned across the sticky tabletop. "Redmond, we killed their son. We owed it to them."

"What is someone with a conscience doing in this business?" Redmond tried to laugh, then took a bite out of his jam-smeared toast. "Besides, *we* didn't kill the guy. If his parents didn't want him to do it, they could have stopped him at any time." He slurped his coffee, then spooned in more sugar.

"Not in Japanese culture, Redmond. Once a son comes of age, the parents must follow his wishes. Mr. Takahashi decided to send his mother and father home. They had no choice in the matter." The waiter returned with Michael's tea. Absently, after the man had left, he took a sugar cube and laid it on his saucer, crushing it with the rounded bottom of his spoon, then tapped the sugar into his tea. "Their steamer should have departed for Japan at dawn today."

"You haven't heard yet, eh?" Redmond snickered, another bite of toast poised halfway to his mouth. "The old man was so excited that he dropped stone dead on the dock. Spilled Junior's ashes all over the place. Can you imagine the expression on the old lady's face?"

Michael stopped stirring his tea and looked straight into Redmond's muddy green eyes, searching for some sign of a practical joke. "How do you know this? Why did no one tell me?"

"Nobody could find you! As far as I know, you disappear off the face of the Earth when you don't want to be found. I got a telegram from a flustered delivery boy. Seems he'd been running all over Hollywood looking for you."

Michael remained silent for so long that Redmond began to fidget. The family had already been through so much. Michael finally muttered, as if speaking to himself, "Their eldest son died fighting the Russian navy for Liaotung Peninsula. On his last birthday, after he'd been gone for months on the battleship *Miyako*, the family set out an extra bowl of rice to honor him. And the son sent his spirit across the sea to join them for the meal. They laughed and talked, but with moonrise the spirit returned to the ship." He lowered his voice to a whisper. "That night, the *Miyako* struck a mine in the Sea of Japan and sank."

Redmond took another bite of his runny eggs. "You mean the ghost appeared even *before* the son was killed? Just what were they doing for their little celebration? Smoking opium pipes?"

"Opium is from China, Redmond, not Japan." With an effort, Michael regained his patience. "Vengeful ghosts are common in our tradition. Anyone who dies violently is certain to haunt those who caused him to suffer. But the Japanese don't believe a person needs to be dead to send his spirit wandering. The family Takahashi truly believes they dined with the elder son on the eve of his death."

"Aww, tug my heartstrings." Then Redmond narrowed his eyes at Michael. "Oh, I see, you're trying to scare me that Mr. Samurai's ghost is coming to get me. Forget it, Mikey. He volunteered. *You* brought him to me."

Michael didn't bother to respond. He stood up, leaving Redmond to pay for his unfinished tea. "Is that all you wanted to see me about?"

Redmond smiled. "I'll be screening my samurai picture in three days, and I need you to run the projector. I've found a private room and five men sufficiently bored with the nickelodeons. They'll pay ten dollars each, if I can deliver what I've promised. Some are worried it might be trick photography, like George Meliés might do."

"Meliés never showed a man disemboweling himself." Michael let no ironic expression show. "Besides, Redmond, who could question your honesty?"

Redmond grinned, then scowled, then drank his coffee.

Redmond insisted on keeping the door locked and the screening room dim, lit only by tasteless red lights behind incense burners. Even more tasteless was his decision to use Takahashi's white blanket—laundered to remove most of the bloodstains—as a projection screen.

Michael mounted the single celluloid reel on the projector as Redmond ushered his clients to flimsy wooden chairs in the room. The director wore a ridiculous Japanese robe, as if to create the proper ambiance.

Michael inspected the five men, who didn't bother to notice the Japanese-American assistant. One looked bored, two were fidgety (wearing obvious disguises); the remaining two frowned with skepticism while tugging on their identical muttonchop whiskers.

Michael wondered what type of lives these men led. Did they beat their wives, or harm their children, or frequent prostitutes—or did they derive enough pleasure just from watching gruesome motion-picture shows?

Of the six pictures on which he had worked with Redmond, this had been by far the most dissatisfying. The first had been a beautiful study of a ballerina's dance; then he had photographed sultry naked women. What might come next after ritual suicide—Redmond killing a baby, perhaps? Michael felt the shame in his involvement, even if Redmond didn't care.

After this evening's spectacle, Michael had made up his mind to disappear, as he had done so many times before, simply cover his tracks. He had enough skill and connections to find work elsewhere, even with his Japanese heritage. Perhaps he would go to New York City, though the majority of filmmaking had shifted toward the Los Angeles area with its variety of scenery. . . .

As Michael fed the celluloid film into the projector and checked the bulb, Redmond began to explain, inaccurately, the traditions and lore behind *hara-kiri*. Michael considered leaving the room after he started the projector, just to avoid seeing Takahashi die yet again, but decided against it. He would see this project through to the end, then be away from Redmond for good.

"Gentlemen, please enjoy the first screening of Redmond's *Scarlet Sword*." The director placed his hands together to imitate a Japanese bow, then stepped away from the bloodstained screen. As the projector began to flicker and whir, a sepia image of Akira Takahashi appeared on the screen. Michael focused quickly.

The five men in the audience watched as the grim young man sat cross-legged in his robes, staring at his sword. The film was intensely sharp and remarkably clear, showing too many details.

Takahashi withdrew the katana from its sheath and took the cloth from his father's gnarled hand. The clicking projector made the only noise in the room. The men leaned forward to watch; Michael was reminded of crocodiles lurking on riverbanks, alert for prey.

Takahashi placed the point of the sword against his stomach. He drew a deep breath, ready for the thrust.

Along the top of the screen appeared a deep crimson line, startling in its intensity against the black-and-white world. The red line widened, covering about a quarter of the screen before it began to drip like thick blood down the screen.

The five men muttered in amazement at Redmond's technique, how he'd been able to superimpose such a brilliant color onto the dull sepia tone.

"Mikey!" Redmond said, his voice a confused growl.

On the image, Takahashi stared down at the curved sword, oblivious to the thick red streams oozing across the screen and obliterating everything.

Feeling a growing horror, Michael tapped the projector lens. A shadow of his fingers should have fallen across the stained-blanket screen, but it didn't. Droplets popped out of the movie reel itself, like juice from a pomegranate seed. Michael touched the film feeding into the projector. His fingers came away wet and sticky.

The five men in the audience began to grumble. The crimson blot prevented them from seeing what the samurai was doing. Redmond swallowed several times; his freckled skin looked a sick gray in the red light.

The curtain of blood spilled to the bottom of the screen and covered the entire picture.

A roaring wind numbed Michael's ears, making him giddy. His vision went fuzzy, and then an empty coldness swept over him. The wind stopped abruptly, and a surreal fuzziness filled the screening room.

"Mikey!" Redmond's voice cracked like a pubescent teenager's.

The projector had stopped, though the screen still glowed like a window onto a scarlet landscape. Michael stood beside the motionless reel of film, but he could not move. Neither did the men seated in the wooden folding chairs. It was as if time had stopped, as if the apparatus projecting their lives had frozen on a single frame.

Except for Redmond, who stormed back and forth. "What the hell is going on here?" He seemed to know the answer, but could think of nothing else to say, no other way to pretend having command of the situation.

Will Vengeance suffice? It wasn't a voice. It wasn't even words. Michael heard Japanese, but the other men in the room seemed to understand as well.

Redmond made a strange sound between a gulp and a scream. "What do you mean? I did everything I promised!" He paused, as if spinning through his memories of everything Michael had told him. "I kept my honor!" Michael could not react, or move, or say anything to help him.

You are a man fundamentally without honor. Writing promises on paper to ensure that you will keep them, profiting by the suffering of others. These five will receive enough blood for their tastes, and my own. Such men deserve to die as common criminals.

The men sat frozen in their seats, but Michael watched as their heads slumped, one by one. He thought he heard a squelching sound and then a haunting series of screams echoing in the air. Michael felt like a helpless bystander, watching and wondering if he himself might be next.

Redmond, you shall have an opportunity to regain your honor.

The crimson covering the screen thinned and began to drip away, revealing a new image of a freckled man dressed in gaudy Japanese robes. He sat cross-legged and holding a samurai sword against his bared abdomen.

"You can't do this!" In the room, Redmond swatted at his robe as if trying to knock away the touch of a phantom sword. The image of Redmond on the screen sat contemplating the blade about to pierce his stomach. "We had a contract!"

I made no contract with you.

"Yes! You signed it, and I fulfilled my part, just like I promised. I didn't cheat you. Look, I'm sorry your father died, but I had nothing to do with that. I can't help it he spilled your ashes on the dock. Please!"

Michael tried to call out to Redmond, but his vocal cords had snapped like so many spiderwebs.

You have me confused with my son, fool. He is content with the bargain he made and with the price it cost him. I am the one who demands vengeance.

On the screen, another robed figure stepped behind the image of Redmond, holding a second sword. Takahashi's old mother, taking up her position to be Redmond's *kaishaku*.

I am the one who suffered most. My sons both gone, my husband. I am left with nothing, and I demand retribution.

"You can't be a ghost. You're not even dead!"

On the screen, the old woman smiled and raised the sword. *Why must a body be dead for the spirit to roam free?*

She nodded to the image of Redmond in the film. He looked into space as if in a trance, then drove the sword into his belly.

The film broke, and the projector bulb burst at the same time. Michael snapped off the machine, and as silence returned he heard a brief remnant of a scream disappearing into time. It sounded like Redmond's voice.

He fumbled for the main light switches. Redmond sprawled on the floor clutching his stomach. The other five men slumped in their folding wooden chairs, arms dangling at their sides.

Michael touched Redmond. The director's skin was cold and rigid. He checked the businessmen, and they were dead as well. He could find no blood anywhere. The sticky redness had vanished even from the film and the projector.

The shock crept up on him, paralyzing him. Why had the old woman's ghost spared him? He himself had arranged for her son's death. But Michael had not deviated from the old woman's conception of honor, as Redmond had. That did not mean Michael was an honorable man. He still had to deal with his own shame.

Shame. The traditions of Michael Kendai's culture had taught him how to cope with shame. Was the old woman's ghost expecting him to follow the traditional course? Redmond had the excuse of ignorance; Michael did not. Would she come after him if he did not kill himself to atone for his crime? But he was too much of a coward.

He rewound the film before he removed the reel. He vowed that no one else would ever watch *Scarlet Sword*. He would destroy it. He knew where Redmond kept prints of his other films, and he mounted the ballerina reel onto the projector. The police would be very confused.

Michael would be long gone before anyone discovered the bodies and turned their eyes toward a convenient Japanese scapegoat. Michael could cover his tracks. He was good at that.

New York looked better and better.

Fighting down the feelings of fear and shame within him, Michael left the screening room. He tried to keep from running as he fled into the street.

Ever since we started dating, Rebecca and I have gone to Renaissance Faires. We enjoy the ambiance, the shows, the costumes (and the food). We have known dedicated Faire people who live on site for weeks at a time, costumers and performers who take their details and time periods seriously. When we were invited to contribute a story to an anthology all about Renaissance Faires, we knew we had to do it. I have always been fascinated by the medieval legends of splinters of the True Cross, artifacts with miraculous properties. In the surreal world of a Ren Faire, with so many merchant stalls and exotic trinkets, we wondered what might happen if somebody might be selling a few splinters. . . .

Splinter

With Rebecca Moesta

Something about the Renaissance Faire beckoned to him like the sound of a hundred sirens luring a lonely sailor from the sea. In spite of the nearly hundred-degree heat of a California summer, he never tired of the beauty of it all— the jostling crowds in brightly colored clothing, the noisy parades of "royalty" and minstrels, the jugglers, the candle-makers, the serenity of a young mother with ample breasts exposed suckling a newborn child as if it were the most natural thing in the world. He loved the spectacle of a hundred different kinds of entertainers and artisans and food vendors, all putting on Elizabethan micro-performances minute by minute, doing their utmost to lure money from the cash-fat pockets of the faire-goers.

And it was those cash-fat pockets that brought Wil to these open-air festivals year after year. He never tired of the magic of thousands of bodies jostling together, muttering loudly, kicking up dust . . . never noticing the slender young man with the wispy beard and peasant clothing who expertly and discreetly relieved them of their excess valuables. Pickpocket, thief, rogue, highwayman—after all, that was a legitimate part of the time period, too. Certainly more authentic than either the churro or cappuccino seller.

It wasn't long before the first opportunity presented itself. Wil had learned to recognize those opportunities while he was still in high school, furtively watching for an unguarded purse or backpack; by now his instincts were so well tuned he hardly had to think about it. He had just passed the booth from which he'd shoplifted his own costume two years earlier, when he came upon a couple in casually elegant street clothes. They were having a heated discussion just outside a palm reader's tent.

"Why not?" the young woman said. "Are you afraid she'll tell us we should get married, after all?"

The young man scoffed. "Come on, they only say what they think you want to hear, anyway."

Quickly assessing the situation—it was important to be a good judge of character—Wil deduced from shoes, hair, makeup, and demeanor that the young woman would be carrying the money. *I'm even doing them a favor,* Wil thought. *A few arguments about money will give them a more accurate sense of their marriage compatibility than any palm reader could.*

He conveniently joined a cluster of people passing by, allowing himself to be crowded into the arguing couple. It took only one brief bump and a mumbled "Excuse me" to liberate an expensive Tumi wallet from the young woman's equally expensive Dooney & Bourke leather purse.

A little farther on, Wil ducked between two booths to determine the value of his acquisition. He was immediately impressed with himself: $281 in cash, and the wallet itself would fetch a good price at the local flea market. Wil tucked his prize into an interior pocket of his billowy brown knee breeches and moved on with a spring in his step. He would dispose of the credit cards, of course. Too easy to get caught using stolen cards.

And he didn't plan to get caught. Ever.

The next two hours proved considerably less satisfying. Discouraged, Wil bought a roasted turkey leg, then re-moved the pewter tankard he wore at his belt and had it filled with chilled ale. He sat down to eat on a bench in a small amphitheater where two jugglers were throwing knives at each other while making witty banter.

After polishing off his lunch, Wil tossed the turkey leg bone to the ground, not even bothering to look for a trash can. If someone scolded him about it, he could argue that his gesture was certainly truer to the Renaissance spirit than using a trashcan was. If it really bothered some do-gooder, let *him* dispose of it. Wil had never believed in much except himself . . . and he'd gotten over himself long ago.

Wil headed up a rocky, hay-strewn path, his eyes begin-ning their automatic sweep. His vigilance was quickly re-warded when he spied a middle-aged man with a chest-length salt-and-pepper beard counting out bills from a leather pouch at his waist. One of the bills fell to the ground and was caught by a hot breeze and blown a few feet behind him onto the path. Noting that the foot traffic was light and no one else was watching, Wil bent smoothly for the merest second, plucked the bill from the ground and continued up the path before the bearded man even had a chance to turn and look for the fallen money.

Wil passed a tarot card reader and a cluster of college students singing madrigals beside a fake wishing well. At the glass blower's tent, he spotted a man in his mid-thirties making a purchase. He wore safari shorts, a golf shirt, designer sunglasses, and sockless leather loafers. A grade-school-aged boy and girl pranced impatiently beside him. A quick glimpse told the pickpocket that the man's wallet contained enough cash to pay Wil's expenses for weeks.

"Come on, Dad! You promised we could see the story-teller."

"And that's just what we're going to do." The man slid his wallet into the front pocket of his shorts and accepted a wrapped package from the glass blower. Wil hung back and decided this man might be worth following.

The man began herding his children up the path. "Why'd we have to buy Mom another glass unicorn?" the boy said.

"We get her one every year, Evan, whether she can come or not. It's not her fault Grandma broke her hip," the girl answered. "What a stupid question."

"Now, Orli, don't call your brother stupid."

Wil gritted his teeth as he watched Perfect Family Guy, more determined than ever to interject a little bit of gritty reality into the pampered PFG's perfect life. Wil was an old hand at rationalizing to himself. He had been making up excuses and explanations for so long that he had almost come to believe them. Almost.

They came to a small pavilion, where half the floor was littered with hassocks and colorful overstuffed cushions on which children sat or reclined. A man with a leathery face and white shoulder-length hair walked among them, telling stories. Wooden tables running along one side of the breezy tent held books bound in hand-tooled leather. The sign over the pavilion said, "Tales of Glorye."

Wil watched as Orli, Evan, and Perfect Family Guy seated themselves on cushions. Pretending a casual interest, Wil entered the pavilion and began browsing the books. The storyteller spoke in a rich, expressive voice. Wil let the words wash over him, but his concentration was focused on PFG.

When the tale ended about ten minutes later, many of the listeners came up to drop money into a hat beside the old storyteller. Most of the audience left, but Wil's three marks lingered to ask questions. He suppressed an impatient sigh, picked up another leather-bound book and leafed through it, pretending to admire the meticulous hand lettering.

The storyteller plopped the hat full of money onto a table not far from Wil.

"So what happened next?" Orli asked the old man. "I mean, after the knight went back and told the King."

"Ah, now that's a much longer story."

"Do you have a book that has the story in it?" PFG asked.

"Over here on the table." The storyteller moved closer to Wil and selected a thick tome with a burgundy leather binding.

Perfect Family Guy showed it to his daughter. "Say, aren't you worried about leaving all that money just lying on the table?"

Finding the comment particularly ironic, Wil glanced over to see the old man smile. "I find that when you take care of the really valuable things, everything else takes care of itself. That's why I keep everything that's truly valuable to me right here in this pocket," he said, patting the left side of his leather breeches.

"I can admire that philosophy," PFG said.

"Look," Evan said, pointing at the pages of the book. "There's the story he told today."

"And two stories that come before, and three that come after it," Orli said. "Daddy, can we get this?"

PFG stroked his daughter's hair. "It would be the perfect souvenir."

Wil gritted his teeth again. *Perfect.* The very perfection of this family was driving him insane.

"Let me wrap that for you." The storyteller moved to Wil's right, reached under the table, and came up with two sheets of heavy paper that looked handmade.

The children began looking at the books on another table. PFG got out his wallet and began counting out the money. When the storyteller laid the sheets of paper on the table and began wrapping the book, Wil saw his chance. The pocket that held the old man's "true valuables" was within a foot of Wil's hand, so he clumsily dropped the book he had been looking at. Pretending to reach for it, Wil awkwardly bumped the old man with his hip, at the same time slipping his right hand into the pocket and apologetically steadying the storyteller with his left hand.

The whole maneuver took less than a second. Wil felt an uneven lump in the pocket, something strange—but just as his hand closed around it, a searing pain shot up his arm. It was like nothing he had felt since the age of ten when he'd lost control of his bicycle going down the driveway, veered into the neighbor's yard, fallen, and ripped his leg open on a sprinkler head.

With another jostle, Wil snatched his hand back and bent to retrieve the fallen book. He fumbled around, momentarily blinded by the pain and sucked in a sharp breath.

The old man put a hand on his back. "You all right, lad?"

For a panicked second, Wil wondered if the old man knew he'd been pickpocketed, but when his eyes focused on the kindly face, he saw no suspicion. "No, I, uh . . . sudden migraine." He put a hand to his head. "Probably the heat."

He handed the book back to the storyteller. As quickly as it had come, the scorching pain subsided, but Wil's hand still throbbed as if he had slammed it in a door.

Perfect Family Guy was beside him. "My wife gets migraines. They can get pretty nasty. Maybe you should lie down somewhere in the shade."

"There's plenty of room on the cushions," the old man offered.

"No," Wil said a little too quickly. "Thank you. I, uh, probably should take some medication for this. It's out in my car." Damn. Now that both men were so solicitous of him, Wil stood little chance of slipping in under their radar.

The storyteller regarded him with solemn eyes. "I hope you feel better really soon. Sometimes there's a trick to it."

"Do you need help out to your car?" PFG asked.

"Thanks. I'll manage." He left the pavilion, cursing himself for attracting so much attention from two potential marks. Surely he could have toughed out just a little bit of pain when he stood to profit so much. Already the searing stab had receded to a mere pinprick in his mind. It had been foolish weakness, but he would not call attention to himself again.

Once he was out of sight of the pavilion, Wil hurried to put as much distance between him and the two annoyingly helpful men as possible. Safely on the other side of the faire, he scanned the crowds once more for opportunities. *This is easy.* He struggled to focus. *You're a natural.* But nothing felt natural right now.

He was filled with a sensation that was simultaneously pleasant and unpleasant, a fizzy alertness of the mind not unlike the way he felt when, after an all-nighter, his body replaced sleep with pure adrenaline. Wil forced himself to move into the flow of shoppers and sightseers.

There. Wil saw his opportunity. A young woman with hot pink polish on the nails of her manicured fingers and pedicured toes was pushing a baby carriage. The mother stopped and bent to comfort the child as it continued to wail. Her attention was fully focused on the brat and not on the purse dangling from the stroller's handle.

He moved in. This was almost too easy. A simple swoop would do it.

His hand dipped into her purse, but the moment he touched the wallet, a lightning bolt struck the index finger of his right hand, shot through his wrist, traveled up his arm, and spiked into his brain. He simultaneously jerked his hand away and fell to his knees. The young mother looked up in alarm, her concentration startled away from her child who, also startled, stopped crying for a moment.

"Sorry," Wil gasped. "I tripped."

"You okay?" She moved around to the back of the stroller, darting a cautious glance down at her purse.

"Yeah, I'll be fine." Wil forced himself back to his feet and dusted off his breeches. "Good as new."

He backed away and lost himself in the crowd. That had been close. Damndest thing about his hand, too. In a patch of bright sunlight he examined his finger. It still stung, as if something small and sharp was embedded in it, but he could see no burn or blister, no cut, no sliver, *nothing.* Yet the pain—the pain in his hand, his arm, his head—had been real. He frowned. Maybe it was a pinched nerve, or maybe he really was having a migraine.

Wil always kept a bottle of ibuprofen stashed in his glove compartment, so he headed out the front entrance, remembering to get his hand stamped for re-entry. The parking lot offered no shade at all, and Wil considered waiting for the "shuttle," a wide, canvas-covered horse-drawn wagon that ferried attendees to and from their cars for tips. But the wagon was at the far end of the lot, and Wil didn't want to wait.

By the time he got to his battered '83 Dodge, he had worked up a substantial sweat. He got the bottle of extra strength pain reliever, took twice the suggested number, and washed them down with a grimace and a swallow of the flat, and by now hot, soda he'd left open in his car.

He rolled down the windows and took a short nap in the front seat to give the analgesic time to work. By the time he woke up it was late afternoon. The faire would be closing in a couple of hours, and parts of the parking lot had already begun to empty out. Wil felt greatly refreshed, in spite of the heat, and decided to get back to work.

He got out of his car and strode through the lot in the general direction of the entrance. As he walked, he glanced through car windows, looking for wallets, merchandise, purses left behind by faire-goers in the "safety" of their locked cars. For the most part, he ignored the older cars, like his, which usually weren't worth the trouble. He also avoided anything too new and too likely to have an alarm. Within ten minutes he had found one with a purse on the floor of the passenger side, "hidden" underneath the morning paper.

He grinned. "Haven't lost your touch, Wil."

All the doors were locked, of course, but he easily found a substantial rock that would remedy the situation. After a quick glance to make sure no one was around, he hefted the rock and swung it toward the window.

Several seconds later, Wil opened his eyes to escape the blinding white explosion in his head. He found himself flat on his back in the dirt, still grasping the rock. The slicing, stabbing, burning pain that grated up his arm was less intense now, but still impossible to endure.

When he dropped the rock, the pain finally began to subside. He hauled himself back to his feet, looked at the car window, and blinked in surprise. The window was not broken. Not even a crack. But he couldn't have missed—not with the force he'd used, not at such short range, and yet . . .

Carefully, afraid of triggering the terrible pain again, he picked up the rock, this time with his left hand. He swung with all his might at the window—

Bam! Flat in the dirt again. Wil's head pounded as if a grenade had gone off in his right ear, and his right arm felt as if an elephant had walked across it. He whimpered—something no one had ever heard him do. He wondered if he might be having a heart attack. Wouldn't that be the left arm? It was hard to think.

His fingers let loose of the rock, and he lay on the tire-flattened grass until the pain had subsided to a mere pricking in his right index finger. He brought it up to his face and studied it again, but still found nothing.

Something was very wrong with him. Wil didn't have medical insurance, but there was a first-aid tent inside the faire. He could describe his symptoms, maybe have them examine him. At least it would be free.

He got up slowly, not even bothering to brush the dirt

off. It might add an air of authenticity when he explained his symptoms, make the first-aid workers take him more seriously. On his way to the entrance, much to his chagrin Wil passed the Perfect Family waiting to take the wagon shuttle back to the parking lot. The wagon was coming, the horses clomping forward, the people pushing closer to get a seat aboard.

Wil hoped to walk past the annoying family unnoticed, but Perfect Family Guy saw him right away and managed to look genuinely concerned. "Hey, how's that migraine doing?"

Wil's first instinct was to lie, but what was the point? "I thought it was gone, but it seems to keep coming back."

The little girl, Orli, trotted out in front of the wagon, grinning. "Look—what pretty horses! Where's the video camera, Daddy? Can you take a picture of me with them?"

Two rowdy young boys began to clatter against each other with wooden swords they had purchased as souvenirs.

PFG nodded his sympathy toward Wil. "Could be one of those cluster headaches, I suppose. They come and go, and they can be as bad as migraines." Wil made a noncommittal response and stepped around the crowd, wanting to be away.

A younger boy, frustrated at being left out of his brothers' sword fight, pulled out his "Renaissance souvenir" pop gun and pointed it at them. "I'll get you both!" He fired the pop gun, augmenting the sound with his own yell, "BLAM!"

The hot and tired horses responded to the noise. Startled, they flinched in their harness, snorted, and lurched forward. Orli was standing right in their path, still waiting for PFG to film her with the video camera. The wagon driver wrenched at his reins, the horses lifted their hooves, and the girl shrieked.

Because he had been trying to get around the crowd, Wil was closest to where the girl stood. He jumped forward, knocked Orli out of the way, smashed into the nearest horse, and fell to the ground. Before he could roll away, he felt a hammer strike his chest. The girl had fallen backward to sprawl in the dirt and had already begun to sob, but the weeping came more from startlement and confusion than from severe pain. Wil, on the other hand, thought he might have cracked a rib or two.

The wagon driver backed the wagon up several feet and jumped down from the buckboard, and other people hurried forward to Wil and the girl. The horses snorted, as if embarrassed by the incident. Orli continued to cry softly, and her father quickly checked to make sure she was uninjured before moving to take a look at Wil. "Wow, that could've been bad! I don't know how to thank you. Are you all right?"

Surprised was the first thing that came to Wil's mind. He had acted completely without thinking, with no regard for his own safety. Stranger yet, he felt very little pain. "Fine." And he found it was true. His entire body was suffused with a pleasant tingling sensation. "Better than fine. I'm great."

Perfect Family Guy still looked concerned. "Could just be endorphins and adrenaline talking. You'd better have a doctor check you out."

A distant part of his mind seemed aware that his body was hurt. He pulled open the loose neck of his muslin peasant shirt and looked inside. A red flush of bruising was already beginning to appear beneath the skin. How odd. After the inexplicable agony he had experienced several times today—each time while trying to ply his trade—now he felt euphoria when he should *really* be hurt. And he'd only been trying to help someone, after all. There was definite irony in that: invisible pain after trying to steal, and a feeling of well-being when trying to help, despite a visible injury.

Wil's eyes narrowed as the thoughts flashed through his mind. *Was* it irony, or was this something more sinister? It had all begun after he'd tried to pick the storyteller's pocket. Had the old man done something to him, administered some sort of drug or hypnotized him?

He smiled up at the PFG. "You're probably right. I'll head back inside to the first-aid tent."

Perfect Family Guy still looked concerned. "They won't be able to do much in there. You might need an x-ray. Do you have insurance?"

Wil shook his head. PFG pulled out his wallet and removed a business card. "Here's my card. If you end up needing to see a real doctor, I'll make sure that your expenses get covered."

"Thanks." Wil glanced down at the little rectangle of paper, then put it in his pocket. *Bentley Watson-Taylor III, Attorney at Law.* "I hope I won't need it. I'm just glad Orli's okay." A tingling rush of good feeling started in Wil's hand and swept up his arm and through his body.

"Thank you, Mister," Orli said, and gave him a hug. "I hope you're going to be okay."

Wil knew the hug against his sore ribs should have hurt, but he didn't even wince. "I'll be fine. You just stay out of trouble."

Back at the entrance he showed his hand stamp, went through, and headed toward the storyteller's pavilion.

On the way, he tested his theory. He tried to pick a pocket and received a fresh jolt of pain. Then, after helping an older woman push her husband's wheelchair up an uneven slope and position the man where he could watch a troupe of players perform humorously abbreviated Shakespeare plays, Wil felt the rush of euphoria again.

The old storyteller had definitely done something to him.

When Wil reached the pavilion, the old man had just finished spinning a tale and the few late-afternoon audience members left quickly. Wil walked straight toward the storyteller, stepping over the scattered cushions. The leathery face registered recognition and concern, but no surprise.

"What did you do to me?" Wil demanded. His voice was rough with mixed emotion.

The old man considered the question. "I shared something with you, as I do with all who listen to me. How is your headache? Are you feeling better now?"

Wil felt an acid spurt of frustration burn in his stomach. "You know it wasn't a headache, and no, I'm not feeling better. You tricked me."

The old man's expressive eyebrows climbed a millimeter up his forehead. "How so?"

Wil cast about for an answer. He wasn't sure how he'd been tricked or what had been done to him, but he traced the strangeness back to *here,* in this tent with gauzy walls and cooling breezes, and this enigmatic man from whom he had tried to steal something of "true value."

"You . . . you tricked me by saying you had something valuable in your pocket."

The old man nodded soberly. "You heard that, did you? That is true. I carry what I value most in my pocket. But how is that a trick?"

Wil seethed inside. Wasn't the answer obvious? "Because you knew I'd hear you, and that I'd try to find out what was in your pocket."

"Ah." The storyteller's voice was barely a whisper. "And . . . ?"

"*And?* When I touched whatever was in your pocket, it gave me a jolt of some sort. It hurt so much I let go and fell to the ground. That's how you tricked me. What was it? Some kind of trap?"

"I admit, I did speak the truth in your hearing, yet no one can choose what another person will do with the truth once they hear it. I did not make that choice for you."

Wil couldn't believe his ears. Was the storyteller actually implying that this was all his own fault? "Oh no you don't, old man. You still did something to my hand, and I'm betting you know how to undo it. Every time I try to practice my . . . business, my hand, my arm, my body, my brain, *everything* hurts like hell. Well, fine. You made your point. Picking pockets is bad. Stealing is bad. I get it." He raised a fist. "Now make it stop or I'll—"

An excruciating pain sizzled up Wil's arm and blinded him for a moment. As soon as he lowered his arm and forced his fist to relax, the agony began to fade. "For God's sake, just make it stop."

"Make it stop? For God's sake . . ." The storyteller looked troubled. "Let me tell you a story—it's what I do. Please, sit down."

Wil wasn't sure why, but he sat. And listened.

"In the time of the Third Crusade, the Year of Our Lord 1190, many brave knights, greedy lordlings, and hapless soldiers traveled across Europe by boat or by foot, in order to secure the Holy Land from the evil Turks. Some crusaders truly felt a calling from God, but the real reason for most of the lords and commanders—third and fourth sons without lands to inherit—was to capture new domains to rule. Other knights simply came for the chance to fight, to kill the infidel, to find glory on the battlefield.

"One such knight—let us call him Roderick the Brash—

led his soldiers into battle, cutting his way through Turkish lines to establish a foothold in Jerusalem. There, while attempting to occupy the ancient holy city, Roderick came upon a kindly old leather worker, who went by the name of Julius. The leather worker did good deeds for his neighbors in Jerusalem, without giving thought to whether they were Christians, Moslems, or Jews. He claimed to have been a centurion in the Roman army in the time of Jesus Christ."

Wil scoffed. "That would have made him over a thousand years old."

The storyteller simply looked at him. "It's a story. Would you like to hear more?"

"As long as there's a point."

"Julius himself was present at the crucifixion and had come into possession of a fragment of the True Cross, and a Splinter from this remarkable artifact had kept him alive for so long. Though he wasn't wealthy, the leather worker had sufficient means to meet his needs and was content. No doubt he experienced the same euphoria you did when you performed a selfless deed."

"That's a stretch. Are you telling me—"

The old man calmly went on. "When he learned that Julius the leather worker had such a treasure, this holy relic, Roderick the Brash came at night into his shop and demanded to see the fragment. Julius told him the story I just told you. And then Roderick struck him down with his sword and took the fragment for himself."

The old man's gaze was distant, and his voice hitched. After a brief pause, he reached into the pocket where he kept his treasure, where Wil had felt the first sharp sting. He withdrew an oddly shaped and unimpressive lump of very old wood, less than two inches long. "When the fragment encounters someone who needs its . . . assistance, it shares a part of itself. A Splinter.

"Roderick the Brash had great need of it. After touching the fragment, Roderick attempted to ignore the message of the Splinter. He continued to fight and kill until the pain became so overwhelming it rendered him unconscious, and his men left him for dead on the battlefield. After that, Roderick had no choice but to change his ways. He performed his penance for many centuries, made his way through the world, and found his own contentment. And, over the years, the fragment grew smaller, bit by bit, as it found others who needed it."

Wil's impatience mixed with wonder, annoyance, and indignation. "So, I'm supposed to believe that you're a knight named Roderick the Brash, who lived during the Third Crusade? And that I've got a Splinter of the True Cross stuck in my hand?"

"I simply told the story." The old man gave him a noncommittal look. "Believe what you wish."

Wil blew out an angry breath, looking at the lump of wood. It wasn't the least bit impressive. "If I believe that's a real holy relic with magical powers, and an invisibly small Splinter is embedded in my finger, then I'd also have to believe that I no longer have free will. I'm just a rat in a maze, and God is some sort of cosmic experimental researcher dispensing either treats or electric shocks, depending on whether or not I do what He wants."

The storyteller did not answer the accusation directly. His pensive gaze seemed to look through Wil. His eyes seemed very, very old. "There are many possible interpretations—some harsher than others. Some say that the Splinter is a sort of . . . conscience for anyone who has discarded the conscience that God gave them. But I don't believe that.

"Others believe that because the cross is a symbol of sacrifice, a Splinter of the True Cross might bestow peace and happiness for every deed that is selfless or sacrificial, while selfish acts are rewarded only with pain."

The storyteller paused. "But I don't believe that either. All of my experience and knowledge have led me to conclude one thing, that a Splinter is distilled truth. No more, no less."

Wil wanted to object, to interrupt and call the man's words bullshit. He didn't believe in Biblical morality or in miracles and had never felt a need to go to church. He had certainly never let himself be bound by superstition. But something kept him silent.

"Each Splinter senses the good or bad potential of a person's actions, then gathers those effects, concentrates them into the *now,* and transmits the truth back to its owner. If a thief takes a wallet, he causes financial injury to the person he steals from. He also steals some of that person's time, and robs him of his feeling of safety. Like a pebble dropped into a pond, there are ripple effects."

Wil rubbed his forefinger but felt no twinge of pain. "Now you're getting pretty esoteric."

"It is concrete enough. Perhaps the thief's victims would not have enough-money to buy necessities for themselves or their families. Imagine that a person needed to fix the brakes on his car. If there wasn't enough money to fix the brakes, and the brakes failed, then a terrible accident could result. All these things factor together and are condensed by the Splinter into a single manifestation of pain, great or small. In the same way, a kind or unselfish deed helps both the giver and receiver. The Splinter concentrates consequences, intensifies truth."

"But . . . but, if I believe you, then you've just taken away my livelihood!" Wil squawked. "That's how I survive.

You don't have any right."

The storyteller smiled. "Imagine what the ruthless warrior Roderick the Brash must have experienced. How difficult it was to give up hatred, pillaging, and violence, stranded in a hostile foreign land, suddenly prevented from looting and killing. . . . Still, he learned to get by. So can you."

Wil squirmed. Something about the old man's interpretation rang uncomfortably true. "So is there anything I could do to get rid of it? Short of amputation? I mean, if I did a lot of good deeds would it go away . . . and leave me in peace?"

"I have met a few people who tried amputation. Strange, no matter how much they cut off—finger, hand, arm—the Splinter stayed inside them, as if it were in their blood. Perhaps you stand a better chance of finding peace if the Splinter remains in your finger."

The old man began to stack up his fine tooled-leather books. With a callused finger, he rubbed the intricate designs and workings, smiling at the craftsmanship. "It's not so hard to learn a new trade, given a little incentive, although you might find it comforting to revisit . . . familiar surroundings from time to time."

Outside the tent, criers were announcing the closing of the Renaissance Faire for another day.

Wil just stood, unsettled, staring at the storyteller, not knowing what to do. "This is impossible. You don't really expect me to change who I am and what I do for a living just overnight, do you?"

"No, my friend. But you will have plenty of time. After all these centuries, who would know better than I?" He paused for a moment, holding up one of his ornate books. "You might discover talents you never knew you possessed.

You already have quick hands, sharp eyes. Think about what you could become."

The old man's words were too much to absorb all at once. Wil had to let the implications sink in, and questions piled up in his mind. "I have plenty of time . . . ?" Then, as he began to consider the possibilities, a familiar pleasurable sensation tingled in his hand. "You mean I could be a fine artist, a poet, a rock guitarist, even a surgeon? How would I choose?"

A small smile flickered at the corner of the storyteller's mouth. "Why choose? You could do them all. But use your abilities to help people, and you will find contentment."

The pleasant warmth seemed to be growing stronger. "Well, I guess I've always wanted to see other countries. Maybe I could join a service organization and travel while I learn some job skills—new ones, I mean—and some foreign languages."

Now the tingle seeped from Wil's hand into his entire body and, for the first time in memory, he felt a true sense of wonder.

And one last little nasty trick. For many years, myself and several writer friends—including Kristine Kathryn Rusch, Dean Wesley Smith, Nina Kiriki Hoffman, Jerry and Kathy Oltion, and others—each wrote a special story for Christmas Eve, which we read aloud before opening presents.

What does happen to the kids who don't show up on the "nice" list anyway?

Santa Claus Is Coming to Get You!

'Twas the night before the night before Christmas, and all through the house little sounds were stirring . . . sinister, creeping, whispers of noise. Echoes of things better left unseen in the darkness, even around the holiday season.

Jeff stared up at the bottom of his little brother's bunk. Ever since Stevie had gotten rid of the night light, he always feared that the upper bunk would fall on top of him and squish him flat.

A strong gust of wind rattled the windowpane. Wet snow brushing against it sounded like the hiss of a deadly snake, but he could hear that his brother was not asleep. "Stevie? I thought of something about Christmas."

"What?" The voice was muffled by Stevie's ratty blue blanket.

"Well, Santa keeps a list of who's naughty and nice, right? So, what does he do to the kids who've been naughty?" He didn't know why he asked Stevie. Stevie wouldn't know.

"They don't get any presents I guess. . . . Do you really think Mom and Dad are that mad at us?"

Jeff sucked in a breath. "We were playing with matches, Stevie! We could have burned the house down—you heard them say that. Imagine if we burned the house down . . . Besides, it doesn't matter if Mom and Dad are angry. What'll Santa think?"

Jeff swallowed. He had to get the ideas out of his head. "I gotta tell you this, Stevie, because it's important. Something a kid told me at school.

"He said that it isn't Santa who puts presents out when you're good. It's just your Mom and Dad. They wait until you go to sleep, and then they sneak out some presents. It's all pretend."

"Oh come on!"

"Think about it. Your parents are the ones who know what you really want." He pushed on in a whisper. "What if Santa only comes when you're bad?"

"But we said we were sorry! And . . . and it wasn't my idea—it was yours. And nothing got hurt."

Jeff closed his eyes so he wouldn't see the bottom of the upper bunk. "I think Santa looks for naughty little boys and girls. That's why he comes around on Christmas Eve.

"He sneaks down the chimney, and he carries an empty sack with him. And when he knows he's in a house where there's a naughty kid, he goes into their bedroom and grabs them, and stuffs them in the sack! Then he pushes them up the chimney and throws the bag in the back of his sleigh with all the other naughty little boys and girls. And then he takes them back up north where it's always cold and where the wind always blows—and there's nothing to eat."

Jeff's eyes sparkled from hot tears. He thought he heard Stevie shivering above him.

"What kind of food do you think Santa gets up there at the North Pole? How does Santa stay so fat? I bet all year long he keeps the naughty kids he's taken the Christmas before and he eats them! He keeps them locked up in icicle cages . . . and on special days like on his birthday or on Thanksgiving, he takes an extra fat kid and he roasts him over a fire! That's what happens to bad kids on Christmas Eve."

Jeff heard a muffled sob in the upper bunk. He saw the support slats vibrate. "No, it's not true. We weren't that bad. I'm sorry. We won't do it again."

Jeff closed his eyes. "You better watch out, Stevie, you better not cry. 'Cause Santa Claus is coming to get you!"

He heard Stevie sucking on the corner of his blanket to keep from crying. "We can hide."

Jeff shook his head in despair. "No. He sees you when you're sleeping, and he knows when you're awake. We can't escape from him!"

"How about if we lock the bedroom door?"

"That won't stop Santa Claus! You know how big he is from eating all those little kids. And he's probably got some of his evil little elves to help him."

He listened to Stevie crying in the sheets. He listened to the wind. "We're gonna have to trick him. We have to get Santa before he gets us!"

On Christmas Eve, Dad turned on the Christmas tree lights and hung out the empty stockings by the fireplace. He grinned at the boys who stared red-eyed in fear.

"You guys look like you're so excited you haven't been able to sleep. Better go on to bed—it's Christmas tomorrow, and you've got a long night ahead of you." He smiled at them. "Don't forget to put out milk and cookies for Santa."

Mom scowled at them. "You boys know how naughty you were. I wouldn't expect too many presents from Santa this year."

Jeff felt his heart stop. He swallowed and tried to keep anything from showing on his face. Stevie shivered.

"Oh, come on, Janet. It's Christmas Eve," Dad said.

Jeff and Stevie slowly brought out the glass of milk and a plate with four Oreo cookies they had made up earlier. Stevie was so scared he almost dropped the glass.

They had poured strychnine pellets into the milk, and put rat poison in the frosting of the Oreos.

"Go on boys, good night. And don't get up too early tomorrow," Dad said.

The two boys marched off to their room, heads down. Visions of Santa's blood danced in their heads.

Jeff lay awake for hours, sweating and shivering. He and Stevie didn't need to say anything to each other. After Mom and Dad went to bed, the boys listened for any sound from the roof, from the chimney.

He pictured Santa Claus heaving himself out from the fireplace, pushing aside the grate and stepping out into the living room. His eyes were red and wild, his fingers long claws, his beard tangled and stained with the meal he'd had before setting out in his sleigh—perhaps the last two children from the year before, now scrawny and starved. He would have snapped them up like crackers.

And now Santa was hungry for more, a new batch to restock his freezer that was as big as the whole North Pole.

Santa would take a crinkled piece of paper out of his pocket to look at it, and yes there under the "Naughty" column would be the names of Jeff and Stevie in all capital letters. He'd wipe the list on his blood-red coat.

His black belt was shiny and wicked looking, with the silver buckle and its pointed corners razor sharp to slash the throats of children. And over his shoulder hung a brown burlap sack stained with rusty splotches.

Then Santa would go to their bedroom. Jeff and Stevie could struggle against him, they could throw their blankets on him, hit him with their pillows and their toys—but Santa Claus was stronger than that. He would reach up first to snatch Stevie from the top bunk and stuff him in the sack.

And then Santa would lunge forward with fingers grayish blue from frostbite. He'd wrap his hand around Jeff's throat and draw him toward the sack. . . .

Then Santa would haul them up through the chimney to the roof. Maybe he would toss one of them toward the waiting reindeer who snorted and stomped their hooves on the ice-covered shingles. And the reindeer, playing all their reindeer games, would toss the boy from sharp antler to sharp antler.

All the while, Santa stood leaning back, glaring and belching forth his maniacal "Ho! Ho! Ho!"

Jeff didn't know when his terror dissolved into fitful nightmares, but he found himself awake and alive the next morning.

"Stevie!" he whispered. He was afraid to look in the pale light of dawn, half expecting to find blood running down the wall from the upper bunk. "Stevie, wake up!"

Jeff heard a sharp indrawn breath. "Jeff! Santa didn't get us."

They both started laughing. "Come on, let's go see."

They tumbled out of bed, then spent ten minutes dismantling the barricade of toys and small furniture they had placed in front of the door. The house remained still and quiet around them. Nothing was stirring, not even a mouse.

Jeff glanced at the dining room table as they crept into the living room. The cookies were gone. The milk glass had been drained dry.

Jeff looked for a contorted red-suited form lying in the corner—but he saw nothing. The Christmas tree lights blinked on and off; Mom and Dad had left them on all night.

Stevie crept to the Christmas tree and looked. His face turned white as he pulled out several new gift-wrapped boxes. All marked "FROM SANTA."

"Oh, Jeff! Oh, Jeff—you were wrong! What if we killed Santa!"

They both gawked at the presents.

"Jeff, Santa took the poison!"

Jeff swallowed and stood up. Tears filled his eyes. "We have to be brave, Stevie." He nodded. "We better go tell Mom and Dad." He shuddered, then screwed up his courage.

"Let's go wake them up."

THE GREAT OUTDOORS

The outdoors has always been a fundamental part of my inspiration and my writing process. I live in the Rocky Mountains and spend a great deal of my time hiking—and writing. I wander for miles, microcassette recorder in hand, dictating chapter after chapter, or just mulling over a plotline or characters.

These two articles and a short story are an effort to show how the outdoors and the breathtaking beauty of planet Earth have opened up creative windows for men, and to try and explain my obsession to the couch potatoes who "don't get it."

False Summits

I set up my Colorado writing office to look out at the spectacular Rocky Mountains. The scenery, the fresh air, the lower cost of living, all were undeniable advantages. Then my brother-in-law gave me a book about the fifty-four peaks in Colorado over 14,000 feet high, along with maps and instructions on how to climb them all, if one were crazy enough.

Nothing thrills a goal-oriented person more than a *List*. I was hooked and immediately took up the hobby. Over the next five years, I did indeed summit all those peaks. I learned a lot about mountain climbing . . . and its relationship to writing.

I grew up in the Midwest, a place not known for many lofty and craggy peaks. Without first-hand experience, I had the rather distorted impression that "mountains" were pointy gray triangles with a zigzag of snow on the top, as depicted in Bugs Bunny cartoons. Since then, though, I've become an expert of the ins and outs (and ups and downs) of mountains, and I've realized that climbing these complicated and often difficult summits offers a useful parallel to a writing career.

===========================

Peak 1

First submission
First personal rejection
First publication in a small press magazine
First professional publication

===========================

Caution: Metaphor Ahead. As anyone starting out knows, a writing career is a very steep path to follow. The terrain is complicated, the trails not clear, and often forests block your view until you actually get to the top. While struggling up a tough grade, you keep your eyes only on the summit immediately ahead, forcing yourself to push on just to reach the top of that ridge.

It wasn't until I began mountain climbing in earnest that I understood the frustrating and heartbreaking frequency of what are called "false summits." You can glimpse the apparent high point of the trail, barely seen through the trees, and you expend all your energy focused on the goal. The top is there, getting closer—

And when you finally arrive, you see that what you thought was the top of the mountain, your hard-earned destination at last, is only a small subpeak. Right after that ridge, the trail continues farther and steeper toward a much taller and tougher point. You just couldn't see it because the false summit in front of you got in the way.

For many writers starting out, that first hard-to-obtain summit may be getting published, even in a fanzine, or receiving a personal rejection note from a professional market. But once you've achieved that, you have to catch your breath, take in the view . . . and see that you've merely managed to reach a crest of the surrounding heavily forested foothills. The majestic snow-covered mountain peaks are much farther away.

============================

Peak 2
First novel sale
Qualification for SFWA membership
First photo or review in a science fiction news magazine

============================

Many writers at this point simply turn around, enjoy their pleasant day hike, and go home. Others push on to the next ridge, closer to the treeline. From your new vantage atop the foothills, that tree-line peak certainly looks like the summit.

From then on, you struggle to reach *that* point, and once you've succeeded—your first professional sale, qualification for SFWA membership, a novel sold to a publisher—you'll have a better view. You can see more of the surrounding terrain. But you also realize that this still isn't the actual summit. There's another ridge up ahead even higher, up in the rocky tundra with a few patches of snow.

Again, some writers stop here. The true mountain climbers, though, eat their beef jerky, drink some Gatorade, and keep going.

=============================

Peak 3
First multiple book contract
Quit your day job and become a full-time writer
First major award or nomination
=============================

Anyone with experience in the mountains knows there are plenty of pitfalls and dangers. I've sat on the top of 14,014-foot San Luis Peak watching the approach of angry thunderclouds, but when I took my hat off to drink from my water bottle, every strand of hair on my head and arms stood straight upright and the air crackled with static electricity. Needless to say, I beat a hasty retreat as the lightning moved in.

I've been caught a quarter mile from the top of Columbia Peak in a white-out blizzard in early September, where I huddled shivering for an hour until finally, experiencing the first stages of hypothermia, I trudged out into the snow and blindly stumbled down the slope to lower and warmer altitudes.

I've crawled across cliff ledges that would have made Indiana Jones proud, and rappelled down a sheer 150-foot dry waterfall, the only way down from the top of Little Bear Peak, Colorado's most difficult Fourteener. I've even encountered a black bear on the summit of isolated and rarely climbed Culebra Peak.

Similarly, in your "career climb" as a writer, there are plenty of pitfalls—some that you can control and others that are simply forces of nature. Editors quit, publishing houses fold, you miss a deadline. A psycho serial killer announces that he drew all of his inspiration from your novel.

Proceed with caution so you don't slip and fall.

==========================

Peak 4

First bestseller

First movie deal

Friends and acquaintances want to borrow money all the time

Other writers begin sniping at you for your "undeserved" success

Critics blast you because you're "too popular"

==========================

I have found that each time I reach a peak in my career, there is a higher mountain visible in the distance. Once you set goals for yourself and reach them, you can either rest on your laurels, or try to climb higher. Are Tom Clancy, John Grisham, and Michael Crichton comfortably perched and satisfied on lofty Mount Everest? Or do even they see more challenging summits in the distance?

Even though I've climbed all the 14,000-foot peaks in Colorado, Denali in Alaska is 20,320 ft, the highest peak in the US. Kilimanjaro in Africa is 19,340 ft, and Everest is 29,028 ft.

I may have seen a lot of summits, but there are still plenty of higher ones left to dream about. . . .

============================

Peak 5

?

Landscapes

By the time our clunky shuttle finished two weeks in round-about transit to the "designated wilderness" planet of Bifrost, Craig and I were more than ready to stretch our legs on the trails of a new alien world. I just hoped we weren't too out of shape for vigorous trekking.

The uniformed ranger who piloted us wasn't altogether happy with his chauffeur duties, but his gruff answers to our many questions could not diminish my exuberance. We were two hard-working guys, looking forward to having the peace and solitude of an entire world to ourselves, and determined to take the long, risky hike to see one of the greatest sights in the Galaxy. With humanity spreading across practically every habitable world, it was nearly impossible to "get away from it all." Yet time and again we managed it.

Craig had filled out the sheaf of required forms, and I had paid all of the fees. We were not just tourists of the "pull over, look, then drive on" variety. We were *authorized* to be here on Bifrost. We had the best modern backpacking equipment, semi-sentient adventure clothing, and camp supplies—not to mention embarrassingly detailed maps. These expeditions had become an annual ritual for us.

Scenery. Solitude. Adventure. This was going to be heaven.

To minimize the impact of visitors on the environment, our ship touched down in a meadow, the single authorized landing zone for official vehicles. When the shuttle's hatch opened, Craig and I stuffed the appropriate allergen filters into our noses, then took deep breaths of the clean alien air. Ready to go.

"I have been counting down the nanoseconds until today," Craig said. "Oh, I was looking forward to this." He had looked tired and a little withdrawn during the long trip, but now he seemed to come alive again. Though he spends most of his life inside an artificially lit starship cabin, Hawaiian genes from somewhere back in Craig's bloodline endowed him with honey-tan skin, deep-brown eyes, and blue-black hair. I, on the other hand, am freckled and pale as protoplasm; despite undergoing melanin treatments and applying sunfilms, I'd probably burn beet red before the end of the trek.

The ranger unloaded our packs from the shuttle's cargo bin. Craig and I hoisted the heavy loads onto our shoulders, carefully adjusted the straps and clamps for balance, and double-checked each other's equipment as if we were orbital construction workers suiting up for a spacewalk.

For us, no first-person-tourist simulations would do: no 3-D images of scenery, no implanted memories of the perfect vacation. This was the real thing. We were going to be entirely and blissfully alone in the wilderness of Bifrost. Making a memory.

"You've got seven days," the ranger said. "Make sure you're back in time, or I'm gone."

Craig turned his wide face to the sky. "If you don't see us in a week, maybe we don't want to go back!"

"Uh-huh." The ranger expressed an encyclopedia of skepticism in those two syllables.

"How often do you really lose people out here?" I asked him.

"About one in twelve miss the scheduled pickup and are never found."

"Maybe they decided to turn Robinson Crusoe," Craig suggested.

"Probably got eaten." The ranger shrugged. "With budget cuts, the Planetary Wilderness Bureau can't afford to go looking for everybody. It's all in the waiver you signed."

"We can handle ourselves," I said. "We do a wilderness trip every year. Even if we get lost, we know how to find our way back."

The ranger stared at us with a grim frown, convinced this would be the last time anyone would ever see us alive. I see that look on my wife's face every time I leave on one of my outdoorsy expeditions with Craig. She never believes me when I promise to be careful, though I have survived every adventure relatively unscathed. So far.

Craig grabbed his walking stick and tossed the other one to me. "Come on, Steve, we'd better start relaxing as fast as we can. Only seven days to cure a year's worth of headaches."

We activated the staffs, which would help us navigate and could also act as cattle-prod defenses if we were harassed by wild animals—though we'd face severe fines and time on a penal planet if we dared to *hurt* any endangered alien species.

"Right," I said. "Asgaard awaits."

Bifrost vegetation had more blues and oranges than a typical chlorophyll-based ecosystem. We passed between scaly ferns and ethereal lichentrees that looked like upside-down waterfalls, and got a view of an ugly swatch of clear-cut ground where loggers had managed to chop down everything before strict preservation regulations had been passed. Now, gray-white stumps thrust up from the soil like razor stubble on a giant's face.

Neither Craig nor I are foaming-at-the-mouth environmentalists, but when you're utterly alone on a wilderness planet, it changes your perspective, clears your head. The scars left by human greed or carelessness tend to look like a big steaming pile of dog shit right in the middle of a playground—*our* playground for the next week.

"I'm glad I never had to haul freight for lumberjockeys or stripminers." Craig scowled, taking the environmental damage as a personal affront. "In a beautiful place like this, what the hell were they thinking?"

"I thought the company didn't give you any choice about the cargoes you carry," I said.

"Screw the company—they've done it to me enough times. Gotta take a stand once in a while." Frowning, he stumped off, as if turning his back on the problems of his real life. "I came here to get away from all that."

Craig is a long-distance cargo hauler who flies a company-owned transport ship around five systems, picking up percentages along the way. He has always dreamed of buying his ship from the company and becoming an independent hauler—and he's gotten close—though recent months had brought a series of setbacks. I didn't know the details, but I would probably hear plenty during the long trek.

At some point each year Craig and I need to get away, escape our jobs and civilized home lives, no matter how much it costs or how far away we have to go. Forget spas and empathic massages, nightlife and interactive entertainment experiences. Sometimes a guy just wants to get sweaty, be miserable, sleep in an uncomfortable tent, eat bad-tasting food, get lost, and then find the way back again, ready to face another year of reality.

Before long the faint path descended toward the distinctive rushing-wind sound of a wide creek. We picked our way over boulders toward the cascade. Wiping perspiration off his brow, Craig climbed up onto a squarish talus slab and shook his head. "This is a *trail?*"

"It's a *route.*" I flipped the filter over my right eye and turned it on so I could see the infrared cairns, little beacons invisible to the naked eye—and presumably to the Bifrost wildlife as well—that marked the trail without defacing the nearly pristine wilderness.

A ribbon of foamy lavender water etched its way through pockmarked stone. Some sort of indigenous algae gave the stream the peculiar tint that in itself served as a reminder not to drink the water without treating it first. In a narrow spot over the creek, three wobbly looking lichentree logs had been knocked over to form a corduroy bridge.

I gingerly started across, looking down into the angry cascade. Although none of the guidebooks had mentioned the presence of aquatic carnivores on Bifrost, the very idea made me scuttle quickly to the other side. Craig paused, bent over, and ceremoniously spat a glob of phlegm into the water. Although he's four years older than me, being out in the wilderness always seems to transform him into a little kid.

Once we were over the bridge, I let my eyes move back and forth, tracing the discouraging zigzag pattern of steep switchbacks up the other side of the canyon wall. When I groaned in dismay, Craig reminded me, "We do this for fun, remember? Asgaard awaits."

"Yeah, yeah, Asgaard awaits. It's sure better than sitting in my environmentally controlled cubicle."

I had long suspected that Craig envied my stable job with its regular salary, though he assured me he'd rather be footloose, traveling from system to system, than stuck at a desk. For most of the year I work sealed in a cubicle chamber surrounded by screens and interfaces, exploring all manner of networks, following faint data trails. I'm a specialist in tracking certain violations in the business world, a hunter hired by clients to scan the labyrinth of entertainment loops, advertising, and news stories for unauthorized use of someone else's intellectual property. In most cases the perpetrators are too naïve or stupid to be a real threat. Still, just because they're idiots doesn't mean they can't cause disasters. I'm paid to avert disaster. It's a subtle job, and I'm good at it.

Even so, I spend much of my time dreaming of Getting Away From It All, while looking at the images in my *Fifty Most Spectacular Sites* guidebook. Craig does the same on his long-distance hauls. And now that we were on Bifrost, we intended to make the most of our limited time here, and make a year's worth of memories along the way.

Soon after we began the climb, with my thighs pulling every gram of mass against Bifrost's gravity, I found myself regretting all of the supplies I had put into my pack. I reconsidered each item from a new angle: Why should I require a first-aid kit, if I was careful enough? Would I actually miss my sanitation amenities if I left them behind on the trail? And did I really need to eat *every* day? Besides, the ecosystem and indigenous species here were compatible with our biochemistry, so we could just live off the land, despite the potential fines. How would the rangers ever know?

Unfortunately for my weary legs, my ingrained commitment to averting disasters brought me to my senses, and we plodded onward and upward. After two switchbacks, we rested ten minutes, then staggered up two more. By early afternoon we climbed over the canyon rim and were greeted by the glorious sight of a thin, cool stream running across the mesa top. We bounded toward it and stopped on the bank to unlace boots, strip off self-cleaning socks, and dunk our feet into the frigid water.

Craig let out a long "Ahhhh!", put his hands behind him, and stared up into the sky where vulture-sized butterflies drifted about on the breezes. There's nothing like the sheer delight of a simple pleasure when you're tired and dirty. "This is the sort of experience wives just don't understand," he said.

"Some wives do," I said.

"None of mine ever have," Craig said, and a shadow crossed his face. I thought he was about to say something more, but he yelped and yanked his feet out of the water. Several small scallop-mouthed bivalves clung to his bare toes and ankles, nipping at the flesh.

In the stream I saw a swarm of these small nibblers approaching my own exposed flesh and pulled my feet out of the water just in time. Inspecting his toes, Craig found only a pinch mark, no broken skin.

"We're making a memory," I reminded him—a phrase that had become a private joke between us when we ran into something unexpected.

He chuckled to himself as he pulled his socks back onto his moist feet and relaced his boots. I understood what he was thinking: After waiting so long and working so hard to get to Bifrost, we weren't about to let anything ruin our vacation. "Rest stop's over."

On backpacking trips, I prefer to put on an extra kilometer or two the first day, when my energy is greatest. Craig has the opposite philosophy, not wanting to burn himself out too soon, so he likes to break off early. Therefore, we compromised and called a halt exactly where we had decided to stop during the months of planning the expedition.

In a pleasant clearing surrounded by huge blue ferns, we unshouldered our burdens, activated the self-erecting tent systems, strung up phosphors for light, and turned on the discourager beacons to drive away any nocturnal predators. Since regulations prohibit real campfires, we settled for a high-resolution hologram of crackling flames and rough logs. I'd considered bringing a can of aerosol woodsmoke, but discarded it when paring down the weight of my pack.

Craig selected a self-heating gloppy concoction of noodles and sauce while I, in a show of macho fortitude, intentionally chose a Spampak. He looked at me with a frown. "You're crazy. I'd rather eat indigenous invertebrates."

"On the trail is the only place this stuff tastes good." I proceeded to eat my meal with much lip smacking.

We sat outside in the growing darkness under the camp lights and talked. When you're hiking all day, you don't have much extra breath for conversation, so you can let your thoughts wander, clear your head, work out personal problems and questions or, better yet, just think about *nothing*. That's a luxury most people in the frenetic civilized world with families and careers and daily schedule grids don't have.

"I wish my life could be like this all the time," Craig said with a sigh.

"You'd miss the amenities of civilization. Eventually."

He gave an eloquent shrug. "But there are plenty of things I wouldn't miss at all." He leaned closer to the campfire image. "What a year! I don't know how I'm ever going to dig out from under the crap, Steve. Maybe it's impossible."

I waited. Craig didn't need me to ask questions. He'd tell me what he wanted to tell me.

"First, I lost a huge account. A shipment of extremely delicate—and extremely valuable—skreel embryos hatched prematurely while my ship was under heavy acceleration, killing every one of them. In the wake of that disaster, my transspace insurance carrier dropped me."

"Without insurance, how will you—"

"Then, before I could get even probationary coverage, I misaligned my ship in a spacedock on Klamath Station—and *that* caused damage totaling just about my entire net worth."

"Are you going to have to declare bankruptcy?"

From the dark forest came the sound of crashing trees, a loud roar, and a frightened-sounding trumpet as two large animals collided with each other. Craig listened for a minute, then with utter faith in our discourager field, continued, "The company's already planning to sever my contract, and if I declare bankruptcy, I'll lose my ship and any chance at a livelihood. At that point, my options narrow down to submitting myself for scientific research or volunteering for hard labor on a terraform colony."

"I hear terraformers get paid well. At least that's a possibility."

"And where could I spend the credits on a raw world?"

I groaned in commiseration. No wonder he needed to get away. "Trust me, someday when it's all over, this will seem funny."

"I don't think so, Steve. It's hard to imagine."

I might have tried to cheer him up, but then the monsters—any guidebook would have called them "large indigenous animals"—lumbered into view. One, an elephant-sized panther, ripped into a house-sized spiny ungulate that looked like a cross between a porcupine and a woolly mammoth. The ungulate tried to duck into a defensive posture, but the panther-thing slipped under its guard.

They snorted and snarled. Spittle and blood flew. Lichentrees crashed into splinters. The porcupine creature raked a spine down the predator's flank, but the beast didn't seem to notice. The ungulate fled crashing away from our campsite. Without so much as a look at us, the panther sprang after it.

Resigned, Craig said, "Well, that gives me a whole new perspective on my trivial human problems."

"Amen," I said. "I'm turning in."

All the next day the trail led along a sinuous arid ridge dotted with surrealistic hoodoos, hardened clay that stuck out from the softer sandstone like a petrified alien army waiting to advance. I used my clicker to snap large files of images, though Craig just stared in peaceful satisfaction, drinking in the details, taking pictures with his mind. "I store the images in my brain," he'd once told me, "since I'm the only one who really cares about them anyway." I had to agree. There's nothing more boring than looking at pictures of someone else's vacation, no matter what planet it's on.

Late in the afternoon, the wind picked up and the sky congealed with ugly gray clouds, and I became uncomfortably aware of how exposed we were on this ridge. Rain and hail struck with the force of Thor's hammer, stinging my bare arms. I dropped my pack and ducked under one of the hoodoos for shelter. Overhead, sheets of static lightning and blue balls of Saint Elmo's Fire whipped about.

I scrambled to get out my electrostatic rain shield, but my hands were already wet, and I fumbled it. An earsplitting clap of thunder was followed by a rumbling boom, and I dropped the shield projector. Naturally, it struck a rock, and the device sparked and fizzled out. "Great."

Craig crouched under the inadequate shelter with me, his head covered by his own electrostatic umbrella, a twinkling net that deflected the raindrops and the gravel-sized hail. He shifted it over so I could huddle under the meager protection that had never been designed to cover more than one person. "Here, I'll tough it out."

"You're getting drenched and bruised!" I said.

"I'm making a memory." Craig smiled, shrugging the droplets away. "Isn't that part of the charm of this back-to-nature stuff?"

"It's supposed to be a pleasant sort of misery," I said. "The kind that makes you appreciate your everyday life a bit more."

"Bifrost is going to need to toss some pretty big loads of 'pleasant misery' at me."

Watching the majestic storm and waiting for the hail to end, we each ate several handfuls of hyper-granola and chased it with some energized water. Then we passed the time chatting.

Craig was having problems with his current soon-to-be-ex wife Grace, who had filed divorce forms while he was on a long-distance run, making it impossible for him to finish the rebuttal phase in time unless he dropped his cargo and raced back home—which she knew, as did I, that Craig would never do.

"Grace figured out a new tactic for increasing alimony. She claims that since I'm flitting around between star systems all the time, the time-dilation effect, though small, is still significant. Therefore she has effectively put more time into this marriage than I have. She's trying to get 1.3 times the standard alimony calculation."

"Never heard that one before." It was just another nail in the coffin of his disastrous year.

As the storm rumbled and swirled around us, Craig continued to tell me about how all of his previous divorces had gone wrong. I'd lost track, unable to remember which of the women were legally bound wives and which were just long-term live-ins. He never learned to be more wary of the women he hooked up with.

But we were here on Bifrost, with only a few days to forget about the nonsense of our normal life. I tried to get Craig thinking about good times, positive things.

We both got a chuckle reminiscing about the previous year's trip, shooting the Hundred Mile Rapids on Beta Kowalski. No one could survive the legendary whitewater stretch in a traditional kayak or raft, so Craig and I rented armored ballistic projectiles. We both found them uncomfortably similar to coffins with picture windows built into every side. Unable to control our own paths, we simply laid back for the ride, in occasional radio contact, though the thundering rapids drowned out most transmissions as we went over cascades, plunged down giant drop-offs, then shot along the current to the next set of even worse rapids. It had been an adrenaline rush for five hours straight, and we were both so weak and shaky by the time we reached the pickup point that the expedition managers had carted us off for a routine medical check. The recovery facilities and the numerous saloons at the bottom of the cascades proved that we weren't alone in being stunned by the trip.

Afterward, Craig and I each had a different look in our eyes. "Most people don't do that, you know," I said.

He nodded. "Most people aren't crazy."

"Most people are boring."

When we showed my wife the pictures, she was predictably horrified and made me promise I would never try such
an outrageous stunt again. It wasn't hard to agree, since I
didn't need to shoot the Hundred Mile Rapids a second
time. I had already checked that one off the list, and there
were other things to see and do. I had them all in my guidebook, *The Fifty Most Spectacular Sites in Galactic Sector A*.
Everybody needs goals.

The next morning we descended steeply into a swamp,
with rivulets of water snaking around dubious-looking tufts
of dryer ground. I found it ironic that our discourager fields
were effective at keeping large predatory animals away, yet
somehow they did nothing to block swarms of annoying
skeeters. The small biting insects couldn't possibly have a
natural appetite for Terran-based blood, but that didn't
stop them from biting us.

The swamp foliage was so dense and the muddy ground
so uncertain that we had to keep IR filters over our eyes just
to spot the trail beacons, many of which were covered with
moss or slimy fungus. I had to unroll the mapfilm and
uplink to the surveillance satellites and zoom in on the detailed topography.

Splashing across the marsh, Craig misjudged a stepping
stone and sank in up to his knee. He pulled out his foot,
dripping with greenish-black muck so viscous as it crawled
off his boot that it seemed alive. Maybe it was.

Halfway through a thicket, I saw some other hiker's care-
lessly discarded food foils, and my face pinched with annoyance. "Can you believe someone would go to all the trouble
of coming to Bifrost, then be stupid enough to throw litter
on the ground?" I worked my way off the marked trail to
clean up after the slob. When I pulled at a polymer strap

from a hiking pack, it came out of the muck connected to the gnawed remains of a human femur. Now it dawned on me that this wasn't merely careless litter.

"Yeah. I think we've found that one-out-of-twelve the ranger was talking about," Craig said, reading my sober expression. "He wasn't very successful at the Robinson Crusoe bit."

I know it sounds warped, but the only thing I could think of was, "I hope the poor guy got munched on the way *back* from his hike, so that at least he got to see the Asgaard Bridge." Sometimes my priorities sound screwy even to me.

I let the bone drop back into the swamp. "I'd better leave a radio flare so the rangers can come and gather the remains." I took one of the pulsers from my belt, activated it on non-emergency locator mode, and tossed it into the water. If I remembered right, the terms of our backcountry permits required the hiker or his surviving family members to pay all the costs of such a retrieval operation. Maintaining a wilderness planet is serious business. . . .

A large fern sprang back and slapped me in the face after Craig pushed into the dryer forest beyond the wet marsh. I wiped slime off my cheeks. We were both tired, but we had to do at least another kilometer. Otherwise, we wouldn't reach our destination tomorrow, and the whole schedule would fall apart.

We found an adequate campsite just after dusk. Too tired to talk much, we ate our meals. That night we went to sleep early after looking at our guidebooks again and drooling over the glorious pictures of the Asgaard Bridge—certainly one of the fifty most spectacular sights in Sector A, if not in the whole Galaxy. I couldn't wait to see it with my own eyes.

★ ★ ★ ★ ★

As luck would have it, thick fog had settled into the lowlands. The trail took us into a narrow gorge, where we couldn't see anything but a gauzy mist that hung like a suffocating pillow. We moved quickly: After days of hiking, our goal was near. We were about to join the very short list of privileged people who had actually been to the Asgaard Bridge. Mere pictures would never be the same as personally experiencing this wonder first-hand.

We began our long ascent, and once in a while we broke above the low-lying mists and saw outcroppings like islands in a gray-white sea. We climbed toward our destination—the grail. As if by some malicious joke, the clouds thickened even further, making it impossible to see more than a hundred meters in front of us, then fifty, and then twenty. In clear weather, the trail would have been plain, but we had to use the IR cairns just to find our way through the mist.

"Can't see a thing," Craig muttered. "This is *not* the memory I wanted to make."

"We're not there yet."

We kept hoping against hope that the fog would lift by the time we reached the Asgaard Bridge. It was mid-morning, and the sun ought to burn away the fog and leave us with clear skies and a beautiful view. It *had* to.

We reached the top of a mesa, then headed toward the edge of the gorge. Both the map and the IR indicators told us that we had reached our ultimate goal. And we could see nothing. Absolutely nothing. Days of hiking, months of preparations, countless permits, enormous expenses—all to get here.

To see thick fog.

The claustrophobic air intensified sounds, and we could hear the roar of the lavender river charging through the rocks and cascading into the distant gorge. I squinted, demanding optimism from myself, but I couldn't discern even a silhouette.

"The perfect ending to a perfect year." Craig shook his head. "It defies belief."

"You say that every time something like this happens." Resigned, I opened my pack, removing a snack and some juice. "Might as well have lunch."

Troubled and sulking, he tossed pebbles into the unseen chasm, while I opened the map and the guidebook, looked at the image of the Asgaard Bridge again, and tried to calculate just how long we could wait there. This weather couldn't last forever, but it could last longer than we had. We both remembered the ranger's admonition that he wouldn't wait for us—and I couldn't stop thinking of the skeleton in the swamp.

"Three hours is all I'm comfortable with. I sure don't want to miss the pickup shuttle. I've got a performance review and a raise justification when I get back to work."

"Yeah. And I've got my alimony hearing." Craig hurled another rock over the edge. "Sure wouldn't want to miss that."

I started figuring out how fast I could make my way back at top speed, how many extra kilometers I could put on my feet each day, but I doubted Craig could keep up.

On the other hand, I really wanted to see the Asgaard Bridge.

After three hours of growing frustration, the gray mist grew whiter and brighter, thinning. I finished packing up, reluctant to leave but watching my chronometer. We had never turned back before. Never. But our time was up.

Feeling as if a neutron star were weighing me down, I hefted my pack. "That's it." Many other choice words were running through my mind.

Craig didn't move to pick up his pack, just sat staring into the opaque fog. "You go ahead."

"You'll never catch up." My pace was always faster than his.

"I don't have to." He finally turned to me. I'd never seen such a bleak yet simultaneously peaceful expression on his face. "I'm not going. I'm staying here."

What could I say to that? "You're crazy! Come on."

"I mean it. What do I have to go back for? I'd rather go native here. I've got my equipment, supplies, guidebooks." The way he rattled off his justifications, I could tell Craig had been thinking about this for a long time—maybe even before the ranger had dropped us off. "The life forms are compatible, so I can hunt and forage. I can build myself a cabin. I'll be Robinson Crusoe, living off the land. Peace. Solitude. Adventure. *You* of all people should understand that, Steve."

"I understand it as a *game,* a break, a vacation. Not everyday life." Craig's expression wavered. I was articulating his own doubts. "Sure, we like doing this primitive thing every year, mainly because it makes our regular lives tolerable by comparison. The only reason we have fun getting miserable is because we know we're going back to reality when it's over. It gives us an appreciation for the simple pleasures."

"I don't have any simple pleasures left," he said. "I've got nothing. No job, no money, no ship, no wife. Tell the ranger that a monster ate me, or that I fell off a cliff. Make up a good story."

I could only stare at him. "You'll regret it in a week, Craig. A month at most. And nobody'll be there to throw you a lifeline."

"No other options that I can see. And I sure don't want to sign up for a bioresearch project. I like camping, roughing it, surviving by my own hands—" He stopped in mid-sentence and jumped to his feet, grinning. "You better take a look, Buddy! Get ready to hear a chorus of angels."

And he was right. The mist parted, and golden sunbeams stabbed down enough to impress even the most jaded photographer. Suddenly, there was the Asgaard Bridge, an impossibly delicate and poignant sliver of rock stretched across a gorge as deep and as sharp as if a cosmic scalpel had sliced the flesh of the sandstone all the way down to the bone. Directly beneath the arch flowed a foaming cascade of pink quicksilver, a perfect strand of water, pouring from between walls of natural diamondplate crystal. Showers of rainbows filled the air all around us. It was more stunning than anything I had ever seen, more breathtaking than any image in any guidebook. High spires of quartz-laced rock rose like crystalline spears on either side of the gorge, dazzling in the light.

Putting aside the crisis for a moment, Craig and I raised hands, and gave each other a high-five. This was exactly what we'd come out here for. "By far the best one on the whole list!" He said that every time.

I pounced. "And if you stay here, who am I going to see the rest of them with?" I pulled the guidebook from my pack. *The Fifty Most Spectacular Sights in Galactic Sector A.* "We've only done seventeen, Craig—that leaves thirty-three more to go!"

He wavered, looking at the Asgaard Bridge, then back at the open book. Just to prod him, as the final part of the ritual, I found the Bifrost page and marked a big fat X on the checklist box. Another one down.

"I really wanted to see the singing cliffs of Golhem," he

admitted. "And the refractory eclipses of Tarawna."

"Don't forget the fungus reefs and phosphor labyrinths on Kendrick Five-A. I was thinking of a way we could combine two separate checklist locations into a single vacation for next year. We *can* bag all fifty, Craig. But not if you're stuck here."

He looked as if his engines and life-support systems had all just shut down. I knew him well enough to read a flicker of doubt in his expression. Even he hadn't been so sure about his decision. "But what else can I do? This seemed like a decent way—make my own home, settle a plot of land. . . . I could pull it off. I know I could."

I had an idea. "If you're going to do that, then why not sign up for one of the terraform colonies instead? Same idea, but you'll get a huge financial incentive and gain title to half a continent. Pick yourself a hardworking colonist wife and form a dynasty."

He scratched his rumpled and sweaty hair. "Terraformers? I always heard that was miserable, living with minimal resources . . . *no* amenities . . ." His words slowed.

"And exactly how is that different from turning Robinson Crusoe here?"

He remained silent. Then, like the mists evaporating to give us a view of the Asgaard Bridge, an uncertain smile broke through on his face. "The difference is, if I become a land baron, *I* can foot the bill for our next expedition."

Though I was anxious to start back, I handed Craig the guidebook and let him spend a few minutes mulling over the images. *The Fifty Most Spectacular Sights in Galactic Sector A*. I set the hook: "You know, there are books like that for Sectors B and C, too."

Craig shouldered his pack and looked at the Asgaard Bridge one last time before returning the guidebook.

Shaken and still uncertain, he took the lead with a new spring in his step. "We'll have plenty to do for years to come, Steve—if you and I make the time to go to these planets."

"We will. As long as we get back to the shuttle in time."

Above the Crowds

Getting away from it all.

I don't dislike people . . . not really. In fact, the ones who read my novels or make microbrew beer are fine examples of the species. However, my profession demands that I spend a lot of time giving talks and making public appearances; therefore, when I'm trying to relax and recharge, nothing interests me *less* than being surrounded by people. When I get away from it all, I like to be far from the chatter and noise of civilization—not just a stone's throw from the crowds, but "Harrison Ford in *The Mosquito Coast*" far away.

It's a basic law of human nature that the more beautiful and more accessible a place, the more people will swarm to it. A mitigating corollary to this, thank heavens, is that if any strenuous effort is required, then the sightseeing public will shy away as if it were a war-torn village in Bosnia.

Thus, in my sojourns I've had to walk farther, climb higher—and ultimately receive even greater rewards with the views, the satisfaction, and the solitude.

When I moved out to Colorado six years ago, I was delighted to discover more than fifty peaks in the state that tower over 14,000 feet high. Better yet, they are all *climbable*. As the icing on the cake, my brother-in-law (and fellow hiker) Tim bought me a guidebook and checklist for all of these "Fourteeners." With a new list in hand, a goal-oriented person like myself was off and running.

418

Some of these peaks are steep, isolated, and treacherous; they have claimed more than their share of lives, from clumsy amateurs to well-practiced experts. Other peaks are easy with well-developed trails. Two, in fact—Pikes Peak and Mount Evans—have paved roads leading all the way to the top. (This creates a most disappointing experience after spending miles on a long trail: A summit crowded with parked cars and gift shops full of plump suburbanites in hot pants and flip-flops buying T-shirts that proclaim "I made it to the top of Pikes Peak!")

One of these Fourteeners, Culebra Peak, is *privately owned* by a surly old rancher who refuses to let hikers onto his property, much to the frustration of those of us who want to bag all 54 summits. However, being accustomed to conquering difficult peaks, I felt I was up to the challenge of pressuring the guy.

Each year, I climb a mountain for charity to support the Emily Griffith Center, a privately funded "rescue ranch" and shelter for abused children. In 1999 I used the charity hike as a crowbar to twist the old rancher's arm, and he grudgingly allowed me and Tim (my "official photographer," as far as the grouch was concerned) onto his property to climb Culebra. This peak is so isolated, we had to chase a black bear from the very summit.

When we signed the trail register buried in the summit cairn, we saw that other Fourteener devotees had found their own ways up the mountain, slipping through the ranch fences and scrambling without a trail up the back route. Peak poachers. Many of them had left angry notes, "No man should own a mountain!" I can't say I didn't sympathize. . . .

Since 1997, I have climbed all of these peaks, crossing them off in my log and feeling insufferably pleased with myself. Now that the goal-oriented, list-checking obsession has been satisfied, I can return to the ones that I enjoyed most.

For this year's Emily Griffith Center charity hike, sponsored in part by *Argosy* magazine, I decided to climb Mount Sneffels (14,150 ft) in Colorado's beautiful San Juan Mountains between Ouray and Telluride. Sneffels dominates the skyline as you drive south from Montrose toward Ouray, a spectacular mountain with a beautiful shape and imposing-looking crags.

Most importantly for a science fiction person like myself, Sneffels has a direct connection with Jules Verne. On September 10, 1874, members of the Hayden Survey were the first to climb the mountain. When they approached the prominent craggy face from the west, one of the expedition members was reminded of the towering mountain gateway and crater described in Verne's *A Journey to the Center of the Earth* (published only two years earlier). Dr. Frederic Endlich of the Hayden Survey agreed and dubbed the peak "Snaefell" after the Icelandic mountain in Verne's novel. Time and misspellings have since altered the name to Sneffels.

The alarm goes off in my tent at 5:30 in the morning, and after fortifying myself with the necessary breakfast of Spam and eggs, I pack up camp and drive for about an hour along a bumpy, pot-holed dirt road to the trailhead. My starting elevation is about 8,800 feet, and the top of Sneffels is more than a vertical mile up, the equivalent to running up the stairs of the Empire State Building 4.5 times. Slurping the first Red Bull of the day and taking a preemptive ibuprofen, I set off.

At first the trail is deceptively peaceful and simple, winding through gentle forests along the rushing East Dallas Creek. Even so, every step is uphill, inexorably gaining elevation. I plod past

two backpackers from Missouri huffing and puffing up the trail.
Twenty-six hours ago, these two were back home at about sea
level. No wonder they're having trouble. I'll probably pass them
on my way back down.

By now I'm close to 10,000 feet. Finally, I circle around, as-
cend a rise, and the trail opens into a broad meadow. There in
front of me, looming in all its majestic and intimidating glory, is
the stone buttress of Mount Sneffels. This is the precise view that
caused the Hayden Expedition to name the peak after Verne's
gateway to the center of the Earth.

I pause a moment to stare at it, mutter several testosterone-
induced defiant challenges, and then keep walking. It looks like
a long way to the top.

The first time I climbed Mount Sneffels in 1998, I approached from Yankee Boy Basin on the Ouray side. At the
time I was doing research for my novel *Captain Nemo* and
felt it was appropriate to reread *A Journey to the Center of the
Earth* while sitting at my campsite in Sneffels' shadow. The
climb from here takes you up a backbreaking and endlessly
steep gravel chute called Lavender Couloir. While not dangerous, it's tedious and maddeningly hard on the knees and
thighs.

This time, though, I decided to climb from the western
side, up and over Blue Lakes Pass and along a direct and
difficult ridge to the summit. This route is much tougher,
involving Class 3 climbing along an exposed ridge where, as
the book ominously says, "You will be in situations where a
fatal fall is possible."

Mountain climbing routes are divided into five classes,
Class One being simply "follow the clear trail and walk
right up to the top" outings. Class Two routes are slightly
more difficult, involving reading a map or following cairns

and subtle trail signs, sometimes climbing steep or slightly loose rock. Class Three trails, like the Blue Lakes route on Sneffels, are significantly more difficult, requiring hand and foot work, good orienteering; certain sections of the trail have perilous exposure and dire consequences for the klutzy hiker.

A Class Four climb requires exceptional route-finding skills, agility across loose rocks and narrow ledges, with ample opportunities for a deadly fall. The most famous Class Four section on any Fourteener trail is the Knife-Edge Ridge on Capitol Peak, a hundred foot-long sharp point like a steep rooftop with more than a thousand foot sheer drop on both the right and the left. You have to scoot along on your butt, one leg dangling over each side.

A Class Five climb requires ropes, pitons, and a great deal of mountain-goat skill. No thanks. Fortunately, every Fourteener in Colorado has at least one route to the summit that is no more difficult than Class Four.

After an hour and ten minutes I reach the Blue Lakes at the 3.3-mile point. I've gained almost three thousand feet of elevation so far. Not bad—but as I look up to see the steep wall of Blue Lakes Pass and from there the forbidding south ridge of Sneffels, I know that the hardest part is yet to come.

The Blue Lakes are a popular hiking destination, and here I meet clusters of hikers and backpackers. It's a pristine and colorful alpine meadow, and the lakes themselves are shallow turquoise jewels. If you've never seen a clear lake in an alpine basin, you've never witnessed the true potential of what a "lake" can be.

To reach the top of the pass from here is another two and a half miles and close to two thousand feet elevation gain. Time to put away the tape recorder and the camera, drink another Red

Above the Crowds

Bull, and start climbing in earnest.

Reaching the pass is a nightmare, an endless succession of switchbacks. It's all I can do to plod from one end of a zig-zag, rest, then plod to the next. The top of the pass never seems to get any closer. My feet hurt, my legs are sore, I'm out of breath— but when I finally clear the top and I stand on the boundary between two spectacular mountain valleys, none of those difficulties matters. Not a bit.

Inevitably the question comes up—why would anyone want to do such a thing? The facetious but nevertheless truthful answer is, If you have to ask, you'll never understand. Some people are born with the "Because It's There" mentality, and others just don't see it.

I have always been one to look up at the mountains, mentally drawing a dotted line along the preferred path to a ridge and then a clean line to the summit. I also used to climb on top of tables or even up on the roof of our house when I was a kid. It's in my blood, I suppose.

The higher you get, the more perspective you have. Even the most jaded person can find such landscapes inspirational—grand vistas, birds and gnarled pines all around, clear air, wildflowers, spectacular lakes and crags.

I usually hike alone, wandering for miles without seeing another soul. When I'm at home in my office, the day is a constant litany of telephone interruptions, background noises, doorbells, package deliveries, questions to be answered, interviews to finish. Simply being able to walk and let my thoughts flow, the imagination wander, is an incomparable rush. I get some of my best ideas this way, plot twists or resolutions to story problems I couldn't otherwise solve. Just having the blissful mental quiet lets my bruised gray matter rejuvenate and catch its cerebral breath.

423

For me it becomes more beneficial in a concrete way. I write with a hand-held tape recorder so that I can dictate and hike at the same time, thereby fulfilling two of my basic needs. As a writer, all of my days are spent creating imaginary things, alien terrains, strange creatures, exotic biologies and geologies, even staging space battles or clashes among armies on the ground. After a while, the batteries of the imagination begin to get drained; they need to be recharged with new input, new sights and sounds and smells.

Sometimes the hikes are specifically relevant. For instance, I have dictated many *Dune* or *Star Wars* chapters while in California's Death Valley or Colorado's Great Sand Dunes. I've also written scenes set on alien polar ice caps while tromping through fresh fallen snow in the Sierra Nevadas. The solitude and the fresh air, the colors, the sounds, are like a high-energy vitamin pill, a Red Bull for my muse.

Another reason to climb the challenging peaks is for the personal feeling of satisfaction, the sense of accomplishment. Though every climb has its agonizing section of gut-busting steep drudgery or white-knuckle perils, once I reach the summit and sit next to the cairn of rocks on the very top, I know that I am the highest thing for many miles around. This brings its own sense of light-headedness (which is not entirely attributable to the altitude of 14,000 feet).

Crestone Needle, historically the last of the Fourteeners to be conquered, was not successfully summitted until 1916. According to the last—and probably out of date—statistics I read, only about a thousand people had climbed all 54 Fourteeners in the nine decades since. (The grouchy old rancher at Culebra hasn't helped matters much for list-tickers in recent years.) Even so, that's a fairly elite group of people.

★ ★ ★ ★ ★

From Blue Lakes Pass, off to the east side is the vista of the Yankee Boy Basin. Today, my hiking partner Tim is also climbing Sneffels with two friends he's trying to addict to the sport. Tim, Bruce, and Bob chose to ascend the standard and much shorter route out of Yankee Boy Basin. If things work out right, we'll meet at the top.

I can see tiny figures of people climbing up and down steep Lavender Couloir. Behind me to the west and impossibly far below is the Blue Lakes Basin from which I've just hiked. The spectacular, bizarrely-shaped peaks of the San Juans are all around—Teakettle Mountain, Potosi Peak, Whitehouse Mountain. I feel like Leonardo diCaprio at the bow of the Titanic.

It's only 11:00 a.m., but the sky overhead is already turning gray with gathering clouds. A distant, ominous rumble of thunder makes me decide that I don't really want to think about the Titanic.

From Blue Lakes Pass I ascend the steep Class 3 ridge. There are occasional cairns—piles of rock left by other hikers to show the way (you have to assume they knew where they were going in the first place). I can also spot scuffs and footprints from other hiking boots. But make no mistake, this is no trail but a "route."

I have to use both hands and feet to climb up boulders, work my way along notches in the rock and scramble up gullies that take me around a particularly nasty pile of unclimbable rock pinnacles. This is a lot of work, keeping my balance on rocks that shift under my feet, climbing higher to pass through a prominent notch—and then, heartbreakingly, lose all the elevation I've just gained, down to the base of a gully so that I can get around another frustrating barrier of rock. Then I have to climb back up again.

After all that work, the summit isn't much closer.

425

★ ★ ★ ★ ★

Sometimes, especially in the final ridges toward the top, my legs are tired and sore. Each step feels like I'm lifting a boulder instead of a hiking boot, but I can see the summit pitch and I plod one foot at a time, count out twenty steps, rest for a minute, then climb twenty more steps. After getting that close, I don't dare give up.

This mulish refusal to see common sense can be almost suicidal. At Columbia Peak on September 8, 2000, Tim and I unexpectedly encountered a white-out blizzard that came upon us with little warning. Earlier that day we had climbed nearby Mount Harvard in T-shirts and shorts, and we wanted to bag a second summit. We had seen the black clouds approaching, but since we didn't hear any thunder, we pushed on. When the blizzard hit, the temperature dropped an astonishing amount within a few minutes, and we had to huddle in a cranny between boulders to wait out the snow so we could push on to the final pitch.

After close to an hour—shivering, teeth chattering—we realized we were encountering the initial stages of hypothermia and decided we'd better leave. As soon as we stepped out into the blowing snow, Tim suggested, "Well, it's not getting any worse. You want to try for the top anyway?"

Of course I agreed. What were we thinking?

After a handful of steps, though, we were unable to press on. "Well, it was only a suggestion." Instead, we turned and slipped and slid in a straight line toward the basin that we couldn't even see far below. However, gravity is a clear enough force that you can follow it, even without finding the trail. . . .

Another time, when climbing down from Windom Peak after what had already been a long day's hike, we still had to

cross a wide basin to climb Sunlight Peak. We looked down
the side of Windom, saw a boulder-filled couloir that led directly down to where we needed to go in the valley. A convenient shortcut! If we followed the actual trail, it would
add an extra mile and another hour of effort to our weary
legs. "That doesn't look too hard," Tim said. "What's it
called?" I looked on the map and identified the topological
feature. "It's a couloir named . . . Widowmaker."

Of course we decided to try it. What were we thinking?

Halfway down, with me ahead of Tim, the large loose
boulders began to shift and roll, and I found myself dancing
atop sliding rocks, each of which weighed a ton or more.
When I finally lost my balance, I jammed my "unbendable"
metal trekking pole into a cranny and held on. My weight
and the crushing boulders bent the stick into an "L" as I
dangled. Luckily, the avalanche petered out. I swallowed
hard, gingerly pried loose my pretzel walking stick, and
made my way over to what I hoped was more stable ground.

"Be careful there, Tim," I called up. "These rocks are a
little loose."

By now it's started to rain. The stones and scree are already
unstable, but now the moisture makes them even more slippery.
In one of the most difficult parts of the climb so far, I have to as-
cend a long, narrow chute full of very loose scree. In the down-
pour, it's like trying to ascend a vertical bowling alley full of ball
bearings and Crisco. I hug the sides, looking for solid rock,
inching my way upward.

Then I hear the thunder again. The metal walking stick in
my hand (a new, unbent one) is perfectly capable of serving
double duty as a lightning rod. But the rain doesn't get any
worse, and though the skies remain gray, the moisture gradually
tapers off. At the top of the chute, I can see the crux of the route,

a summit ridge made of wonderfully rough and solid rock with plenty of handholds (and a sheer throat-tightening drop of about five hundred feet if I happen to lose my grip). As I crawl across it, making sure I have a good anchor before I move one of my hiking boots, I am reminded of that phrase from the guidebook, "You will be in situations where a fatal fall is possible."

Even before I reach the summit, I have already made up my mind that there's no way I'm going to descend via this route. Even though the Lavender Couloir is much longer, drops me into the wrong basin, and requires me to climb back up over Blue Lakes Pass again from the other side—in the long run, it'll save time and maybe a few broken bones.

The top of Sneffels is tantalizingly close now, and I work my way toward it, making a beeline for the summit. But I get stymied by a rock wall that I can't climb over or around, so I have to back off, go down again and around, seeking another way up. In many places I find myself uncomfortably exposed. One misstep and I'll be able to visit spectacular Yankee Boy Basin far, far below. No way is this only Class Three; therefore I must have strayed from the preferred route.

Great.

When you're on top of an exposed ridge or at the summit of a Fourteener, not only are you high above the rest of the world, but you're also much closer to the lightning. Thunderstorms and lightning strikes are the most deadly aspects of mountain climbing, far worse than avalanches or bear attacks.

Upon reaching the summit of San Luis Peak after an exhausting five-hour hike, I sat down to enjoy the solitude. Black clouds were rumbling thunder off in the distance, clumped around other high peaks, but I figured I was safely far away from the storm. Slinging off my backpack, I took out my water bottle, yanked off my hat, and prepared for a nice lunch of beef jerky and granola. Suddenly, every hair on my head and arms stood up straight with static electricity, and the air began to crackle and "ping." I didn't even bother to shoulder my pack, but just ran at top speed back down the trail, losing elevation as quickly as possible.

There are other far less perilous but still unpleasant aspects of a hike. In a Colorado summer hikers are likely to get rained upon (or hailed or snowed). While climbing through Matterhorn Creek Basin on my way to Wetterhorn Peak, I got caught in a Biblical-magnitude hail and thunderstorm. I huddled under my rain cloak trying to make a low lightning-strike profile, then pressed on into the cold wind. I encountered a fleeing German climber scuttling down the slopes of Wetterhorn. When he saw that I was intent on heading up into the furious thunderstorm, his eyes practically bugged out of their sockets. "You can't go opp dere!" he said in broken English. "You're MAD—*mad,* I tell you!" But I saw a thin fingernail of blue sky creeping its way, and since I still had an hour or two before I reached the high ridge, I hoped the weather would pass. Not a particularly sane or conservative hope—but it worked, and I reached the summit that day.

I've talked to women who describe the "joyous amnesia" of childbirth, how after the awful agony of labor an incomprehensible euphoria sets in and they view those memories with rose-colored glasses. Otherwise, no woman would ever have more than a single child . . . and our race would be in deep trouble.

Even though I return sodden and cold, bruised and exhausted from these hikes, it's all part of "having an adventure." In my mind I rapidly revise the misery I suffered, the discomfort and pain, and I can't wait to do it again.

★ ★ ★ ★ ★

The top of Mount Sneffels is incomparably gorgeous. By now the rain has stopped, the clouds have cleared, and I'm sitting in pure sunlight on the summit. (I must have filed all the right paperwork with the weather bureau.) Leonardo diCaprio can have his unsinkable boat; I'll take a mountain any day.

I pull out the cell phone and make my requisite calls, checking in with the Emily Griffith Center to let them know I've made it, and then with my wife to make sure she doesn't worry too much.

Sitting there all alone, I find the register hidden under a pile of rocks. Tim and his two friends have already signed in earlier that day. It would have been nice to meet up with them on the summit, and now I don't have a photo of myself on top of the mountain. But being alone here in this fabulous place is its own reward.

I scribble my name, eat some lunch, and then it's time to go back down.

Accomplishing a task that few other people can, or even attempt to, do is fundamentally exuberating. There's nothing to compare with the feeling of coming home and checking off another peak on the list or putting a map pin in the poster that shows all of the Fourteeners. (Okay, this is something a lot of people don't understand either, but trust me on this.)

I grew up in a tiny town in southern Wisconsin—Franksville—where the sole local industry was the sauerkraut factory. During the annual Sauerkraut Festival, the high point is the kraut-eating contest. People come from across the country and as far away as Germany to see who can devour a full pound of sauerkraut the fastest. The winner receives a glorious trophy proclaiming him or her to be the Kraut Eating Champion of Franksville, Wisconsin. (Moments after receiving the prize, the winner usually dashes backstage to vomit into the sawdust.)

Far be it from me to belittle that person's accomplishments. Though I don't understand it myself, the general concept is the same. One has only to look in the *Guinness Book of World Records* to see list upon list of ridiculous records that somebody has set . . . and others have tried to break. A human being needs to challenge himself, to find his or her limits, to see what it's truly possible to do.

As I start back down, following the alternate route via Yankee Boy Basin, it begins to rain again, making my descent just as slippery. Once I reach the top of Lavender Couloir, the chute is so steep and full of loose gravel I can't possibly hold myself still. Instead I spread my legs wide for stability and balance, prop the walking stick in front of me as a sort of rudder, and try to control my headlong descent.

Fortunately, because I've taken such a long hike, I'm the last person on top for the day. There's no one below me climbing the couloir, so I can dislodge as much gravel as I like without worrying about bombarding anybody.

Off to the west I see the prominent and heartbreaking switchbacks of the trail leading up to Blue Lakes Pass from this side, and my legs ache with the knowledge that as soon as I get down to Yankee Boy Basin I have to climb all the way back up over that pass, then back down to Blue Lakes. Seven more miles of walking to my car.

I stop skidding before I reach the bottom of the couloir and leave the steep gully and head directly over to Blue Lakes Pass. It's not nearly as hard as it looks, but by now it's been a long day. I have a whole new collection of blisters . . . and it hasn't stopped raining. Thunder hits the basin like nearby artillery fire, blasting and echoing off the cliffs like a big-budget Wagnerian opera.

But the hard part is over.

On my way back to the trailhead, there's always a moment when I turn around and look at the stark and seemingly insurmountable peak behind me. I take a deep breath and smile, muttering to myself, "Wow, I just climbed that. I was just on top of there."

It takes me three more hours to reach my car, where I drive the nine miles up the jeep road again to get back to a paved highway and then all the way to Telluride, where, instead of camping, I have arranged for a genuine room with a shower and a bathtub.

That evening I end the hike in the best possible way, by taking a quick shower and then hobbling over to the local microbrewery for well-deserved refreshment. There, by sheer coincidence (or perhaps my own predictability), Tim, Bruce, and Bob track me down and we all go out for a hefty steak dinner.

Afterward, while having a long, hot soak in the tub back in my room, I spend the time flipping through my mountain guidebooks, planning and scheming for the next time. . . .

About the Author

In the past decade, 33 of Kevin J. Anderson's novels have appeared on national and international bestseller lists; he has 16 million books in print in nearly 30 languages. He has won or been nominated for numerous prestigious awards, including the Nebula Award, Bram Stoker Award, the SFX Reader's Choice Award, the American Physics Society's Forum Award, and *New York Times* Notable Book.

Anderson is currently writing prequels to Frank Herbert's classic SF novel *Dune,* coauthored with Herbert's son Brian. The first book, *Dune: House Atreides* became a #1 international bestseller and was voted "Book of the Year" by the members of the Science Fiction Book Club. In solo original work, he has just completed the fifth volume in his ambitious "Saga of Seven Suns" SF epic, as well as fantastic historicals *The Martian War* (under the name "Gabriel Mesta") and *Captain Nemo,* as well as a complex science fiction book, *Hopscotch.*

His *Star Wars* "Jedi Academy" trilogy became the three top-selling science fiction novels of 1994. He has also completed numerous other projects for Lucasfilm, including the 14-volumes in the bestselling and award-winning *Young Jedi Knights* series (cowritten with his wife Rebecca Moesta). His three original *Star Wars* anthologies are the bestselling SF anthologies of all time.

Anderson is the author of three hardcover novels based on the X-Files; all three became international bestsellers, the first of which reached #1 on the *London Sunday Times.*

Ground Zero was voted "Best Science Fiction Novel of 1995" by the readers of SFX magazine. *Ruins* hit the *New York Times* bestseller list, the first X-Files novel ever to do so, and was voted "Best Science Fiction Novel of 1996."

Anderson has written numerous bestselling comics and graphic novels for DC, Marvel, Dark Horse, Wildstorm, IDW, and Topps. In 1997, during a promotional tour for his comedy/adventure novel *Ai! Pedrito!*, Anderson set the Guinness World Record for "Largest Single-Author Book Signing." His thriller *Ignition*, written with Doug Beason, has been sold to Universal as a major motion picture.

Anderson's research has taken him to the top of Mount Whitney and the bottom of the Grand Canyon, inside the Cheyenne Mountain NORAD complex, into the Andes Mountains and the Amazon River, inside a Minuteman III missile silo and its underground control bunker, onto the deck of the aircraft carrier *Nimitz*, to Maya and Inca temple ruins in South and Central America, inside NASA's Vehicle Assembly Building at Cape Canaveral, onto the floor of the Pacific Stock Exchange, inside a plutonium plant at Los Alamos, and behind the scenes at FBI Headquarters in Washington, DC. He also, occasionally, stays home and writes.

www.wordfire.com